ROAD TO FIRE

MARIA LUIS

**""I'm not scared of you."
I meet her gaze. "You should be."**

To all of England, I'm the devil bent on all-out destruction, royal family be damned.

Spy.
Defender of the Crown.
Bound by a secret oath, I am loyal only to the queen.

It's a front that works well, until *she* appears.

Isla Quinn may claim she's only looking for a job, but her hatred for the queen is so palpable, I can nearly taste it.

"Hire me," she begs.

Isla thought she found a knight in shining armor, but she's found me instead.

Savage.
Ruthless.
A man with no heart, no matter how the dead space inside my chest lurches whenever we touch.

And so I lean over, dragging her deep into this twisted game of crowns and thrones, and offer a single vow: *"I could use you."*

Isla

Callous. Cold. Cruel.

I know what's said about Saxon Priest, and it's not desperation that leads me to him.

He thinks me weak, fragile. A charity case.

He knows nothing.

My name is Isla Quinn, and I killed the king.

PLAYLIST

"Rival" – Ruelle
"Twisted Games" – Night Panda
"Like Lovers Do" – Hey Violet
"Dangerous Game" – Klergy
"When Humans Become Our Gods" – Our Last Night
"You Belong to Me" – Cat Pierce
"Waltz of the Damned" – Roxane Genot
"Renfri's Theme (from The Witcher)" – Roxane Genot
"The Curse" – Agnes Obel
"Hross" – Skáld
"Crusader of Glory" – Erik Ekholm
"The End's Beginning" – Sonya Belousova

Road To Fire (Broken Crown Trilogy, Book 1)
Maria Luis

Copyright © 2020 by Alkmini Books, LLC
It is illegal to distribute or resale this copy in any form.

All rights reserved.
No part of this book may be reproduced in any form or by any electronic or mechanical means, including information storage and retrieval systems, without written permission from the author, except for the use of brief quotations in a book review.

Cover Photographer: Wander Book Club Photography
Cover Model: Travis S.
Cover Designer: Najla Qamber, Najla Qamber Designs
Editing: Kathy Bosman, Indie Editing Chick
Proofreading: Tandy Proofreads; Horus Proofreading

To George Washington and the Culper Ring.

A dedication I never thought I'd write, but here we are. Without them, America wouldn't exist as it is today, Alexander Rose wouldn't have written his book about the country's first spy ring, AMC wouldn't have created a TV show, and, well, the Broken Crown Trilogy would never have come to be. It's funny how the universe works sometimes.

Good job, honey.

PROLOGUE

**SAXON
LONDON, 1995**

The king despised me.

He didn't need to say so out loud. Didn't need to breathe a single word whenever Pa brought me to the palace for one of their talks. But I knew.

They always argued and I always sat in the corner, my knobby knees clamped together and my fingers digging into my thighs. Beneath my shoes, a plush, red carpet stretched on forever, winding along narrow hallways and cutting down wide, centuries-old stairwells, before rolling all the way out to the front entrance of St. James's Palace.

Pa and me never entered through the front.

"We're special, m'boy," Pa told me time and again, his hand rooted to my shoulder as he steered me down the alley that skirted Marlborough Road and led to our "special entrance."

But we weren't special. We were *trouble*.

"I told you not to bring him again," the king hissed, no doubt thinking I couldn't hear him. I heard it all, each word slamming into me like a round from the pistol Pa tucked into his trousers at the base of his spine. He didn't think I noticed, but we all did.

Me, my older brother, Guy, and my younger brother, Damien.

The only one who noticed nothing was Mum, but she was sick. Always sick. Just as Pa was always trouble.

"He minds his own business, Your Royal Highness. He's eight, the same age as Princess Margaret." Pa looked over at me, his green eyes, a shade so eerily similar to my own, darkening with sympathy. "He has no friends. No one but his brothers and me and his mum, and I was thinking, maybe, that when you summoned me, my Saxon could play with your daugh—"

The king's fist struck the table with a thunderous *crack!* that detonated like an explosion in my ears. "You forget yourself, Henry," King John seethed with enough heat to singe my skin to ash, even as far away as I sat from them now. "You forget your *place*."

Pa's shoulders stiffened. "Forgive me, sir, but I've forgotten nothing. I took the oath, the same oath as my father and his father before him."

"An oath which you failed to uphold!"

The king shoved away from the table, launching to his feet as he stalked the room like a caged animal. The doors were locked tight, the walls—Guy once whispered to me—were soundproof. If the king killed us, no one would hear our screams. Guy told me that, too.

So, me and Pa scurried into this secret room like vagrants, always fearful that someone might uncover us, spot us.

We were trouble.

The king said so.

Mum said so, whenever the sickness eased, and her

skin wasn't so very yellow.

My knees knocked together, and I fixated on the subtle sound.

Tap.

Tap.

Tap.

"Tell me, Henry," the king snapped, "you're worried about your blasted son not having any friends? My oldest daughter—my heir—is *dead*. Shot during a charity event after *your* family took an oath to protect us."

Tap.

"Sir—"

Tap.

"Two months, Godwin. You promised me two months ago that you'd uncover who assassinated Evangeline. Two *months.*"

Tap.

Tap.

It took me a moment to realize that the tapping no longer belonged to my knocking knees but to the sound of King John's shoes storming over the old wood floors. Toward me. He was coming toward *me*.

Fear clogged my throat.

Trouble. We Godwins were always trouble.

The king's hand circled my bicep and hauled me from the chair. My shoes scraped the floor even as my fingers grappled at the king's shirtsleeve. But he was big whereas I was small, the crown of my head barely hitting his diaphragm when I stood on my tiptoes.

Let me go. Let me go. Let me go!

The words lodged in my throat, threatening to suffocate me.

"John—sir," Pa said, his cheeks red. He fiddled with

the back of his shirt and I knew he was toying with that pistol. *Trouble. Trouble. Trouble.* "I understand your frustration," he went on, his jaw locking tight, every word clipped and precise. "You have every right to be upset. But I've done everything to find Princess Evangeline's killer. I've hunted down suspects. I've employed every possible source to suss out the damned bastard. Paul, the other men and I, we're all working on this."

"You're not working hard enough."

Before the stone fireplace, the king forcibly thrust me into a chair. The unexpected jolt made me bite down on my tongue, and I felt the *pop* of a blood vessel bursting in my mouth.

I wanted to cry out. I wanted to beg Pa to pick me up and take me from this place.

The king hated me.

A flash of steel caught my eye as I tried to spring from the chair to safety. An unforgiving hand yanked me back, and then there was no missing the high sheen of the king's gem-stoned rings that twinkled on his fingers. Yellow topaz like Saturn. Red ruby like Mercury. Blue sapphire like Earth.

My love for outer space felt like a very bad thing when faced with the sovereign king's wrath.

The tip of the blade pricked the sensitive flesh behind my right ear, and only then did I beg, plead, pray. "Papa," I whimpered on a sharp, battered exhale, "help. Papa, help!"

He stepped forward. In his hand he brandished a pistol, and it was aimed at the king.

Trouble. Trouble. Trouble.

"Sir," Pa ground out, his voice quivering with an unfamiliar strain of fear, "you've had a long day. A damn long two months. But my boy Saxon? He's done nothing wrong. We'll keep searching. I won't rest until we find who killed the princess. I swear it on my life."

I couldn't breathe. Couldn't see anything, but for the red sea sweeping over my vision and distorting everything.

Red like the carpet under my feet.

Red like the color of the king's ring.

Red like the whites of my father's eyes when he met my gaze and I saw his terror.

"Put the pistol down, Henry," the king snapped. "Put the pistol down or I'll teach you the taste of true grief."

The weapon clattered to a chair as Pa surged past it. "*John*, fuck, listen to me—"

The blade pressed down on my skin, and a howl climbed my throat.

"Your loyalty," the king said, "swear it on your son's life. We've had your family's fealty for years. Prove it now, Godwin. Prove it to your son that the Crown must always come first."

Pa's red-rimmed eyes locked with mine, and I saw the apology forming in his expression before the words ever entered the space between us. "Saxon, m'boy," he whispered, "keep looking at me. Don't look away."

The king leaned down to utter raggedly in my ear, "Never forget, Saxon, where your loyalty belongs. With the king. With the Crown. An oath that's spanned generations between our two families. Don't break like your father and this moment will never be repeated."

Pain, sharp and insistent, scored the flesh behind my ear. It sank in its claws, twisting and dragging, and the red sea consumed me, swallowing my thrashing feet and flexing fingers and my mouth that parted for a scream that never came.

It didn't come then, in that secret room of the palace

that existed to no one but us. It didn't come that night, when Pa sat me down in our small, ancient flat in Whitechapel, his arms wrapped around me as he rocked my body back and forth, apologies coating his tongue and sounding so very faraway beyond the roaring in my ears.

And it didn't come five months later, when Pa was found dead on the side of Marlborough Road, just yards from St. James's Palace, his stomach coated red with blood.

CHAPTER 1

SAXON
LONDON, PRESENT DAY

The queen enters my pub like she expects to be ambushed.

Not that I'd expect anything less from a woman wanted dethroned by half the country.

Her silver-blond hair is hidden beneath the confines of a black wig that's seen better days. Wide-eyed, her gaze flicks from left to right, right to left; no doubt she's panicking that someone might see through her shoddy costume to the woman wearing it.

It's been twenty-five years since I saw her last, outside of television appearances and snapshots of her in the papers. Only, back then, she wasn't Queen. Not yet. Just a young princess—a princess who was never allowed to play with the spy's sons, no matter that the Godwin family has been integral to the Crown's survival for over a century.

Tossing the damp rag on the bar's oak counter, I drag my equally damp palms over my trousers. Swiftly, I count every patron seated at the bar, then those camped out in the booths, knowing that every person in here would gladly see her dead before they ever bend the knee.

The queen catches my eye and a relieved smile hitches the corner of her mouth.

Relief should be the last thing she's feeling. The bloody woman has entered the proverbial lion's den—and she's done so alone. No bodyguard tailing her shadow. No weapon of any sort that I can see, and I've disarmed enough people in my life to know when someone is carrying, civilian or not.

What the hell is she doing?

Under my breath, I curse her stupidity for coming here. No, her goddamn naivety. Wig or not, if my customers sniff her out, we'll have a riot on our hands.

They want her dead. They want the monarchy dismantled.

And long before I was born, my family was tasked with keeping the Crown exactly where it's been since the eleventh century: at the top of the social pecking order.

Hands on my thighs, I duck under the bar. Tell my barman, Jack, to hold down the fort while I take a piss, and then head for the stairs that lead from the pub up to Guy's flat. Straining my ears, I wait for the telltale sound of a female's lighter footsteps before I start taking them two at a time.

The first rung whines under Queen Margaret, and there's no mistaking the hushed, "Oh, do shut up," that she whispers to God-knows-what.

Sharply, I glance over my shoulder, only to—

Christ.

Is she *trying* to get herself offed? And me right along with her?

As though primping before a mirror, she readjusts the chin-length wig with a sharp pull. A strand of blond escapes to frame her face like a white flag of surrender, shouting, *It's me! Your Royal-fucking-Majesty!* The wig alone is shit, but the fact that she's messing with it is doing her no favors. Even now, her fingers nervously pat the back, unaware of that piece of telltale blond.

Her only saving grace is the fact that she doesn't waste time. She scurries up the steps, chin tucked down, like that alone will ward off any curiosity. It won't. She walks like a royal. Moves like a royal. And, when she utters my name, it's safe to say that she speaks like a royal too. Posh. Proper. My very antithesis.

"Mr. Godwin, I wasn't sure if you'd recognize me."

I'd have to be an idiot not to recognize the most powerful person in the commonwealth. But she'd have to be an idiot to use the surname that the Crown itself scrubbed from every public document after Pa was murdered—and do so in my own pub, no less.

"Priest," I correct gruffly, my eyes locked on Guy's front door. I haven't answered to anything else in over twenty years. The Godwins died right along with my father. Died, and never resurfaced.

"Oh, yes. I—" Rustling echoes behind me, like she's checking the stairwell for any potential lurkers. "Mr. Priest. I do apologize. I wasn't thinking."

Not thinking will land her in the same predicament as her father: dead.

Maybe recklessness is a family trait, passed down through the generations. I can see it. King John was a tyrannical bastard who never thought five steps ahead, let alone one. He single-handedly turned this country back four hundred years. Keeping parliament in place has been nothing more than a case of smoke and mirrors—everyone is all too aware of who's running this country, and it's not the politicians who continue to fill the seats of Westminster.

With a father like that... Well, no wonder his own daughter thought showing up to a fucking anti-loyalist pub would be a grand idea.

Long live the queen.

Shoving the key into the rusty lock, I turn the knob and push the door open. Immediately, my gaze darts to the tiny kitchenette, where my older brother stands, shirtless, as he pops open a can of beans. "Ready to turn in for the day already?" Guy drawls sharply, barely sparing me a glance.

Barely sparing the *queen* a glance.

I shut the door behind her, turning over the lock. "We've company."

"You know how I feel about people."

"Then dust off your manners. I'm sure the cobwebs could do with a breather."

Guy's blue eyes finally lift. They land on me, then zero in on Queen Margaret to my left. He says nothing, not at first. But his eyes narrow and his body visibly tenses and then he's dropping the can onto the counter and sauntering toward us.

Toward the queen.

"*Guy*," I growl, my tone thick with warning. My brother has no boundaries. Not with me or Damien, not with the other Holyrood agents—others like us who've been recruited to serve the Crown. And sure as hell not with the hundreds of people who we've schemed and lied to and stolen precious information from over the years. Information that was never meant to reach the pinnacle of Britain's power.

Expression stony, my brother ignores me as though I

don't exist.

He reaches out, his fingers grasping the queen's wig, and tears it straight from her head.

"Mr. *Priest*," she hisses, her own fingers jotting upward, as though to make a grab for the fake hair, despite being a second too late.

With casual dismissiveness, Guy tosses the wig to the side, where it slides across the floor and catches under the leg of the coffee table. Only then does he offer a dramatic dip of his head, playing the part of ever-dutiful servant.

For fuck's sake.

The queen's blond hair is in disarray, locks strewn this way and that and sticking up like prey confronted by something bigger, meaner. "That—that was *unacceptable*. If my father—"

"Your father's dead, Princess."

Princess. As if she didn't watch her father be brutally shot down in front of her—and an entire rally—just two months ago. The blood that spattered her face and clothing in the aftermath has been stitched into every highlight reel on the telly ever since. I look at her now, eyeing her expression critically, and wonder how many times she's tried to eviscerate the memory.

Hundreds, I imagine.

More, probably.

And now my brother, ass that he's been since birth, is throwing sludge in the already gaping wound.

I elbow him to the side. "What Guy means to say is that you shouldn't be here, Your Majesty." I shoot a pointed, *fucking-behave-yourself* look in my brother's direction. Nothing in his expression gives me any reason to believe that we're on the same page. Blowing out a frustrated breath, I give him my back. "It's too dangerous.

You ought to have gone through the usual channels. We put Clarke with you for a reason."

Queen Margaret flinches, and I nearly start a mental countdown for the inevitable hysterics. "I needed to come here myself," she says, her voice nothing stronger than a break in the wind. "Your father . . . I remember that he used to visit St. James's whenever there was something troublesome to discuss."

It's my turn to withhold a flinch.

I step back, putting distance between myself and the queen before I do something regrettable. Like remind her that it's *my* family that's been sacrificed time and again for the sake of hers.

Sacrificed, splintered, and forever altered.

"Those days are over." I move to the sink, then pour myself a glass of water from the faucet. I don't drink it, but it's best to focus on something else when I speak, otherwise the words might stop coming. *Just as they did when the blessed king branded me.* Habit has me wanting to lift my fingers to the raised flesh behind my ear. Self-control, however, wins out. As always. "We run a pub widely known for its political leanings. What do you think would happen if someone caught us at St. James's? Hell, if someone catches you *here?*"

"*Boom*," Guy answers, his thumb cocking the safety of a fake finger pistol that he touches to his temple. Then, planting his hands flat on the counter, he juts his chin forward and stares the queen down. "We don't exist to you, Princess. This"—he shuffles a finger between them—"shouldn't be happening. We've spent years establishing this place, its reputation . . . *our* reputation."

"Which is what?" she asks softly.

"Isn't it obvious?" Guy leans in, wordlessly baiting her

to do the same—the way I've seen him do countless times in the past, just before he snatches a man by the shirt collar and bashes his head against the closest flat surface. But instead of pulling that maneuver, the same one he taught me the summer I turned eleven, he only issues a slow, humorless smile. "We want to see you break."

She flinches again.

Weak, so fucking *weak*.

If I weren't so desperate to keep my country from crumbling, I'd tell the queen exactly what I think of her: she's timid, as poor a fit for the throne as her deranged father was before her. He ruled as a dictator and, so far, she's ruled like she's terrified of her own shadow. We'd all be better off with her still prancing about in the Scottish countryside, doing whatever the hell she's been doing for the last twenty-some years. With the monarchy disassembled—

No.

The condensation on the glass dampens my palm, turning it slick like the blood that coated my nape when King John carved a number into my flesh.

502.

The fifth generation of spies in my family to work alongside the Crown under the umbrella of Holyrood, an off-the-books agency that was originally named after Holyrood Palace in Edinburgh. It's where my great-great-grandfather was awarded a medal of valor after saving Prince Robert's life during the Second Boer War.

Over a hundred years later, and here we are.

Guy is 501, Damien 503.

But only I have my life's purpose branded into my skin like I'm nothing but cattle to be sold at auction.

Prove it to your son that the Crown must always come first.

A hard lesson to learn, but one that continues to hum

in my veins like a poison with no antidote.

I force the words from my throat, refusing to succumb to silence: "Putting it bluntly, ma'am, our customers would love nothing more than to see you end up just like the king. Dead. Out of the way. A nonissue. Let your mind fill in the blanks, and then come up with something ten times worse."

Her cornflower blue eyes widen, then narrow sharply. "I-If the two of you are done with the lectures, I came here today because I have something that can't be passed through Clarke. There's no time for that, and I thought . . ." Awkwardly, she fumbles with her handbag, her fingers visibly shaking, and it occurs to me, now, that while my brothers and I have spent our entire lives with the royal family at the epicenter of our respective universes, she hardly knows us.

She knows our names. She knows our history—at least as far back as Pa, I'm guessing—and I'm going to assume that she knows the basics about Holyrood: some of the other agents, our central location, even. But beyond that . . . us Godwins are veritable strangers to her.

Our hopes, our dreams, are nothing but a speck of dust on her gilded radar.

With a hushed curse under her breath, she pulls out a mobile smeared with dirt. "I found this in the gardens while I was walking two mornings ago. The same morning that . . . that—"

I exchange a glance with Guy, who scrubs a hand over his mouth.

"They were caught," he grits out, voice hard and unforgiving. "Clarke told you that we suspected something was off with them, and—"

"I didn't listen!" The queen whirls around, her free

hand clenching into a fist at her side. Her signet ring glistens under the light. Ruby red, a hand-me-down of her father's that I well remember. "You can say it, Mr. Priest. Go on. I didn't listen to your advice to not wander the grounds on my own until you could be sure of them. The only fool standing in this room is *me*."

The phone is thrown on the counter where it careens into the wall.

"They were only teenagers, and I couldn't"—she presses a hand to her mouth, her knuckles whitening with tension—"I couldn't make myself truly believe that they'd been sent to kill me. That they weren't anything more than stable hands. I should have listened. *I should have listened.*"

Soft.

It's not that she's weak, it's that Queen Margaret doesn't have the heart—the iron spine—to do what needs to be done in today's tumultuous climate. After suffering the last twenty-five years under King John's reign, parliament has become the equivalent of a brutal brawler's match since her father's assassination two months ago. And, equal to her rabid supporters are the millions who would see the crown stripped from her head and the jewels torn from her fingers.

"The king," Guy says now, his stare locked on the queen's face, "is to blame, not you. He ruled with fear after your sister was murdered. Anyone who opposed him went straight into a jail cell—assuming they didn't disappear completely. You know this, ma'am. You see the polls. You see what's blasted all over the news every night. Don't tell me you don't."

She pauses, just for a moment, her fingers wringing together in front of her. "All of it, Mr. Priest." A tick pulses to life in her jaw. "I see it all."

My brother beats a fast-paced tempo on the counter with his thumb. "People don't like the amount of power your family still wields, especially after everything that's happened. With your father gone, they want the same of you. That's no secret."

Lifting her gaze to the ceiling, her throat works with a hard swallow. "Tell me what to do, then."

"Go back to your palace."

"The mobile—"

"We'll take care of it," I say. We'll take care of the problem just like we've taken care of everything else: by leaning into the pub. It was a Holyrood decision for the so-called Priest brothers to open it ten years ago. It made sense. On paper, Guy, Damien, and I don't exist. A perk, if you will, for being born into a family whose sole duty is to keep the royal family thriving for yet another generation. While the other Holyrood members once had lives, before their recruitment, this is all my brothers and I have ever known.

Survival.

Deception.

Responsibility.

The Bell & Hand is the culmination of all that—a haven for those with a rebellious streak who seek a Britain without the lords and the ladies and the pomp of the royal family.

Absently, I reach up to the scar that I keep hidden with my hair. The pads of my fingers trace the scarred flesh.

As much as I want to tell the queen to piss off—the same way I wanted to tell her father—I never will.

Loyalty to my brothers, both those bound by blood and not, keeps me locked in a prison, generations in the making. The world sees the Priests as traitors, the scum of the earth.

Loyalists see us that way, I remind myself as I turn my back on the queen and snatch the phone off the counter. To those loyal to the Crown we're radical anti-loyalists, but to others . . . we're bonafide heroes.

Even if it's a façade composed of nothing but lies.

CHAPTER 2

ISLA

I'm fucked.

Or, better yet, I'm desperate.

Desperate for a life where I don't count every quid in my purse, always worried that the lights might be turned off at the flat I share with my two younger siblings.

Five years ago, I was prepared to move to the States. A new fancy job beckoned me across the pond, and then there was Stephen, my fiancé, who, even though he didn't quite make my heart race, was still the perfect foil to the life I'd created for myself.

Then the riots began. The streets of London lit with anger and hate, and my parents—two middle-aged folks from Yorkshire who'd been in town to visit—were caught in the wrong place at the wrong time.

They were dead before the sun kissed the horizon good morning.

I never made it to America. Never took the fancy job. Never went anywhere with Stephen after that.

Most days it feels like I'm twenty-nine going on eighty-nine.

I tip my head back, lifting my chin so I can scan the black-and-gold sign hanging above the pub's diamond-paned front window. The Bell & Hand. The ampersand has been scraped to within an inch of its life, the black peeking through the faded gold paint. I trail my gaze south, over the glossy black door and the shiny brass knob—move to the right, where potted plants sit in window boxes. Despite the fact that it's March, the flowers are in full bloom, the poppies bright pink and yellow—a direct contrast to the dour-looking bloke gazing out the window.

No finely tailored suits like I saw regularly at the network.

No fancy smart watches encircling thick wrists.

No red poppies pinned to their lapels, in silent support of the royal family.

It's for that reason specifically that I've come to apply for a position. Five years ago, before the Westminster Riots, I hadn't heard of The Bell & Hand, not even in passing amongst friends. But now . . . well, now it seems like the perfect place to be, given our shared beliefs on the Crown.

The black door swings open and a dark-haired man steps out, a newspaper clasped to his chest as he draws a hat atop his head.

"Sorry," he mutters, when he finds me loitering on the pub's front stoop.

We sashay right, then left, and with an upturn of his lips, he finally steps around me. I keep the door open with the toe of my shoe.

I swallow past the lump in my throat. Straighten my shoulders with single-minded purpose. Duck inside, and then draw in a sharp breath at the scent of cigars and pub food and anti-loyalist blood. It's a heady concoction, made only that much sweeter when I catch sight of croissants being delivered to a table.

Delicious.

I've always been a sucker for a good pastry.

With my folder tucked under my arm, I edge farther inside.

Online, I read that the Priest brothers own The Bell & Hand. Like the pub itself, the Priest surname wouldn't have registered five years ago—but nowadays, it feels like I know everything that's ever been reported on them . . . Not that there's much.

Unfortunately.

I do know this: The brothers are notorious among anti-loyalist circles. Spoken of with complete reverence and only ever mentioned in passing, it's like everyone is aware of their existence though no one dares dive any deeper. I didn't stumble across any pictures of them online. No firsthand interviews, either.

Because people are terrified of the repercussions if caught dishing out that information?

It's not the first time the unnerving thought has snuck up on me, and I quickly stamp down a spark of worry.

I'm in need of a job, and if I have the opportunity to take one that won't shove "God Save the Queen" propaganda down my throat, then there's simply no better fit.

"Looking for somethin'?" asks one of the servers in a thick, Cockney accent when he spots me hovering by the bar. His graying hair is thin at the crown and seems to have migrated to his bushy beard. "The boss ain't in."

From all accounts, all three Priest brothers manage The Bell & Hand. "I want to apply for a position."

His shrewd, brown eyes drift down my body, taking

leisurely time to stop at my breasts and hips before he sucks his teeth behind his bottom lip. "Sorry, no openings."

Before the riot, before my chance for freedom was ripped away by circumstances out of my control, I worked as a celebrity publicist. I can read a schemer when I see one, and this man? He schemes with the best of them. I bet he wouldn't know honesty if it crawled out of that unruly beard of his and waved 'ello.

Reaching for the closest chair, I drag it out, purposely allowing its spindle-wooden legs to scrape against the floor, then sit down without an invitation. I tip my face up, all the better to meet the bloke's stare head-on. "I have time to wait."

I don't, actually, not with Josie and Peter in and out of school, but that's not this man's business. All *he* needs to know is that I won't be moving until I speak to one of the Priest brothers. Lucky for him, I'm not picky. Any of them will do—I'm certainly not about to start playing favorites.

The server grumbles under his breath, but anything he might have said next is forgotten the moment a dark-haired woman comes flying out from the hallway beside the bar. She hustles between the tables, moving slow enough to not crash into anyone but fast enough that I notice the harried way she peers back over her shoulder, once, twice, before darting out the front door and disappearing out onto Fournier Street.

Curiosity seeps into my veins when I hear a rumbling voice bark, "Jack!"

The Cockney server whips around, torso twisting sharply. His back snaps straight, and mine does, too, at the sight of the man entering the pub.

Savage.

My nails scrape the table as the thought flares to life.

He's big, large in a way that most men can't even compare. But it isn't his intimidating frame that kicks my pulse into overdrive.

It's his face.

I stare openly, unable to wrench my gaze away from the harsh line of his crooked nose or the angry, ragged scar that gravely distorts his upper lip. My knees squeeze together under the table, feet involuntarily pulling inward as though prepared to send me running. The response is completely instinctual. *Fight or flight*. He's not a man to anger, that I already know. His cheekbones are high, and his lack of beard surprises me.

Doesn't he want to cover that scar? Maybe he likes it, the way it stops people dead in their tracks and makes them nervously avert their eyes. Maybe he even finds a certain thrill in their fear. It seems impossible that he might be a man who cowers with insecurities himself—

Not when he storms over to Jack, the server, arrogance lining every stride.

Not when they jump into conversation about an order that was late on delivery, and I sit in my chair, wondering if I'm about to make a massive mistake.

Not when Jack says something under his breath, waving an arm in my direction, and I learn firsthand how the scarred man feels about a stranger seeing him for the very first time.

The palest green eyes I've ever encountered fixate on me. Fixate, and don't waver, as though that one glance has gifted him the opportunity to bare my soul and steal every last one of my secrets. Including those I plan to keep buried. A harsh breath billows over my lips as I struggle to hold my ground.

At my old job, I came across men like him frequently.

Not savage men, not men with faces that could terrify small children and send full grown adults scrambling. But men who felt the need to assert their dominance, no matter the battlefield. Even Stephen, for all his public support of women, never missed the chance to remind me that he'd chosen me and not the other way around.

The only thing I miss about my ex is his eight-inch cock and even that's forgettable. A big knob means nothing if its owner is pure shite in the bedroom.

With smooth, controlled movements, I set the folder down on the table. Then lift my chin, boldly meeting those pale eyes once more. In the center, near his pupils, the green becomes a tawny yellow, a color so unique that I feel uneasy just being under their unrelenting stare.

Devil eyes. Soulless eyes.

"Are you Mr. Priest?" I ask, sweeping my attention up to his dark hair. Despite scouring The Bell & Hand's website for information about its owners, the About Us section was dreadfully dull beyond the basics. Dates of upcoming events. An award won here and there. A mission statement that preached the belief in an establishment that welcomes all patrons, so long as their favorite whisky is Scottish and not Irish. A joke, I suppose, but not one that does much in the way of giving up this man's secrets.

And nothing to help differentiate the three brothers from each other aside from their names.

Guy. Saxon. Damien.

I study the man before me, refusing to quiver under his hard stare, despite the nervous fluttering in my belly, and take a wild guess that he's the middle brother.

Saxon the Savage—it has an appropriate ring to it.

The man's scarred lip curls. "Who's asking?" he bites out, dismissing Jack as he faces me fully. Lord, he seems even bigger now that he's within touching distance. He's dressed casually in dark-washed jeans and a ribbed, black jumper that matches the hue of his hair and does little to conceal the wide breadth of his shoulders.

Jack clears his throat. "She's wanting a job. I told her that we aren't hirin'." He swivels his head to scowl at me. "Which we ain't. Hirin', that is."

The man steps forward and, helpful as always, I hook my foot around the leg of a nearby chair and shove it back. "Feel free to take a seat," I say, going for humor-laden friendliness. All the better to butter him up. I need this job—no other will do.

Desperation at its finest.

Green eyes narrow imperceptibly in my direction. "I own every chair in this pub, including yours." It's said without inflection, and he gives me no time to think of a comeback before he grabs the chair by its back and drags it so close to mine that the wood grazes my knees. The feet clatter loudly against the floor when he roughly sets it down, and then he's sitting—collapsing, really—and holding my ground becomes that much harder.

Savage no longer cuts it.

He is ... he is *terrifying*.

My fingers curl helplessly around the edge of my folder. *Don't let him see how unnerved you are!* Maybe if he weren't only centimeters away, with his muscular thighs straddling mine, I would feel ten times more confident about putting him in his place. As it is, it takes every ounce of fortitude to lamely quip, "So you *are* one of the Priest brothers?" I should have looked harder for pictures of them online, done more research, but other than those few mentions in the articles I found, the Priest men might as well be ghosts. They exist nowhere and everywhere, all at once. "Saxon?" I test, hoping I'm right.

He leans forward, his inner thighs scraping my bare leg, where my skirt has ridden up to just north of my knees, and then swipes the folder from under my hand. "We're all out of openings," he murmurs instead of answering my question. His black hair creeps over his forehead as he skims my CV. "Although I'll be disappointed to pass over such ... outstanding references."

The patronizing note in his voice sets my teeth on edge. "I'm more than capable of serving food, Mr. Priest." I feel my nostrils flare as I stare him down. "It doesn't take a rocket scientist to get a plate from Point A to Point B."

He keeps his focus locked on the sheet of paper when he drawls, "No, Miss"—his finger traces my name—"Quinn, you're right. It doesn't."

"Then I ought to be a shoo-in. I've worked in some form of customer service for my entire life."

"If that's the case," he says, once more fixing that unholy stare on my face, "then hearing the word *No* shouldn't be out of the norm."

My entire body stiffens. "On the contrary. When someone like me does their job to perfection, all I hear is *Yes* and *Let's have more of that, please.*"

The words fly from my mouth before I can regulate them—or even consider how they might be interpreted—sexual, aggressively forward—and my cheeks instantly heat like I've baked under the sun for hours, naked. This is a nightmare, an absolute, bloody nightmare.

"That isn't—that's not at all what I—"

Saxon Priest is clearly no gentleman. Instead of allowing me to wallow in my own embarrassment, in solitude, mind you, he ends my stammering with a raised brow. "The Bell & Hand isn't that kind of establishment,

Miss Quinn."

He hasn't just—

He didn't just imply that I'm a . . . that I'm a—

"For that sort of work, I suggest Paddington instead."

My eyes go wide.

What. A. *Wanker.*

Not that it matters, but I haven't shagged anyone since Stephen. The prized land between the valleys is experiencing a years' long drought, if you will. And even if that weren't the case, I would *never* consider sleeping with a man for money.

Although money is exactly what I need right now, and it's the only reason I'm still sitting here and not introducing him to my swinging fist.

Gritting my teeth, so hard that I swear I can hear my molars grinding to dust, I purse my lips into a tight smile. "A miscommunication. I'm here to apply for a front-of-the-house position. I can clean tables, refill drinks, that sort of thing."

Shifting his weight back, he reclines like an animal, predatory down to its marrow but content to watch its prey feel the anxiety of the hunt. One muscular forearm rests on the table; one long leg stretches out past mine. Having effectively blocked me in, his mouth—scarred and all—curves upward. It's wicked and uneven and lacks all signs of warmth.

A foreboding shiver streaks down my spine, even as I bite back my pride and allow myself to beg. For the sake of my siblings. For the sake of my long-term goals. For the sake of survival.

"Hire me," I whisper. "Please."

"Apologies, Miss Quinn, but the answer's still no."

Tossing my CV on the table, he makes a move to

stand. And this time it's despair that kicks my arse into gear. I jerk out my right leg, cutting off his upward momentum by kicking him in the soft flesh of the back of his closest knee.

"*Fuck—*"

His weight destabilizes, big hands clutching and releasing the air as he fights for purchase. I sweep his chair forward, hooking my toes around the wooden leg, then plant my hand against his stone-hard thigh—and push.

With his balance already unstable, he topples backward, once more collapsing in the seat.

Raw, undiluted fury flares in his expression. In a voice pitched so low that I can barely hear it over the other customers in the pub, he growls, "Get. Out."

Stand your ground.

You need this.

He called you a prostitute!

Swallowing a healthy dose of unease, I shake my head. "I cannot."

Those pale eyes of his empty of any and all patience—not that he had much to begin with. "Give me one good reason why I shouldn't toss you out on your ass."

It's now or never.

This moment is five years in the making. Five years of putting myself directly in the fire and stoking the flames. Five years of planning and doing everything in my power to prove that my parents didn't die in vain.

That my siblings will live in an England—in a *world*—where a king or a queen can't cause chaos with a flippant flick of the wrist.

The man seated across from me may *look* savage but looks can deceive. Souls . . . souls can't, and mine was lost to a riot that tore my family to shreds. I can only hope that somewhere, deep inside, his humanity outguns his frigid personality.

There's one item missing from my CV.

One achievement that can never be listed.

I'm Isla Quinn, and I killed the king.

For my siblings.

For my country.

And for vengeance.

"Time's running out, Miss Quinn."

Leaning forward, I smile at the scarred man seated opposite me. I need him, and though he doesn't realize it yet, he needs me too. "I have a proposition for you, Mr. Priest, and I think it'd be in your best interest to hear me out."

CHAPTER 3

SAXON

In my world, Isla Quinns are a dime a dozen.

Women—and men—who think they can hack it in London's underground and offer something crucial to the anti-loyalist cause. Oh, they do their best to rise to the occasion, I'll give them that. They stand side by side with the other protesters, hoisting posters high above their heads with slogans like, *Death to the Monarchy!* or *Long Live Democracy!*

But then trouble—as it always does—snakes its way in. Shackles clank around wrists. A friend finds himself sprawled on the ground, trampled by the crowd. A semi-automatic goes off—something no civilian ought to have in the first place—and you look down to find that your fingers come away with blood after touching the growing, sudden ache in your chest.

Boom.

Where dissent goes, trouble always follows.

And Holyrood creeps in afterward, snipping the lifelines of those who would do more than just shout about the injustices of a British monarchy.

I look at Isla Quinn now, and in her blue eyes I see that same misguided belief that she has what it takes to make a difference.

She doesn't.

No one does.

If, for no other reason than because Holyrood won't allow it.

Savior. Devil.

I suppose, depending on your stance, we play both sides of the fence—and we do it to perfection.

Except for the king's assassination.

My chest grows tight, and I'm not sure if it's because Isla is studying me like I might pounce and tear her apart, limb from limb, like some savage beast, or if it's the ever-present awareness that I failed. *We* failed.

With finality, I shut down those thoughts.

Cracking my knuckles, I slide my ass to the edge of the chair so I'm centimeters from her. Strawberry-blond hair touches her collarbone and frames her face in soft waves. Freckles mar her skin, heavily concentrated on the bridge of her nose. In that prim skirt and blazer set she's wearing, she looks like a teacher hell-bent on correcting a student's errant ways. Otherwise innocent and naïve, but that husky voice of hers . . . the way she maneuvered my much larger frame, tells me that Isla Quinn is harboring secrets of her own.

Doesn't mean she's not unnerved, though.

Go ahead, I want to taunt when her blue eyes bounce from my face to my chest and then back up again, *show me how you really feel.* Any moment now, she'll start squirming. They all do. I know what I look like, and this isn't the first time—nor the last—that I'll use my face as a method in getting people to fuck off.

We're locked in a silent standoff. No words. No movement.

Until her full lips part and she utters for a second time, "Hire me."

My palm flattens on the table as I lean forward, close enough that I note the way she draws her shoulders together like she's facing off against the enemy. *How ironically accurate.* "I'm not interested in your propositions, Miss Quinn."

"Will you listen to what—"

"You have nothing that I want."

Long lashes flutter as she blinks back at me once, twice, thrice. And then, just when I think she's about to accept defeat, her pert chin thrusts forward and she jabs a finger into my chest. "You don't even know what I'm offering, what I'm willing to bring to the table."

I catch her finger, then slip my hand around her wrist before she can issue protest. She's dainty, small-boned despite being relatively tall for a woman, and I use my hold to yank her into me. By her ear, I hiss, "Listen to me carefully, Miss Quinn, because I'm going to say this only once: you're out of your league."

Pulling at her caged hand, her mouth grazes my cheek. Furiously, she whispers, "That's your opinion, which you're absolutely entitled to. But you don't know me from Adam. I'm more than capable of handling myself."

Maybe, but unlikely.

I've heard this same story a million times over since we opened The Bell & Hand. Isla Quinn isn't the first to show up here with so-called *propositions* that we can't live without. No, she's only the first to pretend that she's hoping to make a career out of serving tables before dropping the tall act and revealing her true motives.

"I don't know what you thought you might get out of coming here but I'm no pillock. You're wanting more than a job, and I hate to break it to you, but we aren't recruiting for anything else." I release her sharply then shove back my chair and climb to my feet. "You want to throw your hat into the ring? I suggest volunteering at a local charity, for the kids who've lost their parents after the last riot."

I barely make it two steps before her voice has my knees locking tight: "Who do you suppose those kids grow up to become, Mr. Priest? Perfect, law-abiding citizens? Adults who meekly accept their lot in life, despite the fact that it's been ripped to shreds, so much so that it's barely recognizable?"

Body frozen in place, my gaze locks on Jack, who watches us with sharp eyes while he collects dirty plates from a table. The man's been with The Bell & Hand almost since the day we opened. Reformed bank thief. Crude around the edges but unrivaled when under pressure. Absolutely, wholly, despises the Crown.

Maybe it makes me a fool but I'm the one who's kept Jack out of prison over the years. Me, not Guy or Damien. *Me.* And perhaps that's my Achilles heel—forging connections with people who hate the monarchy, who hate King John, the way I did.

The way I do, even now.

Even still.

Duty is not voluntary. And, sometimes, loyalty isn't a gift but a threat. A persistent, barely concealed warning to exist within the structured lines before you find yourself permanently disciplined. *Just like Pa.*

Voice gruff, I edge out, "You have ten seconds to make your point, Miss Quinn."

Her chair scrapes back, the sound echoing loudly in my ears. "My siblings are just like those children that the charities support. Twelve and thirteen when my parents were murdered in the Westminster Riots. You don't recover from something like that . . . *I* can't recover from something like that."

Slender, feminine fingers graze my forearm, and I immediately step out of reach. "Five seconds," I grunt, as I turn to face her. "Four, now."

Luminous blue eyes retrace their path up my chest, to my neck, and then, finally, to my face. If she's terrified, she doesn't show it. Instead she only frames her hips with her hands. "I can't go back to the way things were, which means I can't work in a position with people who don't understand me, what I've gone through, what I've survived. They report the news, but their lives are otherwise untouched. *Pristine.* Working here—knowing what The Bell & Hand stands for—is what I need to keep going."

My molars grind together. "We don't take on charity."

"Trust me, I'm not looking for hand-outs. I'm only wanting to make a difference—to find a place where I belong."

I almost laugh.

If only Isla Quinn knew that the queen was here, less than an hour ago. How's that for belonging? I wear deception like a monk does his robes. And because I do, I only smile, slow, dangerous and—*there we go*.

The fear.

It widens her gaze. It straightens her spine. And though she tries hard to hide her visceral response, fear hastens her breathing too. Her own body has betrayed her.

"If you know what's good for you," I murmur, my voice pitched low, "you'll leave, and you won't come back."

She audibly swallows. "I'm not scared of you."

I meet her blue gaze. "You should be."

"Mr. Priest—"

"We don't have a position for you, and whatever your proposition is, I'd advise keeping it to yourself—unless you want your siblings to find themselves without their older sister, too."

Her mouth falls open. "Are you *threatening* me?"

"Not even close." I step back, lending much-needed space between us. "But I recognize a lost soul when I see one, and I can promise that you won't find what you're looking for here."

"You don't even *know* me."

I tilt my chin toward where I left her CV on the table. "All I need to know is on that paper. A girl like you, quitting her job at a big news network to work in a well-known anti-loyalist pub? You're clearly living off anger, nourishing it like it's your only sustenance." The Isla Quinns of the world only end up in one place: six feet under. Too stubborn, too shortsighted, and too hell-bent on rectifying a wrong that can never be undone. Emotion will get you killed. *Hate* will get you killed. I shake my head. "You'll be dead before the end of the year because you're too damned blind to see when someone is doing you a favor."

"I didn't ask for a therapy session," she snaps, the fear in her voice displaced by irritation.

"Brilliant," I tell her, turning away, "then get the hell out of my pub."

I don't meet Jack's gaze as I stalk past him. Instead, I duck under the bar and grab a tumbler and the bottle of Lagavulin off the oak shelf. The amber whisky hits the glass with a splash, and as I bring it to my lips, I watch

Isla Quinn storm out the front door in a flurry of strawberry-blond waves and tailored black clothes.

I lost my soul in a secret room in St. James's Palace. *No,* a little voice says in my head, *it was destroyed.* Destroyed by a king who used a child to keep a grown man in place. I never got it back, not then, not when Pa was discovered dead on Marlborough Road, not when Jayme Paul, my father's second, shepherded my brothers and my mum and I out of the country and into Paris, where we lived with next to nothing for years.

But sometimes . . . sometimes I still find it in myself to do the right thing, the *noble* thing.

It would have been all too easy to use Isla's anger to my advantage.

Even easier to use her as prey to lure in all the bastards on the hunt for Queen Margaret. A pretty girl like Isla? They'd all come running, each and every last one of them.

A visual of glittering blue eyes storms my brain.

Some of us gave up our souls long ago, but others . . . *Isla*—not everyone is a lost cause. Not everyone is lost, permanently.

"To the heroes," I mutter, tossing back the rest of the Lagavulin like it's nothing more than a gin and tonic, and welcoming the fiery burn as I swallow, "and to the villains."

And to me.

A man lost to duty.

To the Crown.

And to the death of every soul who's tried to change the direction of fate.

God save the queen.

CHAPTER 4

ISLA

"Well?" my younger sister demands as soon as the front door to our flat closes behind her. "What's the verdict?"

Absolutely pitiful.

Five hours after Saxon Priest shut me down, I force the brittleness from my expression just as Josie cuts the corner into our kitchenette and drops her ratty school bag onto the table. With a sniff of the heavily scented air, she leans around me to check out the curry I'm whipping together. All it takes is one look at the bubbling sauce for her to bump me out of the way and take over stirring.

Her blue eyes slide toward me with impatience. "Are you going to spill or what?"

For as long as I'll live, I'll never forget a nine-year-old Josie leaping from the treehouse Dad built for her and Peter, back in York. She'd jumped because Peter had pulled the same daredevil stunt, first, only to fracture his ankle, snap his tibia, and be relegated to crutches for months on end. He'd moaned about the pain all night and groaned about his limited mobility all day. That is, until

Josie followed suit, flying from the treehouse with all the reckless abandon of a baby bird tumbling from its nest.

Amidst her crying, I'd demanded to know why she'd been so insane as to risk her own neck. Her only answer was that Peter had looked so dejected, always propped up on his crutches and hobbling from room to room. She'd wanted him to know that she understood his need to fly.

Josie at nearly seventeen is no better than her at nine with her hot-pink leg cast and gap-toothed smile. She still sees too much, senses far more than she should, and has the annoyingly persistent habit of pushing until I crack.

"Great news!" I squeeze her arm in a gesture that I hope she'll interpret as genuine excitement. The frown that immediately mars her face suggests otherwise. *Bollocks.* Hastily, I add, "They requested a second interview."

Liar.

I am. Have been for years now.

I tell myself that I have no choice if I want to keep Josie and Peter safe, but sometimes I wonder who I'm fooling. Myself? The memory of my dead parents, who I've already failed countless times in the last five years?

The familiar sting of regret sits like a brick in my stomach.

One day soon, Peter will move out of our small Stepney Green flat, and my sister will follow not long after, and I can't even think about it all without my pulse erratically skipping a beat. But it doesn't matter how deep fear burrows under my skin when I think about us not being under the same roof every night. And it doesn't matter that the last time we were separated, Mum and Dad died. To go through that again ...

Stop. You have to stop.

"Isla?"

At Josie's concerned prompting, I swallow, thickly, and turn toward the cabinets before she can get a read on me. "We'll see how it goes, yeah? I'd say that I'm more than equipped to handle a few plates." To prove my point, I grab three from the shelf and make an exaggerated show of setting them neatly on the table after elbowing Josie's bag to the floor. Lifting a brow, I brush my hands together in a *job-well-done* gesture and look to my sister. "What d'you say? Should I ask for a raise already?"

My poor attempt at humor barely earns me a smile before Josie rolls her eyes and returns to the curry. Her red hair, a shade that looks like gold bathed in sunlight, sweeps forward to hide her face. "You shouldn't even be working at a pub," she mutters, her shoulders hunched as she stirs vigorously, "you had a job. Your dream job. And then you *quit*."

Except that I didn't quit. My position was "terminated."

While protesters disappeared without a trace and the king grew more irrational, I sought to rip back the velvet curtains and show my fellow Brits that the concept of a constitutional monarchy was dead in the water, if it had existed at all in the last twenty-five years since Princess Evangeline's death. I took the job with the news network to destabilize the status quo. Get dirty. Get real. *Make a difference.*

And the network? So much evidence dumped in their laps and all they'd wanted was for me to piss off.

"The pay was stagnant," I tell Josie, lying, once again, for the sake of keeping our family united. *A team of three, for now, for always.* I don't want them to worry. Better they think that I looked at our finances—meager though they are—and determined that leaving the station wouldn't further ruin us.

Josie's stirring pauses. "Because working at The Bell & Hand will make you more?"

"It'll be fine, I promise."

She turns the hob off, her slim shoulders straightening as she slides the steaming pot onto the back burner. "Well, it'd be even more than fine if I took a gap year like Amanda and Bea."

I smother a groan. "Jos, we've talked about this. You're going to uni, just like I did, just like Peter is doing now."

"Who says I even *want* to go?"

"Life isn't always about doing what you want." If it were, then I'd be in America, working some posh publicist job and reminding celebrities to wipe their arses before they walked the red carpet. But here I am—in London, in this hovel of a flat, having the same bloody argument with my sister that we've hashed out a million times over. "Go to uni. Get a good job."

"Like you? Do you suppose your diploma from Bristol will get you that raise at the pub?"

Grinding my teeth to the point of pain, I mutter, "When I went to uni, this blasted country hadn't gone straight to hell yet." Ripping open one of the cabinets, I grab three glasses off the shelf. "The little things that made life worth living are gone. They don't exist. Which means, if you want any sort of life at all then you can forget about the gap year. We're lucky the universities are still open."

Because she's sixteen and thinking short-term, my sister spins around, frustration etched into her delicate features. "You say no to *everything*! I can't even—" She breaks off, drawing in a sharp inhalation. "Maybe if you stopped pushing us for the things that *you* think we want, then we wouldn't feel the need to go around your back.

It's not like we don't know what happened."

It's not like we don't know what happened.

My stomach freefalls and it's a miracle I don't drop the glasses on the floor. Sticking them on the table, I immediately grip the edge for stability. My legs feel like Jell-O. My head feels like it's been shoved inside a water tank and I'm dreadfully low on oxygen.

How could they know? *How could they* know? About the king. About what I did. About the fury that lit my veins when I pulled the trigger.

Fury and resentment and a keen self-awareness that I was altering my life course forever.

I don't regret it. Maybe that makes me cold-blooded. Maybe that means I've abandoned all morality—morality that I've always clung to during the hardest times of my life. Maybe that makes me as vile as King John.

Someone murdered Princess Evangeline and someone else murdered my parents and I murdered the king in return.

Three wrongs don't make a right, but that didn't stop the satisfaction from flooding my body when I saw his shocked expression, seconds before he stumbled backward into his daughter, Princess—*Queen*—Margaret.

Liar. Murderer. Hypocrite.

Three words that I whisper to myself every night when I turn off the lights and slip into bed. It's not who I was born to be, but it's what I've become. But none of that explains how Peter and Josie discovered that I'm the one who killed King John. The police don't even know—though I'm not entirely sure if that's because I did a damn good job of covering my tracks or on account of the fact that, like parliament, the Metropolitan Police's infrastructure is also crumbling.

Uneasy, I press a balled fist to my stomach. "Josie, I—"

"The network fired you," my sister tosses out, cutting me off. When my brows shoot north in surprise, she snaps up her chin defiantly. "Peter found the termination letter in your desk. We both know, and we're—we're tired of you acting like we're children! We're not and we're certainly not *your* children. I'm old enough to decide if I want a gap year and Peter is old enough to decide if and when he joins the protesters, no matter that you tell him he's not allowed."

Instead of experiencing a rush of relief that my secret is safe, I feel nothing but a blade of fear. It twists and plunges, churning my insides, leaving me chilled. My gaze flies to the clock on the wall and I note the time with a punch of dread.

Dammit, Peter.

I push away from the kitchen table. "Where is he?"

Josie crosses her arms over her chest, stubborn to the very end. "In class."

Peter attends Queen Mary University, which is less than a ten-minute walk from our flat. It's Thursday, and even when his class runs late, he never misses a meal. The world could actually be ending, and my brother would take his last breath with a plate of Yorkshire pudding in one hand and a cheese pasty in the other. In every other part of his life, Peter is the very definition of predictable but with the ongoing protests . . . Bloody hell, I'm going to wring his neck.

I meet my sister's stare. "Answer the question, Jos."

"Or what?" she retorts, eyeing me over the slope of her nose. She's taller by a scant few centimeters, has been since she turned fourteen, and never fails to remind me of it. "You won't let me do what I want? Newsflash, I might as well be under house arrest as it is." A sly smile curves her lips as she thrusts her hands forward, wrists kissing like she's prepping to be handcuffed. "Make it official, yeah? Might as well lock me up because I won't be spilling anything about Peter—"

Beeeeeep! Beeep! Beep!

My head snaps toward the window that overlooks Alderney Road at the same time Josie reels backward, her fingers drifting toward her midsection like the wind has been knocked right out of her.

It might as well have.

I remember a time when London's streets weren't outfitted with alarms at nearly every intersection. I took everyday city noises for granted, then. Better to fall asleep to the mundane sound of drunks stumbling down the street than the utter stillness of people waiting for the next tragedy to strike. But this is how we live now—this is what we've become—and fear and retribution and defiance are ingrained in every breath we take.

The not-so-peaceful protests. The all-and-out riots.

The violence.

The death.

Because that's what the siren signifies. Another protest. Another person with their life source snuffed out much too soon.

Without another word, I head for the front door. Shrugging into my coat, I check the inside pocket for the outline of the knife that I've carried with me for years now.

Behind me, I hear Josie's cautious footsteps. "You can't go," she whispers, all trace of angry teenager already abandoned. "It wasn't supposed to get bad. Peter, he told me that it would all be fine."

"The sirens went off."

Fingers wrap around my wrist, tugging sharply. "Isla, you can't go. You *can't!*"

Ignoring the chill of disquiet skating down my spine, I shake my sister off and shove my keys into my pocket. The ridged edge cuts into my palm, and for a moment, I relish the bite of pain. *I'm alive, I'm alive, I'm alive.* A mantra that always feels like I'm baiting fate to prove me wrong.

Over my shoulder, I meet worried blue eyes. "Is he out there?" I ask, unable to silence the tremor in my voice.

There's no question as to who *he* is. Peter. Our brother. The third leg of our tight-knit trio.

Josie sweeps her stare down to our feet, like she can't bear to maintain eye contact. "Yes."

Fuck.

My hand grips the doorknob. "Where, Josie?"

"B-Buckingham Palace." Her fingers dart up to her red hair, threading through the strands. "Some of the kids from his student union were going and . . ." She chokes on a sob, and though my heart aches to comfort her, the way I've done since Mum and Dad died, I stand my ground. "I'm sorry, Isla. I'm so, so sorry." Stepping forward, she holds out a hand, reaching for me. Her fingers curl inward, grasping nothing but air when I don't move, before she drops her hand back down to her side. Dejection flattens the corners of her mouth. "Please don't be mad. He said you would never find out and I-I'm *sorry*."

"Lock the deadbolt and don't answer to anyone else if they come knocking." Opening the door, I slip out into the hallway, only to pause on the threshold. I glance back, my gaze zeroing in on Josie's forlorn expression. She's young, so much younger than I was when we lost Mum and Dad, and yet she carries none of the innocence that I did at her age.

ROAD TO FIRE

That elusive fire that coursed through my veins when I killed King John two months ago returns with a vengeance.

"Jos," I grit out, my hand locked around the door frame. When she looks at me, lashes wet with silent tears, I dig my nails into the wood as though that alone will keep me upright. "I'd do the same for you," I tell her, raw honesty clogging my throat, "I'd do the same for you."

CHAPTER 5

ISLA

Ambient light from the circling helicopter slashes across the crowd, creating an eerie glow over the protesters gathered outside the iron gates of Buckingham Palace.

A crooked nose. A thin-lipped mouth. A heavy pair of brows that snap together when someone shouts, "*Death to the queen!*"

Those within hearing vicinity echo the words like a battle cry: "*Death to the queen! Death to the queen! Death to the queen!*"

I suck in a sharp breath as bodies crowd inward from all sides, cutting off any chance for escape. Hands graze my hips, my arse. Feet stomp on mine as I slip through the angry throng. Pain registers in my toes before I find myself bobbing beneath an arm bent like a chicken wing as its owner thrusts a poster board in the air again and again, each time more vigorously than the last.

It's utter mayhem.

"*Peter*!" I shout, knowing it's futile but unable to stop myself from trying. *Again.* On the thirty-minute tube ride in, I rang him no less than fifteen times. Even now, I reach into my coat pocket for my mobile, sending a hasty three-word text: **WHERE ARE YOU**.

No sooner have I hit SEND that someone rams into me from the side and my phone flies from my grasp.

"Fuck," I mutter, making a hasty swipe for it as it falls out of sight amidst all the feet storming past, "fuck, *fuck!*"

Another body jostles roughly into mine, this time from behind, and I don't feel an ounce of remorse when I jab my elbow backward and hear a telltale masculine grunt. A hand clamps down around my wrist, jerking hard.

I don't waste precious moments exchanging pleasantries.

Instead, I duck low, catching the man off guard, and snatch my hand back before he can reel me in. The heat of his palm ghosts over the crown of my head, but I hustle away quickly, dragging my right foot over the gravel in a pitiful attempt to come across my lost mobile.

Nothing.

Nothing.

Frustration boils deep in my belly.

If—no, *when*—I find Peter, I'm going to kill him.

How could he be so stupid? So incredibly naïve as to think that these protests won't take a turn for the worse when the sun sets and darkness blankets the city? They do, each and every time. And, sometimes, they catch fire, gaining traction and vitality outside of The Mall until it spreads like the plague.

People get hurt. People *die*.

I cannot lose him, too.

Bracketing my mouth with my palms, I bellow, "*Peter!*"

His name is swallowed by a horn honking loudly, off to my left, followed swiftly by the sound of gushing water and startled yelps.

The City Police. The water cannons.

"Bloody hell."

The words have barely escaped before the crowd swoops in more tightly, dragging me deeper into the fold. Elbows knock against mine, unfamiliar hands landing on my spine to roughly usher me forward, toward St. James's Park. Fighting against the push would be akin to fighting a current, and I accept the trajectory with a shaky breath that rattles in my lungs.

"Go!" someone shouts. "Move faster!"

"Bugger," another voice cries out, each syllable merging with the sound of water hitting pavement. It might not be tear gas—water cannons are more humane, some say—but it still hurts like the devil and has the power to lift you clear off your feet if you're caught in the crosshairs.

My own feet stumble forward out of gathered momentum, but I manage a desperate glance over my shoulder to search the crowd. The cone of light from the helicopter continues to dance over faces, but none are recognizable. No blue eyes or short, jaggedly cut hair in desperate need of a trim. No Queen Mary pullover in dire need of a wash. No *Peter*.

Don't think the worst. Don't you dare think the worst.

Easier said than done, especially when screams erupt around me and my back dampens with water. The ground turns slick beneath my shoes, and I know my fate seconds before I hear the horn.

I go down in a sea of scrabbling hands and slipping feet, sucked under thrashing bodies all fighting for survival.

Terror clamps around my heart like a restricting vice, and then I hear nothing.

Not the yelling.

Not the whirring helicopter up above.

Just . . .

Nothing.

CHAPTER 6

SAXON

I reach down, grabbing the man by the threads of his shirt, and turn him over onto his back.

Under the moonlit sky, his face appears ashen. Blood pools beneath his right nostril. His upper lip is busted, his left cheek sliced open—a gift from another bloke's fist, I imagine—and it takes me less than three seconds to catalog the rest of him.

Blue tracksuit. Black trainers with untied shoelaces and blood spattered across the toes.

Seems I'm not the only one with my sights set on Alfie Barker tonight.

All around me, the protest at Buckingham Palace is a cacophony of chaos. The air crackles with tension—fear at its most formidable. And as I slip my thumb over my target's throat, I can't help but wonder if Queen Margaret is watching tonight's festivities.

We told her to stay away, to remain hidden.

If I were a betting man, though, I'd place every last quid I have that she's perched in one of the palace's windows, unable to tear her gaze away from the frenzy.

Because that's what this is. A frenzy. A mob.

And there's no stopping it.

With one palm hovering over Barker's throat, I use my free hand to search his pockets. A stick of chewing gum. A fiver. A purse stuffed full of identification cards. *Multiple.* All with different home addresses and different surnames though the picture remains the same and the first name never changes. Burner IDs. Shoving the wallet into my trousers, I make quick work of moving to his next pocket.

The throat beneath my palm gasps for air. I feel the withdrawal, the innate desperation, in the split second that it takes for him to exclaim, "Get away from me! Who the *fuck* do you think you—"

The rest of his sentence ends with the heel of my hand pressing into his larynx. He gurgles immediately, his fingers grasping my wrist to tug fruitlessly for release. When I don't ease up on the pressure, and instead continue searching for the mobile he's carrying, his knees hike up in a futile attempt to kick me away.

In the light of day, someone might care about this man dying. In the dark of night, though, secrets are kept with infinite care. No one steps in to help. No one shoves at my frame to push me off. *No one gives a damn.* Everyone is too busy saving themselves.

"Please," he grunts, squirming from the chest down, "please don't kill me."

I lean over him, digging my knee into his abdomen until he folds like an accordion. "Where is it?"

He swallows under my grip. Claws his nails over my wrist, my forearm. Yanks so hard on my sleeve that my hood falls from my head. "What? Where is *what*?"

"Come now, Alfie," I say, my tone eerily pleasant, "a

man like you visiting the palace so late after hours? The Guard won't let you through those front gates, which means we both know what you planned to do." I drop another centimeter, until my mouth hovers by his ear and I can hear his every unsteady intake of breath. "Killing a queen in real life doesn't work the way it does in film. In *this* life," I murmur, applying enough pressure on his throat that his lungs inflate with need, "traitors are caught."

Then dealt with.

But I need that goddamn phone first.

It took Damien only minutes to crack the mobile that Queen Margaret brought by Guy's flat, before remotely putting a tracker on Barker's phone. My younger brother is a genius. Had he been born in any other life but this one, I have no doubt that he would have wound up creating new technologies that people around the world could enjoy. New computer software, maybe. Something with artificial intelligence. Only, he's not in that world—he's stuck in this one, just like the rest of us—and so Holyrood is the only entity that reaps the benefits of Damien being the most brilliant person in any given room.

Hacking phones is child's play for him.

Just as intimidation is for me.

Alfie Barker, older brother to the stable hand who tried to kill the queen last week, thrashes around beneath my weight. The queen was right about one thing: it hadn't been the stable hand's idea to orchestrate an assassination in the middle of her garden, in broad daylight. No, it was Barker's.

Beneath my palm, I feel his Adam's apple bob. Fear widens his gaze and his struggle gains renewed strength. "Please, *please*—"

Abruptly, his body goes slack.

His eyes roll into the back of his head.

Fingers fall limply from my wrist to the pavement.

I check the man's pulse. Feel it flutter beneath my fingers. Not dead—not that I expected he would be. It takes more than ten seconds to strangle a person, and I've no interest in squeezing the life out of anyone who'll prove more useful alive than dead.

"Priest!"

At the Scottish-accented voice rising above the cries of the protesters, I glance over my shoulder to see Hamish angling his way toward me. He palms an innocent bystander, pushing them out of his trajectory, until he's standing an arm's length away.

Close enough to speak but not close enough to imply that we know each other.

I cut the Holyrood agent another swift glance. Emblazoned across his chest are the words, *I Stand With The People*.

"It's my protest shirt. Works like a bloody charm," he says, plucking at the fabric when he notices the direction of my gaze. "Figured it's best that I blend in with the crowd."

One of us has to, and with my face, I'm more likely to take a turn in these people's nightmares than look like a knight in shining armor. Drawing my hood up over my head, I take advantage of Barker being temporarily dead to the world and finish my pat down.

"Ye find it?" Hamish asks out of the corner of his mouth. "Because I'm still having flashbacks to that cavity search we did. Ye think you've done it all until ye're bare-fisting a man the size of a mountain. Who the feck shoves a—"

"Enough."

My brother-in-arms promptly shuts up.

A second later, I'm yanking up Barker's joggers at the ankle and thanking a God I don't believe in when I spot his phone tucked into his right tube sock. Not as stealthy as he probably imagined the hiding place would be.

I toss the mobile to Hamish. "Take this to Damien."

Hamish's stare drops to the man still comatose on the pavement. "Any preference on where I dump him?"

"Not dumping him," I mutter, sliding an arm beneath Barker so I can haul him upright—bloody heavy bastard. "Not yet. Bring him to the Palace."

We both know I'm not referring to Buckingham.

Hamish looks from me to Barker then back again. "Ye sure that's a good idea?"

Whether it's a good idea or not doesn't matter. The man won't be leaving Holyrood's compound in anything but a body bag, if that, and not until we've wrung him dry for information.

Instead of answering the question, I shuffle Barker's weight in my arms. "Take him before we start attracting notice. I'll meet you there when I can."

"Always leaving me to do the hard work," Hamish grumbles good-naturedly while he throws an arm around Barker's waist. "See ye, brother."

Hard work is stripping someone of their life when they don't suit the cause. *Hard work* is taking the emotionally strenuous assignments so that your brothers, both those linked by blood and those by choice, won't have that stain forever imprinted on their memories.

My jaw tightens as I watch Hamish and Barker disappear into the crowd, Barker's body limp against the agent's side. Only when they're out of sight do I twist away and allow myself to get lost in the fray.

Before Princess Evangeline's death, Pa always said

that being a Godwin was a lucky hand of fate. Times were good. *Brilliant*, was his particular word choice. Sure, we lived in a tiny flat that smelled of mold and, yes, things could change at any time. But danger rarely lurked around the corner. For the first time in nearly a century, since the first Godwin found his life entangled with the royal family, there was no impending threat.

I wonder what Pa would think of today's turmoil. A nagging, vile part of me doubts he could hack it. Pa was good at heart. And it was that bleeding heart of his that got him killed in the end. Henry Godwin wasn't meant for this life, no matter that he inherited Holyrood's legacy the second he was born.

With my hands stuffed in the pockets of my jumper, I follow the crush of the crowd toward St. James's Park.

And then I hear it—the horn.

Fuck.

Picking up the pace, I dart around a group of uni kids all carrying their posters, just as the first note of gushing water breaks through the din. It's followed by surprised cries, and then mayhem erupts.

People push, shove, run.

I drift to the right, spotting a break in the crowd some twenty paces away. Angling my body around a weeping woman, I head for that gap, my hand on my waistband. The last thing I need is for someone to realize that I'm carrying—or, worse, to accidentally ram into me and grab the pistol itself.

Water spritzes my back, dampening my nape, my jumper.

It seeps like a slow-gathering stream beneath my feet.

The gap widens then narrows off to a point as people turn frantic.

We Godwins always find trouble.

It never fails.

I throw myself toward that break, just as a torrent of water rumbles to my left, sweeping multiple people off their feet.

"Go! Please, go!"

The cry is followed by more, each one more viscerally haunting as bodies slip and slide, tumbling forward onto the rough pavement. My knees lock still. *There's nothing you can do for them. Move!*

The horn blows again, and this time, light from the circling helicopter descends on The Mall, as though the heavens have cracked open to shine down upon all us sinners.

I shift left, cursing myself as I pick through the soaked figures littering the ground. Damien would tell me to save myself. Guy would never find himself in a situation like this. And Pa . . .

Trouble.

Always bloody trouble.

The horn blows again, closer now, and I mentally prepare myself for what's to come.

And it does.

Water blasts me from the left side. People scream.

I don't.

My body crashes against the pavement with the brute force of being mowed down by a train. The taste of metal erupts in my mouth. Someone trips over my outstretched legs, but they never stop or look back.

They run. They *all* run.

I wish I felt that same pressing fear. Wish that it might pick me up and propel me forward, like the dogs of hell were nipping at my heels. Instead I twist my head, grit my teeth, and spit out a wad of blood.

My shoulder, the one that caught the brunt of my fall, spasms as I drag myself up onto all fours. Movement rushes past me on either side. A flash of trousers. A glimpse of bare calves and high heels.

Whoever thought wearing pumps to a protest was a good idea is a goddamn fool.

I lift my head, prepared to haul my ass off the ground, only to finally get a look at what's stopping the break in the crowd from nipping closed.

Trouble.

She's curled on her side, knees drawn up to her chest.

Trouble.

Arms wrapped around her strawberry-blond head, that pencil skirt she wore to The Bell & Hand ridden up to mid-thigh.

My gut lurches at the sight of her—

Isla Quinn.

CHAPTER 7

ISLA

I'm weightless.

Pressure digs into my abdomen and blood rushes to my temple, and my fingers—bruised though they are—search for purchase.

I touch nothing but air.

Open your eyes!

Except that I cannot. Nausea swirls in my belly and my head feels as though it's been stuffed with cotton and, God, but this might be the worst of it all: my body aches as though I've been pummeled.

Repeatedly.

Through sheer force of will, I peel my eyes open and promptly wish I hadn't.

A man's shoes enter my periphery. Black combat boots. The sort soldiers wear. The kind that I imagine hurt like the very devil when they connect with human flesh. And those boots, they're moving.

I'm moving.

Alarm slithers into my veins as my gaze involuntarily tracks north: black trousers, a gray pullover that looks like it's seen better days. It's drenched, same as my own clothes, and clings to a set of impossibly broad shoulders that . . . that . . .

The pressure to my stomach.

The weightless sensation.

I've been hauled over some man's shoulders like a sack of potatoes. *A stranger's shoulders*, my brain supplies, *not just any man's*.

I'm going to die.

There's no other explanation, save for the obvious: someone discovered that I murdered the king, and now I'll pay the consequences.

No!

The word rips through my entire being like fire incinerating my skin. I grab the fabric of the man's jumper, fisting the material tightly between his shoulder blades, and use my grip as leverage. Taking advantage of the man's loose hold on the back of my thighs—completely unsuspecting—I drop my weight toward the ground in the same moment that I swing my right leg over his head.

My abdominal muscles protest.

My arms, holding the majority of my weight, cramp under the pressure of keeping myself aloft.

And still I squeeze the man's neck between my thighs, praying with every bit of my soul that he'll be startled enough to let me go, to let me fall, to let me *escape*.

He doesn't.

There's nothing but the sound of an involuntarily masculine grunt. Deep, guttural. A shiver screams down my spine, chasing away my confidence, and I have no time at all to reorient my pounding head before I'm hoisted up in the air and then coming down just as abruptly.

My cheek meets damp grass a second before the rest

of my body follows suit.

I gasp, biting out a curse as pain twinges in my elbows, the base of my spine. *Don't give up. Don't. Give. Up. Think of Peter. Think of Josie.*

Lightheaded from the fall, I fumble hastily with my coat, angling my fingers for the knife I stowed inside. Grazing the smooth hilt, I tug it free—*No!*

A big hand grabs my wrist, tearing the knife away, and, as my gaze follows in fear, he stabs the sharp blade into the earth, out of reach. A knee presses heavily into my lower spine, immobilizing me, and then that same hand that stripped me of any chance for self-defense anchors down beside my head.

I feel his bulky weight shifting, feel the heat of his breath on my bare neck, and then there's nothing but the sound of his raspy voice in my ear.

A voice I well recognize.

A voice that belongs to a man with a scarred face and soulless eyes and a heart which I swear does not beat.

"Going somewhere, Miss Quinn?"

CHAPTER 8

ISLA

Saxon Priest.

I'm not sure that the reality of him is better—or worse—than being kidnapped by a stranger with a personal vendetta. At least with the latter, I know what I'm up against. With Saxon, all bets are off.

He turned me away today. Hell, he didn't just turn me away; he practically laughed in the face of my desperation.

Arsehole.

When I lift a sore wrist in a last, feeble attempt to snatch the knife, Saxon's hand flattens mine to the grass, his hold uncompromising. I swallow, hard, then turn my head just far enough so I can see his profile.

The distorted upper lip. The harsh slant of his dark brows. The crooked nose and sharp, angular jawline.

I've been pinned down by the devil himself.

"Try it," I mutter, my voice still hoarse from shouting Peter's name. "Whatever it is you plan to do with me, do your worst." I pause, gathering steel fortitude like a mental blade poised to strike. "I bite."

"Something tells me that you'd enjoy it." The weight on my hand doesn't let up. Not even a little. If anything, Saxon only hovers there, his bulk covering my frame, his face so very close to mine. "I should warn you—*I bite back*."

Before I can summon a response, he's flipped me over. My clothes, already soaked through, meld with the damp grass. Any attempt to wrestle my way out of this mess is thwarted when he pins my hands above my head and straddles my thighs.

Though the position is intimate, the look on Saxon's face is anything but.

The cast of light from one of the park's lampposts reveals his expression to be nothing less than merciless. Mouth firm, jaw locked, he stares down at me as though I'm an inconvenience.

"I found you unconscious," he growls, his lips barely moving as he spits out the words.

Unconscious.

The all-too-vivid memory of being swallowed by the crowd twines its way around me like a thorny vine. Bodies rushing to safety, feet trampling my hands, my legs. Every time I'd attempted to stand back up, someone else had knocked me down until it seemed easier, less strenuous, to simply hold on tight until it was all over.

The irony of life, I suppose.

I meet Saxon's steady green gaze. "I thought you were kidnapping me."

"I'm many things," he says stiffly, still restraining my hands, "but a kidnapper isn't one of them."

"Brilliant." I wriggle my fingers. "Now that we've established that, will you let me go?"

His thumbs press down on my inner wrists, right over my pulse. "Do you still plan to stab me?"

"I'm many things but a murderer isn't one of them."

I utter the words primly, and it must do the job of convincing him well enough because the brawny pub owner releases his grip. Electricity shoots up to my fingertips from the sudden release of pressure, and for a single moment, I find myself staring at his rough-hewn features, this man who speaks without a hint of warmth but still saved me from being crushed by the crowd.

Who are you really, Saxon Priest?

Finally, as though he's confident that I won't double back on my word, he lifts off me and climbs to his feet. Still sprawled out on the ground as I am, he appears all the more intimidating as he rises to his full height. Those broad shoulders block the light from the lamppost behind him, so that I see nothing of his face but shadows.

"Can you stand?" he asks, abruptly bending low to swipe my knife from where he buried it to the hilt in the soil.

"Will you carry me again if I say no?"

He pauses, blade in hand, and angles his head down to look at me. "Have you forgotten already, Miss Quinn? I don't do charity."

At least some things never change.

Rolling over onto my knees, I steady a hand on my thigh as I stand. For a moment, the world goes topsy-turvy and the corners of my vision turn a deep maroon. *Oh, bollocks.* I feel myself sway on weakened knees, only for warmth to circle my bicep at the very last second when Saxon keeps me upright.

"Thank you," I murmur, my mouth dry. "I feel like I've been run over. Once for being in the wrong place at the wrong time; twice just for sport."

His grip slides south, to my forearm. "I didn't take you for a rabid dissenter."

"I'm not."

"And yet, here you are."

"My brother—" I cut off as guilt takes a sledgehammer to my lungs. If I hadn't fallen, would I have found Peter by now? The thought that he might be alone, that something even more disastrous may have happened to him than it did to me, hastens my breathing. If he's been hurt . . .

Stop. Don't think like that.

"Your brother?" Saxon prompts, his voice low, emotionally untethered.

"I forbade him from coming to any of the protests. What happened to our parents"—I shake my head, forbidding myself from going there, to those memories I wish I could erase forever—"could happen to him. He doesn't see it that way because he's too damned stubborn to think he's anything less than immortal."

"How old is he?"

"Eighteen."

Saxon steers me toward one of the park's paved paths. "Eighteen-year-old boys are hard-headed." When I snort under my breath in agreement, he only pulls me along, keeping me beside him. "But something tells me that stubbornness is a uniquely Quinn trait."

I open my mouth to protest, but clamp it shut a moment later. Begrudgingly, I mutter, "You're not wrong."

"Didn't think I would be."

My teeth crack together at his impassive tone. "Do you ever feel suffocated by your own arrogance?"

"No."

Good God, the blasted man is rigid as stone.

Standing in his presence is like being thrust, naked, beneath the icy surface of a frozen lake. Even my pulse feels sluggish, as though the very chill of him is now seeping into every one of my extremities. Another ten minutes of this halfhearted banter and there's a good chance I'll have frostbite.

I tug at my arm, and he lets me go without issue. "I need to find Peter."

"You're swaying again."

He's right, I am. But there's nothing to be done about that right now.

Squaring off my shoulders, I plant my hands on my hips. "You have brothers. How would you feel knowing that they might be out there, hurting but unable to save themselves?"

"They're self-sufficient," he says, sounding particularly untroubled by the fact that his heart must be as dead as my hope in his humanity.

"They're your *brothers*."

"They're grown men, Miss Quinn, and they can handle themselves."

"Isla."

Of everything I've said, it's *that* which prompts a reaction out of him. Shadows dance across his face as his head snaps back. "What?"

"Don't call me Miss Quinn. It makes me feel old. Which, all right, my soul feels positively ancient, so I guess there is some truth to it." Aware that he's openly scrutinizing me, I offer a loose-armed shrug. "I doubt we'll ever see each other again. It's an odd twist of fate that you found me at all. So, Isla."

I don't go so far as to stick my hand out for him, and even if I did, I doubt he would accept the offer for what it is: an olive branch.

Instead, he only studies me silently, his gaze flicking

over my face. Then, brusquely, he mutters, "You're bleeding."

"I am?"

He lifts a hand, reaching for my head—but at the last second, he veers off course and rakes his fingers through his dark hair. "Right temple." He points to his own forehead. "It's not awful but you ought to visit a doctor." A small pause and then a rather lackluster, "I'll take you home."

Take me *home?* Absolutely not.

"What? Is this your way of making yourself feel better for being a complete arse during our interview?"

He casts me a single, inscrutable look before striding down the paved path, as though he knows I'll follow. And, damn him, but I do. Like some bumbling puppy determined to please its master. Which I'm not, of course, and even if I were, it certainly wouldn't be *him* who I'm trying to impress.

I'd rather freeze to death than be sucked dry of all warmth by a coldhearted bastard like Saxon Priest.

When he doesn't answer, I demand, "*Well?*"

"I wasn't an ass," is his only reply.

My temper, already simmering from my argument with Josie earlier, threatens to ignite. "You told me I'd be dead within the year."

"Based on how I found you tonight, I'd say that I was right."

No doubt about it, I should have clobbered him over the head while he had me hanging upside down from his shoulder. From between gritted teeth, I seethe, "I was trying to find my *brother*, which is clearly a concept you're too boneheaded to understand."

"Boneheaded, eh?" Sharp eyes find me over his shoulder. Any other man would have the decency to walk face-first into a lamppost, but not him. *Never* him, I'm starting to realize. "Suppose it's unfortunate that I didn't hire you, after all."

"Why is that?" The words come out clipped, annoyed.

"Because, Isla, I would enjoy nothing more than to sack you."

My feet stumble to a stop, just as we hit a main street—Birdcage Walk—where a black car is parked along the curb. Despite the fact that it's a no-parking zone, the car looks like something yanked straight from a Hollywood-studded action movie, sleek and gleaming and utterly luxurious. My surprise ratchets up another notch when Saxon moves to the driver's side door and pops it open.

He meets my gaze. Tilts his chin toward the vehicle. "Get in."

I don't even hesitate when I reply, "You're out of your bloody mind."

His big hand curves over the door, near the top. "I'm not the one with a possible concussion."

As if he needs to remind me that my head is pounding like I've been thwacked with a two-by-four. "I don't get into cars with strangers."

"I saved you."

"You want to sack me!"

"Semantics." He thumps his hand down on the roof. "Either you get in or you walk yourself across London—to Stepney, isn't it? You're quite a ways from home."

I'm starting to regret showing up to The Bell & Hand with my CV. No position is worth this aggravation. Not. A. One. And since the Tube shuts down when protests take a violent turn, I'm right and truly stranded. Although I could hail a cab . . .

Reaching for my interior coat pocket, I pat around for my purse. *Wait—where—?* My heart sinks when I brush nothing but the inner silk seam.

"Looking for this?" comes that taunting, antagonistic voice.

I snap my gaze to his, only to find him holding my canary-yellow purse between his index and middle fingers. My jaw drops open. "You . . . you pickpocketed me."

Saxon doesn't give me the satisfaction of looking the least bit guilty. He twirls my purse between his fingers, murmuring, "Now pickpocketing I have experience with," and promptly tosses the purse into the car. "It'll go to your flat, with or without you."

Without waiting for a response, he slips into the front seat and slams the door closed.

Self-righteousness wars with frustration as I turn to look at St. James's Park. The likelihood of Peter already being back home is greater than the alternative. I know that. In my heart, I feel that he's safe.

Wouldn't I know—wouldn't my *soul* know—if he were gone, just as I'd felt with Mum and Dad? I'll never know the exact moment they died, but I'd felt their loss all the same. Like a candle being snuffed out while basking in the sun, I hadn't needed their light, their guidance, but their absence struck me down anyway.

And the terror of losing them has yet to fade.

It stirs my paranoia.

It steals my sleep when I rise from bed at night to make sure Josie is beside me before checking on Peter in the other room.

I'm going crazy.

My palms are caked with dirt and gravel, but I drag my fingers through my hair anyway, in a pitiful effort to abate the anxiety.

Peter is okay.

He *won't* be okay when I give him an earful at home, but—

Saxon honks the horn and the sound nearly has me flying to the ground for cover.

The entire night is clearly catching up to me.

With slow, measured steps, I round the car's bonnet and eye the man in the driver's seat. He sits like a panther in wait, his wrist resting nonchalantly on the steering wheel, but the passing of another vehicle, coming from the opposite direction, illuminates his face. What I see there doesn't do anything to alleviate the heavy weight in my stomach.

Saxon Priest may have saved me tonight, but as I open the passenger's side door, I can't shake the feeling that I'm entering the killer's lair.

I suppose that puts us on equal footing.

He guns the accelerator at the same time that I lock the seatbelt into place, my purse returned to my coat pocket. I force myself to draw in a steadying breath.

The ride is anything but pleasant.

Saxon drives like a madman, like a *savage*, winding us in and out of lanes. With his hood down and his sleeves rolled up, he looks less like a businessman and more like someone who has lived and breathed the streets of London for his entire life.

Not once does he ask me for my address.

We drive past Trafalgar Square and over Blackfriars Bridge, past the Custom House overlooking the Thames and then, soon after, the Jack the Ripper Museum, until finally he's pulling in front of my flat on Alderney Road.

The hum of the engine descends into silence.

I let out a slow exhale that tightens my chest. "Well, this is it. I suppose I should thank you again for not kidnapping me—"

"Today, you told me that you had a proposition to make."

My head snaps to the right, so that he's all I see. And my heart... suddenly, the chill is rapidly thawing as hope eternal springs to life. "I . . . Yes, I did. I *do*."

He's stillness personified. No quirk of his lips. No drumming of his fingers on the steering wheel. Even when we tumbled into the grass earlier, his breathing never escalated from the exertion, and it doesn't now, either. But he watches me—with that same, steady expression that he wore when he flipped me over onto my back, the one that suggested I was an inconvenience—and I find my knees clenching together as I wait him out.

What it would take to breathe fire into a man like Saxon Priest, I doubt the world will ever know.

"You won't work at The Bell & Hand," he says, his voice deep and arrogant, as though he knows my back is up against the wall and I have little in the way of options, "but I could use you."

A shiver snakes down my spine and my dirt-encrusted fingers knit together in my lap. And a visual, the kind that's best not to imagine while in the midst of company, slips to the forefront of my mind and won't let go.

Big hands traveling up my naked back, pushing me down to my knees. A dark, sinister voice whispering in my ear just before my hair is wrapped in a possessive fist and yanked sharply to the side, to make room for his imperfect lips on my neck. Saxon Priest would rule my body the same way he rules his emotions: tightly, with no give or hint of softness.

I'm instantly ashamed of the way heat floods my core at the mere possibility of a man like Saxon fucking me.

Which he won't be—*ever*.

Lifting my chin, I ignore the irrational flutter of my pulse. "Didn't we already settle this? I'm not for sale."

Nothing in his expression shifts, but I'm all too aware of the way he wraps an arm around the back of my headrest. Warm breath wafts over my face as he leans in, intruding in my space, until his mouth is scant centimeters from mine. If he wanted to, he could close the narrow gap between us and I would be stuck, cornered, *his for the taking*.

My chest rises with a sharp inhale, just before his raspy voice echoes in the quiet of the car: "You couldn't handle a man like me." Indignation sparks on my tongue, but not before he cuts me off: "And I would never fuck a girl like you."

Callous. Cold. *Cruel.*

My heart slams against my rib cage and I don't hesitate in planting a firm hand on his hard chest to shove him backward. "I don't need your pity."

I don't miss the less-than-subtle glance he throws at my building. I've done what I can with the place, with my landlord's approval—a newly painted front door, some potted plants on the front stoop—but even in the darkness, there's no missing the signs of age . . . nor the way the homes on either side of mine look more than a little worse for wear.

"Ten tomorrow morning at the pub," he says, turning the key in the ignition. "If you don't show, I'll know you're not interested."

"Interested in *what*?"

"Money, Isla." He growls the words like I'm insipid, and the temptation rises once more to bash him over the head, to hell with the consequences. "Show, don't show," he adds when I don't reply, "doesn't make a difference to me."

But it makes a difference to *me*, and the bloody bastard knows it.

I throw open the door and slide out from my seat.

Walk away. Go upstairs. Leave him to rot.

I do none of those things and instead bend at the waist so I can peer into the car. Darkness envelops him like a second skin, but I stare at him anyway, hoping he can feel the fire behind my words when I vow, "I will never sleep with you, even if you get down on your knees and beg."

I don't wait to hear him respond, if he even does.

The vibration of the engine roars to life as I let myself into my house, but it's not until I'm unlocking the door to my flat that I remember Saxon still has my knife—*Dad's* knife—which means he's left me with no choice.

And he knows that I'll show.

Josie is sound asleep when I crawl into bed beside her, and it's not until early in the morning that I hear the front door crack open and Peter's heavy footsteps pad inside.

He's home, he's safe.

That should appease the knot in my belly, but something tells me I've bargained with the devil . . . and it's not my brother's arse that's now on the line.

It's mine.

CHAPTER 9

SAXON

"He won't talk."

"Freely, probably not." With my arms folded over my chest, I sink my weight back to half sit on the metal desk behind me. Through the one-sided mirror, I watch Alfie Barker tug at his restraints, panic pinching his ashen features. "But a man will do just about anything to keep a pulse."

A man with a cause would, anyway. A man who has something to live for.

And from what Damien's already discovered about the bloke, Barker fits under both categories. He's a father, a widower. One wrong move on his part and his two little girls will find themselves as orphans before the night's through.

I cut a sharp glance over to my younger brother, who's seated at his monstrosity of a computer. *Boy genius*, Guy and I used to call him. Damien despised the nickname—still does—but it was entirely too apt. Holyrood, pre-Damien Godwin, might as well have been operating out of the Stone Age.

Old equipment. Dated tech.

The older agents, men like Pa, relied on their fists and wits to uncover information. Our return from Paris, almost six years after Henry Godwin was murdered, changed all that.

Or rather, Damien changed all that.

With a soft cap pulled down over his ears, my brother clicks through a series of pages on the monitor, so fast that I'm unable to keep up. Doesn't help that we've dimmed the overhead lights to the barest glow, so Barker, in the interrogation room, won't realize that he has company stalking his every move.

"I sent Jude to follow his family this afternoon," Damien says, extending a hand to tap the computer screen. Pinching his fingers, he glides them apart and the picture he's uploaded grows larger. It's a blurry shot, taken at a park somewhere in the City, by the looks of it, but there's no mistaking the two little girls that a nanny is corralling toward a swing set.

Damien pauses, his fingers falling to the mouse. "Cute kids."

"Don't get attached."

If I'm the frozen tundra, then my brother is a volcano. At first glance, he's just another figure in the Holyrood landscape but with the added potential to destroy everything in his path with a single touch of a button.

Not that he would.

"You sent Jude?" I ask slowly, running my gaze over his frame. "Or you went out on your own?"

Damien's shoulders visibly tense. "I sent Jude, like I said."

"You've fresh dirt caking your trainers."

"Get your head out of your fucking ass, Saxon," he

hisses, spinning his chair around to face me. Blue eyes, a mirror image of Guy's, stare me down. "I'm not Jude, not Hamish. You don't get to run my life and bark out orders. I'm not some bloody animal and I won't be confined to this goddamned place just because—"

"We're not the one who's wanted."

"And whose fault is that?" His gaze, usually so clinically impersonal, burns with mirthless fury. "Not mine."

"I know."

"You say that like it's been you stuck in this house for months on end. Except that luxury belongs to *me*." He shoves a finger into his chest. "And, to make it worse, you won't let me rip his fucking heart out."

"You can't kill the police commissioner. There'll be questions."

"As if that's ever stopped us before."

I don't move away from the desk. Arms still crossed, I shoot a quick glance over to Barker, who's yet to realize that the key for the handcuffs sits beneath the cup of tea we offered him. Intimidation is not always about brute strength. Sometimes it's subtle, a game of deceit, the sinister process of removing a person's options, one by one, without him realizing it at all.

The key may unlock the cuffs, but the door leading from the room is barred shut.

Blinding hope leads to crushing disappointment, which leads to further desperation.

I turn my attention back to my brother, picking my words with care. In all my life, they've never come easily. I go mute when I should speak, then speak out of turn when silence would be best. I suppose a therapist might place the blame squarely on what happened at St. James's Palace, how my terror yielded to nothing but more violence and death and tragedy.

I blame the world we live in where words are meaningless.

People lie, people cheat—*but not with them—my brothers.*

Quietly, I say, "You're seen as a terrorist. You can erase every article that pops up online about you, but it still won't change the facts."

Damien's lips tighten. "I was doing my fucking *job*."

"I know."

On the desk, his hand clenches into a fist. "How long do we let the world see me as the Mad Priest, then? The man responsible for breeching parliament's security. A year? Five? The rest of my goddamn life?"

In the other room, Barker's head snaps up, as though he's heard Damien's escalating frustration. I bite out a curse beneath my breath.

"Keep your voice down," I growl, pushing off the desk to head for the outlet on the wall. I dim the lights even further, until we're nearly encased in darkness. Only when Barker's returned to uselessly trying to pick the handcuff's lock with his fingernail do I continue, "You don't punch out at this job. There are no exit points." Against my better judgment, I reach up to skim the branding behind my ear. The king destroyed the nerve endings when he scarred me, and although I've told my brothers that I can still feel the slightest touch, it's yet another lie that I've given to keep up appearances. The skin there is numb, much like the rest of me. "This job takes, brother, and it rarely gives back. You either accept it for what it is, or you fight against a tidal wave that you won't survive."

"And you?" he asks, so softly I nearly miss the question.

"What about me?"

Damien tips his head back, his gaze locked on my face. Unbidden, a memory from our youth pushes its way to the surface—the first time my younger brother spotted my scarred mouth. It was worse, then, bloody and horrifying, before the doctor did what he could. And since we were poor and ensconced in Paris, like criminals, the doctor we could afford couldn't do much at all. At the sight of me, Damien burst into tears. He was young then, maybe eight to my ten, but was unable to smother his emotions and beat them into submission.

The boy genius with a heart of gold.

These days, he's changing. Turning into someone I hardly recognize. Bitterness and anger bleed from him. Although I'll never admit it out loud, keeping him here is starting to feel necessary to protect him from himself.

I lied to Isla tonight—if I knew my brothers needed me, I would give my own life for them. And I would do it, with no consideration of my own.

"What about me?" I prompt again.

He runs his palm over the back of his skull, ripping the cap off his head and tossing it on the desk. "Would you fight the tidal wave? If it meant freedom and peace of mind, would you do it?"

"No."

"*No?*" he demands, never once tearing his gaze away from my face. "Just no? That's it? You wouldn't even try—"

The sound of fists pummeling a door jerks my head up, and cuts Damien off.

"Looks like the bastard finally drank his tea," my brother mutters, turning back to the computer. His fingers fly across the keyboard and, seconds later, a projector lowers from the ceiling in the interrogation room. Against the opposite wall, a video that Damien—*not*

Jude—captured earlier today begins to play.

Barker's little girls running in the park, blond ponytails swinging as they hop from the swings to the seesaw to the sandpit. They look innocent, happy . . . free.

I move to the one-sided mirror, hands in the front pockets of my trousers, and watch the reel of emotions unravel across Barker's face. The elation at seeing his daughters, followed swiftly by the shattering realization that we not only know exactly who he is, but have access to those he cares about most. Fury combats horror as he stumbles backward, his hands clapped over his mouth, the blood on his nose now dried and flaking.

"Tell me what you want!" he shouts, spinning on his heel as though he can find us hiding in the crevices of the empty room. "Tell me what you fuckin' *want!*"

I press a finger to the intercom button to the left of the mirror. And then I give him the last ultimatum he'll ever hear: "The names of your co-conspirators, Mr. Barker. All of them."

I don't need to bring up the obvious: no cooperation and his daughters will suffer the consequences. He knows what the exchange is, what it's worth, and when he crashes to his knees on the floor, helpless in his grief, the montage of his daughters still playing out on the wall, I sift through my soul to find remorse.

The inner self-loathing of what I've become versus the boy I once was.

I find nothing.

Wordlessly, I turn to leave the room, only to find myself pausing at Damien's side. "I used to think that I'd survive if only I could manage to ride the crest of the wave," I tell him, my voice low. "Save the Crown, protect the status quo, do my job. But it doesn't work like that—

you know it just as well as I do. Holyrood is like quicksand, where one bad deed leads to sinking deeper, until everything that once made you *you* is destroyed."

Damien remains silent, and I wrench the words from what's left of my beating heart to drop them at his feet, humbling and raw. "I fought the wave, brother. I fought it and I lost."

I don't wait for his response.

Instead, I slip from the room and grab a pair of brass knuckles from the box outside the interrogation room.

Life in Holyrood—in this chaotic world that's swallowed us all—is easier when you've accepted fate. Death comes for everyone.

It's only a matter of how soon.

CHAPTER 10

ISLA

Twenty-four hours after my first meeting with Saxon Priest, déjà vu hits me like a boulder upside the head as I cross Fournier Street toward The Bell & Hand. The flower boxes are the same. The bloke seated at the window with his newspaper—I swear it's the same man from yesterday, too. And when I go to open the glossy front door, a patron steps out and we commence with an identical awkward shuffle-shuffle-shuffle.

The dark hair. The tweed flat cap. Even this man is the same, though today he doesn't offer a smile before taking off down the street. Even so, my gut still churns . . .

Pure déjà vu. It's uncanny.

Fighting off a wave of nerves, I step into the pub and take in the familiar scent of coffee and pastries. Seconds later, a familiar figure comes barreling to a stop at the sight of me.

"You again?" Jack, the cranky server, demands irritably. "How many times do I have to tell ya? We ain't fuckin' interested."

"Saxon asked me to meet him here."

"*Saxon* now, is it?" His bushy brows furrow as he inches toward me, a half-step that seems to span the distance of ten. "You think you can just waltz in here, and what? We'll bend over backward to cater to y'er every whim—"

"Jack."

The tiny hairs on my nape stand tall at the terse voice that cracks like a whip through the pub—*Saxon's* voice. Last night, after I crawled into bed, I was unable to stop replaying the entire evening in my head. Like a hot brand to the skin, I felt his muscular frame straddling my thighs ... but instead of holding me captive, my traitorous brain turned me down a different path.

A path where he *did* use me: his scarred mouth devouring mine and his calloused hands pinning my wrists to the soft earth, so I had no choice but to accept the pressure of his weight, his feral kiss. In my dream—a nightmare, really—he hadn't released me, and fear mingled with lust to create an addictive concoction that felt like it would be the very death of me.

Now, as I watch him stride purposefully toward Jack and me, I feel heat rise to my cheeks.

Please don't let him notice.

When he's an arm's width away, he kicks his chin toward the bar. "Leave us."

Jack does a double take, volleying his gaze from me to Saxon and then back again. "You takin' the fucking piss, Priest? Don't tell me you're actually *hirin'* her?"

But I could use you.

As if composed from stone, Saxon's expression reveals nothing. "If I wanted your opinion, I'd ask for it."

Jack's shoulders square off. He opens his mouth, clearly prepared to fire off a comeback, before seemingly thinking better of it. Nostrils flaring, he glowers at me before storming off toward the bar.

Silence closes in and I fight the urge to turn tail, which is a shock all on its own. I've never been one to run from my problems. Even after my parents died, I stepped up and did what needed to be done without hesitation. But standing here now, under the cold stare of Saxon Priest, my fight is dwindling fast.

Flight seems like a much better option for getting out of this alive.

Discreetly, I run my gaze over him, taking in his black leather loafers and the crisp black trousers that cling to his thighs and the charcoal-gray pullover that hugs his brawny torso. Even his thick hair is combed over, lightly styled. Unlike last night, he looks the part of perfect gentleman—except for his knuckles, I notice, which are bruised and scraped raw.

Did he get into a fight once he dropped me off at my flat?

The thought leaves me rattled, but I raise my chin, anyway, and adopt a nonchalance I don't feel. "Well, I'm here." I splay my hands out, as though bowing to his infinite greatness—insert all the sarcasm. "As was demanded of me."

Saxon doesn't take the bait. Those pale eyes of his dip south, charting a slow path from the black choker encircling my neck all the way down to the black, lace-up boots on my feet. I made a concerted effort this morning to ditch all pretenses with my wardrobe. If he wants me here, then he'll get me as I am. Blunt. Badass. Me.

Pulse racing faster than I'd like to admit, I wait for a reaction—anything at all.

Rather predictably, he doesn't give me one. Only says, "Walk with me," before striding toward the pub's front door. Not a request but a command that practically begs me to defy him.

I don't.

This morning, I spent thirty minutes lecturing Peter on the idiocy of not thinking for himself. The rest of the world may be content to fall into line like a flock of sheep, but we Quinns are smarter, *better*, than that. Wolves, never sheep. And yet, here I am, not two hours later, proving myself to be, once again, the worst kind of liar.

When we cross Fournier, I finally find my voice. "Where are you taking me?"

"You'll see."

Five seconds later, he cracks open a wooden door on the eastern side of Christ Church Spitalfields and ushers me to enter. I pause on the threshold, my feet locked in place. "I'm Catholic."

Saxon's eyes narrow at my bluff. "Go in, Isla."

I don't move. "This is a partnership. I have something that works for you and you have a plan that involves me. Ordering me around is not inspiring a bout of goodwill, just so you know."

He plants a hand on the door frame, his forearm grazing the back of my head. "If I wanted to kill you, I would have done so last night. I sure as hell wouldn't need to lure you into a church to get the job done." His arm drops south, and I feel the pressure, the very heat of him, against my shoulder blades in a not so subtle reminder that he's blocked my only exit. "This is what you wanted, isn't it? A chance to strike back at the Crown. A place to work where people understand you."

I turn in place, so that we're chest to chest. Or rather, chin to chest. "If you understood where I was coming from, you wouldn't feel the need to mock me," I hiss, locking my fingers around his arm to use as leverage when I stand on my toes and shove my face close to his.

His muscles flex beneath my grip, and for a second, I'm half-convinced he might throw me to the side. Restraint renders him motionless. But his mouth flattens, and the hollows of his stubbled cheeks seem only that much more pronounced as he stares, unflinching. "If I were mocking you, you would know." His mouth brushes my ear, and a harsh breath fans out over my lips. "I don't play games, Isla. Now, walk your ass inside or go the hell home."

Against my better judgment, I walk my arse inside.

You're doing it for the money.

The lie sits like a ton in my belly, and I force myself to take in my surroundings before I do the smart thing—the *right* thing—and leave exactly the way I came in, to hell with Saxon Priest.

The soles of my boots echo on the marble flooring, a quiet staccato amplified by the near silence of the church. Wooden pews line the length of the nave. White Corinthian columns stretch tall, extending north to barrel-vaulted archways that draw the eye up, up, up, to an intricately carved ceiling. Early morning light filters in from the massive windows, splashing sunshine on the detailed lines of a centuries-old organ in the west gallery.

Saxon's large hand brushes my back before yanking away just as abruptly. "Come."

I tear my gaze from the awe-inspiring organ and follow Saxon down the nave's left flank. With each step toward the unknown, my pulse drives a little faster. Unease quickens my breathing, and the sensation of being watched doesn't fade—especially when Saxon stops beside a confessional and cracks open the wooden door.

My jaw falls open. "Absolutely not."

"Get in."

"This is the third time in less than twenty-four hours you've told me that, and each time I'm struck with the resounding realization that you've taken my good sense and tossed it into a blender of utter destruction. First, the car and now—"

Movement snags my attention and I turn, just in time, to see the heavy, black robes of a priest swish around the corner. Gray-haired and balding at the crown, the man keeps his head down, eyes rooted to the floor. And yet, there's no denying the small, telling pause he gives us before slipping silently into the confessional.

I haven't been inside a church in nearly a decade but even I know this is highly irregular. Nor can I recall the last time that I saw a confessional booth inside an Anglican church, if I ever have.

Something isn't right.

Adrenaline turns my palms clammy as I back up, guided by instinct alone.

A solid male hand collides with the center of my spine. Then, in a voice carved from devilry itself, Saxon orders, "In, Isla."

Damn him, I go in.

And he—*Saxon*—follows right after before promptly clicking the door closed.

Oh, *bollocks*.

His left thigh is plastered to my right, his elbow digging into my side. His massive frame seems that much larger, that more brutish, when confined to a small place meant for only one. Not that he makes an effort to keep to his side of the bench. I'm sandwiched between a stationary wall and the mountain of a man that is Saxon Priest. Even if I tried to escape, I'd be forced to climb over his lap, and where would I be then?

His hand gripping my knee, perhaps, to draw me back. His touch brazen and hot on my flesh, that cold, dark voice of his growling a domineering order in my ear. Something like, *"Don't even think about moving,"* or *"No matter how far you run, I'll find you. Catch you. And drag you right back."*

My imagination is a dreadful, dreadful place.

I squirm in my seat, seeking space from everything that he is—and find no reprieve. His thigh kisses mine, his elbow remains firmly planted in place, and I . . .

Saliva sticks in my throat as I try to swallow.

Beside me, Saxon rumbles, "Bless me Father, for I have sinned. It's been four days since my last confession."

Four *days*?

Eyes widening, I grip the hem of my coat between white-knuckled fingers.

A brief silence, and then, "What of your friend?"

Saxon's head turns, his chin lowered. He eyes me like I'm a selection of cheese at the local outdoor market. But whereas I fancy cheese, *all* cheese, like it's God's greatest gift to mankind, Saxon dismisses me easily, severing eye contact on my next breath. A chill spreads through me when he replies, "Never, Father. She's new . . . but useful."

Useful. That word again.

It's beginning to feel like less of a compliment and more like a threat.

"Ah," the priest murmurs softly, thoughtfully, "and does she pray?"

Instead of hurling myself over Saxon to flee, instinctive reflex has me gripping his thigh, rather murderously, as I wait for his answer. I don't know what sort of game he's playing, and even if I knew, I wouldn't partake. I don't pray. Don't attend church. If Saxon thinks he can wipe all my sins away, he clearly doesn't realize that he has his work cut out for him.

"Faithfully," Saxon finally says, his gaze trained on the shuttered screen dividing the confessional.

I squeeze his leg again, nails digging into his hard muscles, and the blasted man doesn't even hiss in pain. As though women regularly try to maim him, Saxon only plucks my hand off his leg and flattens it against my thigh, growling, "*Patience*. Find some."

With a warning squeeze, he releases me and casually reclines on the bench, his shoulder propped up by the door, his long legs spread wide like he owns the air we breathe, as well as the plank of cushioned wood beneath our arses. His foot finds mine, but not to play footsy and certainly not to flirt. Catching my gaze, he slowly applies pressure.

A clear order to step back in line and follow his lead, if I've ever felt one.

"She hopes to better herself—shed societal judgments."

I want absolutely *none* of that.

It's on the tip of my tongue to tell Saxon to sod off when the priest's smooth London accent catches my full attention. "The congregation grows wary, my son."

Grows . . . wary?

It's an odd comment but no odder than Saxon dropping his elbows to his knees, his head bowed as if in prayer. I wouldn't be surprised if the only being he worshipped is Satan. Figures the two of them would be best chums. "We continue on our path to salvation," Saxon says, "no detours, no change in plans."

My eyes narrow.

A soft chuckle echoes from the other side of the

screen. "Youth gives you ambition."

"Age gives you foresight," Saxon replies evenly.

"Touché." Another genteel laugh and then the priest sighs heavily. "You vouch for her fidelity, then?"

For the first time since we met, Saxon visibly hesitates. With one elbow still planted on his knee, he scrubs a palm over his scarred mouth and flicks his gaze in my direction. Muted sunshine, from the slatted wood of the confessional, slants across his face in stripes of shadowed black and golden warmth.

I feel the weight of his stare like an iron anvil chained to my ankles, seconds before I'm thrown overboard into a swirling sea.

Opening my mouth, I'm fully prepared to take my fate into my own hands when Saxon cuts me off with a firm, "I do."

The priest hums his approval. "Very well. Your friend will come to confession in your place, then, yes?"

Words of protest bubble to the surface, threatening to jump to freedom, but I stifle them at the last second . . . and wait.

Instead of responding, Saxon reaches down and tugs at the hem of his trousers. Fastened to his calf is Dad's knife, which he removes from the leg holster with a familiarity that speaks to years of handling weaponry. A good thing to know, considering we find ourselves at odds more often than not.

With his knees spread wide, he balances the knife on a single finger, as if testing its craftsmanship. The blade wavers, straightens out once more, and then Saxon tosses it up in the air, catching the knife by the hilt, and holds out the only possession of Dad's that I allowed myself to keep after his death. Tantalizingly within reach and yet feeling farther away than ever.

Stomach tightening, I make a swift move to grab the knife, only for Saxon to pull back. "Give the holy father your answer," he says, his voice pitched low for my ears only.

That patience he told me to find? It snaps like a twig.

My hand shoots out to circle his wrist, and it's only thanks to years spent training in martial arts that I catch him off guard. I tilt my father's knife toward Saxon's throat, bending his wrist at an angle that I know must ache like the very devil. The sharp tip punctures his skin and I despise the prick of guilt that echoes in my heart. King assassination aside, I don't find a thrill in hurting people.

Wolves, not sheep, I remind myself.

It takes every ounce of self-control to keep Dad's knife steady when I spot blood beading beneath the blade, coating the metal with a glossy red. My stomach heaves. "You have some nerve," I whisper.

Saxon's eerily colored eyes never leave my face. "And you have none."

My grip on the knife goes slack at the unexpected cut of his words. Mistake number one. The confessional is tiny and the next thing I know, he's leveled the blade with my collarbone, and I see it then, my entire life flashing before my eyes.

And it's pitiful.

No big dreams.

No great ambitions.

No hope for anything but survival for myself and my siblings.

I draw in a ragged breath, at the same time that Saxon presses Dad's knife into my lap, laid flat, so as not to hurt me. He twists away and taps on the screen separating us from the priest. "She'll be here."

I hear the quiet creak of a wooden bench beneath the priest's weight, as though he's shifted around. "Tell me, my child," he murmurs, clearly directing the statement to me, "have you sinned?"

My fingers curl around the knife's smooth hilt. I shot King John with a rifle that I stole then discarded in the Thames. I'd trembled as I lined up the shot. Then brought to mind every piece of advice my father ever gave me during all the times we hunted pheasant back in Yorkshire.

Aim, sweet Isla, he would tell me with a smile quirking his lips, *and don't you dare close your eyes when you shoot or you're likely to hit me instead.*

Pulling the trigger on another human being felt like scraping my soul raw.

In my lap, I grip the hilt of my father's blade tighter, then confess: "Yes, Father, I have sinned."

CHAPTER 11

SAXON

If looks could kill, then I'd already be six feet under.

We've barely stepped outside of Christ Church when Isla storms past me. She manages three furious strides, her blond hair catching in the breeze, before whirling around. Blue eyes blazing, plump lips flattened in displeasure, cheeks reddened from the cold or anger, I don't know, but she gets in my face and bravely—or stupidly—holds her ground.

"What was that?" she snaps, waving a hand at the church.

Involuntarily, my gaze latches onto the freckles scattered across her nose. Innocent, it's how she looks, despite the all-black attire today—but bloody hell if she isn't one step away from blowing a gasket. I've never had another woman repeatedly try to kill me. Maim me, yes. Kill me? Not so much. It'd give me a complex if I weren't already such an emotionless bastard.

I catch her wrist. "You're making a scene."

"Oh, *I'm* making a scene? Right. I don't even—" She snaps her mouth shut, tongue running along the seam of her lips. "I don't appreciate being jerked around for your entertainment. You saw ... You ..." Shaking her head, her gaze drops to the ground between our feet then returns north, to land somewhere in the vicinity of my throat. "You don't do charity and I don't beg for scraps. If we've learned anything about each other in the last twenty-four hours, it's that, which means I'm being fully transparent when I say this: I'm running on fumes. Financially, emotionally, *mentally*, I'm one step away from calling it quits and dragging my siblings to the farthest corners of this bloody country and setting up shop as a ragtag team of hermits. And don't you tell me I won't last roughing it out in the wilderness."

"I wouldn't dare."

She kicks her chin up, ignoring my bite of sarcasm. "Tell that priest of yours I won't be attending Mass or confession or whatever the hell it is that he thinks I'll be schlepping myself over here to—"

"You will."

Her muscles twitch under my grip. "Bark another order at me and I'll finish off what I started. My knife, your neck, one happily-ever-after."

My teeth clench tight. Fuck, she is *infuriating*.

I yank her close, her captive hand trapped between us. "Had you waited five more minutes, I would have filled you in at the pub."

"Instead you're the one making a scene," she retorts, sharply rotating her hand as she fights my ironclad hold.

"No, Isla," I grind out, drawing my thumb over her fluttering pulse at the heart of her wrist, "I'm giving you what you bloody asked me for."

"By trying to frighten me, clearly."

"By trying not to get you *killed*!" My temper spikes

at her implication that I might do her bodily harm. I don't know the last time I raised my voice, but here I am, standing in the middle of a public street, fighting a losing battle that has my blood boiling in a way that I haven't felt in years, if ever. "Your parents may have been murdered but somehow you're still living with your head in the clouds. Any other man would take your proposition and spin it to his advantage. Last night, any other man would have dragged your skirt above your hips, kept your body locked under his, and taken what you didn't offer him freely. You're so goddamned keen to insert yourself into this world of which you know absolutely *nothing*."

I feel her knuckles brush my chest as she furls her fingers into a fist. "You're no gentleman," she whispers roughly. "If you're trying to paint yourself as a man with a heart of gold—"

"I have no heart." I issue the words without fanfare before releasing her hand. Then drag my palm over my trousers, as though that alone can rid me of the last vestiges of her warmth. "And I'm not some knight in shining armor here to save you. Don't twist this into something it's not."

She draws her hand up to her chest, then closes the other over it. "Then why help me? Why bother with any of this?"

I don't know.

I asked myself that same question throughout the night and I'm no closer to discovering the answer now than I was yesterday. But then I remember seeing her lifeless form at the riot, her arms cradling her head and her legs drawn up tight like a cocoon, and that lurching sensation returns with a vengeance.

Isla Quinn is nothing to me.

Her happiness means little, her survival even less so, and yet I haven't walked away. Haven't even considered it.

Needing space, I fall back a step and dig my fingers into my hips. Swing my gaze right, then left. Commercial Street is busy this time of day: people going to work; others headed out for lunch or errands. Adjacently, Fournier remains quiet. Aside from patrons entering The Bell & Hand, no one bats an eye at us standing in the middle of the street, nor do they approach. Even so, I lower my voice to keep us from being overheard. "Father Bootham holds confession—think hard on that. His congregation runs a mixture of loyalists, anti-loyalists. He hears *all*."

Isla's brows hike up. "You say this as if you know it firsthand."

"I say this because he reports everything that he hears back to me." Hands still locked on my hips, I lean forward. "*Everything*, Isla. But the man is devout, and he feels better spilling secrets when it's under the guise of asking God for forgiveness."

Her mouth forms what looks like the words *four days* then hitches into a smile that exudes no humor. "So, you go to confession?"

Stiffly, I nod. "Twice a week. Sometimes more."

"And he wants the queen off her throne."

"The man's an Anglican priest, Isla, a dedicated member of the Church of England. Do you really think he wants Margaret gone?"

A frown tugs that humorless smile of hers into nonexistence, and my jaw stiffens as I hold her gaze. Slowly, as though she's working out a difficult maths problem in her head, she says, "I don't understand. You want the queen dethroned and he wants her to stay exactly where she is. Which means he would only be feeding you information on anti-loyalists, which tells you nothing new. Am I missing something here?"

"Knowledge is power." I twist my body so I can indicate Christ Church with a tip of my chin. "Father Bootham only wants peace. He's . . . kind. Too kind. His parishioners know that, and they feel comfortable coming to him. His first loyalty is to God, his next to the queen. And it doesn't hurt that he thinks my brother once worked for Mi5."

"*What?*"

"He never has." I study Isla's face. Working for Holyrood means bending the truth to fit a particular motive. Father Bootham is a diehard loyalist who feels threatened by the violent uprisings. All of London may see the Priests as men running campaigns against the Crown, but not the good father. To him, Damien's warrant for arrest is a clear front that he must have been acting on behalf of the Security Service to gather intelligence on a divided parliament that's determined to do away with the monarchy, for good.

Father Bootham's not completely off course with that assumption—though the Security Service has no idea Holyrood even exists—and I use it to my advantage. I pay my penance, sitting in that damned confessional twice per week, and play the part of misunderstood loyalist. Bootham reports his findings, and I promise to pass the information along to Damien.

But Isla . . .

She's sharp, quick on her feet. Any run-of-the-mill excuse will send off alarms, and she'll be breathing fire down my neck within days of Father Bootham telling her one thing and me saying another.

I settle for a half-truth: "He believes Damien is loyal to the queen."

Isla's mouth falls open unceremoniously. "Loyal," she says, disbelief echoing in every syllable, "to the queen."

"Yes."

"Has he heard *nothing* of what you all have done? Half this city is prepared to kiss your feet while the other half wouldn't mind stringing you up by your necks."

My nape itches at the thought. Over the years, I've found myself imagining how I'll end up going—stabbed to death like Pa, shot to death like the king. Being hanged wouldn't be my first choice. "A person hears what works in their favor—what aligns with their personal beliefs. And, in me, the priest hears a man who's finally found the right path after a sinful past."

"And you're wanting me to ... what, do the same? Lie to Father Bootham for information?"

"You were sacked from the news network."

Her gaze leaps to mine, shock swirling in those blue depths. "I-I never told you that."

"You admitted as much just now."

A blush stains her cheeks as she twists her face away. "All right," she says, her voice hushed, "yes, I was ... let go."

"Because?"

Her shoulders rise with a sharp inhale. "Because I wanted to do more to show the world what was really happening. I was—*am*—tired of the fighting and the violence and the fact that the queen sits inside her palace, impervious to it all."

Except that the queen isn't impervious to anything.

It eats at her just as it eats at the rest of us, but I keep those thoughts to myself as I nod along, playing the part required of me. Because it's a role. My entire life is a continuous string of roles that I feed small portions of myself to, for the greater good of Britain.

The queen.

Holyrood.

"You get me every bit of intelligence Father Bootham is willing to reveal, and I'll give you what you want in return."

Isla visibly swallows. "Aren't you curious as to what I want to propose? So we can even the score? I don't do well with owing a debt—to anyone."

Something tells me that whatever she plans to offer would pale in comparison to what I'm doing for her— and what she's giving me in return. Father Bootham may choose to see me as a man worth saving, but the rest of London doesn't feel the same. Continuing to visit him would not only put an eventual target on his back, but another on mine. As it is, I'm walking a tightrope that might snap at any moment.

Isla working as a go-between nets me the continual information from Bootham while keeping me out of the limelight. It's a perfect arrangement, and I'm not interested in learning anything that might fuck it up.

I shake my head. "No debt owed. Attend confessional, put on your best redemption tour, and I'll see that you get paid."

It doesn't take a clairvoyant to read the relief that spears Isla's expression. "How much?" When I list off a sum, her eyes go saucer-wide. "Saxon, no. I-I can't accept that. That's way too much."

My skin prickles at the sound of my name coming off her tongue, and I force myself to take another step back. "It's not nearly enough. The wrong person catches wind of what you're doing, and you'll be wishing you hadn't agreed to a blasted thing."

Her gaze finds mine, wary and bold, an alluring combination that tugs at the frayed strands of my conscience. "I can handle the pressure. I don't crack."

I think of the way she held the knife to my throat. A wry smile tips the corner of my mouth and Isla stares at me, as though she's witnessed a ghost. *Or just what's left of my humanity.* "Monday," I tell her, letting my arms fall to my sides as I head for the pub. "Come to me immediately after confession."

A second passes, and then she calls out, "Am I to call you boss now?"

My shoulders stiffen at the unknowingly suggestive tone in her voice.

I will never sleep with you, even if you get down on your knees and beg.

I didn't lie when I told her she couldn't handle a man like me. A woman like Isla Quinn will want to make love, and that act doesn't belong in my limited vocabulary.

I don't kiss.

I don't whisper sweet words guaranteed to make her come.

I fuck.

I rut like a wild animal.

I'm the devil in disguise, and it's best we both remember that.

Glancing over my shoulder, I find her standing in the same spot I left her, her hand loosely wrapped around her strawberry-blond hair to keep the strands at bay. Her features are drawn, suspicious, despite the fact that she's essentially placed her life in my hands, and I nearly bark out a laugh.

To think, for even a second, that she might be insinuating something more—*I'm* the one living in the fanciful world. Me, not her.

"Call me whatever the fuck you want," I tell her, voice curt, because it won't make a difference at the end of the day.

Beauty and the Beast may have triumphed in the fairytales, but in reality, the only thing I'd manage to do is lead her straight to the grave.

CHAPTER 12

ISLA

"We should celebrate."

At my announcement, both Josie and Peter pause, Josie with her soupspoon halfway to her mouth and Peter mid-sip from his water glass. They exchange a quick look, and not for the first time do I wish that my parents hadn't waited so long to have more kids. I'm eleven years older than Peter, almost thirteen older than Josie, and am soundly on the outs when it comes to their secret communications that include brow lifts and nose twitches and silent stares that I can't decipher worth a damn.

Josie dips back into her bowl for more beef stew. "What are we celebrating?"

I sit back in my chair. "I got the job."

Well, not *the* job. Not the one I applied for, at any rate, but I figure it's best to keep the details to myself. Something tells me they'd both read me the hypocrite act if I confessed to the fact that I'll be spying—sort of spying?—on Father Bootham for the foreseeable future.

Josie blinks. "The server position, you mean? At The Bell & Hand?"

"That's the one." I reach for the plate of bread and snag a piece. "I start Monday."

"Monday?" Peter echoes, reaching up to run his fingers through hair the same shade as my own. "You start *this* Monday."

Hearing the agitation in my brother's voice, I purposely make eye contact to reassure him. "It pays well." More than well, actually. *Maybe because spying will prove dangerous and you might die.* I swat the thought away, ignoring the ball of anxiety gathering in my throat. "I know that it's not as posh as the network, and it definitely isn't my old publicist job with the firm, but—"

"It's not the job," my brother interjects tightly, setting down his water glass with a heavy clunk on the table. "You'll be working for the fucking Priest brothers, Isla. Are you out of your mind?"

I cut him a sharp look. "Language, Peter."

"I've heard worse," Josie pipes up, swirling her spoon in the bowl. "Much, much worse. Usually from you."

"The Priests," Peter spits out, undeterred. "Have you really heard none of the rumors? The youngest brother—Damien—he's wanted by parliament. The Mad Priest, they call him. There's a *bounty* on his head. A bounty, Isla, like he's some modern-day Robin Hood or something when in reality he's clinically insane. The man hasn't been spotted anywhere in months. And that's not even considering the middle brother."

At the mention of Saxon, the lump in my throat grows, and I feel a sharp heat when I try to swallow past it. "What about him?"

Peter stares at me as though I'm dense. "Everyone thinks he killed the king."

Oh, God.

The silverware falls from my grip, clattering to the table.

Mistaking my startled silence for horror, Peter thrusts his fork in my direction. "See? You can't even handle the thought of the bloke killing King John and you think that you could work for the lot of them?"

If Peter knew even a quarter of what I've done, he'd realize that it isn't the literal bloody matter of King John's assassination that's inciting my paranoia but the fact that the world apparently thinks *Saxon Priest* did it.

I stare at my water glass and wish I could transform it into wine. Or something stronger, preferably, to wipe clean the feeling of heightening anxiety.

The good news: if all of Britain thinks Saxon murdered the king, then that would imply I'm in the clear. *For now.* I crossed every *T*, dotted every *I*. The rifle went in the Thames and my clothes in a furnace, same with the gloves I wore to ensure I didn't leave behind any fingerprints. On my way out of the building, situated across the street from where King John spoke at a rally, I hastily scrubbed down every doorknob that I touched. Perhaps it was overkill that I'd also worn ill-fitted shoes too.

Just in case.

The bad news: if the rumor has already reached Saxon, then he'll be looking to clear his name, and the search for King John's killer will start again.

My fingers tremble as I grip the lip of the kitchen table. "Why would everyone pin the blame on him?"

"Or maybe it's just uni talk," Josie says, throwing our brother an arch glance. "The lot of you don't have much luck distinguishing fact from fiction. Remember what happened last time? You got a poor bloke imprisoned for something he never did."

Unable to ignore the peanut gallery, Peter clenches

his jaw. "It's not fiction, Jos, and that was a mistake."

"A colossal mistake, I'd say. And how do you know for sure?" Josie's spoon hits the side of her bowl with a clang. "Because I watch the news every night and they aren't ever talking about any of them. The Priest brothers, I mean. Not even the mad one."

"And you really think the news is telling you the truth?" Peter turns his hard-blue eyes on me. "You lied every day that you worked at the network. Tell me otherwise."

I press the heel of my hands to my temple. "Let's not do this."

"Why not?" My brother shoves his bowl forward. "I'm right, aren't I? The news is just a puppet for parliament, for the queen. Feed the people whatever lie suits your purpose today, never caring about what's actually true."

"Don't you think I know that?" I demand in a rush, dropping my hands to the table. "They sacked me, Peter! Because I wouldn't settle for half-truths. Because I *refused* to keep my mouth shut when good, innocent people died on account of me omitting facts that could have kept them alive." When he remains mulishly silent, I add, "I'm not your enemy. I'm only trying to understand what you've heard, not criticize it or you."

Looking somewhat appeased, my brother nods. "All I'm saying is, there are pockets of information. Everyone talks at uni." He shoots a dirty look at Josie but presses onward with the conversation. "And *everyone* talks about the Priest brothers. They've been vocal about wanting the monarchy overthrown for years now. But since the Mad Priest hacked parliament's computer software, I guess it's been easy to link Saxon to the king. Everyone agrees."

"And they know for sure Damien did it?" I ask, internally cursing my failed internet searches. How I missed this news bomb, I have no idea. Plus, isn't Damien the brother that Father Bootham believes works for Mi5? There are so many rumors, so many sides to a single story, that I don't know which way is up or down any longer. "It could have been anyone."

"Could have, I suppose. It was all hearsay and conspiracy theories until someone leaked his identity. Some police officer. Not much the Mad Priest can do to defend himself now. At least, that's the word on campus."

I try to think back to life before my parents died. Much like grasping at straws, the memories feel like they belong to someone else. Mum and Dad visiting me every two months, like clockwork. Walking into my old office each morning and feeling so incredibly accomplished that out of every person in my department, I was the one climbing the ranks the fastest. And Stephen—I don't miss him, necessarily, but I do miss the touch of a lover, of the warm contentment that comes with intimacy.

England has changed in so many ways, but what's changed the most is the decided lack of trust.

Opposing views on the Crown have distanced communities until we're all nothing more than distrustful strangers ready to stab or be stabbed.

If Peter and Josie found out what I did, I'd lose them too.

Softly, I murmur, "I thought you'd support the Priests, alleged king killer and all."

My brother shifts awkwardly in his chair, flicking his stare over to Josie, who's watching us like we're a highlight reel of a high-stakes tennis match. "It's not that I don't . . ."

I reach out and lay a hand on his arm. "Just say it," I

tell him, gently, "go on."

His Adam's apple bobs as he looks down at his untouched stew, indecision flitting across his features. "It's not like I back the royal family."

"None of us do," Josie puts in, going for another spoonful of food. "It's because of the king that Mum and Daddy are dead."

Even though I agree wholeheartedly with her, my heart twists at the utter conviction in her voice. I wouldn't wish this life on her, on my brother. *I wouldn't wish this life on me either.*

Peter pulls away, leaning back in his chair with his arms linked over his chest. "I think it's risky, is all," he says flatly. "Going to the protests is one thing. We're anonymous there. The police don't know my face or yours or even Josie's. They can't track us back home. We could pack our belongings tomorrow, if we wanted, and move to the Outer Hebrides. No one would stop us."

I swallow, thickly. "Fair point."

His lips thin as he shakes his head sharply, like he's coming to some unwanted conclusion in his head. "But you working for the *Priests?* Already, two out of the three of them have targets painted on their backs. How long until one ends up on yours? A month? Six months? All of this is only going to get worse and I-I can't do this without you, Isla." His voice cracks, the syllables emerging strangled. "*We* can't do this without you. I don't even want to fathom it."

Hell.

Feeling the prick of tears, I dig the heels of my palms into my eyes, this time to stem the inevitable flow. I've already put my family in an impossible situation by allowing rage to fuel me. As a five-year-old girl, I can remember playing with dolls done up in the then-Princess Margaret's likeness. I waved the Union Jack flag with pride and often wore clothes with it stitched into the fabric. I looked forward to every summer, while in primary school, when we took the train down from York to visit Buckingham Palace.

And the summer that Mum and Dad brought me to Holyrood Palace in Edinburgh? I nearly collapsed with anticipation because Queen Mary of Scots—my favorite of all our monarchs—had lived there some five centuries ago. The blood that stained the floor from where Lord Darnley murdered her private secretary, David Rizzio, damn near sent me into a tizzy of squeamish delight.

But that life feels so far removed from this one that it's impossible to pretend, for even a second, that I'm the same girl geeking out over British history.

This is history in the making. One day, some little girl will study the time when the British monarchy was finally threatened—and there will be people on the winning side of history and those on the losing.

How this all turns out, I have no idea, but I can only do what feels right in my gut.

Spying on Father Bootham, gathering intelligence for Saxon Priest, feels . . . Well, it doesn't feel good. But it feels necessary, like I'm doing my part for the cause.

My fingers interlace in my lap, and I force myself to say the words that I know will change the course of history—*my* history—forever: "I'm taking the position."

Disappointment darkens Peter's blue eyes. He drags in a shaky breath then blows it all out in one go. "Then there's something you should know."

CHAPTER 13

SAXON

The door hasn't even shut behind Guy before he's stripping off his damp jacket, throwing it on the sofa, and dropping news I could have easily done without. "Clarke caught one of the Queen's Guards trying to enter her apartments last night."

For a moment, I only stare. Let my brother's words infiltrate my head, turning them over for a quick analysis, and summon the only likely reasoning I can think of: "An imposter?"

"No." Guy's mouth twists in a self-deprecating sneer. "We aren't so lucky as that."

Luck has never been on our side. Not as Godwins, not as Priests either.

Plowing my fingers through my hair, I tug sharply at the strands and then drop my hands to the miniscule kitchen island in my brother's flat. I came over to catch him up to speed on Alfie Barker, but this . . . *fuck*. As if we aren't already embroiled in enough pandemonium to last a century, the last thing we need is the queen's own security turning on her. Which then begs the question:

how many more are biding their time before making a move? It's the sort of thought that'll keep me wide-eyed at night, working out all the probabilities.

Although I have a feeling that I already know the answer, I ask, "Was he armed?"

On cue, Guy reaches for his waistband and removes a gun from its holster. "With the bayonet they all carry," he answers, briefly meeting my gaze before moving toward the bedroom to my right. "Claimed he only wanted to check on the queen after he heard a commotion from his post."

"Sure he did—all the way from a different part of the palace. Stupid bastard." I grunt out a disbelieving breath, my flattened hand balling into a fist. Days later, my knuckles are still bruised from my round with Alfie Barker. Bruised and sore and itching for another bout. Lady Luck may not grace my family, but she's visited Barker, and done so under my watch. The man is still alive. Breathing without the aid of an oxygen tank, too, which speaks more to my own self-restraint than any particular resilience on his end. Barker knows more than he's letting on, and until he spills his soul—and possibly his guts—at my feet, he'll stay exactly where he is: miserable, alone, and cuffed to that tiny table in the interrogation room.

Which is far more than can be said for the guard, I'm sure.

"Clarke took care of him?" I call out to Guy.

"I did."

Narrowing my eyes, I push off the stool, trailing after my brother. Noise echoes from the bedroom—the clang of a drawer slamming shut, the rustling of fabric. I pause in the doorway, leaning up against the frame. "How."

It's not a question.

Bare-chested, Guy shoves his arms through the holes

of a fresh shirt. "Don't worry, Mother, I didn't attract any notice." His tone verges on mocking as he draws the shirt down over his head. "In, out. I could have done it in my sleep."

Knowing Guy, he probably has.

"And the queen?"

"Properly teary-eyed and terrified." A humorless smile stretches my brother's mouth as he draws on a pair of loose joggers. At my silence, he rolls his eyes. "I'm taking the piss, Saxon. She won't be seeing me in her nightmares anytime soon. I waited for Clarke to bring the bastard outside. For all she knows, the man's only been let go of his position."

"She's no fool," I mutter, turning to follow my brother as he brushes past me. "You don't think she looks out her window every night and knows that she's hated?"

"It doesn't matter what I think."

My shoulders stiffen as I swallow back a low growl of frustration. I won't deny my own apathy to the cause. I give because I must, and I bleed because it might as well be a rite of passage to protecting the monarchy, but I do it. Always. And I never waver. "You're the head of Holyrood," I grit out, "and if anyone's opinion should be slapped on a banner across the Palace's entrance for all to see, it's yours."

"We knew it would come to this." My brother snatches open one of the upper kitchen cabinets and pulls out a lowball glass then seems to think better of it. With the tumbler returned to the shelf, he nabs a bottle of whisky off the top of the refrigerator. "The night that the king was murdered, you called it."

"Revolution was too strong of a word."

Tipping the Glenlivet 15 toward me, the lines of

Guy's face draw tight. "Call it whatever the hell you want, it's all the same in the end." He cracks the bottle's cap, the aluminum top clutched in one hand. "The country knows what they're after: Queen Margaret out of Buckingham on her pert little ass. Dead, preferably, but I'm sure they'll take her broken crown however they can get it."

First Princess Evangeline, then the king. The possibility of three dead royals in the span of twenty-five years wouldn't be an accident; it's a statement. One that I'm not entirely sure Holyrood has the resources to tackle. We're good at what we do, the entire lot of us. We have our fingers dipped in every pot; men stationed in every corner of the country; and better technology than even Britain's military, thanks to Damien. Holyrood is a well-oiled machine dedicated to a single-minded purpose: protecting the Crown.

But I have no delusions.

When an entire population is hell-bent on tearing a queen from her place on the throne, it doesn't matter how good we are at keeping her tucked away. Unless Queen Margaret is willing to take drastic action, she's stuck in a palace surrounded by her enemies.

The inevitable is staring us dead in the eye and waving a bloody white flag of surrender to boot.

"She's going to end up dead."

Instead of replying, Guy takes a heavy swig of whisky. His throat works, his knuckles turning white around the bottle's neck. "What she needs is to get out of the City."

"She won't."

"She will if she knows what's good for her." My brother sets the Glenlivet down, rotating the amber bottle so that its label faces him. He traces a finger over the raised font, his other hand planted firmly on the laminate counter. "Æthelred II fled," he says after a moment, never peering up from the whisky, "in 1013. The King of the Danes had just invaded England."

Before Pa died, Guy spent years reading books about English monarchs. He stole them from the local libraries, never to be returned, and devoured them while holed up in the room he shared with me and Damien. Used to stay up all night with his nose glued to the musty pages. Whereas words have always been the bane of my existence, they were once Guy's anchor to reality. He read and he debated and he shoved God-knows-how-many trivia points down my throat during those early years—before we fled to Paris, before Mum died from a sickness we couldn't cure, before he learned that using one's fists is ultimately more effective in achieving a desired outcome.

Still, I'll never forget when he asked me how we could even begin to serve the royal family today when we knew nothing of all the dead kings and queens who came before them.

I didn't have an answer for him then, back in that tiny flat in Whitechapel with its thin walls and shit space heaters and ancient floors that always whined beneath our feet. All those stolen books never made their way across the channel to France with us, but it seems my brother has forgotten nothing of what he once believed in so fiercely.

Now, I only stay silent as he taps his thumb against the glass bottle.

"They called him Æthelred the Unready. Not a weak king, just an ill-advised one. But he planned—once the Danes took over, Æthelred plotted and he waited. Less than a year later, the Dane King was dead and Æthelred saw a glimmer of opportunity." My brother's mouth curves, like he's imagining the long-forgotten battle from centuries ago playing out before him now. "He came in on the Thames. Danes lined London Bridge with spears, prepared to fight till the death. But Æthelred's soldiers were bloody brilliant. They pulled the roofs off the houses that they passed, then used them as shields when they came in on the river." Guy pauses, head cocked to the side, his thumb still idly tapping the Glenlivet bottle. "Could be a dramatized version of events—read it in a Norse saga—but still. The Danes were driven out of London that day."

Watching my brother closely, I fold my arms across my chest. "Why are you telling me this?"

"Because our queen isn't ready to deal with her fate. She's no King Æthelred, just biding her time until she can make a big move. She *has* no moves." He thrusts the Glenlivet away, and the bottle nearly teeters off the island before he rights it at the last second. "You know who does, though? The Guard, who are meant to protect her, but are now sneaking into her rooms so they can slit her throat while she sleeps. Men like Alfie Barker, who swarm the streets, waiting for the right moment to take her out."

"So we take Hamish or Jude and introduce the queen to her new bodyguards. Establish more protection around her."

Frustrated blue eyes flit in my direction. "For how long? How long until the Guard isn't only coming for her but for Clarke, for Hamish, for Jude, for the men that we *put there?*"

"They knew the risks when they were recruited."

"Do you hear yourself? Really fucking *hear* yourself?" Guy bites out. "They were *recruited*, which means there's no more getting out for us than there is for any of them.

They didn't make it through training, they died. They tried to opt out of training, they died. They decide, at any point in time, that they're done with this life, they *die*. Holyrood is a one-track journey to the grave, and I'm not trying to bury them any faster."

He's right, of course. My brothers and I always knew what life in Holyrood entailed. We saw its ramifications, first with Pa, then with Mum. But the other agents—men like Hamish and Jude and the scores of others who work for Holyrood—knew very different lives before this one. Asking them to risk even more, when they've already given so much, would be selfish.

I set my hand on the counter. "Then I'll do it."

"You will *not*!" It's an all-out explosion. Barely leashed rage twists Guy in my direction, his chest heaving, his hands coiled into fists at his sides. "You hear me, Saxon? You. Will. *Not*."

Steadily, I meet my brother's wild gaze. "You're not a king doling out orders, brother—just a man. The queen needs more protection and I'm volunteering." I pause, letting that settle in, then add, "We both know that if there's anyone in Holyrood who can hold his own, it's me."

Guy charges forward, hands lifted like he's considering throttling me. He wouldn't be the first to try. "I taught you everything you know."

Instead of answering, I tilt my head in acknowledgment.

My silence fails to mitigate my brother's fury. He's taller by three centimeters—though leaner—and when he steps in close, his breath ghosting over my face, I know he's seconds away from wheeling back and trying to knock sense into me.

With his fist.

"Holyrood is mine," he seethes, his blue eyes glittering, "do you hear me? *Mine.* If I say that we aren't sending any more men to babysit the bloody queen, then you fall *in line* and do as I tell you."

I've never been all that good with following orders.

Guy Godwin may be the head of Holyrood, but he's no god. And his word certainly isn't the law. Ironic, perhaps, that Damien said the same thing to me just the other day when I reprimanded him about leaving the Palace.

"We took an oath," I say, roughly.

"We inherited an oath," Guy returns, each word clipped out from between clenched teeth, "and I'm fully aware of the difference. We have a queen who can't even wipe her own ass without someone trying to murder her, a parliament that's tearing itself apart from the inside out, and at least a thousand people outside the gates of Buckingham every goddamn night. She doesn't need more men; she needs to *leave*."

"She needs us to do our job," I growl.

Guy slants me a harsh look before turning away. "She needs to find her spine before it, too, ends up strangling her in her sleep."

Breathing deeply through my nose, I run my hand over the side of my face. I don't remember the last time Guy and I argued. Maybe when Damien was outed by the Met's police commissioner as having hacked parliament's internal software. Accidentally outed, if you're to believe his piss-poor excuses. The only reason Marcus Guthram is still breathing is because we have use for him yet.

Ethical or not, I'd wanted Damien to place the blame on someone else's shoulders.

He could have done it. He had the technical skills to rewrite history, if not the lack of conscience.

Guy had ordered our younger brother to remain

unseen, an informal house arrest that limited him to Holyrood's main compound an hour outside of the City.

If they can't find him, Guy had said, his expression stony, *they can't have him.*

No, they couldn't, but at the risk of Damien's own sanity.

Beyond that, Guy and I have always been on the same page. He taught me to shoot a pistol—how to defend myself. He held me up when Mum died, his then-bony arms wrapped around my shoulders like an anchor keeping me close to shore.

But this . . .

I shake my head. "We're working with borrowed time. There's no point in arguing when I'm willing to—"

"No."

Bloody fucking hell.

Turning on my heels, before I say something that I'll regret, I pinch the bridge of my nose and seek out the calm. The numbness that's been a constant companion for years now, always there, always prepared to ice over my vulnerabilities.

I don't have the chance.

A knock sounds on the door and then it's cracking open, revealing Jack and . . . and—

"She came looking for you, boss," Jack sneers, none too gently shoving her forward into my brother's flat.

Her.

Isla Quinn.

I'm so caught off guard by her presence that I don't have time to strip the frustration still coating my skin. It bleeds into my icy crevices, blending into heat, into a startled awareness that drags my chest in for a sharp breath. My gaze finds hers—annoyance and unease swirling in those blue depths—and I feel myself step forward, toward her.

Guy cuts me off.

"And who do we have here?" he asks, his voice low, pleasantly curious. But I recognize that tone for what it is, and the startling heat that coiled within me at the sight of Isla dies instantly.

Jack, still standing in the doorway, clicks his tongue in disapproval. "Saxon's newest hire."

"For the pub?" Guy gives me his back, his entire focus centered on Isla. I step to the right, needing to keep her in my line of sight.

"She ain't workin' with me," Jack mutters. "So, no. She's Saxon's little, special pet."

I grit my teeth. Over the years, I've saved Jack more than once from being sacked. He mouths off to customers. On occasion, he's been known to mouth off to me. But the day I hired him, I exacted only one promise: his loyalty. To *me*, not to Guy or Damien or The Bell & Hand. Petty jealousy isn't a good look on him, but neither is the anger that'll no doubt steal over him tomorrow when he realizes that I'm letting him go.

Maybe you're not so unlike King John, after all.

The thought churns my stomach. Sacking someone is not the same thing as murdering them, which is what I suspect happened to Pa after he failed to find Princess Evangeline's killer.

My stare cuts to the barman. "Leave us."

Mouth curling, Jack offers a short, mocking bow that has me wanting to grasp his thick neck and drive his head into the closest wall. "You got it, boss," he says, straightening to his full height, "not a problem, *boss.*"

The door slams shut behind him, the second time it's closed so loudly in the last hour, and then it's only the three of us.

Me.

Guy.

And Isla.

Who, after a moment of halted silence, murmurs, "Well, this is cozy."

I feel my lips twitch at her sarcasm. My heart doesn't squeeze, and my lungs don't ache with laughter, but that twitch . . . It's more than I've felt in years, and I move. Again. Toward her. *Again.* My feet walk of their own volition, and I blame the inexplicable pull on our strange relationship. In less than a week's time, I've saved her and she's saved me in return. Her willingness to mediate between Father Bootham and me is nothing less than the only bout of luck I've received in life. And, so I move, my lips once again firm and my heart beating at its normal pace and my skin cool, but that pull drives me forward, nonetheless.

Her blue eyes cling to my frame and, for the first time since we've met, I don't sense fear.

Guy, the bastard, steps in front of me. He shoves a hand toward Isla. "We haven't met."

I can't see her face, but I hear the familiar iron steel of her voice when she responds, "Isla Quinn." A small pause that gives me the impression that she's looking him over, sizing him up. *Does she like what she sees?* I demolish the thought with the crushing of a mental boot, ignoring the strange, fist-like vice that lingers in my chest. "You must be Guy."

My brother tilts his head, just as I step in beside him. "Figured me out, have you?" he says, the earlier curiosity returning swiftly as he drops his untaken hand. It drifts into the front pocket of his joggers like he never offered it in the first place.

Isla only stares at him, her expression clear. "I'm the eldest of three, too." She says it like they're in some secret club together, as if with that alone they understand each other in a way that I never will. The fist-like vice eases, the icy fingers of ambivalence settling in once more. "And I'm not Saxon's little pet," Isla adds, casting me a quick look before shuttling her gaze back to my brother, "for the record."

Guy issues a soft chuckle that steels my shoulders. "Saxon doesn't do pets," he murmurs, never once glancing in my direction. "The care they take, the gentle touch . . . It's not the way my brother operates."

Everything in me strings tight, like I've had rope tied around my wrists, my ankles. The imaginary restraints pull, chafing my skin in a way that doesn't feel so imaginary. No, I feel it all—the sensation of being dragged in opposite directions whilst moving nowhere at all—and I open my mouth, prepared to put Guy back in his place, but then Isla looks at me.

Really looks at me.

Her gaze skimming my thighs and my waist and then, farther north, to my shoulders and finally, *finally*, to my face. She studies me like she would a framed painting in a museum, like I'm something interesting to look at but nothing you'd ever consider touching yourself.

I will never sleep with you, even if you get on your knees and beg.

That night in my car, her words roused heat within my chest. A certain tightness. A blend of emotion that I never, ever wanted to feel again. And now, under her scrutiny, I put a name to that emotion, a word to the tightness that burns and twists and leaves me feeling decidedly lacking.

Embarrassment.

Bitterness stiffens my jaw, until my teeth are grinding and I'm staring down at this woman—this woman who I saved, who I've offered a position, who's made me feel *lacking*—and she never once averts her eyes from mine.

Like she isn't afraid of me.

Like she isn't considering bolting from this room at the first opportunity.

Like she *sees* me, all of me, and is still determined to go toe to toe, no matter what I say, what I do that ought to have her running in the opposite direction.

Holding my stare, she murmurs, "I don't do pets either. The human variety or the four-legged kind."

Guy's bark of laughter echoes in the room. "A match made in heaven." As though this is a casual conversation about the weather, he strides toward the kitchen. Grabs the lowball glass from the cabinet that he abandoned earlier, and snags two others. Props them up on the counter, unscrews the Glenlivet, and pours three shots. "A toast," he says.

For the first time in my life, I find myself not trusting the man who practically raised me, who sheltered me and then gave me the tools to shelter myself. "To what?"

His mouth quirks with a half-smile that doesn't reach his eyes. "Welcoming Isla Quinn into the fold." He casts an easy glance her way. "For your new job."

Isla doesn't move, so Guy brings the tumblers to us, balancing two in one hand. He shoves the first at me, then ushers the second into Isla's grasp. Raising his own in the air, he murmurs, "To new beginnings, yeah?"

I feel the rasp of the rope around my skin, tightening even more. "To new beginnings."

Isla doesn't smile. She stares at the amber whisky,

then, without saying a word, tosses the liquid back in one go. Guy grins. I want to take my tumbler and bash it over his head. We both take our shots at the same time, and I should have known that my brother would manipulate the situation to his advantage.

"So, what will you be doing?" he asks Isla, his voice deceptively mild. "Working for one of Saxon's many projects to take down the Crown?"

If she's surprised by Guy jumping straight to the chase, she doesn't show it. "Something like that, yes."

"How intriguing."

And then he turns to look at me, and it's only through an entire lifetime of knowing him that I read every bloody thought crossing his mind.

I've never pulled an outsider into Holyrood business, and certainly never a woman like Isla.

Never. Not once in over a decade.

He knows it, just as I do.

Guy smiles. It's slow and crooked and just this side of menacing, and the invisible ropes cinch tight, threatening to cut off circulation. "Has he told you everything, then?" he asks Isla while still staring at me. "How we've spent years working toward protecting the—"

"*Guy.*"

He stops, lifts a brow, and there it is, in all its glory of complete self-destruction: the ultimatum he's prepared to throw in my face should I not back down.

Either I agree that I won't put myself in more danger by personally protecting Queen Margaret or he'll tell Isla, who believes in the allure of the Priests, that we're loyalists at heart, loyalists bound by a duty spanning over a century. He's crazy enough to do it, too, of that I have no doubt.

I want to murder him.

But would you act any differently if the roles were reversed?

I want to say yes. I want to believe that I would put the queen above all else, but that isn't true. My brothers come first. They will always come first, no matter what—the queen and the monarchy be damned.

Bitterness and acceptance rise in my chest as I issue a short nod of acquiescence.

Guy grins for real this time, relief flickering through his blue eyes before he turns toward Isla and lies through his teeth: "We've used The Bell & Hand as a stronghold for anti-loyalists since we opened it. It's the only thing like it in the City. Have another drink, and I'll tell you everything."

CHAPTER 14

ISLA

Saxon hasn't taken his eyes off me since his brother invited me to another drink.

Leaning against the cabinets, he grips the lip of the counter in a pose that's deceptively casual: heavy boots crossed at the ankle; arm muscles corded and straining under the thin fabric of his shirt; head dipped just so, so he can keep vigilant watch over me while his brother rambles on about The Bell & Hand and its origins.

Awareness ripples down my spine, no matter that he's only in my periphery.

I *feel* him.

Feel his sharp gaze blazing a trail over my frame. Feel his desire to drop his hands onto my shoulders and keep me seated on the bar stool. I don't need to look in his direction to know that he's questioning why I've shown up a full day before we were scheduled to meet.

With my stomach tied in knots, I roll the tumbler between my hands and watch the amber whisky coat the glass, like water coasting over the shoreline, desperate to hold on but unable to resist the pull of the sea demanding its inevitable return.

"Enough about us," Saxon's brother says, elbows propped up on the kitchen island. He swirls his whisky, wrist hitched idly as he watches me with vivid blue eyes. "Where are you from, Isla? The City?"

Something tells me that this was his plan all along, to lull me into complacency with liquor and some harmless storytelling before turning the tables around and digging into my life. I don't blame him—clearly, this is a quasi-interview of sorts to prove that I'm not some elaborate loyalist schemer plotting to bring the Priest brothers down.

Even so, I don't trust Guy worth a damn.

I don't trust the way his hard, unforgiving gaze brushes over me, as though he would like nothing more than to toss me, arse-first, out of his flat—despite the fact that he smiles congenially and pours me another shot as though we're all good mates.

And I don't trust the way he tore into his brother either.

If there's one thing I've learned about Saxon, it's that he doesn't cater to the bullshit. He says it how it is, or he says nothing at all. Dad always told me that power resides in silence, and I've never felt that to be truer than when I turned to Saxon, swept my eyes over him, and watched vulnerability skate through his unholy gaze.

He said nothing and yet ...

And yet, I'd felt his rage as my own, as though it were a living, breathing entity skating beneath my skin and turning me furiously hot.

Even now, I clasp the tumbler so tightly that I fear it might shatter into a million little pieces.

Throat dry, I answer, "No, York." I set the glass down, pushing it away with a single finger. It scrapes across the counter, leaving dampness behind. "I've lived in London for nearly seven years now. It's more my home than anywhere else."

"You must miss it, though—family, friends." Guy picks up my glass and carries it to the sink. "I can only imagine what your parents think with you here. They must be worried sick."

"They're dead."

My gaze snaps to Saxon, who only stares back, as though daring me to challenge him. Cold eyes. Unsmiling mouth. Rigid posture. That vulnerability is long gone, if it were ever there in the first place, but still . . . he's rendered me completely silent.

He holds my stare as he continues: "Isla took her siblings in. If there's anyone worrying sick, it's her."

For the first time since I sat down, he jerks his gaze away to focus on his brother. Standing side by side, it's easy enough to spot the similarities between them: the dark, midnight hair and the matching aloof expressions. But the differences take over from there—Guy is taller, leaner. He reminds me of a wolf, always on the hunt, always prepared to take a swipe and make you his very next meal. His eyes are a searing blue and his features, though severe, are unmarred by scars.

Barely restrained energy versus pure ice. Purposely callous opposed to purposefully detached.

As though I've been tethered to a string, I find myself seeking out Saxon, just as he adds, "Reminds me of when we lived in Paris. Us against the world, with you at the helm."

My abandoned tumbler clatters into the sink as Guy lets go. His wide shoulders draw upward, tensing, as if Saxon has breached some agreement to never bring up Paris. Have I read anything about them living there on the internet? No. I don't think so. I would remember.

Curiosity gets the better of me when I ask, "How long were you all in France?"

"Five years." Guy says five like it ought to equivalate to a hundred, as though those five years continue to haunt him still.

Saxon lifts a hand from the counter to pass his palm across his midsection. My eyes catch on the way the fabric of his shirt flattens under his touch, delineating a ridged stomach and what must be steel abdominal muscles. "Our mum died a year after we got there." He waits until my gaze collides with his before saying, "It's been the three of us—him, Damien, and me—for so long that Guy's not one to trust easily."

I hear everything that he isn't saying: *Guy doesn't trust you.*

Too bad.

Coming to my feet, I lift my chin and meet a pair of suspicious blue eyes. "Not that I'd expect anything else since we've only just met, but I promise that I'm not here to tear your family apart. The Westminster Riots stole my parents from me. I suppose you could argue that I had them long enough, but my siblings—" The backs of my eyes sting, and *bollocks!* I need to pull myself together. Unlike Saxon, I've always lacked the ability to smother my emotions. I breathe fire, not ice. "Well, there isn't anything I wouldn't do to keep Peter and Josie safe, and I'll be dead before I come between anyone else's family. But your brother hired me to do a job, and that's why I'm here."

For the job.

Only for the job.

Saxon pushes away from the counter and my lifted chin falls as I feel him at my back. The pressing heat, the tangible tension. I swallow, hard, and immediately regret passing over my whisky tumbler. I need something to do with my hands, anything. As a last resort, I rest my fingers on the kitchen island and brace for another round with Saxon Priest.

"You weren't to meet with Father Bootham until tomorrow," comes his gravel-pitched voice over my shoulder.

Schooling my features, I glance back at him. "It might shock you to know that I'm fully aware of how the days of the week work."

Gritty laughter trips off Guy's tongue. "You have bollocks, Isla, I'll give you that."

My nails scrape over the island as I turn to face Saxon directly. "Because I don't dabble in BS?"

"Because you aren't terrified to step up to my brother."

I meet Saxon's pale eyes. "He doesn't scare me."

He might not scare me, but my heart whispers another story. It races in my chest, a perfect juxtaposition to Saxon's disciplined composure. As foolish as it might be, I'm tempted to press my fingers to his chest and discover for myself if he does, in fact, have a heart. Do I scare *him*? Logic says no, but there's nothing even remotely logical about the way my own heart threatens to burst from my rib cage when he steps in close and demolishes yet another centimeter between us.

Demolishes it, like it's in his right to make the space disappear.

Demolishes it, like he's determined to discern whether I'll crack and run for the hills.

One of his hands falls to the island beside mine, my pinky and his thumb brushing—I gasp at the contact, and barely manage to suppress another when he clamps his hand down fully on mine and juts his harsh face close.

"Tell me," he orders, his green eyes searching mine. Hesitance keeps the words lodged in my throat, and he must read me well enough because he adds, "You can say it in front of him."

There's no pretending I don't know who *him* is—Guy Priest.

The wild one.

My lower spine collides with the island, which bends my arm at an awkward angle. There's no pain in the position, and even if there were, I wouldn't pull away. To do so would imply that Saxon leaves me flustered, which he doesn't. Not at all. *Liar.*

"Isla."

I crane my head back, so I can maintain eye contact. "My brother attends Queen Mary. He hears all kinds of rumors on campus—"

"Elaborate."

"The particulars don't matter."

"They do or you wouldn't have come here." He squeezes my hand. "*Elaborate.*"

It's now or never.

Licking my lips, I prepare myself to force the words out—words that will either solidify my innocence or guarantee that I end up on his radar. And while I don't think Saxon would turn me in as King John's murderer—especially not when he hates the royal family as much as I do—I find that I need to hear his answer before I tell him anything else. Gut instinct. "They say you killed the king."

Utter. Silence.

It sweeps over the kitchen, and heightened tension knits my shoulder blades together. Saxon's fingers separate mine, as though he's seeking to ground himself. It's his only outward reaction, and I'm once again reminded that power speaks volumes in silence.

Guy curses beneath his breath. "Who the bloody hell is *they*?"

I keep my attention locked on Saxon. "The students at uni. Everyone thinks you've done it."

His disfigured lips part on a growl. "I've done nothing."

Yes, I know.

Since I can't reveal that, I opt for a touch of humor. "Not a kidnapper, not a murderer, either. Careful, you're close to convincing me that you believe in unicorns and happily-ever-afters."

His mouth doesn't so much as twitch. "I kill, Isla, make no mistake. Past, present, future. But I've never met the king, let alone assassinated him."

Past.

Present.

Future.

I feel the weight of his hand on mine and fight the urge to squirm. But . . . But I'm no better than him, am I? *I* killed the king. If the blame belongs anywhere, it's on my head. In the two months since I pulled the trigger, Britain's internal turmoil has taken on a sharp, primitive edge.

That's my fault.

One could say that life under King John's reign was worse. He became something intrinsically vile after Princess Evangeline died, a predator who hunted innocents and turned lives upside down, all on some crusader's campaign to avenge his daughter's death. The kind man that my parents' generation remembered became nothing but a figment of the past.

But I'm not so short-sighted as to believe that Queen Margaret has done any better. Where her father attacked, she's retreated. From the public eye, from Westminster, from her duties as queen. And so, the country has gone up in flames—her supporters want her to take control, as the king did before her, and anti-loyalists see this as their moment to strike and topple the entire political system.

I did that.

I created the ripple effect and now there's no escaping my decisions. I see them every time I turn on the telly and watch coverage on the latest riot. I see them whenever I close my eyes, in bed, and sleep with my remorse for being the reason the death count continues to climb.

And I see it now, too, as I stare at Saxon—a man who's been slandered for a crime that I committed.

If it were possible to choke on one's guilt, I would be dead on the floor.

"I'm sorry," I whisper, despising the tremor that I can't quite disguise. *I'm sorry that you're about to be hunted. I'm sorry that I did this to you—to your brothers. I'm sorry I can't fix this without putting Josie and Peter in danger.* "I'm so, so sorry."

Saxon's dark brows lower, his mouth twisting in self-deprecation. "For what? You didn't put the first gun in my hand. I did that."

"No, I did."

As one, we both turn to stare at Guy, who offers a grim smile. "You were thirteen. Too young for that kind of life. Too young for any of it." Despite the cryptic words, Guy shakes his head, laughing this low, disbelieving sound, like he's been damned from the start and is just accepting his lot in life now. "So, I did that. To you."

Saxon's throat works with a visible swallow, and he pushes away, turning toward his brother. "Guy—"

"No." Hands up, he falls back a step, then another. "We're all right. I need to . . ." He looks over his shoulder, but not before I see the way he slams his eyes shut, like he's seeking reprieve from whatever it is that plagues him. "I need to go—pub business. Fill me in later, yeah?"

Before either of us has the chance to respond, Guy's slipped out the front door.

It clicks softly shut behind him.

And the air . . . God, it's as though I can feel it crackle to life the second Guy's footsteps fade into nothingness. Chest tight, I remain plastered to the island and watch Saxon closely.

Even with his head bowed, he appears virtually untouchable. A king of death wreathed with a crown of torment.

I touch my tongue to my bottom lip. "Would you . . . Would you like to talk about it?"

He's silent for a moment, self-control evident in every line of his body. And then he twists his head to meet my stare. The tawny yellow near his pupils appears starker, more effervescent. "About how I'm a killer?" he asks softly, dangerously. "About how killing is all I've ever known?"

Drawing in a sharp breath, I shake my head. "That's not . . . that's not what I meant."

"Isn't it?" He steps in my direction. Just one foot. Just one step. And yet I feel the shortened distance all the way down to my toes. "The other side of the coin is that killing one person often means protecting another—giving up a corner of your own soul to save someone better."

I understand!

I want to shout the words, to scream them into the void. I thought—oh how I had thought—that murdering King John would mean safety for Peter and Josie. With the monster off his throne, life would return to its former self. A bipartisan government. A figurehead monarch. I was wrong. Stupid. A bloody *fool*.

At my sides, my hands tremble. I've been doused in isolation since that day, so alone with my decisions and my remorse and my fear, and Saxon . . . He knows how this feels. He knows the toll death takes on your spirit.

A confession begs for release but something in me renders it silent.

Hello, thy name is Paranoia.

"You're more than that," I tell Saxon, my voice little more than a ragged whisper. "Sometimes . . . sometimes we're put in hard positions with limited options."

He pins me with a cool stare. "And sometimes we simply amount to what we've always been destined to become."

A killer. A monster of our own making.

Does one decision instantly revoke years of always being good? For my sake, I pray that it isn't true. For Saxon's sake, I would do everything in my power to prove that it isn't.

I open my mouth, prepared to speak, and am soundly cut off when he demands, "Tell me the real reason you're here, Isla."

Oh, hell.

I raise my gaze to the ceiling, searching for the right words.

"Just say it."

Pressing my knuckles to my eyes, I inhale, then let it out slowly. Drop my hands to my sides and spit out the words before I choose to keep them within me forever. "There's been talk that . . . that—"

"*Isla.*"

"You've been marked, Saxon."

CHAPTER 15

SAXON

You've been marked, Saxon.

If I had a fiver for every time I've heard that, I'd be filthy rich by now—but Isla doesn't know that. She stands before me, her fingers wringing together, her gaze anywhere but on my face. *Or maybe the latter's just for obvious reasons.* I shut my wanker conscience up with a mental *sod off.*

I rake my fingers through my hair. "Is that all?"

Isla's mouth gapes open. "Is that *all*? Are you . . .? Did you not hear what I just told you?"

"I heard."

She slips away from the island, prowling toward me with furrowed brows and an unsmiling mouth. "How can you not care? Someone wants you dead. *Multiple* someone's, actually, if we're aiming for full transparency."

Full transparency: someone has wanted me dead at one time or another since we opened The Bell & Hand. Playing two sides of the fence takes delicate balance and always leaves one party feeling particularly heated. I made a habit of looking over my shoulder a long time ago.

"If you haven't noticed, pissing people off is something of a—"

"Personal skill of yours?" Isla stops in front of me, close enough that I spy gray speckles hidden amongst the cerulean blue of her irises. Right now, as she stares up at me like she would love nothing more than to bash me over the head, her eyes are turbulent. Intense. *Beautiful.* "Yes, trust me, I've noticed."

I wrench my gaze away. "If I panicked every time someone set their sights on me, I would drown in worry."

"It's a good thing you have no heart, then."

At the frustrated note in her voice, I slide her a subtle glance that starts at her black boots—the same pair she wore to Christ Church—and ends on her freckled face. "At least you agree."

Instead of cracking a smile, as I expected she might at my sarcasm, she only drops her head back and props her hands on her hips. A sharp inhalation expands her chest and, *fuck me*, draws my attention down to her breasts. "I'm going to come right out and say it: *I* need you to care. If you die, then I'm proper screwed."

The corner of my mouth curls. "Not so altruistic, are you?"

A second passes, and then another, and I'm nearly convinced that her head might explode when she snaps her gaze to meet mine. "*Altruistic?* I'm trying to help you!"

"You're trying to help yourself."

Her lips firm mulishly. "It's mutually beneficial, all right? Yes, I need to keep this position. I'd be a liar if I claimed otherwise." A pause fractures her words, and she takes another one of those heavy breaths that tempts me to look down and keep on looking. "But you saved me, Saxon. I don't . . . I don't want to think about what might have happened if you hadn't found me the other day. If you hadn't ignored that nonexistent heart of yours and carried me to safety."

My mouth grows dry at her utter conviction.

Praise unsettles me. When it isn't offered with some form of quid pro quo attached, then it's given when praise shouldn't exist at all. Theft. Murder. *Lies*. Rarely have I ever done anything worthy of admiration, not after peeling back the layers and revealing my ulterior motives.

And what ulterior motive did you have for saving Isla Quinn?

None.

I hadn't thought twice. Instinct guided my feet forward. Instinct guided my fingers to her neck, checking—no, *praying*—that her pulse would still be fluttering beneath my touch. And instinct guided my arms around her body, swiftly picking her up before any more harm could come to her.

I had no motive—nothing but an unexpected, devastating need to see her safe and out of harm's way.

Softly, I hear my name trip off her tongue, a question hovering within the two syllables.

I swallow, tightly, and twist around to give her my back. "You did try to strangle me," I mutter, all too aware of the grit in my voice.

Isla laughs. "I said that I was grateful, not that I was a saint."

Chest tight, I flatten my mouth, killing a smile before it can even breathe itself into existence. "Nor am I—a saint, I mean." Unable to stop myself, I trace the scarred flesh behind my ear. *502*. A reminder of who I am, now, yesterday, and forevermore. "The only outcome of you telling me who wants me dead is more violence."

"You told me that knowledge is power."

"I did."

I hear her footsteps behind me, coming closer, until she's at my back. Slowly, I slide my eyes shut and simply ... listen. To her steady breathing, to the wood floor groaning beneath her slight weight, to the movement she makes, as though she's tempted to lean forward and lay a hand on my spine—but won't.

"Maybe you're ready to chance death, Saxon Priest, but everything I've done in life has been to run the opposite way of it. I don't ... I don't let people in, not anymore. But you saved me, and I'll be damned if I don't do the same for you."

I spin around, but she doesn't stumble back. No, not Isla Quinn. She holds her ground, cants her head up so that our gazes clash, and even when I growl, "*Don't*," she doesn't obey.

"A group of loyalists want you dead. Peter overheard them when he stumbled across one of their meetings on campus."

"On *campus*?"

Isla shifts her weight from one foot to the other. "At Queen Mary."

I lower my chin, getting close to her face. "You're telling me that a bunch of bloody uni kids want to take me out, and you think I ought to be ... what, *frightened*?"

"Yes," she says simply, like I'm short a marble or two.

"I doubt they're savvy enough to even know where to find their own balls."

When I turn away, Isla latches a hand around my bicep and keeps me rooted in place. I could easily throw her off, if I wanted. *But I don't want.* Every part of me fixates on her fingers squeezing my arm. When was the last time I allowed a woman to touch me? *Really* touch me, with her mouth on my flesh and her limbs wrapped around my body?

Never.

My aversion to being touched has been a part of me for as long as my scarred mouth. No kissing. No touching. It's me who does the fucking, and my interactions with the opposite sex have only ever been about sating the itch until the next time it rears its ugly head and I do it all over again.

Guy was right about me—I don't do pets and I don't do gentle and I don't do affection.

And yet, my fingers close over Isla's and instead of tearing them away, as I've been known to do before with rare, unwanted advances, I find myself soaking up the once-in-a-lifetime sensation of a woman not shirking away at the very thought of laying a hand on my body.

Fucking hell.

Completely unaware of my internal struggle, Isla argues, "You're not immortal, Saxon. I don't care how many times you've come out a scuffle alive, you are not immortal."

The devil controls my tongue when I grunt, "Careful, Miss Quinn, or I may get the impression that you actually care about what happens to me."

Her blue eyes fly wide. "I-It's as I said before, I—"

"Yes, I heard. Without me, you're proper screwed."

"No, not—I mean, bloody hell, yes, that too," she stammers awkwardly, fumbling over her words in such a familiar way that I nearly take pity.

Nearly.

"So, you want to save me." Her hand, still fitted beneath mine, tenses. In fear? Self-preservation? *Lust?*

"What is it that you'd have me do? Drive to Queen Mary and murder every one of those kids? Should I learn where they sleep—slit their throats before they can return the favor?"

Her lips part and snap shut, once, twice. "You're trying to unsettle me."

I drag her closer. "I'm discussing my options."

"No," she retorts, her voice dipped in an emotion that I can't decipher, "you're pulling on the same mask you wore when we met. Cold. Callous. Maybe that act works on your brothers or Jack, but it won't with me. Don't insult my intelligence by pretending otherwise."

"No one said anything about your intelligence," I edge out, heat flooding my veins. "You don't know me, Isla. You have no idea what I've done—what I've *chosen* to do."

"The tortured villain spiel would be more compelling if I didn't already know you're a killer."

Jesus. Christ. The fucking mouth on her.

Releasing her hand, I spin on my heel and put some much-needed distance between us before I do what my hard cock is begging for—to shove her on the closest flat surface, even the unforgiving wood floor, and strip her naked. I'd show her how she's wrong, how coldness is all I've ever known. Her pants torn down around her ankles, her hands pinned down by her sides. Each callous thrust inside her heat would prove to be her worst nightmare.

Cold. Callous.

Me.

If I had any hope of being anything but what I am, that ship sailed years ago.

I plant my balled fists on the kitchen table, my bruised knuckles bearing the brunt of my weight. The tightness of my cracked, healing skin aches and reminds me that I'm human—not immortal, not the icy veneer that I wear like a second skin.

A red-blooded man, just like any other.

I despise the vulnerability, just as much as I despise the idea of being at a woman's mercy.

Isla's mercy.

Harsh, angry words spill from my mouth. "Go the bloody hell home."

I feel her shocked gasp like a knife plunging between my ribs.

"Isla, go *home*."

"Really?" I can almost imagine her shaking her strawberry-blond hair back from her face, her pert chin shoved up with insolence. "I'm to hop to your every command, then? You tell me to run, and I sprint. You tell me to fall on the blade, and I aim it straight for my heart."

I cast her a sharp look over my shoulder. "You work for me—or have you forgotten?"

"You told me to call you whatever I wanted, and the only thing that comes to mind is *coward*."

If she were anyone else, she'd be bleeding out on the floor already.

My nostrils flare at her brazenness. "You're on thin ice, Miss Quinn."

Fiery confidence bleeds from her expression when she counters, "Except for when I've been slung over your shoulder like a rag doll, thin ice is how we operate. It seems my tail has gotten tired of hiding between my legs and can't be bothered to get with the program anymore."

Air comes fast, pumping into my lungs at such an alarming rate that I feel unsteady.

Isla Quinn is thawing me out, and nothing about that sits well with me.

Get this conversation done with—now.

"Tomorrow, after confessional," I say from behind clenched teeth, refusing to even acknowledge what she's said with a suitable response. "Meet me at the pub. Don't be late."

Sarcasm clings to her slender frame when she clicks her heels together and salutes me with two fingers—a *toss off*, if I've ever seen one. "Of course, boss," she says, every word soaked in saccharine sweetness, "I wouldn't *dare* disappoint you, boss."

First Jack, now her.

I've been thrown into an alternate universe that's my own version of hell.

It takes everything in me not to squeeze my eyes shut and burst into a chorus of a thousand curses. "Tomorrow," I reiterate stiffly.

She moves to the door, hips swaying angrily, hair flicking out behind her like a mane of candlelit strands. Ripping the bloody thing open, she pauses on the threshold. Her shoulders rise with a heavy breath, and, in the rarest display of vulnerability that I've ever been shown—by anyone—she touches her forehead to the door frame.

A gift.

That's how this moment feels, like she's gifted me some forever elusive puzzle piece to humanity that's escaped me.

She turns her head, her temple still kissing the wooden frame, before her gaze fixes on my face. "Friends keep each other alive."

Just like that, the imaginary ropes encircling my wrists finally chafe hard enough to draw blood. "We aren't friends," I tell her, my voice hoarse.

She pauses, her blue eyes flitting over me, before she

pushes back. "We could be, Saxon, if only you'd let us."

And then she leaves, as I demanded of her, and I'm alone.

The way I've always been.

The way I'll always be.

Forever.

CHAPTER 16

ISLA

Father Bootham is right on time.

I hear the door to his side of the confessional click closed, and then the rustle of heavy robes being re-situated as he sits.

Without Saxon here to invade my personal bubble, the confessional is surprisingly roomy.

Fucking Saxon.

In the twenty-something hours that have passed since I fled Guy's flat, I've hovered between wanting to skewer Saxon where he stands, with the sharpest object I can find, and the *utterly* inexplicable desire to ask him how he can be so flippant with his life.

It's no secret that he's lived roughly. One glance at his face and I can only imagine the thousands of stories that he must keep locked away behind his formidable, *don't-try-me* attitude. Saxon Priest is no sweetheart, that's for sure, but his barks don't terrify me—they only pique my curiosity.

Father Bootham's voice startles me from my thoughts. "My child, shall we begin?"

Bollocks. One day in and I'm already on the verge of cocking it all up. "Yes, sorry. Apologies, Father." His answering silence stretches on, awkwardly, until I remember that I'm meant to play the dutiful role of a parishioner seeking penance. *Think of the money, think of the money, think of the money.* "Bless me, Father, for I have sinned. It's been"—approximately my entire lifetime since I've done this for real—"three days since my last confession."

"Welcome back, my child." Father Bootham's voice warms, when he adds, "No need to be nervous."

My fingers grip the bench. "I'm not nervous."

"Is that so? If you think any louder, I fear you'll implode."

At his unexpectedly wry humor, a laugh slips off my tongue. One glance at the dark wood around me reminds me that I'm in a church, and the laughter dries up faster than rain falling in the Sahara. "Apologies." I bite my bottom lip. "Again."

"No apologies required . . . again."

I squeeze my fingers around the bench's wooden lip, trying to smother another chuckle.

"Tell me what's on your mind, my child."

What's on my mind isn't fit for a priest's ears. I want to storm over to The Bell & Hand and get in Saxon's face until he ceases to be a complete bellend. I want to feel his strong fingers intertwined with mine again. And, more than anything, I want him to realize that we're *allies* in this, not enemies. We both want the same thing. Why he feels the need to thrust me away, as though I've offered him nothing of worth, feels almost worse than the guilt that continues to gnaw away at my soul.

Yesterday, for the span of a heartbeat, I'd felt united in our misery. Saxon understood. He understood *me*. And then the bloody bastard had to rip the proverbial rug out from beneath my feet and remind me, all too bluntly, that I am *alone*.

Well and truly alone.

A quiet knock on the screen recaptures my attention and I fabricate a lie, just like all the others I've told in recent years. "I feel . . . uncertain." When Father Bootham says nothing, I hurry to elaborate. "In my place here. What I'm meant to say. How much I'm not allowed to say."

"There are no boundaries," the priest replies smoothly. "I give you information. You dole that out. Nothing more, nothing less."

"And you don't worry that the information may land in the wrong hands?" I ask before I can stop myself. But, oh hell, do I wish I could snatch the words back. *Stupid. Stupid. Stupid.* Saxon is going to absolutely murder me—and, given his history, I'm not at all sure that he wouldn't actually do it. "Never mind. I'm sorry, that was a nosy question. Let's forget I even asked."

"I have ears, my child."

I swallow, hard.

He continues in that self-assured, no-nonsense tone of his. "I know the risks I face by helping the Priests. All it takes is one word breathed in the wrong direction and everything I've worked for will come crashing down around me. I wouldn't survive the fallout, that I know."

"Then why—"

"Because we're put on this earth to *believe*, and it is up to us to decide what we believe in. I choose God or, perhaps, He chose me. That belief lives in my veins, in my soul. It is who I am."

"And Queen Margaret?"

"Others may say that He chose her, and so we all

must too."

I slide my arse to the bench's edge. "But you don't think that?"

Silence reigns, casting a chill over my skin. Then, "I believe that the queen has peace in her. I believe that she leads with love, where her father led with fear. I believe that, if we only offered her a chance, she would give us unity, safety, and a country that inspires hope, not never-ending deceit."

Deceit.

Here I am, doing exactly that.

Because I *don't* believe—not in the Crown, not in our queen, not in anything that carries the stamp of King John.

"I think . . . I think that the world needs more people like you, Father Bootham."

He issues a soft chuckle. "My child, the world is already filled with people like me—if only you look hard enough." Before I can edge another word in, he adds, "Now, let us get to it, shall we? The congregation has been chatty, and while most of it sounds quite the norm, one thing leaves me worried."

My ears perk up. "Whatever it is, I'll be sure to pass it along."

"We all carry our struggles," he says, almost as if he's reassuring himself, rather than confiding in me, "and those struggles weigh heavily on our shoulders."

Even though he can't see me, I nod. "Yes."

"You asked me who I believe in. I believe in the Lord, I believe in our queen, and I believe in the Priests. And believing in the latter two is the cross I bear, for when they cross hairs . . ."

I have no idea how Saxon does this twice per week.

Listening, lying to the priest's face, pretending all will be well before turning around and using the information to further dismantle the institution.

Guilt strains my fingers as I knit my hands together in my lap and bite my tongue to keep from shouting, "*Please! Don't tell me!*"

My morals are slipping away faster than I can even think to tie them to me for safe keeping.

"A mother came in," he continues, the angst in his voice weighing down my own conscience. "Her son attends Queen Mary."

Queen Mary. As in the same university that Peter attends, Queen Mary.

Thank God for the screen separating us because Father Bootham goes on, completely unaware that all the blood has drained from my face. "In any other circumstance, I might hesitate to relay this information, but I find that I cannot hold my tongue. When the son visited for family dinner, he was . . . inebriated. He confessed that he had joined a group—led by one of the university's professors—who believe that . . . that Saxon Priest killed the king."

"He didn't do it," I whisper, feeling every bit the liar that I've become. "It wasn't Saxon."

"I know." Father Bootham sighs. "I've been doing this for a long time, you know. I know when someone gives me untruths, just as I know when someone bleeds good faith."

I tremble.

Right there in the confessional, before God, before Father Bootham, I tremble with fear. Saliva sticks to the roof of my mouth, and no matter how many times I swallow, I find myself on the verge of tearing out of this prison box of worship and hightailing it out of Christ

Church, never to return again.

I half expect Father Bootham to wait me out until I confess to all of my misdeeds, but he doesn't, too wrapped up in his own quandary to ponder my sudden silence. "I was told they've hatched a plan to do away with Saxon. The details are sketchy, at best, and not entirely reliable. The boy was drunk, and the mother too horrified that her son was concocting a murder scheme to demand he tell her everything."

Finally, I manage, "Did she go to the police?"

I can practically imagine Father Bootham shaking his head. "The Met is unreliable, as you well know. They'd just as soon put her boy in a prison cell as praise him for doing what most of the city wants done."

The likelihood that *this* boy and the men that Peter overheard talking are two different groups seems far-fetched. Peter told me in warning, so that I wouldn't inevitably involve myself and get caught in the middle. Father Bootham is telling me now so that I can warn Saxon.

Which I've already done to no avail, the stubborn bastard.

I run my fingers through my hair, digging my fingertips into my scalp. "If I tell Saxon, you know what will happen."

A small pause before, "That is my own sin to bear."

"But you believe in him."

"I believe in him as much as I believe in myself."

I'm working with a stubborn bastard and a foolish priest who can't see the truth staring back at him. Saxon Priest is *not* the hero in this nightmarish fairytale. He hates the Crown, and he hates it enough to manipulate a good man like Father Bootham into thinking that they're working together for the same cause.

A man like Saxon, who claims to be heartless, clearly has no qualms about the subterfuge. But I . . . It feels so utterly wrong to sit here and tell the priest that he's doing the right thing in saving Saxon's life, when he's doing nothing more than turning on the people who are actually his allies.

The boy. The mother.

Slowly, I drag in a breath, letting it fill my lungs with renewed purpose. Of why I'm here. Of what I've suffered to be in a position that allows me to chart my life as I see fit. "You said the details are sketchy but if we're to help Saxon, I need more. Did the mother know where her son met for those meetings? Which professor banded all the students together?"

"Yes," Father Bootham answers softly, like the word has been torn from his moral compass. "I know it all."

A pained smile crosses my face as I slip my hand into my coat pocket to pull out a pen. I press the tip to my palm and test the ink. Black beads on my flesh. "I'm listening, Father. Go on."

CHAPTER 17

SAXON

"You're done."

Mouth gaping open, Jack shoves a thumb into his chest. "*Me*? I'm the one who's bein' sacked?"

Elbows planted on my desk at The Bell & Hand, I meet the gaze of the man who's been by my side since we opened. Over the years, I've saved him more times than I count, even when logic told me to let him go. Jack's a loose cannon on the best of days and a walking disaster on his worst. Temperamental might as well be his middle name. Yesterday's backtalk, however, sealed his fate. "Today will be your last shift."

Jack leans across the desk to jab a finger in my face. "Hold on. You're sackin' *me* but you're keeping that fuckin' bint?"

Each word is abbreviated with another finger jab.

"Keep that up, and you'll be missing a finger along with your pride."

Expression hardening, he doesn't pull back. If anything, he thrusts that digit closer. "I know too much about you, Priest. About this entire damned place. You think I won't use that information? You think I won't—"

A squeal erupts from Jack's mouth when I grab his hand, snap that finger backward, and listen for the telltale *crack* signaling a clean break. "Mother*fucker*!" he screams, scrambling back to cradle his hand to his chest.

"Unlike you, I don't make promises that I can't keep." Slowly, I rise from my desk, my knuckles rooted to the wood. "Loyalty, Jack. It's a simple thing."

Still holding his broken hand to his chest, he snarls, "You don't think I recognize a sinkin' ship when I see one? The minute that bitch walked in here, ye've been unable to think with anything but your knob."

My muscles vibrate with barely leashed control. "You have no idea what you're talking about."

"Don't I?" On shaky feet, he strides toward me, only to stutter to a halt when he sees the look on my face. "I see it. We all do. Ye watched her leave that first day like she'd taken the air with her. A fool, that's what you are. A bird like that ain't gonna be doin' you any favors."

Frustration bleeds into me, and it takes every ounce of self-possession not to beat the man to a pulp. He has no idea what the bloody hell he's talking about. Isla is a piece of the puzzle for my long game, that's all.

Nothing more.

I storm over to the door and swing it open. "Change of plans. You're done now."

"You'll regret this, Priest," he snaps, closing the gap with his nostrils flared, his eyes narrowed to slits. "Everything about this pub—I could spill its secrets so fast ye'd be unable to do anything to stop—"

My hand locks around his throat as I drive him into the open door. Eyes going wide, he scrabbles at my fingers.

I'll let go when I'm good and ready.

I thrust my face close to his, until he can feel each of my knuckles cutting off his air supply. "Wasted words," I utter, calmly, evenly. "Turning me in would only convict yourself." I squeeze, so he'll feel the power behind my grip. His breath heaves and mine remains steady, and still I keep him plastered against the door. "The thing about blackmail, Jack, is that it's only successful if you're smart enough to pull it off. Methodical to the very end." I lower my voice. "I'd catch you every step of the way. Every time you thought you'd pulled the wool over my head, I'd beat you at your own game until there's nothing left of you. No hope, no ambition. Save us both the headache."

Red in the face, he breathes, "You're a cold bastard."

"So I've been told."

I let him go with a push out the door. He stumbles forward, his gait uneven, but catches himself before landing flat on his face. Silently, I watch from the hallway as he moves toward the front of the pub. He snarls like a beast at one of the staff, then picks up a glass from a table and hurls it against the wall.

Just like a child who hasn't gotten his way.

At all the commotion, Guy's dark head pokes into the hall, and he glances over to where I'm standing. "Sacked him?"

I give a curt nod.

"Finally," he says, clapping his hands together in mock applause. "This calls for a celebration. I've only been waiting for this moment for almost ten years."

I stride toward him. "Can't. I have a meeting."

His brows knit together. "With?"

"Isla." Pulling my mobile out from the back pocket of my trousers, I check the time. Right on target. "Is she here?"

My brother frowns. "No. Was she supposed to be?"

Yes.

"She's probably running late," I mutter, moving behind the bar.

But when fifteen minutes pass, and then yet another fifteen, with no signs of her strolling in through the front door, I'm forced to consider the inevitable: Isla Quinn quit on me.

Maybe yesterday's verbal match pushed her over the edge. Or maybe that's not it at all. Maybe she looked at her life, matched it against mine, and realized that she's better off letting me rot alone in hell while she saves herself and her siblings.

I wouldn't blame her.

Guy steps in beside me, taking a clean rag to a damp glass. "Still a no-show?" he asks quietly, his eyes scanning the dining area.

"Nothing."

As much as I don't want to entertain the thought of her quitting, it doesn't seem at all like her either. Hell, yesterday she showed up to my brother's flat simply to warn me that I've some university kids looking to cause some problems. That wasn't part of our original terms. She came of her own volition because she wants to repay her so-called debt and keep me alive.

None of this makes sense, and I say as much to Guy.

My brother side-eyes me. "You know her well enough to make a claim like that?"

"Money talks, and she needs every penny that she can get."

"Maybe she's found herself another position."

"In less than a day?" No, something is wrong. I can feel it in my gut, in the tightening of my chest.

My gaze cuts to the front door for what must be the

tenth time in a matter of minutes. Ten seconds. That's all it takes to cross from Christ Church to The Bell & Hand—twenty, if you're purposely dragging your feet and taking your sweet time. I don't want to even consider what could happen in the span of twenty seconds. Getting hit by a car. Being kidnapped right off the street.

I step to the left, so I can peer directly out our window onto Fournier. It's a typical late-winter, London day. Gray skies interspersed with splashes of sunlight. A slight rain—just enough of a drizzle for Londoners to break out their umbrellas.

Nothing out of the ordinary.

My pulse quickens.

"I'm going to run by the church," I tell Guy, who sets his now-dried glass down and picks up another from the rack, running it through with the rag.

"We don't know her."

"She isn't for you to know."

When I make a move to cut around him, Guy heads me off. "And she is for you?" he says, his voice pitched low enough to not be overheard by customers. "Be smart about this. We are *not* on the same side as her."

"I'm aware."

"Are you?" His blue eyes rove over my face, like he's trying to get a read on me. "Because from where I'm standing, the view is crystal clear. Will you ever tell her that the intelligence she gathers is used to betray everything she believes in? Will you fake sympathy, pretending all is well when her own parents are dead because of a king that you protected? The woman I met yesterday would not turn around and kiss you in gratitude."

I flinch.

Stepping forward, I bring my profile close to Guy's,

so that my mouth is directly next to his ear. "Don't go there."

He claps a hand on the nape of my neck, like we're sharing a brotherly hug.

It's anything but.

"You would break a girl like Isla," he hisses, his breath rustling the strands that cover my scar from King John. "You'd break her heart when she realized who you are, and you'd break her spirit the second you put your hands on her."

It's not anything that I don't already know. Hearing it from Guy, however, churns my stomach. I was nine when Mum died. Ten when a butcher dragged me into an alleyway, for daring to steal a slab of meat from his shop, and took a massive blade to my face, severing my upper lip in two and leaving me scarred for life. Twenty by the time I gained enough confidence to sleep with a woman, only for her to ask to be on all fours so she didn't have to see my face while I fucked her.

A shattered soul doesn't happen in a single instant. It's gradual—a fracture that occurs time and again until there's nothing left to stitch together.

For myself.

For Isla.

I push my brother aside.

"Fucking her isn't happening," I say over my shoulder, "but I'll be damned if I don't make sure that she's still breathing."

I don't wait for a comeback, instead picking my way through tables and patrons, hope clinging to my icy heart that she's simply caught up in conversation with Father Bootham.

But finding the priest in his office offers no reassurance.

His wide eyes glance up at me from behind his desk.

"She left nearly an hour ago, Saxon. Told me that she was going directly to the pub to speak with you."

"*Fuck.*"

The good father doesn't even reprimand me for the language.

Cautiously, he settles his elbows on the desk and threads his fingers together. "I suspect I know where she's gone."

My gaze darts to his. "Tell me."

The priest swallows, his Adam's apple bobbing roughly. "I told her . . . I told her that there's been a—shall we say—a certain commotion at Queen Mary University recently."

My tongue feels thick in my mouth. "Say that again."

Father Bootham reaches up to tug at his priestly collar. "At Queen Mary, there's been . . . some trouble."

"Trouble involving *what*?" I demand, dread seeping into my veins like toxin.

"Not what but whom," he says, still fiddling with his collar. "You, Saxon. The trouble involves you."

The priest keeps rambling, but my brain is on a crash-course collision. Yesterday, Isla came to me with news that a group at Queen Mary wants me dead. I turned her away. Both for my own sake—killing loyalists is something I try to avoid at all costs, in respect for my own misguided vow to the Crown—and because the fact is, if I murdered every person who had it out for me, I would bathe in the blood of my enemies for the next two lifetimes.

But for her to hear the same story from Father Bootham, tangled with the irrefutable fact that she feels some strange compulsion to save me, there's no doubt where she's gone.

Isla Quinn isn't a murderer, but that doesn't mean she

won't find herself killed in the process of trying to do the honorable thing.

That strange, sickening sensation swirls in my gut once more. The one I felt when I spotted her curled in the fetal position in front of Buckingham Palace. And the one I felt, even stronger, when I dragged her into my arms for the first time and prayed that I might still find alive.

I meet Father Bootham's dark eyes. "Tell me everything. Now."

CHAPTER 18

ISLA

As I pass the Clock Tower on Queen Mary's campus, wind whips my hair into my mouth and rain turns the grass soggy beneath my feet.

If the weather's anything to go by, coming here was a very bad decision.

"In, out," I mutter to myself, for the third time since I got off the Tube.

That's the plan, at least.

Father Bootham knew just enough to describe the group's gathering place as a grand room with a domed ceiling and busts of literary figures peering down from the upper two galleries.

There's only one place like it at Queen Mary: The Octagon.

Bowing my head to keep my face from being splashed by raindrops, I follow the paved path toward the back of the Queen's Building. It's eerily quiet out, the stormy weather keeping everyone indoors.

Everyone but me, that is.

Because you're a stubborn fool.

No, not stubborn. Just incredibly persistent.

Saxon might not care to know what the plan is to kill him, but I do. I don't allow myself time to reason out why that might be; nor do I allow myself time to dwell on the adrenaline rushing through my veins as I duck past a bicycle rack.

I visited The Octagon once with Peter for a concert, when he first started attending uni. The strings of the violin and cello and harp rose like heaven-sent chaos. Otherworldly. Beautiful. And amplified by the glass ceiling until it was impossible to feel anything but dwarfed by the splendor of each note. We'd sat at long, bench-style tables, alongside every other attendee.

Today that's the last place I should be. I need to get myself to one of the two upper floors without being caught.

My feet slosh through a shallow puddle but I'm too busy scaling the side of the brick building, visually, to do anything but shake out my leg like a dog and keep trudging forward, ignoring the rain pelting down on my shoulders, ignoring the paranoia that sweeps around me, like a lover might, and demand that I turn around and leave.

I lock sight on the front door then search for another, more covert entrance than—

A hand comes down on my shoulder, hard enough to rattle my teeth. "You look lost."

Oh, *hell*.

I pin a smile on my face, turning toward the stranger. "No! Not at all. I'm attending a meeting, but I've never been and I'm gathering the courage to—"

Every word dies on my next breath.

Brown eyes. Dark hair tucked under a tweed flat cap. A weathered face that appears no older than mid-forties.

I know that face.

I know that face.

How. Where. *When?*

The man readjusts the hat, rain catching on his short lashes, and—

The bloke I played side-shuffle with on the front stoop of The Bell & Hand. As in, The Bell & Hand, home to anti-loyalists everywhere. Relief floods my system so hard that I nearly gasp and throw my arms around this man I've only ever seen in passing.

He reaches down, flicks his brolly open, and positions it above my head. A smile curves his thin lips as his brown eyes hold mine. "First time coming to Queen Mary, eh? I'm a professor here."

My breath catches in my throat. *Don't think the worst. Don't you dare think the worst.* Right. I'm letting the paranoia take root again. The likelihood of him being the same professor that Father Bootham mentioned is—

"Ian Coney," he adds, instantly shattering all hope.

Fuck.

I dart a glance over to The Octagon, then the drenched walkway that leads to freedom. There are two options here. I play the flighty sort, thanking him for stopping to check on me, and continue on my merry way. I'm only a matter of blocks from being home, safe and sound, and putting this all behind me.

Or I do what I came here to do.

In the end, Professor Coney, leader of the loyalist group out for Saxon's blood, makes the decision for me. With the brolly still over my head, he says, "Come inside and get out of the rain."

I swallow, thickly, and choose option three. "That would be so lovely!" I smile, all teeth, and shiver for dramatic effect. "It's only that"—I wave at The Octagon—"I'm meant to be attending a meeting. My brother comes here for university and thought I would find the group ... enlightening."

Coney's brown eyes drift over my frame. "And he pointed you here, to The Octagon?"

I nod. "Yes."

"Interesting you should say that."

"Oh?"

He gives the umbrella a little shake. "It's where I'm heading too. Please, let me escort you."

The idea of having Professor Ian Coney at my back sounds less enticing than bathing in a pit of poisonous snakes. I hold my breath, keeping count of every step that brings me closer to learning of their plans to kill Saxon, all while praying that I won't end up dead in the interim.

Coney steps to the side as I open the door, but instead of letting me through, he blocks my entrance with the closed umbrella. "I didn't ask. What is your name?"

Rain soaks the earth, a cacophony that fills my ears as loudly as the blood thrumming in my temples. "Beth," I lie smoothly, "Beth Linde."

"You'll need a password to proceed, Beth Linde."

I stare at the clear, plastic brolly in front of me. It might as well be a broadsword, for all the good it does in appearing harmless. With the umbrella to my front and Coney at my back, I'm well and truly stuck. "A password?" I echo.

"Yes."

Neither Peter nor Father Bootham mentioned anything about a password. Peter didn't because he'd only overheard a few of the members while searching for a book at the university library. Father Bootham didn't because that boy had been too blasted drunk to mention it to his mother.

Think off the cuff!

A bunch of loyalists who want Queen Margaret to keep her throne would use something related to the royal family, I'm sure of it. The possibilities are endless, and time is ticking down. I feel Coney's breath on the back of my neck, and the rain seeping into my clothes, and my own heart threatening to fly from my chest.

Do it. Just say something!

"God save the queen."

Coney laughs, like it's all in good jest, and lifts the brolly blockade. "A lucky one, you are." I nearly collapse against the door frame, I'm so surprised. It must register on my face because he taps my leg with the umbrella, good-naturedly. "Don't look so startled, Miss Linde. Your brother didn't set you up for failure, if that was your worry."

It wasn't at all.

Instead I'd been prepared to find a knife shoved into my back. One wrong move, one wrong word . . . I shiver, for real this time. "We would have had words, if he had."

Coney throws his head back with a hearty chuckle. "In you go now. You're completely drenched, you poor thing."

Drenched, yes, but still alive—for now.

Thank God.

My footsteps echo off the herringbone-wood floor as I take in the selection of chairs all placed in a circle. There's a hodgepodge of people seated, all men: university students wearing Queen Mary apparel, a few blokes who look to be around my age, and two older gentlemen. Whereas an orchestra filled the octagonal-shaped room just last year, excited chatter does now.

Coney grips my shoulder, driving me forward. "We have a newcomer, everyone."

Seven pairs of eyes turn on me, and my stomach careens straight to the floor. Can they see that I'm the enemy? Do I have it scrawled, clear as day, across my forehead: *I killed your beloved king.*

I slip my left hand against my thigh, hoping to hide the rain-smudged words I jotted down earlier when talking to Father Bootham.

"She can take my chair," says one of the uni boys, leaping up from his. "I'll get another."

I don't want him to give up his seat. Bloody hell, I don't want a single reason to look at these people as anything more than obstacles in dismantling the monarchy. To do otherwise would blur too many lines, and I fear they've blurred quite enough already.

"Thank you," I murmur, purely out of good manners.

Like my own private tour guide, Coney leads me to the vacant chair and gestures for me to sit down.

His hand never leaves my shoulder.

Sitting, my calves come together as though a vine of fear has twined around them, keeping me fastened in place.

The last time I was here, I gawked in awe at the beauty of The Octagon. Cast-iron galleries on the first and second floors. A beautiful domed, glass roof. Intricate, cream-colored Victorian-era plasterwork. Thick columns arching high, toward the ceiling, and melding with the bowed walls to create small porticoes where the busts of literary greats observe all. Shakespeare. Chaucer. Byron.

Today, The Octagon's elegance mocks me.

"Shall we start where we left off the other day?" Coney asks, still hovering behind me, so close that I can feel the fabric of his damp shirt against my back.

I take small comfort in the fact that Dad's knife is tucked away in its usual spot.

One of the older men leans back in his chair, resting his ankle on his opposite knee. "We need to move soon. If we wait any longer, we'll lose our edge."

"Being cautious isn't a drawback," argues the boy who gave me his chair. With blondish-brown hair and a baby-face, he looks years younger than the hard gaze he levels on the others suggests. "We have only one chance to do this right. Going in half-cocked, just because we're eager to put the damned bastard down, won't do us any favors."

The first man sits up in his seat. "What d'you know about strategy, Gregg? I have Army boots older than you."

Next to him, a balding bloke nods. "You're both right, yeah? The Priests are notorious, and their underground network isn't something we should discount. They have manpower."

"*We* have manpower," Gregg spits, jabbing a finger at every individual seated in the circle. "I've no desire to sit back and let Saxon Priest get away with what he's done. He'll die, just like he did to the king, with a bullet in his chest. But we must *plan*."

A lump grows in my throat, and the vines twine higher, around my thighs, my belly, until it feels like a struggle to breathe.

As if sensing my inner turmoil, Coney settles his free hand on my other shoulder. "Let's hear from Beth, shall we?" His fingers squeeze, none too gently. "What do you think about our little problem with Saxon Priest, newcomer?" he asks, directing the question to me, though I can't see him at all. "Should we make a move now and save ourselves the trouble of dealing with him, too, when we turn to his brothers?"

Turn to his . . . brothers?

Oh, God. Do they have plans to do away with all

three of them?

Sweat blooms in my palms and words crash on my tongue. Smart. I need to play these next few seconds smart or it won't be only Saxon's head they want served on a silver platter. "I think . . ."

Before I can say more, Coney leans forward, his stomach grazing the back of my skull, which cants my head at an awkward angle. I wait, my breathing suspended, to see if it was a mistake that he'll quickly rectify. Perhaps with an added apology for slipping and bumping into me.

He doesn't retreat. He doesn't apologize, either.

Instead, he only chuckles, soft, low, like it's a fine game that we've decided to play while the rest of the group watches with piqued curiosity, heads tilted, eyes studiously assessing.

I have zero interest in participating.

I shift on my seat, inching away, only to be jerked back into place like an errant child fleeing punishment. My soft grunt breaks the charged silence as my head cranes forward and my shoulders remain trapped within his hold.

"Miss Linde?" Professor Coney prompts.

Focus. Play nice. Do what the crazy tosser says before you end up dead in the Thames.

With my gaze zeroed in on my knees, I utter, "I think you'll be better off taking Gregg's approach. A half-cocked plan is no plan at all."

There's nodding from half the group, including Gregg and the bald man.

I breathe a little easier.

"Funny you should say that," the professor murmurs. One hand comes off my shoulder, and then is followed by a distinct rustling sound, like he's fishing in his pockets. "See, we've been debating how best to—shall we say—

eradicate Saxon Priest for weeks now. Do we recreate King John's assassination? Do we go for something completely different? We can't quite come to a mutual decision."

A thin stack of photographs lands in my lap.

The moment the face in the picture registers, every muscle turns to ice.

Saxon.

His unique green-yellow eyes are bright from the sunlight which bathes his brawny frame from one of the pub's windows. He's speaking to one of the servers at The Bell & Hand, hands fixed on his hips, his scarred mouth set in that rigid line that I've grown to recognize all too well.

Dread keeps me paralyzed as Coney leans over me, his front plastered to my back, his fingers finding the first photo and tossing it haphazardly to the ground. "Of course, I don't believe in doing anything half-cocked," he continues, pointing to the next frame, which shows Saxon bussing a table at the pub. "You learn by watching. Their mannerisms, who they trust, the motives behind their every move."

At my sides, my fingers twitch. "I agree."

"Do you?" Coney's breath warms my face as he turns to stare at me, but then we're cheek to cheek once more. No one else says a word, their attention riveted on us. "Then perhaps you can understand my surprise when I showed up today and found you standing in the rain."

He flicks to the next picture, and it's *me*.

Me standing there, talking to Saxon, that day we went to Christ Church.

Shite, shite, *shite!*

"See, you being here doesn't align with what I've learned of you . . . Isla Quinn."

Swapping to the next photo, it's instantly recognizable: Saxon and I standing next to the side entrance of Christ Church, my hand wrapped around his arm, Saxon's expression murderous, seconds, perhaps, before he told me to get my arse inside the church or go home.

Each picture proves more incriminating than the last.

Anxiously, I scan the others in the group, looking for an ally. A potential friend. Anyone, really, who might prove useful in helping me get out of here unscathed. But as my eyes dart from one man to the next, their mouths stay zipped shut. Poses casual, albeit alert. There's no help coming, not from that lot.

"I've been trying to garner information from him," I edge out, thinking quick on my feet, "that's all. So I could come here and tell you."

"No, I don't think that's the case."

Before I can even plot my next move, Coney's made his.

The hand that showed me the photographs fits around my neck, squeezing, and I scream. I scream so loud that I'm surprised the glass ceiling doesn't shatter.

Coney clamps his other hand over my mouth.

Oh, God. Oh, God. *Oh, God.*

"I think you're as much a traitor as Saxon Priest," he grunts in my ear, below the sound of the other men mocking my strangled gasps for air. Deftly, Coney sweeps his thumb along my jaw as he chokes me.

And he *is* choking me. Every bit of training from my youth flies out the window as pure survival mode kicks in. It isn't pretty and it certainly isn't strategic. My feet skate over the floor, legs twisting wildly as I grab his wrists, yanking hard enough to leave marks behind. But his grip doesn't slacken and dear God, I can't breathe. *I can't breathe!* I wheeze, digging my nails into his flesh, and try to wriggle free.

"No, little bird," he drawls, running his thumb down the column of my throat in an eerily appreciative gesture, "I think you planned to sit here, all prim and proper, before traipsing right back to the traitor to tell him everything you heard. And if you did that . . . we'd all be dead."

It's on the tip of my tongue to shout that I killed the king.

I did it. *Me.*

At least they'd punish the right person. At least I'd earn my penance without costing Saxon his life.

Except that I've never been all that good with accepting my lot in life—I have no interest in dying, not yet. I want to live. I want to fall in love. I want to taste happiness again, in a way that's eluded me for years.

I'm alive, I'm alive, I'm alive.

And damn anyone who tries to take that from me.

I breathe through my nose, ignoring the black web of unconsciousness creeping over my vision, and nimbly snake my fingers into my coat pocket for Dad's knife. By the time the jeering from the others morphs into screams that I've pulled out a weapon, I've already sunk the blade into Coney's thigh.

He stumbles back, releasing my throat with such abruptness that I collapse to the floor, completely lightheaded from the regained oxygen pumping into my lungs. *Crawl. Crawl!* God, I try. I gasp for air and shove myself onto all fours, but fingers grasp my ankle in a vice, stalling my flight, and then Coney snarls, "You fucking *bitch*!"

And then I'm dragged backward.

CHAPTER 19

SAXON

I run.

Rain plasters my shirt to my chest and my feet churn up puddles but there's not a bloody chance in hell of me slowing down when the visions skating through my head are hideous nightmares.

Isla dead before I can save her.

Isla *almost* dead, blood caked in her strawberry-blond hair, her bright blue eyes fluttering closed one last time before she goes limp in my arms.

It can't happen. I won't *let* it happen.

Without hesitating, I hurdle over a bicycle rack marked with Queen Mary University's emblem—a crown. As if I need another reminder that when I reach Isla, I'll be breaking my oath to a different queen, this one the Queen of the United Kingdom.

An oath that we inherited, Guy argued just yesterday.

Inherited or not, I've never strayed from Holyrood's singular mission.

Until now.

Until *her*.

Picking up the pace, I follow the curve of a brick building and feel a surge of relief when I spot the rotund façade of The Octagon that Father Bootham described. I'll need a way in, something more circumspect than the singular door that faces a large quad and more university buildings.

Doubling back, I retrace my steps.

It takes two tries of jiggling handles that won't budge before I crack one door open and slip inside.

Immediately, the rain dims to a dull staccato, matched only by the thud of my shoes as I start down a hallway that ought to lead me directly to The Octagon. Seconds bleed into seconds, and the place becomes maze-like, winding me in, taking me in one direction, before unfurling into an intersection with three options and time ticking away.

Focus.

Within Holyrood, I'm notorious for staying calm. I've fought, and won, with a knife wound that punctured the sensitive flesh just above my kidneys. Broken bones. Bullet wounds. Even a deflated lung. I stop for nothing. *Savage*, Hamish once called me, after we completed a mission to take down a group of Scots who wanted King John dead.

I'm efficient, not savage.

Right now, I'm neither of those things.

No, I'm *unraveling*.

My chest pumps with excess adrenaline and every muscle in my body screams in protest when I push myself harder, faster.

And then I hear it.

A scream that raises the hair on the back of my neck and sends my heart rate straight into overdrive. A scream that will haunt me until the day I die, until I'm six feet under, chained down in hell, and still unable to escape her shrill cry of fear.

Isla.

Red swarms my vision.

Anger. Panic. Retaliation already rearing to strike as the double-wide doors to The Octagon come into view.

I throw my entire weight, only for them to vibrate in place. One glance downward reveals old-fashioned chains threaded through a single lock. Picking it would waste valuable time that I don't have, which means any attempt to remain inconspicuous is about to be shot to hell. Literally.

"So much for making a quiet entrance," I mutter, stepping back to clear the space.

Reaching for my holster, I pull out my pistol.

Aim. Squeeze the trigger. Fire.

The lock explodes. Tossing the broken chain to the floor, I rip the doors open and—

A man straddles Isla's waist, pinning her to the ground. Blood coats the floor around them. It's painted across his legs, on her hands. Between them, a knife gleams under the florescent lighting, revealing more blood dotting the steel.

A violent mural of imminent death.

Rage the likes of which I've never known floods my veins.

Starting forward, I raise my pistol, ready to pick the bastard off.

Only, a body slams into me, full-force, and I stagger to the left. Grabbing the man's arm, I drag him down with me as I fall. Turn us as we crash to the ground so that I land on top, my legs straddling his thick waist, my hand splayed across his face, jamming his profile into the polished floor. I lift my weapon, preparing to shoot to kill, when the sound of footsteps rushing toward us jerks my attention up.

Six, maybe seven men.

All trucking toward me as though they're extras in some B-Grade action film and believe that charging in numbers will save them. Maybe it would have, had they been attacking anyone else but me.

Switching the gun to my left hand, I lock in on the only one carrying a firearm—a bald bloke.

I take aim. Squeeze. Fire.

Down he goes.

The man under me scrambles to shove me off, bucking his hips and pushing at my chest. In a pathetic move, he takes advantage that I've swapped hands and tries to bite my thumb. Not happening. Nostrils flaring, I crack the butt of my pistol over his crown, and watch his eyes roll to the back of his head.

"*Saxon!*"

Isla.

Ignoring the other loyalists on the hunt for my blood, I launch to my feet and run. Toward her. Toward the man trying to kill her.

And, for the first time since King John scarred me, I turn my back on my own destiny.

CHAPTER 20

ISLA

My arms tremble so violently that I fear my bones will snap and I'll have a blade buried in my jugular within seconds.

Hold, I rage with all my heart, *hold on!*

Beyond the roaring in my ears, I hear commotion on the other side of The Octagon.

A gun unloading a round.

Followed by a startled cry seconds before Death steals into the room and claims its first victim.

Saxon came for me.

If I weren't seconds away from death myself, I'd weep with relief.

The knife sinks another centimeter, drawing closer, *closer*, and I let out Saxon's name on a blood-curdling scream. My throat tightens from the effort, my chest constricts with my inability to breathe, and life as I know it becomes nothing more than the man pinning me to this bloodstained floor with my own father's weapon aimed for my neck.

Come for me, please, please, come for me.

I want to shout the words. I want to beg for Saxon to hear me, but I do nothing but hold my position, using all of my strength to grip Coney's wrists and survive another second.

"You think he'll save you?" Above me, Coney's mouth twists in a sneer. Blood is spattered across his neck, the left side of his body. His blood, not mine. "He won't get close enough to even try."

Craning my neck to avoid the knife's sharp tip, I squirm in place. I'm strong. I've *always* been strong. Dad put me in mixed martial arts as a child. He thought it would be a good outlet, since I had the particularly bad habit of picking fights in school with the bullies who targeted the smaller children. Quinns were raised to lead, to do *better*.

I exceeded all expectations.

And now ... And now I've let terror render me useless.

I twist my head, my eyes scouring The Octagon until they land on Saxon, who's fending off two other men and Gregg. He's poetry in motion, a violent storm of sharp jabs and roundhouse kicks.

Turbulent. Powerful.

Savior. Devil.

All in one.

Saxon came to save me, but I'll be dead before he even has the chance.

Muscles faltering, I take a deep breath ...

And let it happen.

Dad's knife descends like a guillotine dropping to sever its victim.

I watch it fall, watch it aim for my neck, and then, at the last second, I slam my hand against its serrated edge and send it clattering to the wood floor, where it slides out of reach. Searing agony erupts in my palm, the metallic scent of drawn blood hanging in the air.

Move.

Move now!

I move, ignoring my quivering limbs and growing fatigue, and hook my legs around Coney's hips. Using his surprise to my advantage, I roll him beneath me and pin his legs down. Alarm splices across his face and he struggles against the restraint of my legs hooked over his, but I hold on. *I hold on.* Self-preservation kicks in, overruling all else, and I circle my hands around his neck, the same as he did to me.

And I squeeze.

Until his face turns a ghastly, unnatural shade of purple. Until my arms beg for relief. Until I feel tears coat my cheeks because maybe I could convince myself that I wasn't a murderer after shooting King John, but now I have two victims, and there's no hiding from the truth staring back at me with lifeless brown eyes and bruises shaped like my thumbprints already blooming on his throat.

I shot King John.

I strangled Professor Ian Coney.

Saxon's words from yesterday haunt me now: *Sometimes we simply amount to what we've always been destined to become.*

A ragged, watery sob catches in my throat, just as strong arms wrap around my waist. "We have to go," Saxon grunts in my ear, "right now. Before the Met gets here."

He lifts me off Coney's dead body.

I struggle to breathe. "I killed him. Saxon, oh God, I killed him."

Large hands frame my face, jerking my attention up to meet pale green eyes. "You're alive. Right now, focus on that." His nose bumps mine as his thumbs cradle the hollows behind my jawbone. "We're going to run. Do you hear me, Isla? If you can't do it, I'll carry you myself. But we have to go *now*."

So, I run, with only one glance back at The Octagon.

Beauty meets chaos. Heaven meets hell.

And dead bodies litter the ground.

We weave through campus, my hand clasped in Saxon's, the heavy rain erasing our sins.

My over-imaginative brain paints nonexistent faces in the windows, all gawking at us as we run past, cataloging our bloody clothes and the tears streaking down my face and Saxon's hard expression that never once cracks.

Has the Met been called yet?

No sooner have I had the thought than sirens break through the monotony of rain pelting pavement.

Saxon slows, his head twisting as though he's pinpointing exactly where the sirens are coming from, and then he drags me to the right. I stumble over an overgrown tree root. "Go," he bites out, pushing me in front of him.

My gaze flies over the narrow snicket. A metal dumpster sits on the opposite end, blocking the exit. "That's not going to work. There's no way we'll be able to get out—"

"We're going to crawl." Hand to the space between my shoulder blades, he pushes me forward. "Unless you want to be caught when those coppers come barreling down on us."

As if to prove his point, the sirens escalate, louder and louder, until one police cruiser, then the next, flies down the campus road we just vacated.

"Get down," Saxon growls, "before the next one happens to look over and sees us fucking *meandering* our way to safety."

This time, I don't defy him.

I drop to my hands and knees and crawl my arse toward the dumpster. Gravel bites into my wounded palm, and I try not to think about the possible infection I'll be battling if I don't clean it soon.

Fighting off the urge to whimper, I opt for a desperate dose of humor. "So, come here often?"

A big hand lands on my arse, just short of slapping the cheek, and urges me to move faster. "Only you would crack jokes at a time like this."

I keep my eyes on the ground in front of me, evading shards of broken glass. "It's either that or cry. I'm doing us both a favor."

"I don't need any favors," he snarls, and immediately, I'm assaulted by the visual of livid, unholy eyes and a scarred, tortured mouth bearing down on me, from behind, "I need you fucking alive."

My heart skips a beat. "Because you care?"

"Crawl, Isla," is his curt response.

We reach the dumpster, and Saxon moves around me, up onto his knees. The rain has dampened his shirt to the point of translucency. Muscles stacked upon muscles, which are put on more prominent display when he reaches toward his hip and retrieves a gun from its holster. Pistol in one hand, he dips a hand into his pocket and reveals the bloody hilt of Dad's knife.

The knife that nearly killed me. I swallow, hard.

Green eyes find mine as he hands it over. "You follow me. Every step. Every pause."

I drag in a sharp breath, only to hiss between my teeth when the hilt collides with my wound. Still, I grip it firmly. Steadily. With every ounce of strength that I have left in reserve. "Where are we going?"

"No questions, just follow."

Severing eye contact, he turns, his big frame hunched like a rattlesnake poised to strike.

More sirens echo in the near distance, sending a chill of fear rappelling down my spine.

The Octagon will be all over the news by nightfall.

Saxon doesn't need to tell me that he left no survivors—he couldn't have, even if he'd wanted to, not with the chance of them telling the police our identities. *Also my fault*. Saxon hadn't wanted to do anything about the loyalist group, even with the mounting target on his back.

I hate that I dragged him here, that I forced more spilled blood on his hands and on my own.

Selfishly, though, I know there was no other option.

I recognized Ian Coney because I'd seen him at The Bell & Hand. And he'd seen me, too. How many others are there like him? How many supporters of the Crown are lurking, biding their time, within the pub that Saxon and his brothers set up as a safe haven for anti-loyalists?

If I hadn't shown up tonight, who knows when they might have attacked.

Perhaps today, tomorrow, three weeks from now.

But they would have, and they would have managed to catch Saxon off guard, perhaps fatally, and I don't know what it says about me that I would rather have the blood of Ian Coney on my hands—literally—than discover that he'd stripped Saxon of his life.

The man in question shoots out an arm, blocking me from further movement.

"Do you hear something?" I whisper.

He tilts his head, listening. "An ambulance," he rumbles, "which means someone isn't dead." Twisting toward the brick wall, he comes just short of punching it. At the last second, his fist curls behind his nape, pressing deep into the flesh there. "*Fuck!*"

"Understatement of the year," I choke out. "They know who we are."

"I know."

"I've got to get home. Peter, Josie, they—"

Twisting around, Saxon's fingers find my chin, his thumb grazing the skin just below my bottom lip. The sudden, unexpected contact clams me up, snapping my mouth shut. "We get out of here and I'll send Guy to them," he says, his gaze searching mine. "But me and you—we need to hustle."

"Hustle." When I nod, his thumb slips over my wet skin and my heart stutters. "I can do that. I don't crack, remember?"

His hand falls to his side, the ghost of his touch erased by rain. "Now's your chance to prove it. Don't disappoint me."

CHAPTER 21

ISLA

I don't disappoint him.

As lightning shatters the sky, Saxon leads me from snickelway to snickelway. Though we've left the sirens behind, it's done nothing to soften our pace. Two months ago, I assassinated the king in a plot that I'd planned for months, ever since it was announced that he would be speaking at a rally, in full sight of the thousands gathered to see him. Today, there is no planning—only the controlled chaos that Saxon sets into motion to shuttle us away from Queen Mary's campus.

I step in a puddle, and dirty street water promptly drenches me from toe to ankle. "*Bollocks.*"

My clothes are soaked, my hair is nothing more than a bedraggled rat's nest that sticks to my face, and if I'm ever able to dry out these boots to wear again, it'll be a miracle of epic proportions.

Holding up a hand for me to stop moving, Saxon peers out onto Mile End Road, his dark head shifting from right to left. I walk this street nearly every day on the way to the Tube, but it all feels . . . foreign. Like I don't even recognize my own borough.

"We can't run all day," I whisper to his back. "At some point, we're going to have to stop, regather."

And save Peter and Josie, too.

I haven't forgotten Saxon's promise that he'll send Guy for them. And while Saxon's older brother isn't exactly on my list of chums that I'd love to grab a pint with, I know that he cares deeply for his family. If he's sent for my siblings, they'll be in good hands. Safe hands.

I hope.

Distracting myself from thoughts that may send me into a downward spiral, I press my back into the building that lines the snicket. My teeth chatter from the chill that's swept over my body. The longer we move, the colder I become. The adrenaline ditched me somewhere near the Stepney Tube station, leaving nothing behind but festering fear and mounting dread.

What have I done?

"Saxon." When he doesn't answer, I reach for his back, laying a hand on his spine to snag his attention. The contact to my throbbing palm has me hissing out a short, uneven breath. "Saxon, please. Where are we going?"

With his hair plastered to his temple, and his skin pebbled with pearls of rain, Saxon looks like an ancient warlord reincarnated. Broad shoulders, hard chest, thick thighs. The scarred mouth and intense stare that he levels on me only fuels the feeling that he could save me, or break me, if he so chose.

He indicates the opposite side of the street with a tilt of his chin. "There."

Slack-jawed, I stare at the appointed brick building.

It's not unlike the tens of others we've passed in the last half hour. A mobile store on the ground floor—two stories above it. Narrow, single-paned windows meshed with a decided lack of character or charm. From our vantage point, it's hard not to miss the crumbling brick façade and the string of rubbish strewn along the pavement. The store's windows are completely boarded up.

My own flat isn't exactly posh, but this . . . "It's a hellhole."

Saxon leverages a hand over his pistol, re-holstering it in one smooth move. "Tonight, it's our hellhole."

"You're taking the piss, aren't you."

"Not even a little."

"The ceiling looks like it might cave in at any second!"

"Only imagine the opportunities if it did," Saxon murmurs, slicking a wet hand over my shoulder and giving me a nudge forward. "Chances to fake your own death don't come around every day."

I take it back. All of it.

Saxon Priest isn't a coldhearted bastard—he's certifiably *mad*.

Tempted as I am to dig my heels in and demand that he bring me home, I trail him across the busy street. Home is dangerous . . . or it soon will be. Realistically, it's only a matter of time before the survivor from The Octagon gives the police our identities. And while the Priest brothers seem to have experience with successfully erasing themselves from the public eye—or, at least, the internet—the same can't be said for me. Even after killing the king, I carried on with my routine, hoping that acting normal would translate to normal *all around*.

Simply put, I'm fucked.

Throwing a hasty glance to the right for oncoming traffic, I spot The Shard's hazy silhouette on the horizon. It stretches toward the sky like a beacon—of what, I have no idea. Stability, perhaps. Normalcy. Not that any part of this day has been remotely normal.

"You do have a key, don't you?" I ask.

He approaches the run-down mobile store with quick, measured strides.

"Saxon?" I scurry behind him, picking up the pace. "Saxon, breaking and entering is *not* going to be what turns this day around for the better. Do you know the owner? Are they on our side? Because I'm telling you right now, I hope you trust them with everything that you are, or we are so fu—"

I grind to a halt when he stops before the shop's front door, swipes his dark hair back from his face, and waits.

I almost miss it. No, I *would* have missed it, had I blinked a second earlier. The door—the *glass door*—reflects Saxon's grim expression before turning a shade of red along the perimeter of his body. An outline of glowing neon that dims a moment later.

What the hell*?*

Slowly, the door cracks open as though invisible hands have tugged on the handle from the inside. Saxon pushes it wide. "Go in."

Déjà vu.

Not for the crazy, high-tech door or this wild, insane day, but for *him*.

The car, the confessional, this boarded-up mobile store. Each time he's told me some variation of "get in," I've found myself more deeply embroiled in this world of chaos. This time, unlike the others, however, I don't have the luxury of turning him down—not that I've done so, yet.

Within hours, I'll be a wanted woman. A criminal. Just as I feared after murdering King John.

I slip past Saxon, my fingertips accidentally grazing

his hip as I knot the fabric of my shirt to squeeze out the excess rainwater. "Well, are you going to explain how all that worked?"

He closes the door behind us, flipping the deadbolt. "Security system."

It takes everything in me not to roll my eyes. "Yes, Saxon, a security system. One that's state of the art, nothing like I've ever seen before, and programmed to analyze a person's identity simply by stepping in *front of it*."

Not to mention that this fancy-schmancy tech security system is being used at a dead-beat phone shop in Stepney, of all places. Which means that this building is either not at all what it seems, or the Priest brothers were in need of a testing zone for another locale and figured this one would do.

Either way, it doesn't make a lick of sense.

How can they afford technology like that? Surely, The Bell & Hand does well—but *this* well? And why in the world do they own an abandoned building in the East End, in the first place? One glance around the space proves that the ramshackle exterior suitably matches the inside. An old register sits along a far wall and aisles take up the majority of the space to my left. Dust and debris crunch beneath my boots as I turn in a small circle.

Hellhole is a grave understatement.

Saxon brushes past me. "Has anyone ever told you that you ask too many questions?"

"Yes, actually." I stare at him, deadpan. "My old employer at the network right before he sacked me for insubordination."

"Seems like he had the right of it."

Deep breath. Take it in; let it out. Do not *kill someone else today.*

Fingers tingling at the memory of what I'd done, just hours ago, I slam the door on those debilitating thoughts before they cripple my wits. "Who owns this building? Just you? You and your brothers?"

He guns me with a quick stare. "Sometimes, the less you know the better."

"You know what I think?"

"Something tells me that you'll say what's on your mind, no matter how I answer."

Disgruntled, I plant my good hand on my hip. "It was a rhetorical question."

"Rhetorical questions are for the weak-minded." I drag in a sharp, affronted breath, just before he adds, "Say what you want or don't say it at all."

"Fine. All right. Then I don't agree with you—knowing less makes you a sitting duck." Restlessly, I dig my fingers into my hip. "Yesterday, you essentially told me that the information I had didn't interest you."

"I said that I didn't want to know anything more, not that it didn't interest me. Two very different things."

"Either way," I bite out, reining in my temper, "you chose ignorance. That's your prerogative, of course, and I was going to do just that. Lay off and let it be—begrudgingly, I might add, because it was *obvious* that something was brewing and knowing less is like throwing a white flag in the air and begging to be caught before the war's even begun."

"Brilliant visual, Isla," comes his dry reply, "really."

Stubborn.

Infuriating.

Man.

"Father Bootham tipped me off today. His and Peter's stories lined up, even though they've clearly never met before." Lifting my chin, I continue, "You might believe that knowing less is better, but I was always taught to gather the facts, then assess the situation when you have it all laid out before you. It's what I did as a publicist. It's what I did on the network, when they allowed me to actually do my job. And it's what I had to do here, too, to make sure you wouldn't be utterly blindsided."

I step forward, only for my wet boot to squeak loudly against the floor. Following the source of the noise, Saxon's attention drops south. He pauses, hands flexing at his sides, and cocks his head. Something in his expression . . . God, there's a rawness there that I've never seen before, not from him. It's not vulnerability, I don't think. Not affection either. Like every other aspect of Saxon Priest's icy exterior, it's impossible to put my finger on it and yet I feel that look anyhow.

Slow heat thaws the perpetual chill in my bones when I say, "You should be thanking me, you know."

"Is that so?"

His voice is deep, guttural, and matched with another deliberate perusal that starts at my feet and meanders its way up my thighs to the nip of my waist, and then, finally, to the delicate slope of my neck. I stave off a shudder. "Yes."

"Why?"

"Because the man—the professor—that I-I—"

Saxon's gaze collides with mine. "Say it."

Heat of another kind kindles in my chest. Remorse. Shame. *Disgust.* "No."

"This is why you first showed up to The Bell & Hand, isn't it?" Slowly, he stalks toward me. One foot in front of the other, the soles of his shoes echoing in the quiet of the room. A predator on the hunt. My heart skips a beat, timed with his heavy step. "That first day you told me that you had a proposition for me. One that I couldn't refuse."

Unease coils in my belly, and I stumble back. "This isn't—what happened today wasn't... *isn't* what I wanted—"

"Except that I saw you."

With my heart in my throat, my stare leaps to his. "What?"

"Today," he says, coming closer still, severing the distance between us with each long-legged stride that intimidates as successfully as it entices me to watch him and never look away, "I saw you, the *real* you."

"I-I don't understand."

"It means that I underestimated you, Isla Quinn. When I had you slung over my shoulder, I underestimated you. When I had you cornered in the confessional, and you held your blade to my neck"—a dark smile curls his scarred mouth—"I never thought that you would actually slit my throat. I underestimated you then, too."

"You didn't. Not at all."

He speaks over me, as though I haven't said a word. "When we met, you said that you had something that I couldn't refuse. It's my own fault for not realizing you'd been offering yourself."

In this moment, I despise him just as much as I hate myself. Silly, foolish me had honestly thought I could work for Saxon as a pay-for-hire. I'd killed once, hadn't I? What stopped me from doing so again?

But now—*but now*—it's so clear that I was absolutely delusional. My hand throbs from the knife fight and my heart hurts from taking another life, no matter that Coney tried to take mine first. In two months, I've not even managed to overcome the night terrors of what I did to King John. I toss and turn; I slip from bed and stare out the window for hours, as though expecting the king's ghost to appear on my front stoop.

I'm being haunted, and hunted, and whatever I thought myself capable of just last week is clearly a moot point buried so far deep it'll never resurface.

Saxon never underestimated me. Because, beneath all my bravado, I've never catered to the darkness lurking within. Until today.

I swallow, roughly. "I'm not a . . . I'm not a—"

"Say the word."

Killer. Monster.

"I can't," I whisper, inching backward. Because then it's true. Because then it's real. Because then where do I go from here, knowing that I'm wholly irredeemable? "Saxon, I *can't*."

"Then I'll say it for you," he grits out, backing me against the wall. His hands land on either side of my head, blockading me in, and *hell*. His damp chest rubs against my breasts and his muscular thigh slips between my legs, trapping me in place. For a man who radiates a chill factor rivaling the Arctic, his skin is so hot I'm convinced that I might go up in flames.

"*Murderer.*" The word is uttered roughly next to my ear, for me and for me alone, even though there's not another soul in this abandoned building. "It makes you ruthless. It makes you broken."

I battle back a ferocious cry. "Wrong. It makes me strong."

"Strong," he murmurs, as though tasting the word on his tongue and finding it unpalatable. "Strong is strangling a man like you did today and finding no remorse, no part of your soul that feels fractured or missing for doing what had to be done. Strong is what you tell yourself when you're fighting your own conscience."

"Then that's your definition, not mine." When his nose grazes the shell of my ear, sensation erupts along my spine. Gooseflesh. Heat. *Need*. My hips curl out of their own volition, seeking his hardness. No! I freeze, immediately. *Focus, Isla. Focus!* "Obviously, we're nothing alike."

"And yet, just yesterday you said that we could be friends." His hand drifts down, never touching my body. But oh, he comes close, so close, to the swell of my breasts, to the flare of my hips, until his fingers land on the wall beside mine.

"You turned me down," I say, my brain threatening to short-circuit.

"So I did." Blunt fingers circle my wrist and drag my hand up, pinning it above my head. The position forces me onto my toes, putting me at the disadvantage. He towers over me, surrounds me, until I see nothing of the shop beyond the broad stretch of his shoulders. Wide-eyed, my gaze flies to his, just as he murmurs, "Guy was right about me, you know. I don't do pets; I don't do friends."

My fingers wriggle in his grip, but I'm not exactly pulling away. *Because you want it. The heat. The tension. The taste of fear from the unknown.* I swallow the truth, keeping it buried. "I don't imagine your charming personality keeps people around long enough to find out if they'd want the same of you."

His thumb presses on my inner wrist, as if testing the pace of my pulse. Fast. It's pounding so, so fast, a fact that Saxon must know because his eyes gleam. "Ask me why, Isla. Ask me why I don't want you as a friend, as a pet."

The feminist in me wants to spit in his face for assuming that I'd want to be a "pet" to any man. Him, most especially. But the rest of me ... the rest of me trembles, and the shaking isn't rooted in fear. Heat blooms between my legs and, beneath the confines of my wet shirt, my nipples bead into hard, little points. If I give this man even a sliver of what he's asking of me, I'll surely drown.

But like when he ordered me to get in the car, or the confessional, or this blasted, run-down building, I succumb to the ice in his veins and the blistering heat that tethers us together.

"Tell me why," I echo.

It's not a question.

It's not me falling to his feet and worshipping the very ground he walks on.

But it's enough, because his jaw locks and his grasp on my hand tightens and his pale green eyes sear me on the spot. "Because I would take everything that you are and make it mine. Your beauty, your humanity, your *fire*. I'd fill every broken and misshapen part of me with you until there's nothing left." He laughs, a dark, gritty sound that tangles my fear and desire into a web that has no exit point, or understanding, but just *is*. "A man like me steals what he wants, Isla, and with every piece of you that I took, I would still demand more, until you begged me for freedom."

The word DANGER might as well be dancing around us in neon lights. I close my eyes, breathing sharply to override the aching need in my core, and I see it: the danger. I open them, and meet green and yellow, and there, in his tempestuous gaze, resides danger at its most visceral.

If I were smart, I'd nail him in the balls and run for safety.

If I were smart, I would do anything but what I do next, which is lick my lips and whisper, "Tell me what you'd steal—from me. Tell me everything."

His nostrils flare and then I feel it—*him.*

Oh, *God*.

Behind the prison of his wet trousers, Saxon's hard-on is huge. He leans into me, giving me his whole weight, as well as the delicious outline of his cock against my stomach. Sweat coalesces on my back. Bloody hell, the devil has come out to play and I'm *burning*. I nearly whimper as I struggle, one-handed, to rid myself of my coat. Saxon rips it from me, and, to the chorus of *this shouldn't be happening* singing in my brain, he repositions me against the wall, keeping me restrained.

"Your taste," he growls, rolling his hips against me in a sensual glide that promises orgasms and good times for all, "right off the wet lips of your pussy." I do whimper, then, and he takes my captive hand and splays it over my right breast, so that I'm cupping myself through my shirt. Beneath my fingers, my nipple pebbles. "Your cries," he rasps, turning his gaze down to our hands. "I'd own them, each and every one. When you scream at the top of your lungs; when you're rendered silent because my cock is stroking the back of your throat and it's either scream or choke."

Fuck.

Arching my back, I shove my breast into my palm, urging him to let me squeeze, to pinch my nipple. Something. *Anything*. Desperation rips a moan from my throat. "*Saxon.*"

His eyes darken.

A tick leaps to life in his square jaw.

In any other man, those small tells wouldn't be enough to imply how much he wants this, wants me. But in *this* man—this cold, stoic man who breathes ice and detachment—those ticks reveal everything and more.

"What else?" I ask, shamelessly. "Saxon, what *else*?"

As one, he moves our joined hands south. We trace my stomach and detour left, to my hip, which Saxon makes me squeeze, as though, through my touch, he's memorizing every line and contour of my body. Seemingly satisfied, he continues our downward path, over the waistband and metal tab of my trousers, past where I'm throbbing and needy, to my thigh.

"Squeeze," he commands roughly, and I do. I clutch my inner thigh, letting his fingers slip between mine to graze the denim. It's wet, painted to my skin from all the rain we trudged through. I can't find it in myself to care, not when I'm hanging on by a thread, following Saxon's every move.

I've lost my damn mind, is what this is.

And, as if he's actually read my mind, he drags our hands up, centimeter by painstaking centimeter, until we're covering the triangle between my legs and I'm shaking so hard that I might combust. He curls my hand, allowing me to cup myself. The slight pressure is everything and somehow not enough, all at once, and I throw my head back, ignoring the bite of the brick wall colliding with my skull because I need more. Right now, right here. *I need more.*

"Your will."

Saliva gathers in my mouth. "What?"

He molds my hand within his, guiding me into a rocking motion that aligns the seam of my trousers with my clit. He's manipulating my body, putting me exactly where he wants me, and the pleasure is so sharp, so acute, that all words take a hike and I simply exist. Here, with him, for as long as it'll last.

"Just like that," he grits out, "just like *this*. I'd make you want me, Isla. I'd make you beg. I'd make you so hard up to come that you'd do anything I demanded. And you would, no questions asked, because you'd get this in return."

Pleasure slices through me, the orgasm so close that I ride my hand—*Saxon's* hand—hard, fast, needy.

Please, please, please.

His hot breath fans over my temple. "I'd grab your hair, like sunshine captured in my fist, and fold you over my lap. Spread your legs, wide, to make room for my cock, your pussy so wet you'd take me in one thrust. And I would fuck you, Isla. I'd fuck you so hard that you'd always remember that it was *me* who did this to you, me who made you come undone. The man with no heart. The man you vowed that you would never, ever fuck. But you did, with my name on your lips—a prayer, penance—and—"

I come, as promised.

With his name on my tongue and our hands sandwiched between my legs, in a building that was meant to be a safe haven from the police but has become something else entirely. Something that I fear will be the death of me as I know myself.

"Tell me, Isla."

My chest heaves raggedly. "You want me to beg."

He removes our hands, keeping them clasped as he shifts them back to the wall. "I want to fuck you."

"I thought you'd never sleep with a woman like me."

"Ruthless. Broken." His voice turns darker, grittier. "It's what I see whenever I look in the mirror—today, I saw it in you."

Is that how he sees himself? Misshapen? Broken? *Ruthless?* A lump grows in my throat. "Saxon, you can't—"

"Let me steal that too." His gaze drops to my mouth, lingering there. "I'm not gentle. I break everything I touch, but maybe—with you—I'd piece all the fractures back together. And, if not, then at least we'd be ruined together."

Everything in me shouts to walk away.

He made me come, yes, but we could go back to our version of normal if we stop now. Right?

Except that I don't want to stop.

I want to feel the ice chip away from his emotional armor. I want to feel his cock slam into me. I want him to take me, his soulless eyes locked on my face when he crashes his scarred mouth down on mine. I want *all* of him—the savior, the devil, and everything in between.

Even now, I feel myself growing wetter just at the thought.

"Yes."

The obedient word slips out and Saxon smiles. It's slow and not particularly kind but it's laced with expectation and hunger, and if he were to demand that I get down on my knees, right now, I'd do it.

Except he doesn't ask me to beg and he doesn't ask me to get down on my knees. He only watches, trailing his heated gaze from my damp hair to my equally damp clothes, and then he growls a single word that sends a chill dancing down my spine.

"Strip."

My heart thuds rapidly. "Here?"

"Here."

"What about you? Turnaround is fair play."

Something in his gaze shuts down, some of his always present coolness resettling into his expression. "Strip, Isla."

I want to press for more but when he fingers the hem of my shirt, giving it a short tug that says more than a thousand words could, I concede. I strip. First my shirt, which I toss to the side. Then my thin bralette, which I send in the same direction.

Warmth tears through me when I catch Saxon's wide shoulders heave with a sharp inhalation, his cheeks crested red with lust. I'd once wondered what it would take to set a man like Saxon Priest on fire and now, I know.

Me.

All it takes is *me*.

Boldly, I cup my breasts, thumbing my stiff nipples. "What next?" I ask softly, as though I'm playing his game instead of orchestrating it.

Jaw clenched tight, his lips barely part when he makes his next demand. "Your finger—lick it."

Like a good girl, I put my finger in my mouth and swirl my tongue around the tip, enjoying all too much how Saxon's gaze flares. *Oh, Mr. Priest, how easily the tides turn.* With a *pop*, I give my finger a little twirl in the air to signal *next-order-please*.

Brows knitting together, the corner of his mouth hitches with competitive spirit. "Tell me, is that how you suck cock?"

I squeeze my legs together. "Never had any complaints before."

It's the wrong thing to say—I recognize the mistake immediately.

That half-smile on his face grows, wicked and predatory in its very essence. Swiftly, he clasps my still-wet finger and tugs my hand down to the button of his trousers. "Get on your knees."

"Is this the moment where I beg for forgiveness for acting like a spoiled brat?" I ask, blatantly teasing him. "Should I cry? Shed a tear or two for dramatic effect?"

He hooks a hand around the nape of my neck, dragging me close. "No, this is the part where you admit that you're scared."

"And if I'm not?"

A small pause that I can't decipher. And then, "You will be."

Maybe it's the conviction in his husky voice that does it or perhaps it's the events of the day finally catching up with me, but I shiver—and Saxon notices. His expression shifts, stiffening, before he nods, as though coming to some decision. "On your knees, Isla."

Slowly, I lower to the ground.

My trousers protect my skin from the dust and grime, but there's no protecting the rest of me from what's about to happen. We're crossing a line—a line that can't be redrawn. We aren't friends. We aren't really lovers, either. We're two lonely people who faced death today and won.

Liar. That's not all this is, and you know it.

With nervous fingers, I ignore the fluttering in my belly that tells me we're feeding the beast instead of cutting off its head, the way we ought, and flick the button through the hole. The zipper sliding along metal teeth sings in my ears as I part his trousers. His briefs are black, much like his soul.

I drag my finger down his veiled length, secretly loving the way his cock twitches under my touch. "Tell me how you like it," I say, my gaze locked on the thick crown already thrusting out from the top of his pants.

He curses beneath his breath, his palms settling on the back of my head.

Hooking my fingers over the elastic waistband, I tug the fabric down—and just barely hold in a gasp. He's thicker than I expected—longer, too. The plump head already beads with pre-come and I have it on good authority that he wasn't exaggerating when he said I'd scream or choke—

doing both, simultaneously, would mean instant death.

"Open your mouth."

I do him one better. Wrapping a hand around his base, I glide my tongue from root to tip, along the ridged vein that begs for attention. Saxon's fingers tighten in my hair, tugging on the strands as though he's torn between yanking me away completely and pressing me deeper.

Taking the choice for my own, I wrap my mouth around his crown, lapping the pearl of moisture away, and swallow him as deep as I can go.

"Fuck." He releases a throaty groan that sounds wrenched from his soul. "*Fuck.*"

I lift my gaze to find that his is already locked on my face. Shock mingled with possession flits through his features, twisting his mouth in a snarl. Holding his stare, I draw him deeper, bobbing my head. I moan around his length because it seems like it's something he might like, and *yes*, he absolutely does.

His hips buck forward.

His fingers shove me down, making me take even more.

I choke on his length, eyes watering, eagerness rising as I shift on my knees.

It's a power move on his part. But of the two of us, I'm the one wielding the torch. *I love it.* Love the way he silently begs for me, with his thrusting hips and deep, guttural groans. Love the way his fingers flex in my hair, as though he's desperate to maintain control but can't help letting go to the sensation of me working him over.

Saxon may be the king of his emotions everywhere else in his life, but in this moment, with my lips moving down his length, then back up, over and over again, he's lost to the chaos. He's lost in *me*.

Giving him one last twist at his base, I pull back, canting my head for a picture of total innocence. "Tell me, Saxon . . . are you feeling scared?"

His lips firm, a promise of retribution manifesting when he fists my hair and growls, "Face the wall."

I raise my brows, egging him on. "Shall I drop trou? Or would you prefer to do the honors?"

A dark cloud washes over him. "If you were anyone else—"

"But I'm not." I stand, already shoving the denim and my knickers to my thighs, then farther down to my knees and ankles, before kicking them away. I keep my boots on. "I'm me and you're *you*."

"And that means what?" he bites out. "Good and evil?"

"No, fire and ice." I smooth a hand over my belly, delighting in the way he tracks the pass of my fingers like a predator does with its prey. His damp shirt clings to his torso, doing a piss-poor job of hiding the twitch of his pectoral muscles when I inch my fingers down my body, tantalizing him with the promise of what lies between my legs. "I breathe, you inhale, and we both go up in flames."

Leaning forward, I take a tentative step toward him. Hand to his strong chest, my fingers graze the corded muscles of his shoulder.

Do it, Isla, take the risk.

He watches me with hooded, wary eyes. Danger lurks in those green-yellow depths, but I take the plunge anyway, testing him with a brush of my thumb over his mouth.

His hand claps around my wrist, yanking me away. "*Don't*."

Steadily, I meet his gaze. "Steal a kiss from me."

He stares at my mouth. Looks at it as if he can picture the kiss now—my lips pliant beneath his, absorbing every thrust of his tongue, every nip of his teeth. Saxon's kiss would be just as savage as the man himself. *Give it to me, please*, I want to beg. But then the moment is gone, utterly obliterated, as he whips me around so that I'm facing the wall. I reach out to the brick to steady myself, only for his palm to land on my spine and lower me, then lower me even more.

The horizontal position exposes me completely. Legs spread wide, I feel the chill in the air along my wet folds, then hear the telltale sound of a foiled wrapper ripping open.

Oh, God, this is happening. *Really* happening.

Me, Saxon Priest, *sex*.

Sex in an old mobile shop. Sex on the run from the police. Sex with the man who would despise me if he learned that I'm the one who killed the king, then allowed the blame to sit on his shoulders.

The head of Saxon's thick cock grazes my core, and my pulse leaps with anticipation. "Last chance to walk away."

There's no walking away, not when I'm already feeling the stirrings of a new addiction. "Ruin me—take me—"

He does, on a single, hard stroke that has my fingers raking the wall and my head falling forward with a startled cry. My palm screams in pain from the knife wound and my core aches from stretching for a man like Saxon Priest and my heart . . . my heart *flourishes*.

Calloused fingers stake their claim down my spine before framing my hips in a bruising grip. He holds me like I might run away at any second. He slams into me, over and over again, with the ferocity of a man who's been starved of the sun for years and has only just stepped under its warmth again.

I'm unraveling.

Desire floods my system and I moan, turning my head to bite down on my arm.

"No," Saxon grunts harshly, his fingers sinking into my hair and dragging my head back, "let me hear you."

I can't deny him.

Another cry falls from my mouth as his fingers tangle with my hair, keeping my spine arched and my head thrown back.

Cold. Callous. But *so damn good.*

This—this is what I was missing with Stephen. No matter what suggestions I gave to my ex, he never delivered. Or maybe I'm looking at it all wrong. Maybe it's less that he didn't deliver and more that my body simply was unwilling to respond, as though it's always known that someone better, someone more life-altering, waited just around the corner.

Someone like Saxon.

He fucks me as I predicted—with tightly leashed control that demands my body and soul obey him—but with an edge that I never could have anticipated. He churns his hips, moving into me faster, deeper, dredging up sensations I've never felt in my entire life. He folds himself over my back, the dampness from his shirt passing a chill through to my body, before tucking his hand around my waist so that he can reach down and flick my clit in time with his strokes.

My heart rate hammers in my temple, tunneling my vision, until all there is, is us, this moment, the fact that I've let Saxon Priest inside me, and I never want him to leave.

"Harder," I whisper, panting, "I want everything."

He pinches my clit, ripping a cry from my throat. "Begging already, Miss Quinn?"

"Yes. Yes"—the flat of his finger circles me, then

retreats, dancing over my clit in barely-there caresses that drive me wild and turn my cries into strangled moans—"Saxon. *Saxon*, oh my God, I'm going to come. Please. Don't stop. *Please.*"

Thrusting harder, he dips his finger along my folds, gathering more of my wetness, before returning to my clit. He rubs, applying more delicious pressure, and my knees threaten to give out beneath me. Another second of this . . . I can't. I'm going to crumble where I stand. I'm going to burst apart at the seams. He fucks me and I . . . I plead, shamelessly, for more of his cock, for more of the rippling heat sweeping over me like I've been thrown in a furnace and left to burn alive.

His mouth grazes the space between my shoulder blades. "Tell me what you are, Isla."

Right now? He wants to have this talk *right now?* I'm on the verge of the most epic orgasm of my life and he wants to argue, and I want to come, and hell, knowing him, he'll probably be the sadistic arsehole that he is and stop if I don't answer quickly enough.

I hate that I know him as well as that.

Reaching down, I graze my hand over his to ensure he keeps stroking me. I feel his dark chuckle against my back, before I answer: "Ruthless. Broken." A small pause that tugs at my conscience. "A killer."

And then he bites my shoulder—*I bite back*, he'd promised—and growls only three words: "No, a warrior."

My lungs squeeze and my clit throbs and his next thrust hits the *exact* spot that I need to instantly shatter. I come, shouting his name and squeezing so tightly around his length that he orgasms a beat later.

He's silent when he comes.

No groaning. No frantic words slipping off his tongue.

But I feel his shattered breathing against the nape of my neck, rustling my hair, and I feel his cock pulse inside me, and for Saxon Priest, a man who allegedly has no heart, I know he's given me something today that no other person has ever had from him—a fractured piece of his soul, battered and bruised, but a piece that's no less beautiful had it been shiny and new.

CHAPTER 22

SAXON

"Ring me when you get to her flat," I say into the receiver, my gaze trained on the woman staring out the window, her fingers listlessly braiding the heavy strands of her hair. "As soon as night falls, I'll bring Isla."

On the other end of the line, Guy curses. "Christ, Saxon. This is a problem."

I hear everything that he isn't saying: *Isla Quinn is the problem.*

It's not anything I haven't thought myself since fucking her an hour ago, despite the fact that we both vowed that this would never happen.

As if sensing my stare, she turns ever so slightly, glancing over at me with big blue eyes and a small, worried smile playing at her lips. *Fuck.* I wish she'd fly at me, arms raised to beat me down for taking advantage of her. I took her like an animal, up against the wall, still fully clothed while she'd been completely bare. Her anger I could handle, even the inevitable disgust at having let me touch her, but that hesitant quirk of her lips is like crossing the River Styx, knowing that paradise will always be forever out of reach.

I'll remember the shape of her lips for the rest of my life. A sharp Cupid's bow up top, a plump lower lip that trembles when she's on the verge of orgasm.

The first pair to ever wrap around my cock and suck me deep into a warm, wet mouth.

The first pair to ever ask me to steal a kiss.

A kiss that you couldn't deliver.

"I know," I mutter to Guy, threading my fingers through my hair and nearly ripping out the strands. Gripping the mobile, I twist away, seeking a reprieve from the lust hammering my body and demanding that I strip Isla naked all over again. "Don't you think that I know that?"

"Right now, I'm not sure that you know anything."

He's probably right.

Everything that I am is solely focused on the blonde warrior who killed a man today, in order to save herself, then got down on her knees to offer me the likes of salvation to which I've never known.

Stop thinking about her.

Unlikely, especially since I have her heady scent still filling my nose. It's on my skin, my clothes. Even now, I can smell her off my fingers from when I circled her clit and made her scream. Like some possessive caveman marked by lust, I'm tempted to never wash myself clean again.

"We'll talk it over when I get us out of here tonight."

Guy blows out a frustrated sigh that rattles in my ears. "Whatever you think that you're doing, be done with it, you hear me? Damien's got news for us—about Alfie Barker—and then we have to figure out the mess that is your bloody face all over the goddamn internet. You've fucked us, Saxon. Absolutely and completely fucked us."

Scrubbing a hand over my jaw, I clench my teeth

tight. "Ring me as soon as you have Peter and Josie."

Hanging up the phone, I toss it on the rickety table that sits in the center of the room. Unlike the ground floor, it's not so dirty up here. Musty, yes, with furniture that had its heyday in the seventies and a rug that's torn and discolored, but not necessarily unclean. It's one of Holyrood's many hideouts within the City.

The fact that I brought Isla here is another problem all on its own.

"What did he say?" Isla's voice drags my gaze away from the table to where she's standing, a finished braid now falling over one shoulder. The hairstyle makes her look younger, innocent, especially with her face scrubbed free of makeup. After today's events, it's safe to say that Isla Quinn wouldn't know innocence if it bit her in the ass.

Ruin me . . . take me . . .

At the memory of her begging for more, my cock twitches in my trousers and I drop my hands to the table. "He's heading over to grab them now."

Grasping the back of a chair, Isla falls into it, raw relief sweeping through her expression. "Oh, thank God. I wasn't sure if . . . Of course, I'd hoped—"

"My brother might be an ass, but he would never leave two kids to fend for themselves."

She bobs her head, nodding quickly. "Like I said, I hoped. But your brother and I, we didn't exactly get off on the right foot."

It's on the tip of my tongue to tell her that she and Guy will never be on the right foot. It's simply not possible. Despite what happened today, we Priests fit solidly under the loyalist umbrella while Isla . . .

I drag my hands over my face. Christ, this is a mess.

Hesitant as I am to bring Isla and her siblings to

another one of Holyrood's hideouts, this one a terrace house in Camden, I don't see another option rearing its head. Staying in Stepney, so close to Queen Mary, won't work. Returning to The Bell & Hand, any time in the near future, might as well be the kiss of death. It'll be the first place the police visit, and it'll be up to Guy to hold down the fort.

All this time, I've managed to walk the tightrope between opening the door to anti-loyalists while still maintaining my position within London's social landscape. It was Damien who had to hide at the Palace, for fear of someone catching him—not me. Ten fucking years of running the pub, and now *this*.

Granted, once Damien has the chance to comb through the Met's databases and strip us of any charges, it might be a different story. But even then, how would I explain to Isla that suddenly we're free to do as we please?

You can't.

Pinching the bridge of my nose, I draw in a breath. "According to Guy, my face is already all over the news. A possible suspect—not confirmed."

Isla's lips settle in a firm line. "And mine?"

"Not yet. Either the survivor didn't get a good look at you or—"

"Professor Coney had photographs of me."

My head snaps back. "What?"

"Photographs." She splays her hands wide, gesturing at her thighs. "He dumped them in my lap right before he tried to strangle me—"

"He did *what*," I bark, low, furious, firing away from the table to stalk toward her. "Explain."

"What else is there to explain?" She motions to her neck, and my gut lurches with barely subdued rage. "He tried to kill me and I . . . I killed him instead." She swallows visibly, then briefly closes her eyes. "What matters is that he knew who I was, Saxon. And I knew *him*."

Coming to stand before her, I drop to my haunches. Tempted as I am to lay a hand on her leg, I keep my fingers locked on my knee. Fucking her once is not a green light to go for a second round. And, considering how epically dysfunctional our relationship already is, taking her again would prove to be the very definition of insanity.

Find the calm. Find the ice. Find yourself.

"How?" I demand, my voice emerging with all the softness of granite.

With only the cast of natural light from the narrow window to illuminate her face, Isla's blue eyes appear darker, a turbulent gray, like the skies that drenched us this morning. "That first day when I came to apply for a position, I ran into a man on the front steps. I thought nothing of it. There are thousands of people that you cross paths with, in a single lifetime, that never mean a thing."

"But?"

"But I saw him again the next day, when you asked to meet." She leans forward in her chair, propping her elbows on her thighs and clasping her hands together, careful of the clean cloth that I wound around her injured hand when we came upstairs. "Déjà vu, Saxon. The same man, the same feeling that I had when I walked in the pub after sidestepping around him. Ian Coney didn't just stop by The Bell & Hand—he was actively staking it out."

"*Fuck*."

Her thumbs crisscross restlessly over each other. "I don't know how many others like him are out there, just waiting until they can make their move on you. I don't think . . . I don't think Professor Coney is an isolated instance, though. You and your brothers are notorious among anti-loyalists. And since you run the pub yourselves, everyone knows where you are at nearly any given time of the day."

Isla isn't wrong.

It's something we actively considered when we agreed to open The Bell & Hand ten years ago. At the time, it seemed like a brilliant idea. We needed a front that gave anti-loyalists a reason to trust us with their secrets. But in building that repertoire, we simultaneously alienated the group of people who should have trusted us implicitly, if only they knew the truth.

Bloody tangled webs and all that shit.

Feeling my throat tighten, I ask, "You mentioned pictures. What were they of?"

"The ones of just you, or the few that included the two of us?"

The fact that the bastard managed to sneak not only pictures of myself but ones of Isla . . . If Ian Coney weren't a dead man already, then I'd deliver him straight to the grave. "The latter," I edge out, curbing my anger.

Isla licks her lips, immediately drawing my attention there.

She wanted a kiss and I . . . panicked, full force. Even if I'd gone for it, I wouldn't know what to do. It's a zone I've never been welcome to, a paradise that's remained forever out of reach. And, beyond the practicality of it all, anything more than a quick peck might have allowed her to feel just how misshapen my upper lip is.

Just how ruined I am.

Pushing up to my full height, I retreat to the table and rest my ass against it.

Blinking at me, like she's confused as to why I abandoned her side so quickly, Isla runs her uninjured palm over her thigh. "The first one was simple enough, just a snapshot of us talking."

"And the second?"

"The second one is"—grimacing, she sinks her teeth into her bottom lip—"the second one is damning, not so much for us as it is for Father Bootham. Coney caught us going inside the church, Saxon. Being completely honest here: I don't know how safe it would be for him if we kept seeking him out for information. I don't even want to think about how many others have caught on already."

Dammit.

I drop my head back to stare up at the ceiling.

For years, I've bided my time, knowing that all the lies we've spewed were bound to catch up to us at some point . . . while simultaneously hoping that they never would. The other Holyrood agents have it easier, and we've purposely kept it that way. Men like Hamish and Jude—the public would never recognize them if they were spotted on the street because they keep a low profile.

The same can't be said for my brothers and me.

We stuck out our necks to gather more intelligence, and it's worked brilliantly. But all good things eventually burn to the ground, and with Damien already out of commission and my face now appearing on every news outlet known to mankind, there's only so much time left before we can't dig fast enough to keep the earth from swallowing us whole.

"But there's nothing on me?" Isla draws out slowly, studying me with an alertness that sets me on edge. "Right?"

I nod my head toward the abandoned mobile sitting idly on the table. "According to the last search that I did, no, you're still in the clear."

"So, we'll use me for whatever needs to be done."

My molars crack together. "Not a chance in hell."

"*Every* chance in hell, actually." Leaping from the chair, she begins to pace the length of the room; the fractured sunlight streaming in through the curtains highlights her pursed lips and stubborn chin. "You were right, earlier. I came to The Bell & Hand because I'd heard just enough rumors to know that I could be useful to the cause. I'm a godawful cook, and I doubt my skills at serving food are any better, but I know how to shoot a pistol, Saxon. I know how to fight. I can *help*."

And what, exactly, would she be helping? A battle that goes against everything that she believes in, all right under her nose? A fight that might land her six feet under and literally breathless by the end of the week?

A visual of her struggling for the knife against Coney turns my muscles to stone. The blood on her hands, the remorse and fear that brought tears to her eyes when I finally reached her side, has me seeing red. We're on opposite sides of this war, and still I can't. Call it selfish on my part. Call it being shortsighted to not use what she's offering, the way I've always done in the past. But I won't put her in a position that might reenact today's events in any fashion.

"No."

Frustration snaps her brows together. "You aren't even hearing me out."

"It's not happening." Planting one hand on my thigh, I jut my chin forward. "Those photographs—where are they now, huh? They aren't here. I didn't even know they bloody existed until ten minutes ago."

"I should have grabbed them before we left."

"We were running, Isla." I shake my head, lifting a

hand to skim the side of my face. "We barely had time to breathe before someone overheard the gunshots and called the police, let alone be stopping to pick up pictures off the ground. It's too late now."

She squeezes her eyes shut, and the rhythmic parting of her mouth gives me the feeling that she's counting to ten. Seeking patience from beating me over the head, I imagine. When she's done, she inhales deeply through her nose.

I breathe, you inhale, and we both go up in flames.

Today, she caught me in an inferno. Any more heat, and I'll turn to ash.

"I hate this," she whispers, defeat evident in the sudden slouch of her shoulders. "Five years ago, I planned to move to America. I'd been offered a transfer to Los Angeles. Sunny, fun LA, land of celebrities and sandy beaches. Or so I've been told."

I go still, watching her closely. "Then your parents died."

She nods curtly, wrapping her arms around her middle as though she can contain all of her hurt. "They were down to visit me from York, the way they did every other month. I was at work, of course, over in SoHo—I'm a recovering workaholic, in case you missed that memo. They wanted to visit Big Ben, and I waved them off that morning." Her features crack, her mouth quivering with anguish. "I thought nothing of it, Saxon. I stood in my kitchen, rinsing their plates from breakfast, and waved them off. No hug. No kiss on the cheek. No mentions of *I love you* or *Be safe* before the door closed shut behind them."

Christ.

Words, forever elusive, escape me. I stand there, mute, and watch devastation sweep over her as though she's stuck in a time warp, doomed to experience that day all over again and suffer the emotional fallout.

"I was on the phone with a client when my coworker shoved her mobile at me and pointed at the article she'd pulled up. I barely gave it another thought. A protest breaking out in London? It's not like that's anything new. But this . . ." Swallowing, Isla furls her hand into a fist and brings it to her mouth, waiting, gathering her thoughts. A single tear slips over her cheek before she swipes it away, like its very existence embarrasses her. "They never came home. I waited up all night, one eye on the clock as annoyance burned away to worry and worry finally spiraled into fear."

My fingers itch to reach for her, to drag her into my arms and offer comfort that I haven't received myself in years, long before our return to England. The last person to hug me was Guy. The time before that? Pa, the day King John scarred me. Age-old self-restraint keeps me chained to the table, immobilized. "When did you find out they'd been killed?"

"The next day. Half-past six. The sun had barely risen when I heard banging on the front door. Foolishly, I thought"—she offers a bitter laugh—"well, I thought perhaps they'd had a wild night out in the City. Gone to a play, perhaps, or rode the London Eye. Mum begged Dad for years to go on it but he never wanted to spend the money. Seeing two officers standing there instead, with pity on their faces, was all the news I needed. They were dead, I was alone, save for Peter and Josie, and the world as I knew it ended."

I'd felt the same when Pa was murdered.

Henry Godwin may have failed, big time, in finding Princess Evangeline's killer, but his death turned our family upside down. His replacement at Holyrood ushered us out of England within days, setting us up in a hovel of a flat in Paris.

"It'll only be temporary," Jayme Paul told us as he led us into our new home, "just long enough for us to know that whatever Henry did or didn't do won't end up on your heads."

We had nothing. Little money beyond what Holyrood sent us monthly. Paranoia that accompanied us each time we fled the dark flat in search of sun and fresh air. In London, at least, Pa had made the most out of our tiny home in Whitechapel. He hung pictures on the walls; cooked us horrid-tasting meals that we pretended to eat happily before spitting out into our napkins when he glanced away; and he tutored us, daily, sitting down every morning to go over our maths and history, since boys who don't exist on record can't exactly attend school without raising eyebrows.

Mum, God rest her soul, hadn't been able to even move from the loo to her bed on her own, let alone keep three boys under the age of fourteen on the straight and narrow.

Guy fed us; he clothed us.

He stole what we needed to survive, never uttering a word of animosity when Damien cried because he was hungry and I asked, time and again, when we could return home to London.

Guy had been saddled with two brothers to raise on his own. Instead of crumbling under the weight of expectation, he gave us more than we could have ever dreamt of. He taught me to use my fists, as well as my wits. He snuck Damien into local classes because our youngest brother had wanted a computer, and Guy, at thirteen, had no way of teaching Damien what he himself didn't know.

So, I understand about worlds ending. I know that

desperate, bleak feeling deep in my veins, where ice runs the thickest. But it still changes nothing in the end, not when it comes down to a matter of life or death.

"As of tonight, you'll be taking a break from the public eye—at least until we can get a good sense of what's coming our way."

"*What?*" Feet stumbling to a halt, Isla spins around to face me. "Absolutely not. I'm not undergoing some version of bloody house arrest just because you order it."

"You don't have a choice."

Her blue eyes narrow, shooting daggers in my direction. "I let you into my body—but trust when I say this: you don't own the rest of me, Saxon Priest."

I wait for the guilt of ordering her around to kick in, the bout of shame for bending her to my will, as though one round of earth-shattering sex will have somehow changed my genetic makeup for the better.

At the end of the day, I'm still me.

Saxon Priest, Holyrood agent.

Saxon Godwin, the ghost of a boy who no longer exists.

Skin cold from the lack of heat in the building, I ignore the quick tattoo of my heart and stick to the plan that gives us both a chance to make it to tomorrow, unscathed.

"We leave as soon as night falls, whether you like it or not."

CHAPTER 23

ISLA

As Saxon promised, we slip out from the downtrodden mobile shop later that night, much the same way we entered: unnoticed and anonymous.

"Keep up," he rumbles, throwing a quick look back at me, "or I'll put you over my shoulder for a second time."

I curse the darkness for concealing the rude gesture I flash him.

"Do that again and I'll put those fingers to better use."

Bastard. I suspect he'd enjoy it too.

As would you.

I silence the taunting voice. Right now, it doesn't matter what I would or wouldn't enjoy. I'm on edge. Both from the worry of possibly not finding Josie and Peter waiting for me—though Guy put them on the phone earlier, so I could speak to them myself—and the frustration of knowing that we'll be putting our heads down after this, for God knows how long.

I'm no fool.

Saxon's plan is smart, even discounting the fact that the media has yet to release any information about me as an accomplice in The Octagon's murders. Still, my gut is screaming that something is seriously wrong.

Why wouldn't the Met announce my identity?

How likely is it that the photographs went missing by the time that the police swarmed The Octagon?

Nothing adds up.

"One more block," Saxon murmurs, his voice deep and impassive, as though today's events are a regular occurrence for him. Based on the way he killed Coney's comrades, without hesitation, I imagine that I'm not so far off base with that theory.

Who are you really, Saxon Priest?

Not the first time I've wondered that, but now that I'm following him into the dark, it's the only question that keeps hammering at me.

"Were you ever in the military?" I ask.

There's just enough light from the passing lampposts to reveal how his shoulders stiffen. "Another block, Isla," he repeats, keeping his attention fixed on the pavement in front of him.

I wait the block.

Hell, I even wait until we're in his fancy black car and driving to some unknown destination before pouncing again. "Well? Were you?"

"Was I what?"

"In the armed forces." Leaning my shoulder against the door, I twist my frame so I can read his body language. "Did you ever serve?"

"No."

Interesting. "What about mixed martial arts? Did you ever—"

His head snaps in my direction. "What's with all the questions?"

"Don't I have a right to be curious about you? After all, you were coming inside me . . . what—has it already been five hours ago now? Time sure does fly when you're having fun."

"*Isla.*"

I stare at his profile. The heavy brows. The crooked nose. The perpetually curled lip. Despite all of my good intentions to remain impartial, I find myself softening. "Saxon, you know more about me than anyone else has in years. But here I am, once again putting my life in your hands, and every part of me is screaming that I can trust you when the reality is that I shouldn't."

White-knuckling the steering wheel, he bites out, "What's stopping you?"

"How about the fact that we're in a car that must cost over a hundred grand? Or what about the front door at the mobile store—that sort of technology is *not* cheap. Not to mention that it's completely unnecessary to anyone who isn't expecting some sort of physical attack." Holding my breath, I tack on, "You own a pub, Saxon. And I don't doubt that it's a successful one, but I can't imagine you're pulling in enough money to afford all of *this*."

When I gesture at the car's fancy dashboard, Saxon snags my wrist. "Don't touch anything."

I mimic his deep, gravel-pitched order while tugging at my hand to no avail. "*See?* First it's only a security system and now I'm meant to sit in my seat like a good, little girl—"

"There's nothing girlish about you."

"—and I've not only put my life in your hands, but I've done the same of Peter and Josie."

"I won't let anything happen to them." His thumb strokes my inner wrist, over my pulse, as he keeps his focus centered on the road. I'm not even sure he realizes that he's done it. "Or you."

I'm positive that he can feel my heart racing, there where he holds me in his calloused grip. Gooseflesh erupts over my skin at the utter conviction in his voice. I twist my head away, needing a reprieve from all things Saxon Priest. The blasted man is sneaking under my defenses, one rigid smile at a time.

As a little girl dreaming of weddings and husbands, I often pictured some variation of Prince Charming. Sometimes he had a thick head of blond hair and bright blue eyes. Other times he was dark, his skin a deep umber and eyes the color of an ancient bronze coin. But always he was sweet and kind and forthcoming with his affection.

Saxon is none of those things.

He keeps his thoughts to himself—except, I suppose, when he's stripping me bare—and rarely allows any glimpses of vulnerability. If I weren't so sure that I felt his heart beating wildly against my back when he thrust inside me, I might be able to convince myself that he's a robot from the future come to wreak havoc on my life.

And, still, I feel the pull between us, however inexplicable that it is.

"Collateral."

I stiffen in my seat, aware of the way my hand jerks in his. "Pardon?"

"I tell you something about me that no one aside from my brothers know," he says, drawing out the words slowly, like he's surprised even himself, "and you have that information . . . should you need it."

Lights from the passing buildings shine into the car, illuminating the bridge of his nose and the tight line of his jaw. He doesn't like the direction of the conversation, that I can see plainly, but he's offering an inner peek into his life anyway.

Because I asked.

"Okay," I say, softly, "yes . . . collateral."

Silence fills the car, so that the only sounds come from the rhythmic tread of the tires zooming us along and the steady pace of Saxon's breathing. Mine, in comparison, traipses at a full-fledged gallop.

"When we lived in Paris," he begins, his voice pitched low, "it was . . . difficult. My mother was sick, the same way she'd been since giving birth to Damien."

Rubbing my lips together, I ask, "And your father?"

He shoots an inscrutable look my way, then returns his attention to the road. "Dead."

"Oh."

"You're not the only orphan around these parts."

"No," I murmur, wishing I could offer my sympathies with a hug or a kiss to his cheek, despite knowing that he would reject it all, "I suppose I'm not."

His lips tighten as he releases my hand to shift gears. He doesn't take my hand back.

"I didn't lie when I said Guy was the glue that kept my family together, especially after Mum died. He was the eldest and to kids that young, it made him the leader. Damien and me, we looked up to him."

I think of the way that Josie and Peter have leaned on me since our parents' deaths. Until recently, when my paranoia has, admittedly, made me a bit overbearing, they've always put me on a pedestal. I kept them safe, I kept them alive.

After today, that's not a guarantee.

Shoving the damning thought away, I focus on Saxon, finding surprising comfort in the husky baritone of his voice.

"But I got older, and with that I wanted to—" Breaking off, he winces, like he's determined to find the right words. "I wanted to . . ."

"Help," I say, studying him from my side of the car, "you wanted to help."

He nods stiffly. "I felt like a burden. Guy's birthday was coming up—he was turning fourteen—and I wanted him to feel good. Happy. *Something*, at least, that wasn't desperation or worry or bloody despair."

It takes everything in me not to ask why they were in Paris in the first place. Had their mother been able to work, despite her being ill? Had she received a work transfer? Or had something happened here in London—maybe even regarding their father's death—that led them across the channel and into France?

I sit on my hands, as though that'll also keep my mouth shut from being a nosy busybody.

The car veers to the right, across an intersection. It's so dark out that I don't recognize any landmarks. If this had been last week, after the protest at Buckingham Palace, I for sure would have thought Saxon Priest was leading me to my death.

"I thought steak would do the trick," he says, straightening out the car. "Not that we had the money."

"Did you work for it?"

His mouth curls bitterly. "No, Isla, I stole it."

Oh.

Pity swims with horror at what he'd clearly gone through at such a young age. While I'd been playing with dolls and scampering around Yorkshire with my parents, he'd been fighting for his livelihood, right alongside his brothers.

"There was this one butcher who hung the meat at

the front of the store, just inside the window. I must have heard Guy mention a thousand times how tempting it was to just slip inside and snag one off the hooks."

My heart pulls. "Saxon . . ."

"I was ten and so not exactly the brightest chap."

"You were a child."

"I went for it," he says, shortly, combing his fingers through his hair. He pauses behind his ear, rubbing the skin there, then drops his hand to the steering wheel again. "I waited until noon, when I knew there'd be a rush, and then I made my move. I wasn't stealthy. Hell, I could barely reach the meat without climbing up on a chair, I was so short back then. It was a doomed mission from beginning to end."

"The butcher caught you."

It's not a question, and Saxon doesn't treat it as one.

"The butcher caught me," he echoes, the impassiveness that I despise seeping into each syllable, "and then he gave me this."

He runs his tongue along his scarred, upper lip.

"*No.*" A shudder tears through me. "How could he do that? And to a *child*, no less? There are so many laws against—"

"I stole from him, Isla."

"This isn't the blasted *Middle Ages*, Saxon! Grown men can't just go around deforming ten-year-old's because they stole a slab of—" I clap a hand over my mouth as my brain goes into high alert. *Deformed.* Oh, shite. Shite! "I didn't mean to say that," I utter hastily, feeling the guilt creep in. Here he is opening a piece of himself to me and I've gone ahead and called him *deformed*. Especially when that isn't at all how I think of him. "That wasn't the right word. You aren't—"

"If you think it's a sight now, then imagine how much worse it was then. I made Damien cry."

"Saxon, I'm so sorry. That isn't at all what I meant; you have to believe me."

"Just a slip of the tongue."

"*No*," I breathe, regret pinching my lungs, "not that, either. You aren't deformed. We all carry burdens, scars. Mine are here"—I touch my heart, wishing I could unload all of my secrets so I wouldn't need to carry their weight alone—"and yours are visible. But it doesn't mean there's something *wrong* with you."

He slows the car, parking in front of a charming, brick, Victorian terrace home. Three stories tall. A garden encased by a cast-iron fence. It's all I take note of before Saxon snags my attention again: "Anyone who dares to ask what happened usually gets the gift of a fist in their face."

Slowly, I meet his stare, fully aware of the tangible current humming between us. The back of my neck tingles. "I demanded that you tell me something."

"I told you out of my own free will."

"Earlier, you said that you'd steal that from me, too."

Holding my gaze, he brings his thumb up to his mouth. Traces the calloused pad over the smooth contour of his perfect, bottom lip, then arches north, to where his upper lip hitches, permanently set in place like he's perpetually angry and out for blood. "If you haven't noticed," he murmurs, "I've made a habit out of taking what doesn't belong to me."

My breath catches in my throat. "Is that a promise?"

"Are you worried that it might be?"

"Maybe," I say, my entire body vibrating with awareness, "but only because of how much I want it to be true." Reaching out, I grasp his hand, then bring his fingers to my chest, right over my heart, so he can feel it race. In the darkness of the car, I can just make out his gaze flaring with a sudden surge of lust. "I like the wrestle of power. You catch me, flinging me over your shoulder, and I—"

"Press a blade to my throat," he finishes, flicking my nipple.

"Yes."

His thumb circles the hard bud, and it's as though the fabric of my shirt and bra aren't even there, because I feel his touch as keenly as I did when I was stripped down before him. When I gasp, he only swirls his thumb again, drawing out the sensation. "Some might think you're mad for this."

I grasp his wrist, keeping his hand in place. "Some haven't felt numb to everything but fear and hate for five years."

Saxon cups my breast, testing the weight in his palm. Oh, *God*, it feels so good, so good that I nearly miss when he muses, "You asked me to ruin you."

"Yes." Warmth crests my cheeks, no matter how chilly it is in the car without the heat blasting. "I did."

"Then consider this a mission accomplished. Us fucking isn't happening again."

Before I can even process what he's said, he pulls away and turns to look out the windscreen, his expression set like stone.

My jaw falls open. "What? Is this because . . . because I said that—"

"I was deformed?" The laugh that falls from his mouth is pure grit. "No, Isla. That's just the truth."

"Then why can't we—I mean, what's stopping us from having sex again?"

I sound desperate and angry but *bloody hell*, what is

wrong with the man? Maybe he shags every Sue, Karen, and Joanne, but I've been going with just my fingers since Stephen dumped me five years ago. I'm tired of being alone. I'm tired of aching for *more* than this violent life I've landed in.

I'm exhausted, down to my marrow, and I want . . . Hell, I just want to be *wanted*.

And not in the way I'll be wanted by the police, soon enough, for killing Ian Coney.

"Saxon?"

A pounding on my window has me jerking upright, twisting for Dad's knife—that is, until I see the blue eyes staring back at me.

Guy Priest.

The man can wait another minute.

"So, what?" I mutter, returning my blade to my coat pocket. "You drop me off and leave, never to be seen again?"

I wait.

And wait.

And wait until finally I scoff under my breath, turning for the door—only for Saxon to catch me by the wrist, stalling me. I feel his heavy stare, centered on the back of my head, and I feel the tightness in his grip, as though he's fighting some internal battle that he'll never win.

Finally, he edges out, "The people I ruin end up dead."

I swallow down the lump of nerves and peer back, meeting his unholy gaze that appears black from the shadows dancing across his face. "And as you've seen today, people who threaten me end up the same. But you make me feel, Saxon—hot and dizzy one minute, chilled to the bone and terrified the next. I like it. No, I *crave* it. Maybe that makes me mad or maybe that just makes me human."

"Isla . . ."

I pull out of his grasp. "Just face it, the only person in this car who's scared is *you*."

CHAPTER 24

SAXON

"Did you fuck her?"

I haven't even closed the door to my security room before Guy's words sink into me like a knife twisting in my gut.

Slamming my eyes shut, I seek patience, the ever-present calm—and sense nothing but simmering irritation. If I'd known coming up here would entail an interrogation about where I've stuck my cock in the last twenty-four hours, I would have stayed away.

Behind me, I flick the latch shut, locking us inside the room, and Isla and her siblings out. "No."

Seated on a plush rolling chair, legs spread wide with his hands linked casually over his stomach, my older brother assesses me with a hard onceover. "Then why did you have your hand on her tits?"

I pause.

Slowly tilt my head from side to side, cracking the crick in my neck, because it's either play this cool or fly off the handle and add another tally to my already astronomical death count for the day.

What's one more—really?

I take the seat opposite his. "How long were you standing there?"

"Long enough."

I don't indulge him with a response.

His knuckles whiten as his hands move to the armrests of his chair. "Since we came back from France, you're the only one I've been able to rely on within Holyrood. Damien's a genius but a complete hothead. Hamish and Jude are loyal but uncreative. Clarke sits with the queen and plays babysitter all day. And don't even get me started on fucking Paul, of all people. But you, brother— you always know what has to be done, and you make it happen, no matter the cost."

"I play by your rules, you mean."

"You don't fuck up!" Guy springs from his chair, hands locking behind his head as he sidesteps the elaborate desk setup and paces the room. "You're ruthless. Smart."

I'm broken.

Isn't that what I told Isla just this afternoon? I recognized the traits in her because I see them in myself whenever I look in a mirror. I won't cover up the damn thing, as if I can't bear the sight of my own reflection. That's never been who I am. I accept my faults. Sometimes I even relish them. But I've never shied away from what I've become, shadows and all.

"What happened today was—"

"A shitshow," Guy finishes, clipping out the words, "today was a bloody shitshow. And while everyone at the Palace was trying to figure out how the hell to pull you out of this mess, you were off shagging the enemy, the *one* person you shouldn't be—"

The rest of his sentence catches on my fist connecting

with his jawbone.

Crack!

His head jolts to the side, his whole frame following in startled shock. Body limp, he falls onto my abandoned chair. But the wheels slide, then teeter off-balance from the sudden onslaught of his bulky weight, and—

He crashes to the floor.

The chair atop him.

His rage swirling and thickening the air around us.

I've never punched him, not ever.

And, as his younger brother, Guy has never laid a hand on me, not once.

Gripping the chair leg, he throws the whole thing to the side, where it slams against the wall. One hand lands on his knee as he hoists himself up and, based on his expression, he might as well have plumes of smoke to rival Mt. Vesuvius steaming from his head. "You ever do that again," he growls, his voice thick with untapped fury, "and I'll make sure my face is the last you'll ever see."

We Godwins always find trouble.

Biting my tongue, I issue a short nod.

Only when my brother has stood do I counter, "Mention her one more time and I'll return the favor—tenfold."

No answer.

"You hear me, brother?"

He meets my stare, his expression tight. "Loud and clear."

Bloody brilliant, then.

Twisting away, I fist my hands on my hips. That wasn't at all how I planned for this to go, but one minute . . . *Christ.* One minute I was collected, as usual, and the next I saw red. Unable to stop myself. Prepared to draw blood. And all because my brother tried to keep my focus trained on

Holyrood and the queen.

Which is our job.

Getting sidetracked is dangerous for everyone involved, and today I managed to upset the balance that we work tirelessly to uphold. I murdered loyalists. *Seven.* I murdered seven. And, if that isn't enough to throw all of Holyrood into chaos, I was sloppy when I left The Octagon.

The survivor.

The missing photographs.

I don't blame Guy for wanting to shake some sense into me, but still my blood heats at the way he spoke of Isla.

"Damien's about to get on the line," comes my brother's stiff voice from behind me. He pauses, maybe even touching his fingers to his already bruising jaw. Then, "Either you're in or you're out."

He's not talking about this room, filled with all sorts of tech that I keep here on the second floor, in case the Palace is ever discovered and we're forced to move headquarters without warning. He means Holyrood as a whole.

In.

Out.

God save the queen or . . . I don't even know what the alternative might be. This life is all I've ever known.

I hear myself rasp, "In."

In, for Holyrood.

In, for my brothers.

In, for the people Holyrood has enlisted over the years who have become family.

Out, for Isla Quinn.

"Sit."

I take Guy's chair, leaving the one he threw for him to deal with, then roll it to the side, giving us some much-needed breathing space. Honestly, we need more than this but since Isla and her siblings are downstairs, in the kitchen, I simply drop into the chair and cross my ankles.

Calm.

Cool.

Christ, it's not working.

My chest shudders with a big breath that does little to mitigate my boiling blood. I crack my knuckles, one by one, before I cave and do what I really want: slam out of this room, trap Isla alone, and show the world that I can fuck her as many times as I feel like it.

Let's just face it, the only one in this car who's scared is you.

I wasn't scared then and I'm not scared now.

I haven't been scared since I was eight years old and being held down by the king, a knife in his hand, while my father watched in horror as I thrashed and cried for help that never came.

Jaw stiff, I motion to the computer. "Get him on."

Guy doesn't ask me to elaborate. He doesn't say anything at all until Damien's face appears on the screen. And my younger brother looks like he's seen hell and come out the other side: unshaved beard, red-rimmed blue eyes, a cigarette sticking out of the corner of his mouth, lit with a tendril of smoke curling in the air.

The only times he smokes is when he's struggling to piece together intelligence.

"Fuck," Guy mutters beneath his breath, echoing my thoughts exactly.

This is not going to be good.

I smooth a hand over my skull. "What happened?"

Damien plucks the fag out of his mouth, stamping it out on an ashtray. "Good news first or the bad?"

I exchange a wary glance with Guy, who only shakes his head and says, "Good. After today, we could use whatever we can of it."

Stiffening at the less than subtle jab, I keep my gaze zeroed in on Damien.

"I spoke with Clarke earlier," he says, leaning back in his chair and propping the end of a pen in his mouth. "We're in the clear for the queen's new security system. The only people allowed in her rooms are Clarke; the select staff she chose, who we've vetted; and the three of us. Anyone else tries and they'll be experiencing the shock of a lifetime—literally." A bitter smile curves his lips. "Granted, I won't be seeing the outside of this estate for at least the next fifty years, so I suppose we're only talking about the two of you."

Guilt plucks at my conscience. "It won't be fifty years."

"You're right—it could be longer."

Ignoring the trace of awkwardness, Guy props an elbow on the desk, wheeling closer. "Did the queen protest?"

Damien arches a dark brow. "What do you think? Of course she did. But Clarke phrased it exactly as you instructed: either she accepts the new security measures or she's out of Buckingham and back to Scotland within days."

"Good," Guy mutters, letting out a sigh, "that's good."

I nod in agreement. "All right. Give us the bad news."

The easygoing expression on Damien's face shutters as he flicks the pen away. I hear the hiss of a Zippo, then watch as he lights a new cigarette and takes a short drag, sucking the nicotine into his lungs before releasing it all in one smooth go. He drops the lighter to his desk. "We've a massive problem."

"When don't we have a problem?"

Damien points the cherry in my direction. "Touché, but here we are. Two words: Alfie Barker."

My fists clench. "What about him?"

The man is still being held at the Palace, since he won't give us the names of his co-conspirators, even after suffering a beating at my hands. Truthfully, I didn't expect him to hold out as long as he has. Men like him—single fathers, widowers—always crack, and they crack early. I don't blame them. If I had a family depending on me, I'd do the same.

But Barker hasn't budged, not that first night, not in the few nights since.

It's . . . unusual.

"We're not going to get through to him."

My gaze collides with Damien's. "You know something," I utter, voice low. "What did he say?"

"It's what he hasn't said."

"Explain," Guy says, his eyes locked on our younger brother, too. "What the hell are you talking about?"

With the filter fitted between his lips, Damien inhales then taps the ashes from the cherry. "There's a lot of time to think when you're on house arrest. And I can't stop thinking about Barker." His blue eyes shift to my face, an almost impersonal wave of curiosity flitting across his expression. "He has two daughters, both under the age of seven. Why won't he break? None of it makes sense."

Drumming his fingers on the desk, Guy says, "You can't discount him being a radical."

"Normally that'd be my first assumption. But the two of you haven't been here—I have." The screen showing my brother's face shimmers, then blacks out before cutting to a clip of Alfie Barker huddled on the floor, his wrists cuffed, his eyes livid with pain. "He cries every day. Begs to go home."

"Nothing out of the ordinary." I ease my gaze away from Barker's defeated posture. "He's torn between saving his family and confessing to his boss that he failed the mission. Tough choice."

"That's the thing," Damien says, switching the monitor so he's back on camera again, "I looked at his phone records. Tore it all to shreds." Another smooth drag of the cig, before blowing out an air ring of smoke. "All random numbers. Burner mobiles, no doubt. He's been receiving instructions from what seems like everyone under the sun."

"What are you getting at?" Guy growls from beside me, his hand a curled fist on his knee. "Get to the bloody point already."

"I think he's been talking to one person, and he just doesn't know it."

My eyes narrow. "How would he not know?"

"Because," Damien says, stamping out his second cigarette in the course of ten minutes, "he's being worked over by a pro. In almost every text conversation, Barker asks where they're located, in case he needs to get himself and his girls out of the City. Glasgow. Chelmsford. Devon. The answer changes every time."

I don't blink. I'm not at all sure that I even breathe. "Damien, where do the mobiles trace back to?"

"London," he answers evenly, "it's always London."

"Fuck." Guy spears his fingers through his short hair. "*Fuck!*"

I concur.

Sinking back, I slouch in my chair. Not wanting to know the answer, but knowing that I need it anyway, I ask, "How many numbers are we talking? Five? Ten?"

"Over twenty that I've counted."

"Christ," I breathe, scrubbing a hand over my jaw. "And Barker doesn't realize any of this?"

My brother shakes his head. "I don't think so."

Guy drops his hand to the desk, his palm open and flat. "What I want to know is how they—him, her, *whoever*—picked Barker in the first place. What makes him special? He roped his brother and the brother's friend into this mess, but it seems that it all starts and ends with Barker. Which, as we know—"

"Isn't common," Damien finishes. "I know, and that's our problem. I can't find a damned thing on the man prior to a year ago. It's like he appeared out of thin air. I haven't found so much as a birth certificate, let alone mention of a wedding announcement in the papers, and we all know that he was married."

That explains the cigarettes and unkempt look, then. *Boy genius* at his finest. There's never been a puzzle Damien couldn't solve, and it must be driving him insane to know that the truth is just out of reach. The Mad Priest in his natural habitat. The irony, really.

It's Guy who speaks up first: "We're working with someone who knows what they're doing."

I dip my head. "Security Service, maybe."

"If not that, then someone with a lot of money to grease some palms." Elbows planted on the desk, Damien props his chin atop his clasped hands. A frown tugs at his mouth. "I've been wracking my brain, trying to piece together a paper trail but it all leads to—"

"Nowhere."

Damien nods at me, his face solemn. "Nowhere. It leads nowhere. We can keep Barker here, maybe bribe him with the possibility of seeing his girls. But with him thinking he's been following orders from an entire network, when it's only been one person, I doubt he'll tell us anything worthwhile. The bastard's in the dark about this as much as we are."

It's not a realization that sits well with me.

Running my finger along the scar, behind my ear, I feel the raised flesh. *502.* Loyalty. Trust. Brotherhood.

"The king," I mutter roughly, dropping my hand to my thigh.

Guy shifts in his chair, aiming it so he can look directly at me. "You're thinking the assassination and this attempt are related?"

"I think that if we can discover who killed John, it might lead directly to the ghost who's working Barker like a puppet on a string. Coincidences don't exist. No one knows that better than us."

CHAPTER 25

ISLA

The bed creaks beneath me as I sit up, my feet landing on the supple carpet below.

The logs in the fireplace have ceased crackling, lending the bedroom a stilled darkness that's only disturbed by the soft moonlight filtering in through the transom window. Silence permeates the home—no footsteps echoing up and down the stairs, no whispers coming from the second floor, where Saxon and Guy disappeared to, hours ago. If it weren't for Josie's rhythmic snoring, I could almost convince myself that I'm completely alone.

It's *stifling*.

Gripping the edge of the mattress, I try to ease the unsettled pace of my breathing. I draw circles on the carpet with my toes, counting to ten on a hushed whisper, then starting again when I reach double digits.

My pulse kicks up, the images from my night terror bulldozing their way in, so that it's not the quiet street I'm staring at but a dead Ian Coney, his brown eyes dull, his lips turning distinctly blue, his—

"Stop it," I hiss, digging the heels of my palms into

my eye sockets, "just *stop it*."

I'm not sure who I'm speaking to—myself, for succumbing to the constant plunge of paranoia each time I close my eyes to sleep, or the ghosts of King John . . . and now Professor Coney too.

A hand grazes my spine and I nearly hurl myself from the bed.

Except that I do actually hurl myself, I realize, once I blink and the room resettles around me. The cool glass of the window at my back brings goose bumps to my skin, and the curtain has wrapped like a noose around my right ankle and thigh.

I'm stuck, just like I am in my dreams.

Unable to move. Unable to breathe. Unable to *think*.

"Isla?" Josie whispers, scrambling to all fours on the bed. "Are you all right?"

Moonlight fractures across her features, highlighting her nose, hollowing out her eyes with deep shadow. I twist my head to the side, clutching the curtain fabric in a fist and yanking it sharply from my leg. It unwinds with an audible snap.

The release does nothing to lessen the cacophony of my erratic heartbeat.

"I need . . ." I wet my dry lips. "I need water, I think."

She swings her legs over the side of the mattress. "I'll get you some."

"No!" I throw out a hand, stopping her in her tracks. "No, I'll go."

"Are you sure? You look like you've seen a ghost."

How ironically appropriate.

"No ghosts," I lie. Grateful for the shadows, I force a weak smile and motion for my sister to climb back into bed. "It's late—early—you'll need more sleep than this."

Josie casts me what I can only imagine is a dubious look before slipping beneath the sheets again. She twists one way, then rolls abruptly onto her left side, so that she can watch me quietly. "How long are we to stay here?"

If that's not the question of the century then I don't know what is.

"Not long."

Another lie—I've lost count of them all, at this point.

Earlier, I explained the basics of what happened this morning. I acted in self-defense and killed a man, and until we're sure the Met won't come for me, we need to keep a low profile. I don't know what it says about the world we live in that instead of appearing horrified by the truth—or telling me *I told you so*—my siblings only crowded around the sofa and wrapped their arms around me.

Maybe they saw the bleakness in my expression and knew I needed their support.

Or maybe we're just so far gone as a society that an *Us vs Them* mentality is something even teenagers accept as part of the norm.

I'm as sickened by the prospect as I am relieved.

Stomach heavy, I move to the bedroom door, only for Josie's voice to stop me. "Are you scared?" she asks, sounding so small and so young that my heart aches. "After what happened . . . are you scared that they might find you?"

There's no mystery as to who she means by *they*—the police.

In a sea of lies that bubble up like the fountain of truth, I give my sister a sliver of verity. "I'm only scared that they'll take me away from you and Peter."

My active imagination surfaces the worst-case scenarios, changing them out like a film I can't bear to watch.

Josie dead.

Peter lost and alone.

Josie starving and cold.

Peter dead.

"But I'm not going anywhere," I add, a stilted smile touching my lips, "which means it's time for you to go to sleep."

She huffs out a laugh but burrows beneath the covers, seemingly content with a world that has me bossing her around.

I barely make it out of the room before claustrophobia rears its ugly head again. I need fresh air, a place to *breathe*.

Guy mentioned that the property has a rooftop garden and I stumble toward the stairs, gripping the bannister and taking the rungs two at a time. Once on the small, second-floor landing, I swing my gaze left, then right, seeking an entrance to the outdoor space.

Nothing.

Unless...

Arms rooted down by my sides, I stare at the door that might lead me to freedom. Saxon told me that I need to stay here, on Lyme Street, but that can't mean I'm relegated to spending every waking moment within these four walls.

I'll go mad. Absolutely and proper mad.

On silent feet, I approach the door, my hand already itching to rip at the knob and lead me to a night spent under the full moon.

There's a fifty-fifty shot that I'll be walking into Guy Priest's room.

A fifty-fifty shot that it'll be Saxon on the other side.

I send up a prayer and test fate.

Twist the knob and step inside.

The room is completely black, the curtains drawn shut. The fireplace hasn't been lit, not the way Peter sparked ours for some heat before we all hit the sack, him in the bedroom next door to mine and Josie's.

It feels like I've walked into a void.

And then I hear *his* voice—dark, cold, chill-inducing—and I'm not sure if it's relief I feel or a growing sense of dread for waltzing into the lion's den and expecting anything less than a skirmish.

"What are you doing, Isla."

A statement thrown down like an iron gauntlet.

Blinking, I search the room, looking for his familiar, broad-shouldered silhouette. When I come up blank, I take a tentative step forward. "I couldn't sleep."

My ears prick at the sound of a chair creaking. Is he standing? Walking toward me?

"Too hot with the fire?" he asks, his voice a low hum that sends a shiver down my spine.

Wait. How did he know that Peter lit the fireplace for me and Josie?

Tempted as I am to learn the answer, I opt for the truth. With him, I feel as though I can. No judgments cast. No raised eyebrows and silent disapproval. Just me. Just the paranoia that won't quit, no matter how much I try not to feed into the fear.

"A nightmare," I tell him, just above a whisper. "I saw Coney—how he was when I . . . when I did what I did to him."

"Describe it to me."

"What?" More movement, this time from my right. Toes digging into the carpet, I turn in that direction, seeking him out. "I want to *forget*, not recall every last detail."

"Trust me, Isla."

Trusting him seems counterintuitive to everything that my gut is screaming at me to understand. I trust him with my body. I trust him with my safety, even. But my heart?

My shattered soul?

It's a risk. A big risk. One that's more likely to blow up in my face than lead to a happily-ever-after with the two of us honeymooning somewhere warm and tropical. Not that marriage to a Priest is on the table for discussion.

Darkness lurks and silence stalks what's left of my confidence.

I cock my head to the side, listening for his approach. "Let me see you—please."

A long beat passes, then another.

And then I sense him coming up behind me. His big hands settle on my shoulders, his thumbs tracing a line from the base of my neck into my hairline. His breath coasts over my bare skin, making my stomach flutter with something that sounds a whole lot like *yes, please, this* with every flip and flop that tangles me even further within his web.

"Trust me," he reiterates. "Please."

Rubbing my lips together, I run my sweaty palms over the silky fabric of my pajama bottoms that Josie snagged from my drawers before leaving our flat. "You're begging."

"No, I'm giving us what we both want."

My breath catches in my throat. "All right."

"Sit down."

At his raspy command, I squint, wishing the fabric of the curtains wasn't so thick in this room. No moonlight seeps in, and yet . . . Where I felt stifled downstairs, I feel only a thrill now, like the darkness isn't a plague but a cure.

"Where?" I ask, reaching up a hand to capture his.

"Lead me."

So, he does.

One foot in front of the other, his palms on my shoulders guiding me through the pitch-black room. The carpet tickles my bare toes and my skin pebbles with gooseflesh from the heat of his hands.

This isn't about sex or lust or getting off.

It's something more, something ... enigmatic.

I breathe, you inhale, and we both go up in flames.

Turning me around, he inches me back another step until my calves collide with the wood frame of a bed and the backs of my knees meet a soft mattress. "Sit."

I sit, already missing the warmth of his touch.

Straining my ears, I pretend that I can hear more than the reigning silence. I imagine the pop and crackle of a fire glowing in the century-old fireplace. I imagine the scratching of a tree limb against the window, soft and insistent, as though begging to be let in. I imagine him pressing me deep into the mattress, his mouth slanting down over mine as he slips his hand inside my knickers to make me cry out his name.

I imagine it all, vivid and bold, then feel an unexpectedly cool breeze as something lands in my lap.

Fabric. It's fabric.

One brush of my finger over the finely sewn seams instantly indicates that it's a shirt.

A shirt that he stripped *off*.

My eyes go wide as I hear his knees crack, then feel the breadth of his back on the inside of my thighs as he kneels between my legs.

"What are you"—I shake my head, heart pounding faster than it has any right to for a man like Saxon Priest—"what are you doing?"

His deep voice hits me in the chest like a sledgehammer out to smash me into smithereens: "Letting you see me."

Oh.

I fist the shirt as emotion stings my eyes. It didn't escape my notice how he kept his clothes on earlier, even after demanding that I remove all of mine. The fabric was his armor, his shield against society. And here he is, on his knees, giving me free reign over his naked torso.

"Y-you don't have to."

"Free will." A small pause. "Tell me what you see when you close your eyes."

On his command, my lids fall shut.

And, just like that, I'm whisked away on the grotesque wings of my worst nightmare.

"Shocked blue eyes," I breathe out, shuddering at the memory as it plays out before me in my mind's eye. "I felt his surprise, right there in my gut. I felt like it was my own. It was . . . something that I couldn't have anticipated, not ever."

"What else?"

I tangle Saxon's shirt around my fingers, winding it in and out between each digit, simply for distraction. Still, I keep my eyes squeezed closed, as ordered. "The fear—the way his hands jolted up like . . . like he could make it stop. The bleeding. His body going into shock. But there was nothing he could have—" I break off, breathing heavily as the memories assault me. It hurts. It hurts so much to remember, and shouldn't I be *satisfied?* I did what I set out to do. I killed the king. But all I can see is his expression and now there's no stopping the shudder that wracks my frame. "I'm sorry. I don't think—I don't think I can do this. I don't want to remember. I don't want to *keep* remembering."

"Touch me."

My hands stop fidgeting. "Saxon."

"See me while I see you."

It's then I hear it, among the imaginary crackling fireplace and the branches clawing at the window—the raw vulnerability underlying the self-assured command.

A protest leaps to my tongue but my fingers have a mind of their own.

I discard his shirt, letting it fall to the mattress beside me, before shifting forward on the bed so I can reach him.

My thumb grazes the corded muscle linking his shoulder with his neck. With the slightest pressure, I skim north, only to find his head already bowed.

"Keep going," he husks out, "breathe for me."

It's not until my palm flattens across his back that I realize he isn't breathing at all.

He kneels, breath drawn in, and waits for me to pass judgment.

There's no light, nothing to guide the direction of my hands, and yet I follow the hills of his shoulder blades and the valley of his spine. I touch him as though I've spent years memorizing every rigid line of his body. And, with each pass, I feel my heart fracture just a little more.

Scars are scattered across his back.

Some overlap, crisscrossing in feathered batches that churn my stomach and remind me that not all nightmares have the luxury of being locked behind a door of slumber.

"Tell me what you see, Isla."

He's not asking about the firm, hardened flesh beneath my fingertips. Collateral, that's how he put it in the car—and yet this moment feels like nothing less than trust being earned both ways.

I can't hide the quiver in my voice when I speak. "In

my dreams I feel remorse like a living, breathing entity. It clings to me"—like thorny veins crawling over my thighs and keeping me restrained—"and holds me captive. When I struggle to escape, I see his blood dripping from somewhere up above. It lands on my hands, my feet, the rest of me . . ."

The base of my palm collides with a scar that stretches from his left hip to just under his armpit. A second later, he takes that much-needed breath, letting it fill his lungs so that my hand rises with the inflation.

"Where did this come from?" I whisper. *Where did* all *of these come from?*

He exhales. "I don't remember."

Something tells me that he isn't lying—with the number done to his flesh, I can't imagine he's able to keep track of each wound and every injury.

I want to wrap my arms around him.

Promise him that he's not alone.

He beats me to the proverbial punch, asking, "How do you wake yourself up?"

Sometimes I scream myself awake.

Sometimes I pray for a reprieve and pretend that none of it is real.

Most times Josie shakes me until I'm stumbling my way out of another nightmare, lying about what I see in my dreams, and then sitting at our tiny kitchen table until the sun kisses the morning sky and I remember what it's like to breathe all over again.

My hands drift north, over the slopes of his muscular shoulders to the soft strands of his midnight hair. "I let it swallow me whole. Until there's nothing left for the guilt to grab onto, until I'm left alone for another day."

When I trace the shell of his ear, dipping to the

hollow behind his lobe, he stiffens. I expect him to jerk my hand away, as he did when I tried to touch his mouth earlier today, but he holds himself still, a map of secrets that he's given me to decipher.

I could live another fifty years and still not understand everything there is to know about this man.

"There's a certain beauty in the dark," he utters gruffly. "The light shows us what we want the world to see, but the night—the blackness that visits each time we lay down to sleep—it understands us. It clings like toxin, like disease, until we remember that it's the shadows that shape us. The sun needs our silhouette, just like we need its warmth."

My fingers fall from his head to grip my knees. "Two halves of a whole."

Silently, he pushes himself to his feet, then loops his hands around my wrists to tug me off the bed. He leads me to the door, then steps to the side. "Good night, Isla."

I want him to ask that I stay.

He doesn't.

"Good night, Saxon." Throat tight, I step over the threshold. Then, pausing, I look back over my shoulder. "When did you learn to embrace it—the darkness?"

"The day I was taught that help never comes, not even when you beg for it."

And then he closes the door, the lock audibly turning over, leaving me stuck on the other side, both with his scars and mine.

CHAPTER 26

SAXON

With one elbow planted on the desk, I rake my fingers through my hair, letting them rest on my nape. Less than an arm's length away, the dimmed computer screen continues to mock me, baiting me to pull the proverbial lever and confirm what I already suspect in my gut.

"Do it," I grunt under my breath, "get it done."

I reach for the mouse, fully intending to do just that, only . . . Only, at the last second, I shove the chair back and launch to my feet instead.

Fuck!

Twisting away, I clamp my hands down over the back of my head. Dig my thumbs into my skull.

It shouldn't be this hard.

I've spent my entire life manipulating people into giving me intelligence, only to pin my target to the metaphorical wall. I do it without remorse. I do it without consideration for how my actions affect anything, or anyone, but the mission at hand. Even with Father Bootham—a man of God and a kind soul at that—I feel nothing but agitation at being confined to a confessional each week.

Ruthless. Savage.

It's what I am. It's *who* I am.

And still, I've sat in this damn room for close to an hour. Deliberating. Seesawing. Battling indecision with resolution, as though I can simply snap my fingers and cut the strings binding me to Holyrood and the queen.

The part of me wanting to lay the blame somewhere puts it at Isla's feet. She came to *me* tonight. Every one of my senses attuned to her entering my bedroom. The quickness of her breath. The way she begged me to step out of the shadows and reveal myself, all while knowing that I wouldn't.

The broken, ruthless part of my dead heart hummed in satisfaction when I stole her from the light to lure her into the darkness.

Which I did, my gaze fixed on the pajama bottoms she wore and the matching top, which was made out of the thinnest material I've ever felt beneath my fingertips.

How easy it would have been to strip it from her. A sharp tug on the shoulder strap would have snapped the seam, allowing me to twine it between my fingers like a lead I could control. I would have pinched the material between my fingers, listening for her husky gasp, before dragging it down. Down past the swell of her breast. Down past the hard bud of one dusky pink nipple. Down so far until the other strap broke free, too, exposing all of her to me. My lips on her flesh, my tongue driving her into a frenzy.

And if I'd done that—if I'd backed her up to my bed with the sole purpose of working my cock deep inside her—then there'd be no indecision.

Fucking Isla again would be infinitely more satisfying

than betraying her trust.

"*Christ.*"

With a frustrated growl, I press my thumbs into my eye sockets.

A few strokes of the keyboard, that's it. One search of Holyrood's database and I'll walk away—

"Knowing that she's lied."

Because that's what it comes down to, doesn't it.

Tonight, she eased the brakes on the fortress built around her. She let me scale her walls, one brick at a time, until we stood on equal ground, her gentle fingers caressing every one of my scars and my mind visualizing exactly what it is that she sees when she slips into bed at night and succumbs to slumber. And now I'll be taking a sledgehammer to those bricks, smashing them all down at once, and stealing information that she hasn't given me freely.

Information that she might *never* give me.

Without allowing myself any more time to hesitate, I turn on my heel. Plant a hand down on the desk and, with teeth gritted, reboot the computer.

Trouble, trouble, trouble.

The word thrums in my veins, turning ice to fire.

I'm aware of the darkness cloaking the room, the incessant drumming of my thumb on the keyboard as I load the browser and type in a name.

The page reloads.

An image pops up in the top right corner of the screen.

And then the air turns thin, practically nonexistent, as I feel my stomach plummet with the truth staring back at me in the form of a dark-haired man stationed behind a desk, much like the one I'm using, with university students gathered before him.

Ian Coney has brown eyes, not blue.

Which means the death haunting Isla at night doesn't belong to the loyalist professor who wanted me dead. No, that honor belongs to someone else.

Someone with blue eyes.

Someone who stumbled back in shock after being murdered.

Someone whose identity Isla doesn't want me to know.

CHAPTER 27

ISLA

"*It's been three days since Queen Mary University faced the most devastating domestic terrorist attack seen on a university campus in this century. The Metropolitan Police have not given up on the manhunt of prime suspect Saxon Priest, who authorities believe has fled—*"

The telly turns black without warning, and I have only a second to prepare myself before I feel Saxon's presence so acutely that I'm surprised the air around me doesn't physically ripple with his arrival.

Though the tiny hairs on my arms do stand to attention like good little soldiers.

I shift on the sofa, tucking one leg under the other. Do my best to beat my battering heart into submission before seeking him out. "So, you've decided to emerge from your cave then? I feel honored."

Saxon rounds the edge of the sofa, tossing the clicker onto the cushion beside me. "Is it a cave when I have fully operational electricity and running water at my disposal?"

Three days.

That's how long Peter, Josie, and I have been stuck in

this house. It hasn't escaped my notice that Guy left the property sometime yesterday but Saxon has stayed. Or rather, he's stayed *away* but remained in the house, like a ghost whom I hear stalking the halls at night though he never appears once the sun graces the horizon.

Against my better judgment, I soak up his brawny frame like I haven't set eyes on him in years.

His dark hair is damp, slightly tangled, like he recently showered and forgot to comb through the strands. The stubble on his face has thickened, signaling the start of a full beard. He's wearing a fitted short-sleeved shirt paired with soft, gray joggers that hug his arse when he hitches the material at the thighs and claims a seat on the coffee table.

Legs spread. Hands firm on his knees. Bare feet.

My skin warms, and it takes every ounce of strength to find the words to quip, "I couldn't be sure, what with you avoiding the sun and all. Peter and I, we've been taking bets on whether you double as a vampire."

"When I said that I bite, that's not what I meant."

"What? Fresh blood doesn't do it for you?" I tease, hungering for the elusive quirk of his lips that he gifts me so sparingly.

I won't dare admit it out loud but I've missed him. *This.*

The aloofness that he wears like a second skin, which always makes me desperate to tear it to shreds and watch the man with a heart beat to the surface. The man who vowed he would let no harm come to me. The same man who stripped off his shirt, knowing that his scars reveal the harsh realities of his life, and knelt before me anyway.

Humbled. Vulnerable. *Real.*

Subdued humor flickers in his pale eyes before he

lifts a hand, scrubbing it over his mouth. To hide a smile, perhaps—at least, that's what I tell myself. "I think I spill enough blood without doing it for sport, too," he rumbles.

"Sport, survival. Two sides of the same coin. Suppose it depends on your outlook."

He tilts his head toward the blank telly. "And what do you say my outlook should be on that?"

He doesn't need to elaborate. My gut clenches with the memory of what happened at The Octagon, and my thinly veiled good mood dissipates, as if I've snapped my fingers and demanded its destruction.

Three days of constant worry. Two sleepless nights of terrible dreams. Seventy-two hours to regret every decision that I've made in the last two months that has led me to this exact moment.

Sighing, I drop my head against the cushions. "You're putting yourself at risk every moment that you stay here with us. That's what I think. You should have left with your brother. Gotten out of the City."

Saxon doesn't move though his brows draw together. "I promised that I wouldn't let anything happen to you."

I hate that my stupid heart melts at his words.

"Yes, you did. But that was before we realized the entire city would be hunting you down." Rising from the couch, I start for the windows that overlook quaint Lyme Street. The curtains are drawn, allowing only a sliver of sunlight to shine through. Hooking a finger around the fabric, I peel it aside. There are no police cruisers driving past. No signs of any neighbors either. Quiet. It's all too quiet. Worry slicks through my veins. "How long until they find us here? Find *you*?"

"They won't."

I let the curtain fall back into place. Turn to Saxon,

who's angled his body so he can watch me. "You say that like you've done this before."

Beneath the short sleeves, his biceps bulge as he drops his elbows to his knees and clasps his hands together. "I know what I'm doing." Green eyes pin me in place, and in them I see nothing but masculine confidence. "Believe me."

"You're seriously not concerned. Not even a little?"

"I've defeated worse odds."

I'd laugh at his arrogance if I weren't so tempted to wring his neck. *Men.* Seriously. Aside from orgasms, what good do they bring to the table? Nothing but headaches and stress and all the blasted anxiety in the world.

"There are too many unknown variables for me to feel comfortable. Plus, with Peter and Josie—" Breaking off, I plunk down on the abandoned sofa, the cushion still warm from my bum. Truth be told, I'm surprised there's not a permanent dent shaped like my arse. I haven't moved in days. "We can't stay here, not forever."

"For now, you have no choice."

My shoulders stiffen at his high-handedness. "Correction: I always have a choice."

"Right now, you don't." Before I can issue another protest, he digs into the pocket of his joggers and retrieves his mobile. Typing in a password, he tosses me the phone. "Guy dropped by your flat last night."

The phone lands in my lap like a ticking time bomb. Something in Saxon's tone, though . . . Apprehension skids across my flesh, cold and swift. "He did? Why?"

"I met him there."

And, just like that, the apprehension morphs into claws of outrage reaching into my chest to squeeze at my lungs. "Sorry, you did *what*?"

"Don't make me repeat myself."

"Repeat yourself?" I echo, launching from the sofa for a second time, the mobile slipping to the floor, forgotten. The carpet is scratchy beneath my bare feet. "I want to know *why*."

Saxon watches me from behind lowered brows. Nothing in his expression so much as flickers, and *God*. How could he have been so stupid? I'm self-aware enough to know that I'm overreacting and yet I can't stop. *I can't.* The worry tangles with anger and then the anger dances with fear until I'm a hot mess pacing the living room, my breathing escalated, terrible visions of Saxon bleeding and injured in some snicket overriding all common sense. Had that happened, I never would have found him. I wouldn't have even *known*. I squeeze my eyes shut, desperate to destroy the images before they drag me down a darkened path that leads to nothing but more paranoia.

I spend my days worrying about Peter and Josie. I didn't think I would need to be concerned with Saxon doing something rash too.

Is there *no one* here who cares if they live to see another day, save me?

Frustration boils over, dictating my tongue. "Do you have any idea of what could have happened? What *might* have happened had you been caught?"

"Trust me, you wouldn't haven't been proper screwed. I had a plan in place."

My own words being flung at my face does nothing to settle the simmering rage hammering at my rib cage, like a beast ready to claw its way out through bones and flesh and muscle.

"And if something had happened," he continues smoothly, "nothing would change. Guy would look after the three of you. You needn't worry about being tossed out on your ass."

The beast emerges, flaying me open, and I explode.

"You bellend, I'm not worried about *me*!" Spinning around, I stop just short of throwing myself at him and beating his hard chest with my fists. "It's you I'm worried about. *You*. There's a bloody manhunt with your name written all over it, and I can't believe you'd be so foolish as to just waltz into Stepney. You could have been taken to prison or, worse, been killed!"

"Foolish?" he echoes, his voice deep and even and sounding as though he's been dredged through the very pits of hell. Slowly, like a panther rearing to strike, Saxon comes to his bare feet. He towers over me, a king whose authority has been questioned. "You want to talk about being *foolish*?"

I stand tall, my shoulders pressed back, my chin lifted.

Words climb my throat but Saxon edges closer and closer, and the look on his face renders me mute. His green eyes are ablaze with emotion—fury, displeasure, and something unidentifiable. Something that makes my heart tumble over itself with fear ... and the sick promise of anticipation.

"Foolish," he growls tightly, "might as well be your middle name."

"How foolish can I be when you've mentioned—repeatedly—how you constantly underestimate me?"

"I may underestimate you, but you've overestimated *yourself*."

He stalks me, hunter and prey, and I'm hyperaware of the door being open. Peter and Josie could walk in at any moment. I'm meant to be Saxon's employee, nothing more, and yet I can't find it in myself to tell him to toss off or get down from his high horse. I'm angry and flustered and upset, but still I don't leave. No, like he's hooked chains around my ankles, I find myself drifting toward him.

"The same could be said for you," I retort archly. "You went to the *one* place in London where we shouldn't be. I've said it before and I'll say it again—you aren't immortal. Maybe one of these times I'll say it enough that it'll actually stick in that thick skull of yours."

He moves before I can even anticipate him.

His hand locked around the back of my neck, dragging me close. His hot breath on my face, a warning if I've ever felt one. His devil eyes narrowed and spitting fire, the entry point to hell, if I dared to look long enough.

At my startled gasp, he snarls, "Do you have *any* idea what it felt like to enter that room and see a knife only centimeters away from your neck? *Do* you?"

I can hardly breathe, not with him overwhelming my senses. I feel his heat, his tension, his wrath radiating like a life source all of its own. "I didn't crack." Digging my fingers into the fabric of his shirt, I coil the material like that alone will keep him at bay. *It won't.* He knows it; I know it too. One misstep, and he'll flay me alive. "You saw for yourself. I did what I had to do."

"You were impulsive." He drives me backward, step by step, until my calves collide with soft fabric and unyielding structure. The sofa. His hand never leaves my nape. "Reckless. *Foolish.* And when I saw blood on you, you fed that recklessness to me. I would have killed anyone just to reach you in time. And I did. I slaughtered every last one. Because I would rather burn in the pits of hell for all eternity than see you die."

Shock widens my gaze.

It's not an admission of love.

No, his words are curt and brutish and more than a

little frightening, given the ferocity with which he spits them, but they feel important. A once-in-a-lifetime sort of declaration from a man who would sooner manipulate someone to do his bidding than reveal even an ounce of compassion.

I lick my lips.

His gaze zeroes in on my mouth, unwavering.

"I'm alive," I whisper.

I'm alive, I'm alive, I'm alive. Within Saxon's arms, I finally know what the word means in its truest definition. The excited rush of my pulse. The pounding of my heart. The nerves that tangle in my belly, like captured butterflies intent on escape. It has nothing to do with survival and everything to do with seizing the moment.

His throat works with a rough swallow. "I'm aware."

"Are you?" Ignoring my trembling knees, I play bold. Confident. *A warrior.* "You've avoided me since that night in your room. Treated me like I'm nothing more than a ghost."

He says nothing.

But his expression shutters, revealing more in this moment than he probably has in a lifetime. And then, gruffly, "If you think I've avoided you, then you simply weren't looking hard enough."

"Then why haven't you—"

"Because us fucking again will lead to nowhere good."

I know, deep in my soul, that he isn't talking about orgasms.

So softly that I can barely hear myself speak over the roar of anticipation thundering through me, I tip my head back. "You care too much."

"You're wrong," he grunts, but his eyes remain entranced by my lips, "I don't care at all."

Kiss me.

Want me.

Touch me.

I rub my lips together, just to tempt him further, before parting them to utter a challenge that will bring us both to our knees: "Then prove it."

CHAPTER 28

SAXON

Trouble, trouble, trouble.

With each word that tumbles from Isla's mouth, my resolve to stay away cracks a little more. She's purposely baiting me, her blue eyes wide with false innocence, my shirt fisted in her grip, keeping me close. So close that there's no ignoring her dilated pupils and the blush warming her cheeks. Beneath my fingers, her neck quivers.

She likes it.

The cast of fear.

The chase of being caught, then submitting to my every demand.

She admitted as much that night in my car, and I can't deny the effect that her lust has on me. My hard cock strains the confines of my joggers and my heart—the damned thing that's done me no good since I first laid eyes on this woman—thumps erratically in my chest.

I want this.

No matter how I promised Guy that I would be done with her for Holyrood's sake.

For once in my miserable, gray-stained life, I plan to

keep something for myself.

I want to be *selfish*.

I graze my thumb down the length of her throat before sweeping it back up, in a caress that tantalizes more than it soothes. Her breath hitches. Satisfaction curls through me, a black ribbon of pleasure wrought from the darkest depths of hell. I press closer until it's only my grip on her neck that's keeping her from collapsing to the sofa.

"*Prove it*," I scoff, mocking her. "You're a total glutton for punishment."

Her fingers tighten their grip on my shirt. "Or maybe I'm just a glutton for you."

I hiss out a breath at the coy flirtation.

This woman . . . Christ, she provokes me something fierce. Strains the limits of my patience, never backing down until she steals a reaction from me. I feed off the challenge as much as I want to own it, own *her*, and do everything in my power to hear her lust-filled moan announcing defeat.

My free hand splays across her back, sinking south to the base of her spine. "Don't think you're working me around your little finger."

"I wouldn't dare try."

At her sarcasm, I squeeze her ass, just enough to lull her into complacency—before reminding her of who I am. Cold. Callous. *Savage.* I turn her around, yank down her joggers, her knickers, and—

Crack!

Her cry shatters the otherwise still room.

And her ass cheek . . . it pinkens as I dig my fingers into the tense muscles, relieving the sting from my hand. Her shoulders tremble when I lean forward, draping my front over her spine. By her ear, I husk, "You were saying?"

"Again."

My chin jerks back. "What?"

She twists her head, until her mouth is hovering close enough that if I dared, I could brush my lips with hers. She knows it, too. The dare burns in her blue eyes. *Kiss me*, that look reads. *Ruin me.*

The temptation to do both is like liquid heat in my veins.

"Don't make me repeat myself," she repeats, throwing my words back in my face. "*Again.*"

Bloody fucking hell. "Isla, you—"

She cuts me off by thrusting her ass backward into my crotch. "I'm tired. I'm tired of running, tired of lying. But, most of all, I'm tired of pretending to want things I don't and crave in secret what no one will give me."

My brain empties of every comeback.

The skin across my back tightens and my toes curl reflexively into the carpet and my cock, Christ, it lengthens. Thickens. Leaks from the tip. I could come, just with my fist and the visual of my handprint on Isla's sweet ass.

She glances over her shoulder and tears down the last of my defenses with a softly uttered, "What are you tired of? The truth."

I give it to her, on a hoarse rasp, unable to restrain the words and keep them under lock and key: "Being cold, down to what's left of my soul."

Her blue eyes darken. "Then burn with me, Saxon."

Fuck.

Head pounding—the both of them—I slip my hand, fingers spread wide, over her throat. Angle her head to the left, so I can work my mouth over the sensitive skin behind her ear. A nip of my teeth, followed by the glide of my tongue to the erase the sting. A shudder tears through her, and her head falls forward, giving me access.

I take full advantage.

Grinding my fabric-covered cock against her ass, tugging her earlobe between my teeth, then lower, a bite to the juncture of her throat and shoulder. She releases a tormented sound that's a cross between a scream and a moan, and her hands fall to the sofa's armrest, her hips rhythmically rocking backward.

Needy. Wanting.

For *me*.

"Don't move," I order.

Isla will always be Isla, though, and she flicks her hair over one shoulder and meets my gaze with fire and excitement dashing across her features. "Or what?"

I catch those candlelit strands in my fist, tugging her so close that her lips part beneath mine. Deliberately, I linger in the moment, baiting her, tempting her, torturing us both, before growling, "Or I'll bend you over my thigh and turn your ass red."

Her lips curve in the most beautiful smile I've ever seen. "All you had to do is ask. No argument over here. Shall I just"—she waves at the sofa, scooting out from under my arm—"sprawl and wait? Maybe a little something like this?"

Mouth dry, I watch as she climbs onto the cushions, hiking up her shirt around her waist so that her round ass is on display. Swaying. Tinted pink. To say nothing of the glistening wet folds between her legs that have me pressing a hand to my cock, just to relieve the mounting pressure.

I open my mouth. "You—"

"Yes?" Isla flops over, settling into the corner of the sofa. One leg falling open to the floor. The other bent, toes pointed into the cushions. Her cunt mine for the taking.

And I *will* take it.

Instead of answering, I head for the door to close it. I don't know where her brother and sister are but this moment, it's for me and Isla. The woman who needles her way under my skin. The woman who ought to take one look at me and run the other way. The woman who's rapidly destroying what's left of my tattered heart.

She asked me to burn with her and I'm going to do just that. Nothing held back. No desire left untended. Either we survive this together or not at all.

I twist around, reaching for the hem of my shirt to pull it over my head. The material lands on the floor, abandoned. Forgotten. I'm already rounding the sofa, my gaze latching onto Isla's, as though we've always been fated to land here in this crossroads together.

The devil in disguise.

A fallen angel with broken wings.

The two of us—ruined, untamed, and desperate to feel alive.

I sit on the sofa, spread my legs wide, and cut my gaze to hers. "Come here."

She doesn't need to be told twice. With an elegant sweep of her feet onto the carpet, she approaches. Her fingers dance along the collar of her shirt, contemplation furrowing her brows as she visually traces my naked chest for the first time. The raised scars she felt beneath her fingers. The tattoo over my left shoulder: inked swirls of blue and green, abstract in perception—a maze of my own life, with no way to escape. Stuck. Cornered. Saxon Godwin never made his way out.

Licking her lips, as though she's desperate for a taste, Isla drops to her knees before me at the same time that she draws the shirt over her head and throws it aside, exposing small breasts and dusky-rose nipples that beg to be worshipped.

Perfection. Fucking perfection.

Her hands land on my thighs.

"No," I grunt, gripping her upper arm, "not there."

Head jerking up, her mouth parts. "No? I thought—"

"I made you a promise." Still holding her, I pull her off the floor. Frame her hips with my hands and turn her around, so that her ass is all I see. And that fading handprint. Christ, knowing that I've marked her—however temporarily—calls to something inside me that I've never allowed to crest the surface.

Possession.

Hope.

Right now, Isla Quinn belongs only to me. Mine to pleasure, mine to take, and mine to ruin.

Manhunt be damned. Holyrood be damned. The queen be fucking damned.

Keeping my legs spread, I drag her onto my lap. A small gasp flies from her mouth when her rear collides with my rock-hard erection, but I don't let her get comfortable. Sweeping my hands down the length of her smooth legs, I tug them sharply outward, so that she's forced to loop them over the backs of mine.

She's splayed wide, vulnerable.

Just the way I want her.

"Saxon?" comes her hesitant whisper.

"Fulfilling my promise," I return, just as softly, while circling her wrists with my fingers and tugging her arms backward. I crisscross her wrists behind her, at the base of her spine. I can only imagine the visual that she must paint—breasts thrust out, lean body arching, her clit throbbing while her legs tremble atop mine. I keep one hand fisted around her wrists, restraining her, while brushing the other along the outer swell of her breast. "To own every one of your cries. To steal the taste of you right off your cunt. To make you remember who it is that does this to you."

My fingers make direct contact with her peaked nipple, pinching the sensitive nub, and she moans, low and throaty. Squirming in my lap, she yanks at my ironclad hold. I drop my mouth to her shoulder blade. "You can't run, Isla. Not until I'm done with you."

Her answering whimper emboldens me.

This is the first time a woman has ever begged for my touch and I'll be damned if I rush the moment. No. I plan to sample every bit of her, to memorize what makes her grind her hips, seeking my cock. What makes her scream and come back for more. And then, masochist that I am, I'll do it all over again.

She's made an addict out of me.

Flicking her nipple one last time, I flatten my hand and skim the length of her stomach. I follow the shallow grooves of her abdominal muscles then the curved flare of her waist. Her desperate gasp is my only soundtrack when I bypass her pussy and trail my fingers down the inner slope of her thigh instead.

I smirk against her back when she releases a frustrated groan, her muscles flexing within my grasp.

"Isn't this what you craved?" I murmur, tracing my fingers up, up, up, so close to where we both want them, before veering south all over again. "You like the push, the pull—the fear of the unexpected that comes with the pleasure."

"I-I—"

"Cat got your tongue?" I brush my mouth over her skin, the center of her spine. "Maybe I should help with that."

Before she can speak, I move my hand from her thigh and slap her—there, between her thighs, right over her clit.

She screams my name.

I feel her entire body shudder, even her toes that are hooked around my calves. She shudders and I burn alive and I will never—*never*—forget this moment for as long as I live. Isla Quinn, warrior that she is, crying out my name. I cup her core, easing the burn. Already on my fingers I can feel how wet she is.

Wet and wanting and waiting to be fucked.

I dip my fingers through her wetness, capturing the essence of her, before grazing my fingertips up over her belly button, up over one hard nipple, up to her soft, plump lips. "Taste yourself."

She obeys immediately. The tip of her tongue flicks out against my fingers, a gentle caress at first. But then she seems to realize that there's no judgment here, not between us, and she wraps her lips around me and sucks them deep. One knuckle, two. Like it isn't my fingers she's tasting but my cock.

A groan reverberates through my chest, unchecked. "*Christ.*"

She grinds down, her ass circling over my crotch. Lips still staking their claim on my fingers, licking them clean. Giving as good as she's getting.

I'd expect nothing else from this woman.

Pulling myself free of her mouth, I don't wait for what I know will be a sarcastic remark before rendering her speechless all over again. My wet fingers go to her clit, applying pressure, then dance away when she grows stiff in my arms and tries to wrestle back control. Because I'm a starved man with no qualms about stealing what I need to survive, I plunge two fingers deep inside her.

"Saxon," she whimpers, "oh, God. I can't. It's too much."

"Wrong." I regrip her wrists, keeping her captive. "It's not enough. It won't ever be enough, not with us." Tension lines my body, winding me so tight that I might splinter. "Tell me what you see," I growl into her back, my voice thick, "and leave nothing out."

"*Please*, I need to—"

"Tell me, Isla." I curl my fingers within her. Press my thumb down on her clit. "And I'll consider putting you out of your misery."

A cry wrestles with a frustrated hiss. She struggles in my embrace, seeking more, her hips churning. I let her have her moment. For a second. And then I'm pulling away, flipping her over until she's flat on her back, her ass lined up with the edge of the sofa, and I'm the one on my knees.

I spread her legs wide, forcing her to hold her knees against her chest.

A breath away, she's soaked. Dripping. It's a view I've never been privy to before, but one I have no doubt that I'll enjoy.

I lift my hungry gaze to hers. "Uphold your end of the bargain."

It's all I say before I palm her inner thigh, bow my head, and feast.

CHAPTER 29

ISLA

The first touch of his tongue to my clit is heaven-sent. Knees clutched within my hands, there's no stopping the cry that rips from my throat. The feel of him, the *strength* with which he pins me, holding me in place, is as much a turn-on as the sight of him between my legs.

Midnight hair in disarray. Green eyes burning bright, determined and narrowed. That surprising, unexpected tattoo of his fluttering with each hard contraction of his muscles. Mouth wet and glistening as he swirls his tongue and brings me to what must be Dante's undiscovered tenth circle of hell.

Nothing has ever felt so good.

Nothing should *ever* feel as good as this.

I breathe out his name. Sink my nails into my shins because it's either that or claw the sofa cushions to shreds as I writhe under his persuasive mouth.

Uphold your end of the bargain.

His husky demand pervades my consciousness and I lick my lips, desperate for words to give him when all I seem capable of is begging for more. His thick stubble scrapes the inside of my thighs and his tongue causes chaos with each and every flick. And then he ups the ante by sliding a finger inside me.

No, *two* fingers.

They stretch me, circling in time to the rhythm of his tongue lapping the tiny bud of need at the hood of my sex.

I cede all control. Release my knees and crank my body up on the sofa so I can sink my fingers into his hair and scrape my nails down the back of his skull. He wraps a big hand around my thigh, splitting me wider. From this angle, there's nothing but the top of his head and the muscles playing in his back as he kneels on the carpet, his face still buried between my legs.

He's winding me up like a mechanical toy. Torturing me with every drive of his tongue and every sure thrust of his fingers. Never have I felt this way. Never have I felt so *wanted*.

"It's too good," I moan, swaying my hips forward to chase the pleasure. "Saxon, *please*—"

Another finger. It's a tight fit, almost too tight, but then he eases the pressure by withdrawing, then slipping his tongue against my entrance. Crude. Vulgar. Clutching his head, I feel my entire body vibrate around him.

I need him to know what he does to me. I need him to know that there is no other man who has ever made me feel this way, like I'm coming out of my skin.

"Touch yourself."

The words come from me, dirty and desperately hoarse.

He pauses. Lifts his head. "You want to watch."

It's not a question, and I wouldn't do him the disservice of lying anyway. There are too many already—or, at least, one really, really big one—and isn't this what I asked for? The truth? His and mine?

I dip my chin. Then, "I want to watch."

Nostrils flaring with lust, Saxon grasps my legs and plants my feet down on the carpet. He shucks off his joggers as he stands, kicking the material away. Yes. *Yes.* My gaze is rooted on his hard-on when I hear him mutter, "Then I'll give you a show that you won't soon forget."

One second I'm sucking in air and the next Saxon's hand is cupping the back of my neck, his other choking the base of his erection.

He stands so close that the tip grazes my mouth.

My eyes go wide, darting up to his. Feral. Demanding. That pale gaze sears me alive. And, as though he's demanding that I repay the favor, I plant my foot on the sofa. Place my fingers between my legs to find myself throbbing and achy, just as Saxon's tight grip slides up his length and twists the plump crown.

As his hips pulse forward, I lick the head.

Because it's there.

No, because it's *Saxon*.

My heart races in my chest and my fingers delve between my folds to sink in deep. I thrust them in time with the way he fists his cock with angry, aggressive strokes that leave me panting. His abdominal muscles tighten, and a groan wrenches from his throat as I watch come leak from his slit. I want to lick it away. Before I'm given the chance, he runs his palm over the head, smearing it, and then dragging his fist down to the root.

It's lewd.

Brutal.

And the stuff my dreams are made of.

"I can hear you," he grits out, his thumb sweeping up to my jaw. "How wet you are around your fingers."

I curl them, my head falling back into his hand to let him cradle the weight. Then I turn, slightly, and bite the tip of his thumb, never taking my eyes off the show before me. I want him to come across my chest—or in my mouth. I've never swallowed before, but I would for him. Gladly. Eagerly. "Saxon. Saxon, I want you to—"

His guttural voice breaks me off: "Would you be that wet around me?"

"*Yes.*"

He doesn't need further encouragement.

His hands fit under my armpits to lift me up, but as I feel him turning me around, I stay him with a palm to his chest. Over the feathered scars that speak to so much horror. I meet his hot gaze. "Don't hide from me. I want to see you."

"*Christ.*"

But he doesn't say no.

Hauling me off the sofa, he links his hands under my thighs and props me up on the hard back. My legs wrap around his waist, hands landing on his shoulders. I graze my thumb over the water-colored edge of his tattoo.

Brows drawn together, he mutters, "You'll regret this."

I won't regret him—ever. Me and Saxon, we were never meant to be, but that doesn't stop me from soaking him up and breathing him in.

"Take me," I whisper, reaching between us to line up his cock with my core. "And I'll let you know what I regret or not."

Jaw cinched tight, he searches my eyes, as if looking for any lingering doubt. Then finds the crease of my hips to hold me steady—and drives himself home. I cry out, my head falling back. I feel him move, his hips pistoning sharply, his mouth landing on the underside of my jawline. His grip never loosens. Faster. Harder. He thrusts into me like he has a point to prove—or maybe like he's determined to make me regret nothing at all.

Either way, my skin burns and my lungs squeeze and I glance down to watch his thick length fuck me, again and again. No condom. I should panic at the realization, but I'm too far gone to care.

I cling to Saxon's broad frame. Accept his hard, punishing thrusts like they're my due. Each one belongs to me, each one catapults me higher, until I'm quivering and moaning and cupping the side of his face and forcing him to look at me.

There's nothing cold about this man.

He's stripped down.

Stripped bare.

Groaning deep in his chest. Hips churning faster and faster, hitting me in just the right spot that I feel the drag of him against my clit on every forward stroke. Scarred mouth parted and gasping for air.

Welcome to the fire, Saxon Priest.

"Please."

It's all I say, all I ask, and his broad shoulders tense while his thrusting hips slow to an excruciatingly devastating pace. His unholy gaze fixes on my mouth, and I see the want there, the craving for what I'm offering him.

"Steal it," I whisper, running my eyes over his stiff, uncertain features. "I breathe, you inhale, and we both go up in flames. Remember?"

Something in him implodes then.

I feel it in the way his arms bind around my back, securing me to him. In the way his mouth curls, but instead of snarling—or clamping his mouth shut before storming away—he confesses, "You're my first, Isla Quinn. And, more than likely, my only."

Then his mouth, ragged scar and all, crashes down on mine.

And I was wrong. So very *wrong*.

The rest of him may be taking me ruthlessly, as savagely as I once perceived him, but his mouth is the sweetest torture I've ever felt. He sips from my lips, drawing out a swallowed gasp from me, before taking full advantage of my surprise. His tongue plunges into my mouth to tangle with mine, and I feel myself squeeze around his length.

We both groan.

I frame his face with my hands, holding him still.

Show him with my lips how to segue the kiss from passionate to teasing to all-destroying. Because that's what this is: something more than sex, more than casual shagging. We're burning together, willingly, and chasing the flames with everything that we are.

He cants my head to the side. Presses deeper.

I open my eyes, only to find green already blazing a trail of heat. He's watching me. Studying me. *Devouring* me with his gaze and his mouth on mine and his cock that's hitting me just right, just so, until I feel the familiar spark of fire tingling in my belly.

Ripping my mouth from his, I pant, "I'm going to come."

"Not yet. Not until I ruin you more."

His teeth graze my bottom lip, sucking the sensitive flesh into his mouth. He bites. I claw my fingers down the front of his bare chest, over the scars and the gruesome reminders of his past. He tempts me into another kiss, this one so soul ravaging that I feel the prick of tears. And then there are his fingers, claiming my clit and rubbing in tight circles designed to drive me wild.

I come, just like that.

My mouth claimed by his.

My core throbbing.

My heart—utterly and completely ruined.

He thrusts again, deeper, rougher, his breathing ragged in my ear. When he comes, it's still him, still Saxon. Not overtly loud or vocal, but he groans deep in his chest, as if he's being tortured. He pulls out of me, one hand locked around the base of his cock, and releases all over my stomach. White jets of come land on my pelvis, the soft swell of my belly.

Slowly, the seconds tick by.

And then he meets my gaze, a stark vulnerability in those green-yellow depths that wraps around my heart like a knotted rope I have no hope of ever untying.

"I liked it," he rasps, as if surprised.

Reflexively, my legs tighten around his hips. "The sex?"

"Yes, but no." A small shake of his head. "Your kiss, Isla. I liked your kiss."

An altogether different sort of pleasure winds its way through my limbs. Hesitantly, I ask, "Your first?"

His throat works with an audible swallow. "Among other firsts today."

My stomach flutters at the embarrassment caging his tone and I rewind the clock in my head, moving from moment to moment, getting hot all over again from the eroticism of his touch, his dirty words, his mouth on my—

Oh.

"You've never—?"

"No."

"And you never wanted t-to"—I wave a hand at my lap, desperately searching for a word that won't make me sound like an idiot—"eat?"

Utter. Failure.

He drags his upper lip behind straight, white teeth. Breathes out a shuttered sigh, and then confesses, "I'm not sure I've ever wanted anything the way I crave you."

It's not a direct answer but it stills fill in the gaps.

He's never kissed anyone.

Never gone down a woman.

Not until me.

"Saxon?"

"Yes?" he hums.

"Do you believe in fate?"

He twists his head up to stare at me, a shadow passing over his face. "No."

"Well, I do." I cup his face and sit up tall, so I can brush my mouth over his. "And I think, somewhere deep down, you were waiting for me. For us, whatever this is. So that I could be your first."

And, more than likely, my only.

Saxon's lips curl in a smile, a *real* smile, and if I weren't already sitting, I suspect I'd be bowled over by his handsomeness.

Saxon Priest will be the death of me, of that I have no doubt.

CHAPTER 30

SAXON

Drawing my joggers up the length of my legs, I watch Isla pull her hair out from under her shirt collar. Still damp with sweat, the strands stick to her neck, forcing her to coil them around her fingers and tug the heavy weight into a loose knot atop her head.

I want to fist those strands myself, bend her over my arm, and lay claim to her.

My mouth on the underside of her jaw. My mouth brushing the all-too-sensitive flesh behind her ear. *My mouth devouring hers . . .*

"If you want it, take it."

Stiffening, I cut my gaze to hers. "What?"

"A kiss." Those strawberry-blond waves cascade around her shoulders all over again. But with her attention solely trained on me, she seems perfectly content to let them go untamed. "I'm not some gift you're only allowed to open on special occasions. I promise that I'm just as willing fully clothed as I was naked with you thrusting into me."

Christ, her tongue.

Bold and beautiful and sweet to the taste.

In this moment, I feel like the fumbling schoolboy that I never was in my youth, mainly because I was never a schoolboy to begin with. I've carried the weight of the world on my shoulders for most of my life and have more than my fair share of scars to prove it.

But one woman—*this* woman—has stripped me raw.

Guy was wrong.

It's not Isla who ought to be scared of what will come of us—it's *me*.

One touch of her lips on mine and I feel shaken, down to my core. I'm warm, doused in my need for her, and my heart—the fucking thing won't quit thudding double-time in my chest. When she finally wriggles into her sweats, then loops the ties into a knot at her waist, I'm forced to acknowledge that I've lost my bloody mind.

She's fully clothed and here I am, heart still racing, cock still hard, my skin on fire.

I want Isla Quinn like I've never wanted anything else in my life.

Focus, man. Focus on anything but *her.*

Feeling like I've been dealt an impossible hand, I clench my teeth together and snatch my discarded shirt off the floor. "We need to talk about what happened at your flat."

"I'd rather we discuss why you've gone from kissing me like your life depends on it to skirting around me like I've contracted the plague." She pauses, serving me with a swift once-over. "For what it's worth, you've probably been infected already. Mouth to mouth, you know. I'm sorry to say that you're doomed."

Against my better judgment, my lips twitch. "Have you always been so cheeky?"

Her blue eyes skate down my chest, to my stomach, as I lift my arms and draw the shirt down over my head. "How egotistical will I sound if I say yes?" she asks.

"On a scale of one to ten, I'd put you at a healthy twenty."

A flirtatious smile curves her mouth. "One kiss and the sarcasm is already out to play. Just imagine what a few more might do for your oh-so-charming personality."

"And here I remember you telling me that I was lacking in that department."

"I have the right to change my mind at any time, Mr. Priest. It's a woman's prerogative—or hadn't you heard?"

Laughter, unfamiliar but true, reverberates in my chest.

If it were possible for her smile to widen any more, her cheeks might crack in two. "You should do that more often," she says softly, her gaze guileless as she stares at me. "You're handsome as it is when you're snarling and acting like a complete wanker, but your laugh?" She presses a hand to her heart. "It sinks in here, like I can feel your heat even though we aren't touching."

Everything in me grows still. "Isla, you don't need to lie. I know that I'm not . . . that—"

"No. You don't get to tell me how I should feel."

The laughter dies as I swallow past the sudden boulder in my throat. Awkwardness—that damned fumbling schoolboy syndrome—returns swiftly, like a punch to the gut. I've torn apart families, I've put my body on the line of duty more times than I can count. *Savage*, they call me. But in this, with Isla, I don't feel like Saxon Priest, Holyrood spy.

I'm a Godwin again, grasping hope with both hands and feeding it life, even if it leaves me completely exposed.

Gruffly, I ask, "And how do you feel?"

She approaches me on silent feet cushioned by the

carpet, her hand already outstretched to settle on my hip the second she steps in close. Her face tips back, so much trust lighting her expression that my mouth turns dry. Quietly, she confesses, "Like if you tucked me into a dark room, I'd always be able to find you. Deep, raspy. Magnetic. And I'd follow that sound, tethered to it like a string that can't be snipped, to a man whose heart beats in time to a rhythm meant only for me."

I don't wait.

Don't hesitate.

I take it—*her*.

My fingers sink into her thick, still-damp hair, cradling her to me, and then I brush my lips over hers. A second kiss that feels like the first all over again. Or maybe that's how it's meant to be with the woman who's singlehandedly battering down every one of my walls. Where it could be the hundredth kiss or the thousandth, but still tastes like the first.

I wouldn't know.

But I lean into this one like it very well might be my last, my only, a kiss meant to carry me for whatever years I have left.

I drag Isla closer, aligning her chest with mine. Breathe in her scent as my tongue flicks out against the seam of her lips to demand entry. A feminine whimper breaks from her, and I bask in the sound. That whimper is for *me*. Awe coils with desire in my veins, quickening my pulse even as I tug on her hair to tip her head farther back, crushing my mouth down over hers like she's mine to devour, now, tomorrow, forevermore.

Another small moan. Her fingers dance over my hip. She rocks in my embrace, swaying closer still.

In film, couples always seem to keep their eyes closed

during a kiss like it's some rudimentary rule that to taste fully, you need to be blanketed in darkness. But I've spent a lifetime in hiding—within Holyrood and London, with women who'd rather fuck a lamppost than an ugly son of a bitch like me—and I won't do it here, not with Isla.

So, I watch.

I watch her lids flutter when I graze my teeth over her bottom lip, nipping sharply at the sensitive flesh, and I watch her forehead crease when I delve deeper, raking my mouth over hers and thrusting my tongue into her mouth with all-out possession. Her hands jump to my chest, clutching the fabric of my shirt, and there's a moment—brief, paralyzing—when I'm convinced that I've been too rough, too demanding, too *me*.

Only, she doesn't push me away.

No, she stands on her toes and pulls me closer and moans deep in her throat, needy, appreciative.

Yes. *Yes*.

I skate one hand south, to the space between her shoulder blades. Keep her locked against me, for better or worse. Our tongues tangle, dueling for control, neither of us willing to concede defeat. My fingers drift down, down, down, until I'm cradling the curve of her ass in one palm and groaning at the feel of her in my arms. And when she reaches up to cup my face—sweet, so fucking *sweet*—I growl my approval into her mouth and feel her smile against my lips.

An honest-to-God smile.

I don't know whether to kiss her harder, just to erase it from existence, or smile back because, for the first time in my life, my chest feels light. Airy. Like I'm actually living instead of simply existing from one mission to the next, always ready for the anvil to drop and trouble, ever present, to sink its claws into my flesh.

Wrenching my mouth away, I press my forehead to hers. Words bubble up, too many of them, all at once. Words of affection and words of frustration, for not being able to sort my emotions properly and pluck out the good ones, the words another man might have no difficulty saying. Any man who isn't me. Scarred. Broken. Cold.

"If I have a heart at all," I husk out, feeling my face heat, "it's only because you've put it there."

Her fingers on my face flex. And then they smooth down, down even more, until her palm is on my chest, resting against the organ that has no business beating for her, a woman opposite me in this war.

"Sometimes we only amount to what we've always been destined to become," she whispers, and the words are familiar, so familiar that I strain my memory to remember who said them, but then she kills the effort completely by leaning forward to kiss my chest. My heart. *Christ.* She holds still, as though soaking me in, and then pulls back long enough to murmur, "You could steal every piece of me, Saxon Priest, and it still wouldn't change a thing."

My breath catches, even as my stomach drops at the negative implication. It shouldn't matter. I've known what I am for years, and I've never once cared. Never once tried to do better. And still . . . "No?"

She nods, then lifts onto her toes to kiss me. Soft, a promise of more. Against my lips, she breathes, "You've had a heart all along. If I've done anything, it's just to show you that it's okay to melt every once and a while and be *you*."

Fuck.

I'm trembling. Shaking. Whatever the hell word you want to use because it's all the same in the end. I open my mouth, wanting to say *something*—anything to express the range of foreign emotions sweeping through me—only for banging to start on the door. Loud, insistent.

And then, "Isla! *Isla!*"

Blue eyes dart up to my face. "Peter. I don't . . ." She fists my shirt, dropping her forehead to my chest. "I'm sorry."

I tuck one finger under her chin, lifting. When our eyes meet, I touch my mouth to her temple. "Don't apologize for wanting to look out for him."

"I distinctly recall you telling me that he was old enough to handle himself."

There's a teasing edge to her voice, so I return the favor tenfold. "I did, and I distinctly recall you telling me that I'm a coldhearted ass."

"Not so much in those exact words."

I grin, crooked but genuine. "We can argue about it later. But don't forget that we really do need to discuss what happened at your flat. We can't put it off, not for any longer than we already have."

Except, when Isla opens the door to let her brother inside, the look on his face tells me that trouble has risen its ugly head yet again. A fact he confirms a second later when he rushes for the television and turns it on. The screen shimmers, pixels recalibrating as he switches channels, and then a newscaster's voice fills the room, each word more damning than the last:

"After receiving a tip from an anonymous source this morning, police have discovered the long-time reverend of Christ Church Spitalfields, William Bootham, dead in a Stepney flat this afternoon. The flat belongs to twenty-nine-year-old Isla Quinn."

CHAPTER 31

ISLA

My legs collapse beneath me, and it's only thanks to Saxon that I don't go crashing to the floor.

His muscular arm wraps around my waist, drawing me into his side. "*Breathe*," comes his gravel-pitched command in my ear, his nose rustling my hair as his palm slips under the fabric of my shirt to rest on my stomach. Across the room, my brother studies us with narrowed eyes. "Isla, breathe for me."

Dramatics aside, I don't think I'll ever breathe again.

With my attention locked on the BREAKING NEWS notice scrawled across the telly in blood-red font, I watch in horror as uniformed medics wheel a stretcher, carrying what can only be Father Bootham's body, down the narrow walkway leading from my front steps to the waiting ambulance on the street. Officers move in efficient lines through the open doorway, their faces somber. A quick pan of the camera reveals my landlord speaking with a journalist.

I look again to the stretcher, just before the ambulance's aluminum doors clang shut, and my stomach bottoms out for a second time.

Three days.

Only three days ago, the priest sat opposite me in the confessional and told me that he worried for Saxon's safety. Bloody hell. Why hadn't he been more hard-pressed to worry about himself? Why hadn't he stopped to think about what telling me would inevitably do to *him*?

As though sensing my inner turmoil, Saxon's hand settles more firmly against me, his thumb caressing my skin. Back and forth, back and forth. Maybe, under different circumstances, I'd find his touch soothing—I would have, even five minutes ago—but this . . . *this*.

Dear God, Father Bootham.

Ruthless. Broken.

Murderer.

The guilt of yet another death sits on my doorstep—quite literally this time.

Move. I need to move.

Yanking away, I escape Saxon's hold on quick, purposeful feet.

"Did you know?" I demand, my voice cracking pitifully as I stumble backward, putting several meters between us. I need to breathe. I need to *think*. And with him so close—even now—I might as well be a lost cause, forever destined to seek him out.

Saxon Priest has made me a convert.

Despite my floundering, he remains stubbornly fixed in place. Shoulders pressed back. Green eyes hard. Hands fisted down by his sides. An unholy king that refuses to kneel, even in the face of utter destruction.

If only we were all so lucky not to feel blindsided by this news.

"Saxon, did you *know*?"

"No."

"You said there was something you needed to tell me about my flat, that when you went there—"

"Someone broke in," he says stiffly, keeping his whole focus centered on me. On my periphery, I spy Peter shifting his weight from foot to foot after turning off the television. "Someone who fully intended for you to be there when they did."

Dead.

They—whoever *they* are—wanted me lifeless. Saxon doesn't need to say so out loud when all the confirmation I need is already written across his face.

This is the moment I've dreaded these last two months. Does it really matter if I'm wanted for the death of King John or Ian Coney when it's all the same in the end? My identity has been blown and I'm being hunted—and then framed for the one murder that I didn't commit myself.

You lasted two months longer than you predicted.

Ignoring the stamp of trepidation, I grit my teeth against the onslaught of paranoia. Breaking down won't do me any good. *Crying* won't do me any good. Either I fall to my knees and accept defeat or I grasp the torch I've been passed and dredge up whatever strength is left within me to keep pushing onward.

A new fight. A new war to be won. A new reason to look myself in the mirror and marry the Isla of old with the blood-stained woman who now stands in her place.

Saxon's gaze skates over my face. "Bootham's death is a warning. They're wanting to push you out of the shadows."

The illustrious *They* again.

As in, the blasted loyalists.

Good men like Father Bootham, my brain reminds me. Not all loyalists are bad, but the majority of them—

idiots, the lot of them. They're sheep all falling into line, unable to see the catastrophic effect the Crown has set into motion over the last twenty-plus years. Anger swirls in my belly. All I need in this world are the people in this house—Josie, Peter, *Saxon*. Everyone else can rot in hell, and I'll be damned if I deliver myself to those faceless, traitorous bastards with my tail between my legs like I'm ashamed of what I've done.

I'm not.

I'd do it all over again if it means surviving yet another day to see them fall.

"They'll have me once I'm good and ready. Not a second before."

"They'll *never* have you," comes Saxon's dark, sinister growl. It's a threat as much as it is a vow, and a thread of desire sweeps along my spine. "I'll tear their fucking hearts out first. Mark my words, Isla. *Nothing* will happen to you."

My back collides with cool glass and fabric warmed by the sun. The window. The curtains erasing the outside world from view. Out there, London is reeling from the sudden death of a beloved priest. In here, it's the quiet before the storm. We can't stay hidden forever. I don't *want* to stay hidden forever. That's not the sort of life any of us deserve. And, hell, Father Bootham deserved his ending least of all.

He did nothing wrong. Nothing besides believing in his queen and supporting her right to keep the throne. Now he's dead, and I may as well have been the one to deliver the final blow.

"If we have any hope of coming out of this unscathed, we need to figure out how he was murdered," I mutter beneath my breath.

Maybe he was slaughtered inside my flat. Maybe he was brought there after the deed was already done. Either way, my nerves twist and my calm disintegrates like a water balloon striking a hard surface, and it's as I'm drawing in a deep rush of air that I catch a blur of navy blue launching toward Saxon.

"Peter, *no!*"

My brother ignores me completely.

His arm swings, fist at the ready, and aims for Saxon's face. I flinch, expecting to hear the crunch of cartilage breaking or a pained growl from the man who brought me to orgasm, multiple times over, just an hour ago.

I should have known better.

With quick reflexes, Saxon bobs the punch, grabs Peter by the wrist, and yanks my brother around until his back is flush with Saxon's chest. Bigger, stronger, Saxon binds an arm across Peter's front, forcing my brother's arms to dangle uselessly by his sides.

"Let me go, you bastard!" he cries, wriggling in Saxon's immobile hold. "You did this. You *did* this."

I step forward, only for narrowed green eyes to pin me in place. "Don't move."

At Saxon's order, I go deathly still, my stare flitting to Peter, whose face crumples with misery. Red cheeks, flared nostrils. His eyes are squeezed shut but if they were open, I know they'd be bright with fury. And that fury would be directed at the wrong person. Saxon did nothing. He offered me a position when I begged. He saved me—twice—when I faced down the proverbial barrel and was seconds away from inevitable death. He brought us here and gave us shelter, when he could have easily walked away and wiped his hands clean of all things Quinn.

Saxon isn't the devil in this situation.

No, that honor belongs only to me.

"Peter." When he doesn't so much as acknowledge my existence, I repeat, more urgently, "Peter, *look at me.*"

His blue eyes snap open, zeroing in on my frame. "I told you," he says, the words escaping on an angry hiss, "I told you what would happen if you struck up with the bloody Priests and you didn't listen!"

Behind him, a vein throbs in Saxon's temple.

I defy his command and take another step in their direction, laser-focused on my brother. "You're right, I didn't listen. But it was my choice to make and I did what felt right."

He barks out a humorless laugh. "How's that worked out for you so far? You've killed a man and now *another* man—a priest, Isla, a fucking priest—is dead in our bloody flat. Who killed him, huh? You? Is all this talk just some elaborate ploy to play the victim card?"

My legs shake and my heart pounds feverishly fast and, still, I stand my ground, unwilling to break. "You know that I wouldn't do that."

"Wouldn't you?" he snaps back, jutting his chin forward with rash teenage abandon. "After this last week, I don't even know who you are. *My* sister isn't irrational. *My* sister wouldn't hurt anyone, let alone play God and take someone's life. And my sister wouldn't be fucking a goddamn Priest!"

Saxon's grip on Peter visibly tightens, his features so frighteningly cold that I'm surprised my brother doesn't immediately turn to ice. "You don't know anything, lad. And if you speak to her like that one more time—"

"You'll *what?*" Peter snaps, thrashing his arms but making no dent in Saxon's ironclad hold. "You'll fuck her again? We all heard. Me, Josie. The bloody queen probably heard." Angry blue eyes land on my face. "You had it all, Isla. The job, the money. Maybe we weren't rich but *killing* people? You talk about it like it's nothing. I figured the self-defense thing was a lie—an exaggeration, maybe—but now I know that it isn't true at all. Mum and Dad would be disappointed, you know that?" He spits at my feet. "You aren't the girl they raised. You're not even *half* of that girl."

Air seesaws in my chest, clouding my vision until all I see is the boy who I held throughout the night when I showed up in York, no parents in tow. His distraught wails have haunted me ever since.

But now—right now—all I feel is rage boiling deep in my gut.

Rage at the world, yes, but rage at him, too.

You're not even half *of that girl.*

When Saxon opens his mouth to speak, I throw up a hand to stop him.

All these years I've sheltered Peter and Josie, but, clearly, it's time that I strip off the blinders. He wants the truth? Then he'll have it.

The cold.

Bloody.

Truth.

I step forward, bringing my nose centimeters from his, knowing that Saxon will keep him restrained. "You don't get to cast stones from your high horse, little brother," I utter tightly, like a wound drawstring bound to spring free, "you don't have that luxury. Not today, not tomorrow. For five years, all I've done is protect you."

He snorts, this disbelieving, rude sound that ignites my temper.

I grip his chin, taller though he is, and force his gaze

down on me. "You claim I'm not who you thought I was, and you're right—I've had to become *this* woman. Mum and Dad were murdered, and I never saw it coming. Not once." I feel Saxon's hot stare on my face, but I ignore him, focusing only on Peter. "And I'll be damned if the same happens to you or Josie."

"What would really happen to us? Answer me that. *What?*"

"Do you know how many people have disappeared in the last five years?" I demand sharply. "Do you?" When Peter averts his gaze, silent, I hiss, "Seven hundred and ninety-three, not counting the hundreds, if not thousands, who were never reported as missing in the first place. And you know what all those people had in common? They had family or friends or acquaintances who spoke out against King John."

"That has nothing to do with us."

Still holding his chin, I thrust my face close to his. "Wrong. It has *everything* to do with us. Because Dad and Mum saw to it. Oh, they were just middle-aged folks who loved nothing more than to traipse around the country with their kids. That's what they showed the world. That's what they showed *us*."

But it wasn't the whole story.

A fact that I didn't know until I was forced to sell our family home in York to pay off my parents' debts. Debts they'd accrued by secretly donating swaths of money to anti-loyalist movements here in London. Sure, they came to visit me every other month because they loved me. I don't doubt my importance to them. If anything, my moving to the City only bolstered their ability to have a firm hand in what was happening here to take a stand against King John.

They died in a revolt of their own orchestration.

The coded letters I discovered in the vault, in their bedroom, revealed all. Letters I then burned to protect my siblings and myself. If they'd fallen into the wrong hands ... Well, we'd be in the same position that we are now.

Turns out the universe is an ironic bitch like that.

"They wanted the king dead," I tell Peter evenly.

"Everyone wanted the king dead," he seethes, "that's no secret."

I shake my head. "But they planned for it. And on the day that they—" I breathe harshly through my nose, fighting the well of tears that never fails to spring up when I think of them both. "On the day that they died, they staged that protest, Peter. King John was due to head into Westminster, to sign into law that parliament would be no more, and Mum and Dad, they were going to make a move. They organized it all."

His eyes go round. "No. No, you're lying. Mum and Dad, they wouldn't—"

"They did."

I'm so wound up that I nearly miss the tension seeping into the room. Saxon's knuckles are white where they clutch Peter's arms and I'm sure ... God, I'm sure he feels betrayed that I haven't told him any of this. He trusted me. He *saved* me. And I repaid him by keeping secrets, no matter that he would have understood them all.

I look to him now, begging him silently to not hold a grudge against me, and I try not to feel slayed by the startled expression on his face.

Bollocks. I can't—I can't deal with him right now. Peter. I need to concentrate on Peter.

I turn to my brother. "They died alongside more than a hundred other people. And the king walked away unscathed."

A ragged sob wrenches itself from Peter's throat.

Welcome to the truth, brother mine. The cold, ugly truth.

The truth that's kept me up at night for five years. The truth that's guided every decision that I've made in all that time. The truth, for better or worse, that's led me here to this exact moment, prepared to tear the safety net I've cast over him in two.

Completely irreparable.

"You say that you don't know me," I say, steel lacing every word, "and you're right. I walked alone for years, knowing every piece of information that they'd gathered and sharing it with no one. I watched it all unfold, Peter. The increased disappearances. The gradual number of Brits who found themselves locked up or, worse, dead— and all because they had the wherewithal to stand up to a man so inflated by power that he couldn't see the storm he was brewing among his own people.

"So, yes, I left the fancy job." I smile, a thin, grim smile that bears the weight my soul has carried for more than a thousand days. "I'd hoped that working with the network would satisfy Mum and Dad's goals. Give the people what they ought to know though no one else dared to do so. But *I* dared. Me, the girl you say our parents would be so disappointed in."

"Isla." This from Saxon. His voice is cut deep, as though filtered through the frozen tundra, and I swear I almost feel icy fingers grazing down my spine. He repeats my name again, harder, rougher, a pleading note turning the vowels curt. "Isla, what did you *do*?"

I meet his gaze head-on.

There's a commotion in the hallway, the sound of pounding footsteps on the stairs, but I'm too far deep to stop now.

So, with my stare held captive by the man restraining my brother, I finally confess: "I did what my parents failed to do five years ago—I killed the king."

CHAPTER 32

ISLA

Saxon's scarred mouth moves, parting to speak—

No sound emerges.

Meanwhile, my heart hammers so erratically that I hear nothing over the thunderous din of adrenaline. *You did it. You confessed.* I should be nervous. Scared, even. *Something*, at least, given all the night terrors and anxiety that I've experienced in the last two months.

The fear doesn't arrive.

Not in the ten seconds post-confession. Not in the next thirty either.

All there is, is pure, sweet relief when I seek out my brother's gaze, then Saxon's, wishing I could throw my arms around them both without appearing positively unhinged.

"It was me," I hear myself whisper, as though they didn't catch it the first time around. "I did it. I shot the king."

Peter makes a strangled, wretched sound, even as palpable emotion spreads like wildfire across Saxon's face. Dark brows knitting, a vein pulsing in his temple. The brush of relief fades to a dull throb when he rasps, "You lie."

No.

No.

"I wouldn't—"

"Don't, Isla," Peter counters, his tone begging, "you've done nothing but lie for years."

Self-preservation drives me physically backward, away from the barbed comment that feels as precisely aimed as an arrow straight to the heart. He isn't wrong. But, dear God, the words *hurt*. The surge of relief drains from the gaping wound my brother struck, leaving behind a hollowness that already feels ten times worse than all of the night terrors combined. I look to Saxon with a tendril of hope.

"I'm a lot of things," I admit hoarsely, holding his gaze, pleading, "but a liar isn't one of them. Not today. Not about this."

Something twists in his expression.

Horror. Disgust. Doubt.

Maybe even a tragic mixture of all three.

"I should have told you." I lick my lips. Scrape a sweaty palm over the fabric of my shirt. Flick my gaze to Peter, who's staring at me from the prison of Saxon's arms, and then back again. "There were so many opportunities and I . . . I never said a word. For that, I'm sorry. So, so sorry."

"Fucking *hell*."

At the rough curse, Saxon releases my brother and twists away abruptly. Fingers clamping down on his nape. The hem of his shirt lifting to expose a strip of golden skin.

His green eyes are everywhere but on me.

Look this way, Saxon. Please.

He doesn't.

As though tethered to his energy, my feet pad toward him.

One step.

Two—

A hand circles my wrist, and it's Peter holding me back. Peter who warned me away from the Priest brothers. Peter who fessed up about the loyalist group at Queen Mary because he wanted to see me safe and aware of all signs pointing to danger.

Had it been anyone else but Saxon on the proverbial chopping block that day, I don't know . . . I squeeze my eyes shut as the startling truth reverberates through me. I don't know if I would have risked my own life for anyone but him.

Saxon and I have known each other for only a week. And yet . . . And *yet*, it feels like our lives were always meant to cross paths. An intersection. A juncture with the sort of hard-hitting collision guaranteed to alter life forever after.

He may not believe in fate, but I do.

Saxon Priest has always been my destiny.

Desperate, I shake my brother loose and try again. "You saved me." At my sides, my fingers tremble. I curl them into fists, not out of anger, but to keep myself from reaching for the man who still won't spare me a single glance. "And I returned the favor by lying—first by omission and then completely outright. You didn't deserve that. You *don't* deserve that. The world thinks you murdered the king but—"

"Stop."

"—I did it," I finish, raising my voice to speak over him. How many times did the confession sit on the tip of my tongue, waiting to be freed? And now that I've opened the gates, every grim, bitter detail is begging for escape. "All this time, it was *me*. Maybe you're right— you and Peter both—because I'm exactly what you said.

Ruthless. Broken."

"I said *stop!*" Saxon whips around, his face a mask of anguish. Because I killed the king? Or because I lied and allowed the blame to fall on him? I don't have the chance to voice either question. In three powerful strides, he demolishes the space between us. "I don't want to hear another word, Isla. Not another fucking word."

"Saxon, you—"

"No." His big hand clamps down on my shoulder, driving his rough-hewn face centimeters from mine. So close that our noses touch. So close that I can feel his hot breath on my mouth. I shudder. "Never again," comes his low hiss, his devil eyes locked on my face. "Do you understand?" He shakes me, fervent, demanding, torture written in every tense line of his body. "Promise me right now that you'll never repeat any of this. *Promise me.*"

"The damage is already done." I sweep my hand over his, squeezing once. "Father Bootham was found dead in my flat. Whoever stole those pictures obviously set me up, just as they did to you. There's no stopping what's coming, Saxon. I killed King John, and not even you can save me."

Above the roar of paranoia, I hear Peter curse beneath his breath followed by a short, pained, "I-I don't want you to die."

Josie.

Oh, God.

Without missing a beat, Peter launches forward, his arms already outstretched to comfort our sister. He disappears behind the breadth of Saxon's shoulders, out of my line of sight, but when I try to follow, Saxon blocks my path. There's nothing but his broad chest and strong, stubbled jaw and his hand on my shoulder that shifts to cradle the base of my head as his gaze flicks between mine, searching.

"Promise me."

At the roughly uttered command, I cave. "Yes, fine, I promise. Now please move so I can see my—"

"Isla Quinn, the king killer," interjects a new voice, all-too-pleasantly. "It has quite the ring to it."

The masculine timbre is instantly recognizable. Sharp hostility congealed with a mocking friendliness that instantly squares off my shoulders for battle.

Guy Priest.

I lift my gaze to Saxon's, aware of our audience, and barely move my mouth around the words, "Let me go."

His response is instant: "You don't know what you're asking of me."

I move a second time.

Again, the stubborn man mirrors the side shuffle, firmly planting himself in my way, as though shielding me from prospective harm. A hopeless, frustrated laugh climbs my throat. There's no danger here, not in this house. Nothing besides the very real possibility of crushed emotions if I don't smooth the troubled waters before the waves drown us all in one go.

I lower my voice, intending my next words to be only for the two of us. "She's young. This isn't"—I draw in a sharp breath—"You need to step aside, Saxon. Please. Right now."

He drags his thumb along the side of my neck to settle over the plump center of my bottom lip. I feel that one touch all the way down to my toes. But in his prolonged pause, I can't help but wonder if he's weighing his choices. Maybe debating whether or not to throw me over his shoulder, the way he has before, and do away with *my* choice altogether. Then, jaw clenched tight, he slams those brilliant green eyes of his shut. Without a word, he tears himself away.

The loss of him is immediate. Overwhelming.

Don't reach for him.

Not right now, at least, when I desperately need to give Peter and Josie my full attention—while somehow managing to ignore commentary from the arsehole peanut gallery.

Sole attendee: one.

"Jos," I say, casting my gaze past Guy, who's propped up against the door frame, and turn to my sister. She's huddled under Peter's lean arm, hauled up against his side. Her blue eyes remain rooted to the floor, avoiding mine. "Please . . . please don't be scared of me."

Wordlessly, she shakes her head.

"Josie, please—"

"You're all over the telly."

At the droll statement, my head jerks toward Guy. Arms linked over his chest, he watches the scene play out before him with an avid curiosity belied only by his shrewd stare. I press my lips together, refusing to take the bait. "I didn't kill Father Bootham."

"But you *did* murder the king."

Saxon stiffens beside me. "Guy, stay out of this."

"What? I'm only looking out for her." He kicks away from the door frame and ambles closer. A lion on the prowl. A jackal poised to strike. It takes every ounce of willpower to keep my feet fixed in place. "The way things are going, your little pet will be stuck behind bars any day now. She needs a place to hide—somewhere outside of the City."

"*She,*" I snap, "is standing right here. Either talk to me directly or don't bother at all."

The corners of Guy's lips curl in a small, self-serving smile. "Should I tell you how I'm jealous, then?"

Unblinking, I meet his stare. "Do you really need an invitation? I imagine you already plan to tell me why."

His smile kicks up another notch as he leans forward. "Jealous," he murmurs slowly, as though tasting the word, "because you managed the one thing that we've all been angling for, for years—the king dead. Total chaos ensues. Absolute anarchy."

A knot forms in my throat. "That's not what I want at all."

"No?"

"No one wants anarchy."

"You're right," the eldest Priest says, stepping close. I catch a hint of his aftershave—something masculine, sharp—when he claims a small perimeter around me. Only once he's at my back, leaving me with a full view of Josie and Peter, does he add on a raspy whisper, just for me, "I wanted revenge."

The memory of Mum and Dad leaving for Big Ben slams into me with such force that I nearly keel over. Revenge. Vengeance. Anger. Five years with only those emotions fueling me, governing every one of my actions. Even now, as I stare at my siblings clustered together, like they don't know whether I'll turn on them next, I find myself succumbing to the rage all over again.

With my gaze on my brother and sister, I dip my chin. "Revenge was all I had."

A masculine hand—firm and tanned and unbruised, so unlike Saxon's—lands on my shoulder to slowly twist me around. I catch a glimpse of broad shoulders and a strong chest before Guy bends, next to me, to say, "I was twelve when our father was murdered. He was another victim of the king. Bled out on the street. Stabbed fifteen times."

Realization dawns and I breathe a single word: "Paris."

"How smart you are, King Killer. We fled the country in the middle of the night. And, somehow, I can't even find it in myself to be disappointed that you took what I wanted right out from under me." A rough chuckle grazes my ear. "But I think . . . I think I'll call in a favor to even the score."

I run my tongue along my bottom lip. "What favor?"

"Let my brother be the hero in this story."

Unbidden, I look to where Saxon stands by the window. Nothing in his posture reveals that he's overheard his brother's bargaining chip. I wait, heart in my throat, for him to glance my way. I want him to *see* me. But he doesn't return my stare and, if I weren't already positive that he does, in fact, have a heart beating under all that steel muscle and hard flesh, I might have been able to convince myself that he's completely tuned us out.

Steeling my own body, I shrug Guy off. "I don't need a savior."

"We never know what we need until it's too late."

Ominous.

Gooseflesh erupts over my skin, turning the tiny hairs on my arm on end. "What do you know that I don't?"

"I know that you can't stay in this house forever." Guy slants a critical look toward the curtained window. "At some point, you'll need to leave. You and your siblings, and Saxon—why don't you tell her what you told me?"

Shoulders rounded with one hand planted on the wall, Saxon's back expands with a heavy breath. Slowly, that open palm drags into an angry fist, and I swear I can feel the scrape of his roughened fingertips over my skin.

His gaze catches on my face, his eyes clear and calm and collected.

Like ice.

"We have a house in Kent."

I pause. *Another* house? The retort sits on my tongue, ready to spring. At the last second, I ditch it in hopes of getting answers they might actually deliver. "So, you want to shuffle us from one spot to the next."

"I want to keep you safe."

Dammit, Saxon.

Joy sparks heat and, despite everything that's happened, I struggle with biting back a smile. Destiny. There's no other reasoning for why one comment like that from him has the black clouds hanging over my head dissipating within seconds.

"You have a heart," I tell him.

He holds my stare. "Only for you."

CHAPTER 33

ISLA

"Get in."

I ignore Saxon's order to slip into the car and quickly survey Lyme Street instead. It's eerily quiet, just as it's been since we arrived on Monday night. No signs of life. No movement of any kind. Even the array of cars parked along the curb seem frozen in time. Three days of me watching the outside world—this small strip of it, at least—and there's nothing to indicate that these homes are actually in use.

"Do you own it all?" I ask quietly, aware of Peter and Josie, who have already made themselves at home in the back of Saxon's sleek car with our single duffel. Our entire lives—all three of ours—shoved into one bag of poorly sewn polyester. "The street, I mean. Do you own all these houses?"

His hand finds the small of my back, beneath the fabric of my shirt. "Yes."

Startled by his unexpected honesty, my gaze lifts to meet his. "*All* of them?"

"All of them on this block."

Camden might not be Notting Hill or Mayfair, even, but it's not dirt cheap either. There must be at least ten properties on this block. Maybe even more. Questions fly at me from every angle, my curiosity begging to be satiated, but only one seems important enough to ask: "Do *you* live on this street?"

Though his face remains expressionless, his fingers give him away.

They flex against my skin, the roughened pads of each digit digging into my spine. He's not pushing me into the car, no matter how he might be tempted to do so, but it feels like an involuntary response. One that segues into uncomfortable silence before a slamming door steals my attention.

"Don't take M20," Guy calls out as he pounds down the front steps and strides across the narrow street. He throws a set of keys in the air, then snatches them midflight as they fall victim to gravity. "We can't risk anyone taking a good peek at one of the tolls."

Like a naughty schoolboy caught doing something he shouldn't, Saxon drops his hand away from me. "We'll see you there."

"Don't be late."

With that, the eldest Priest brother climbs into an equally sleek, two-seater vehicle. The hum of the engine sounds impossibly loud against the otherwise quiet street. Not two seconds later, he's ripping down the road and disappearing around the next block.

Saxon clears his throat. "Get in the car, Isla."

I stand my ground. "Answer the question and I will."

"You touched my scars in my bedroom," he mutters, his voice low and painted with exasperation, "and I made you come on my sofa." Jaw tight, his impatient green eyes flit over my face. "Will that suffice?"

"I—"

My mouth clamps shut as the words sink in. *Really* sink in.

He took us into his home, no questions asked. He fed us, let us sleep in his guest rooms, and never did he ask for anything in return. And, if I hadn't pressed just now, I have no doubt that he would have been content to let this information go unsaid—forever.

Temptation sweeps through me, demanding that I stand on my toes and press a kiss to his mouth. A *thank you* kiss. An *I see you for who you really are* kiss. A kiss that reflects trust and loyalty and, bollocks, I can't find the inner strength to stop myself. Rising onto my tiptoes, aware of Peter and Josie probably gawking from the backseat, I leverage my weight with a hand on his ripped waistline and brush my lips to the underside of his stubbled jaw. Then another, this one to the corner of his mouth after I gently angle his head so I can touch his lips with mine.

"Thank you," I whisper.

Long fingers wrap around my wrist, tugging me away. "We have to leave."

This time, I don't ignore the husky command.

Climbing into the front passenger seat, I slide the seatbelt home and fold my hands in my lap. Immediately, I sense the stares from Peter and Josie. One curious, one judgmental. It doesn't take a rocket scientist to decipher which vibes are coming from whom.

Peter wanted me to stay away from the Priests.

Josie just wanted me alive.

I disappointed them both but for entirely different reasons.

As quickly as Guy fled Camden, we do the same. Saxon keeps the radio turned off, leaving the four of us to sit in awkward silence for the entire length of time it takes to leave the City and merge onto East Rochester Way, heading southeast toward Kent.

Beyond the motorway's guardrails, we pass open fields and quaint farms. Cows and sheep dot the landscape, along with a few old cottages that seem as blended with the scenery as the animals themselves. The weather is forgiving today, considering the time of year: bright blue skies matched with warm temperatures that allow us to crack open the windows.

Inside this car, and despite the fresh air, it's utterly *stifling*.

A short breath expands my lungs, and I drop my chin, my fingers lifting to massage my temples. "Ask me," I edge out, over the rush of wind tunneling into the car, "ask me whatever you want and I'll answer."

Peter doesn't miss a beat. "What did you do with the gun?"

"I threw it in the Thames." As if it happened only yesterday, I struggle not to succumb completely to the memory. The cold breeze teasing at the hem of my coat. The pinch of my toes, from wearing a pair of shoes a size too small. The utter terror of possibly being caught as the metal railing dug into my belly when I hurled the stolen rifle into the black water. "By the Middle Temple Gardens," I add, my mind's eye still replaying those crucial moments when I tossed my trainers into the river, as well. "I wanted to get farther away—my plan was to toss it near the Royal Airforce Memorial. But all I heard were sirens and screams and I panicked."

"You came home late that night." Josie's sweet voice

rises to be heard over the wind. "You told me that you'd met a man at a pub."

Out of the corner of my eye, I watch Saxon's grip on the steering wheel turn impossibly tight. Jealousy, maybe? One glance at his face reveals nothing—as expected—and I force myself to answer my sister's question instead of alleviating Saxon's concern. There have been no other men but him, not since Stephen.

"I booked a room at a hotel. It was cheap and not particularly clean, but it had a fireplace . . . I, ah, burned my clothes. Every last stitch that I wore."

"Clearly, you thought of everything."

At the slightly caustic remark, I cut my attention to the man driving the car. Strands of dark hair fall across his forehead. On anyone else, the unkempt look might appear boyish, but it does nothing to soften his hard edges.

I'm starting to suspect nothing can, not even me.

Tucking my fingers between my thighs, I keep myself fully on this side of the center console. "I planned. Ever since it was announced that King John would be speaking at St. Paul's, I tracked every possible route away from the cathedral to the Thames." Pausing, I clasp my hands. Do my best not to recall every fraught moment of that day, as if it hasn't already been imprinted on my brain. "I ran those routes for three months. In the morning, late at night, until I had each one memorized."

"Æthelred," mutters Saxon, shaking his head.

Blankly, I stare at him. "Who?"

"Nothing." He guides the car onto the off-ramp and circles an empty roundabout. "It's nothing. We're almost there. Ten minutes, maybe fifteen."

He says it with all the excitement of a prospective visit with the dentist. Clamping my hands down on my opposite forearms, I tip my head back against the plush headrest.

"There was no boy," I tell Josie, looking into the rearview mirror so I can glimpse her face, "and there were no late nights spent at the network. I lied. I lied for *years* and I can't take back any of that." Swallowing tightly, I rub my thumb against the jut of my elbow, needing to do something with my hands. "I thought . . . I thought, maybe, that with the king dead, the country would revert back to how things were before. Parliament at the forefront of our politics. Nights where we didn't worry about hearing the sirens, announcing another death at yet another riot. I thought we'd be safe. Maybe not me, but you, Josie, and you, Peter. I thought the two of you would be *safe*."

"You were naïve," Saxon utters roughly, "so bloody naïve."

I don't even bother to defend myself. "I was."

Truthfully, I still am.

Peter's hand gently folds over my shoulder, squeezing. "I don't want you to think that I hate you. I can't . . . Fuck—"

"Language, Peter," Josie admonishes, and from the way Peter jolts in his seat, I have the sneaking suspicion that she poked him.

"Dammit, Jos, I'm trying to say something here."

"No one's stopping you."

A small, battle-weary smile lifts the corner of my mouth. "Josie, let him talk."

Squeezing my shoulder again, Peter goes on. "We all wanted the king dead. All of us. But I wouldn't have done it myself. That's not, uh . . . That's not the sort of person I am, I suppose. But you've always been braver than me, Isla. You do what no one else will, and I-I just wanted to tell you that. It's not naïve to trust your gut—it just makes you human."

Tears prick the back of my eyes and I reach up to grasp his fingers. Overwhelmed by emotion, I kiss the back of his hand, the way Mum used to do to us as children. "You have no idea what that means to me," I say, my voice ragged. "I love you."

"What about me?" Josie pipes up, jabbing me in the other shoulder.

I glance back at her, and she is just so *Josie*. Tough and brave and so much older than her sixteen years, but her blue eyes reveal everything she won't say out loud: she's terrified of me dying, of somehow leaving her behind to fend for herself. "I love you, too," I tell her, snagging her hand before she pulls away completely. "There isn't anything I wouldn't do for you."

Even kill the king.

For the first time in the hour-long ride, the radio punches on and music floods the car. Saxon's palm hits the steering wheel with an audible *thwack*. "Five minutes."

Letting Peter and Josie go, I settle a hand on his upper arm. "Are you okay?"

He issues me a stiff nod but says nothing for the remainder of the ride. Trees bracket the two-lane road, their scraggly branches eclipsing the clear sky above. The stifled air has returned, and not even the upbeat melody playing from the speakers can do much to erase the unease seeping back into my veins.

The road opens some, revealing a quaint stone house on our right before Saxon takes a left at the fork. And then it's nothing but a narrow, single lane road leading us deeper and deeper into the woods. The brush grows thicker, the sky disappears altogether, and I can't even imagine what it must be like to drive here at night.

Pure, all-encompassing darkness.

I sit up tall in my seat. "How much farther?"

Gravel crunches under the tires as Saxon eases us down a small drive lined with trees on one side and a short brick wall on the other. "We're here," he says, and then we are.

A landscaped lawn comes into view, followed shortly by a paved path that winds around a pond and a small stream. Stone bridges arc over the water, and if I lived here, I know—without a shadow of a doubt—that I would spend most of my days seated beside that stream, taking in every splash that nature has to offer.

I lower my window, hoping to catch the sound of rippling water.

"What is this place?" Josie breathes from the backseat.

"We call it the Palace," Saxon answers, turning the music off with a flick of his fingers. "It was built for Henry VIII. A manor house that he never visited." He looks over at me, pausing, before returning his attention back to the road. "In the chapel, the ceiling has artwork that the architect had done to commemorate Henry's marriage to Catherine of Aragon."

Peter releases a boyish chuckle. "I bet that didn't pan out well in convincing Henry to come on by for a wee visit."

"It didn't, but it's been"—Saxon brushes his thumb over his mouth—"in our family since the late nineteenth century."

"Like a home base?" Josie asks curiously. "Do you belong to a secret organization, Saxon?"

The car slows to a stop. And then, "Something like that."

More unexpected honesty.

Something unfurls in my chest, an emotion I've never felt before, and I reach for his hand on instinct alone.

Crazy or not, I feel like I could take on the entire world, so long as he's with me. A team. An unstoppable unit. Saxon balances out my rashness. *Reckless*, he once called me.

I suppose he was right.

But he's not as cruel or savage as I once believed him.

"We'll get out here," he murmurs, squeezing my hand before letting go.

As one, we follow as he leads us down a gravel-paved path sandwiched between neatly mowed grass and untamed green ferns. The grounds are a treat for the eyes, a beautiful blending of acutely designed parterre gardens and wild foliage allowed to grow free of heavy hands and sharp shears. If I believed in fairy tales, then this would certainly be the one I wished to live in.

And then my jaw actually does drop when the medieval-styled manor house comes into view.

I stumble to a stop. "There's a moat."

Peter brushes past me, our duffel bag looped over one shoulder. "Bloody hell. Is that a *drawbridge*?"

"My brother had it installed as a joke about five years ago," Saxon murmurs, his fingers thrust deep into the front pockets of his joggers. "We all had a good laugh, and then we promptly locked him out for the night. Couldn't even swim over because these walls were built over five-hundred years ago. There's no scaling them when the bridges are up."

"Was it Guy you pranked?" Josie asks, skipping forward with her arms spread wide.

"No." A small pause. "My brother Damien."

"Oh, the mad one," she singsongs, turning back to us with a wriggle of her brows. "Or that's what I've heard, at least. But since I heard that *you* killed the king, and obviously you didn't, I'll withhold judgment on the Mad

Priest. For now."

Saxon mutters something that sounds suspiciously like, "You really shouldn't," before speaking louder, "Why don't you and Peter go ahead? Guy will be waiting in the Great Hall. I want to show your sister something."

Peter and Josie require no further encouragement.

Like the children they once were, they race each other over the wooden bridge. With a shove at the front door, which looks like heavy oak, they disappear inside. Only then do I turn to Saxon. "You're full of surprises."

His green eyes land on my face. "I have another to show you."

I lift a brow. "Oh?"

Removing his hand from his pocket, he holds it out for me to take, palm up. "After your grand reveal today, I thought this might interest you. Come with me."

He doesn't need to tell me twice.

As we walk, I take in the elaborate garden that spans from the back of the house to a building that looks like it was once used as the estate's stables. Tall and constructed of brick and exposed wooden beams, it's a more modest version of the Palace. Smaller, though not by much. My palm is sweaty within Saxon's when I murmur, "I'm sorry that I didn't tell you earlier . . . about the king, I mean."

"You've already apologized."

Rueful, I shake my head. "I know. *I know*. But I should have told you sooner. The world thought you did it and I never corrected the assumption."

"You would have been dead," he replies stiffly. "Correcting the world would have done nothing but put a mark on your head."

"Which has happened, anyway."

Saxon falls silent as he props open the door to the

building and releases my hand so I can pass him. I go willingly, only pausing once I'm inside.

Dark-paneled walls.

Slate flooring.

I turn in a semi-circle. "You've clearly done some restoration work in here. It's not at all what I expected."

"It's where we work." Saxon's hand claims its spot at the base of my spine. "Our headquarters."

Curious, I slant a look at him. "Are you admitting that you aren't just a pub owner? That you're actually as Josie said—a secret agent or something?"

He meets my stare with no hint of hesitation. "Surprise," he says on a husky rumble, and a chill skates down my spine. "You wondered about the car and the houses and the security system at the Stepney place . . . Josie wasn't wrong."

"And you work together with your brothers?"

"For better or worse."

"Interesting." I continue down the short hall, listening for Saxon's footsteps and realizing that he's so light on his feet that his stride barely makes a sound. "What did you want to show me?"

"It's right down here."

He motions for me to turn right when the hallway ends, and I slow, just a little, to trail his heels and survey the space around me. More dark walls and dark, polished floors and it's as though I've been thrust inside a maze. Had there not been any light from the diamond-paned windows lining the left side of the hall, I would be completely lost.

I watch Saxon's broad shoulders as he stops and waits for me to catch up. When I do, he taps his fingers on a fancy-looking panel, and shock riots through me when I realize that we're actually standing before a door. A *glass* door.

My jaw falls open. "Is that . . . is that a—"

"An ally to the queen," he answers, his voice completely impassive. "His name is Alfie Barker."

I stare, open-mouthed, at the man huddled in the corner of the room. His clothes are bloodied, his stare blank, and I barely manage to choke back a gasp. My fingers graze the door, the glass cool to the touch. "He can't see us."

It's not a question, and Saxon doesn't treat it as such. "A one-sided mirror. We can see in but he can't see us. He can't hear us, either, unless I want him to."

Which I don't.

Saxon doesn't say the words out loud, but I hear them, nonetheless.

Something that feels acutely like discomfort swirls in the pit of my stomach. I drop my hand back to my side. Rub my fingers along my hip, hoping to erase the bite of cold from the door. Loyalist or not, that man—Alfie Barker—looks . . . broken.

"You've beaten him."

Saxon's answering pause lasts so long that I look up at him. Only then do I realize he was waiting for eye contact. Slowly, softly, he confesses, "I told you that I have no heart, Isla."

I swallow, hard. "But you have choices. You could choose to treat him kindly instead of—instead of—" I wave my hand at the door, to the man ensconced inside who looks like he's been to hell and back.

The wave is all I can manage, and Saxon catches my hand in his. "You had a choice, too. With the king."

"I did." Lifting my chin, I add, "And maybe I made the wrong one but, in that moment, it felt right. It felt like the *only* option."

"Then maybe you can see that I feel the same with Barker." A tick appears in his jaw. "I had no choice. I've never had a choice. That was decided for me a hundred years ago, and it's either family or—*fuck*."

A hundred years ago? Is his secret organization with his brothers truly that old? A hundred years ago, life in Britain was normal. Unmarked by domestic unrest. But knowing what I do now—about my parents and this world that keeps so many secrets—I wouldn't be surprised if there's always been a group like the Priests who have wanted the royal family stripped of their crown.

Wanting to comfort him, and with my back to the cell imprisoning the queen's ally, I intertwine our fingers. "Clearly, I don't agree with your methods. But I don't . . . I'm still on *your* side, Saxon. I breathe, you inhale, and we both go up in flames, remember?"

His features splinter.

With relief? Gratitude?

Then, voice raspy, he says, "There's one more person I need to show you. Come."

With my heart lodged in my throat, I follow.

Five steps.

An erratic pulse.

Sweaty palms.

Saxon pauses at the room beside Alfie Barker's, his face turned away as he plugs a code into the panel on the wall. I don't know what to make of him keeping this all a secret—some government organization that he's never once hinted at—but I trust him.

I trust Saxon Priest with my whole heart.

The door cracks open.

"In here," he tells me.

"Are we . . ." I lick my lips, suddenly nervous. If the other room held a supporter of Queen Margaret, God knows who this one houses. "Are we supposed to go in, just like that?"

His stare ensnares mine. "I have you, Isla. Go in."

I listen, just as I did a week ago when he ordered me to get in his car. I obey, just as I did when he told me to slip into the confessional at Christ Church Spitalfields. I trust, just as I did after he saved me at The Octagon and brought me into his home like I belong with him.

Like I belong *to* him.

My steps are silent as I enter the room, and instantly, I note that it's empty.

Completely.

Utterly.

Empty.

"I don't under—"

A soft but still deafening *click* has me whipping around, mid-sentence.

Saxon peers back at me from the other side of the door, and this one—this glass isn't single-sided. I can see him, clearly, and I can hear every damning word falling from his scarred lips as I stand, shocked to my core, and he levels me with a truth I don't want to believe.

"Don't breathe for the enemy, Isla. Don't breathe for *me*."

The *enemy*?

Heart beating so frantically that I hear nothing beyond the roar in my ears, I rush to the door. "Saxon, let me out." I pound my fist on the glass, again and again and again. "There's a misunderstanding. Whatever this is, it's just a misunderstanding. Please, let me out. *Please*."

"I'm a spy for the Crown, and you killed the king." Green eyes spear me from behind the barrier separating us. "The only misunderstanding is that I didn't know sooner or you'd be dead already."

He steps away from the door.

Steps away from *me*.

"Saxon, let me go." I smash my fist into the glass. "*Saxon!*"

And then the door goes opaque, a double-sided mirror no more, and I scream. I claw at the glass. I cry for mercy.

Help doesn't come.

I breathe, you inhale, and we both go up in flames.

Liar.

Liar.

Liar.

Saxon Priest has turned me to ash and I've never been more alone.

CHAPTER 34

SAXON

I see only Guy's face when I enter the library.

Smug.

Victorious.

My boots land like anvils on the eighteenth-century Persian rug. I hear Damien call my name. Barely acknowledge Hamish when he toasts me with a celebratory cigar and a tumbler of whisky. I ignore Paul completely.

"Saxon, tell me. How is the king killer finding her new accommodations?"

It's the only thing Guy says, and he says it like he's discussing whether or not he needs to take a piss. But his blue eyes remain trained on me with a certain glint that threatens the last vestiges of my sanity. Any chance of him saying anything more is obliterated two seconds later when I snatch him by the shirt, haul him from the chair, and plow my fist directly into his face.

His head snaps to the side, a grunt pulling from his mouth.

Undeterred, I punch him again.

The left side, this time.

The audible crack of bone breaking shatters the room, followed only by Damien's urgent shout, but there's only rage. Rage that swarms my vision. Rage that has me snarling, "You fucking bastard," as I rear back, prepared to deliver another blow.

Strong hands grapple at my forearm at the final moment, swinging me around.

"Jesus," Damien grunts, shaking me, "*stop*."

I don't stop. "Let. Me. Go."

"Are you *mad*?" When I try again to jerk away, Damien tightens his unyielding grip around my chest. His blue stare, so eerily similar to Guy's, hardens with irritation. "What the fuck has gotten into you?"

"Isla Quinn."

At the rasped remark from behind me, I shove Damien off and turn on my heels to stare down my older brother. I want to tear him limb from limb. Carve out his dead, unforgiving heart and drop it at his feet. My chest expands with heavy, ragged breaths, and it's only a matter of self-restraint that keeps me from starting round two.

"I told you what would happen if you mentioned her again."

Guy digs his thumb into the cut below his left browbone. When his finger comes away with blood, I feel not an ounce of regret. Given the chance, I'd do it all over again. "And I told you what would happen the next time you hit me." Without even a grimace, he drags his bloodied thumb across his white shirt, leaving behind a trail of red. "But here we are, both of us still alive. You're losing your touch."

Baring my teeth, I lunge forward, only to have a heavy arm band across my stomach and limit my forward mobility. I swing my gaze to the side. "Get your hands off me."

Damien shakes his dark head, offering a bitter laugh. "So you can kill him? No chance."

I drag my elbow back, nailing him in the gut. "Better him than—"

"Who? Your precious Isla?" Guy taunts, stepping forward until he's so close that I could almost headbutt him. Almost. Just another few centimeters. *Come closer, dear brother.* "The big, bad Saxon Godwin has lost his mind over pussy. I never thought I'd see the day."

Out of sight, Hamish makes a gurgling sound, as though he's choked on his drink. "I don't think provoking the beast is the best course of action."

"He wants to provoke the beast," I growl, never taking my eyes off Guy's bruised face. The imprint of my fist from the other day has yet to fade, and I find a sick sense of satisfaction in that. "Because he thinks everyone should have to listen to his preaching."

"And here I was remembering our conversation," he drawls, "when you told me that, as the head of Holyrood, it's necessary that I give my opinion. So, here it is." He shoves his face close to mine, wrath dancing in his blue irises. "You cast the blame everywhere but on yourself. That scar you touch when no one is looking? You *earned* that. Pa knew how much John hated when he brought us along, but you wouldn't quit. Every bloody day you begged." His voice pitches higher, like a child's, when he says, "*Take me with you, Pa. I want to go with you.* And he told you, every time, that the two of you could get in trouble if he did."

Stiffening, I jerk my head back. "I'm not the reason he's dead."

"No, but you're the only reason why you're deformed."

"Jesus, Guy," breathes Damien.

But my older brother will not be deterred. His words flays me alive. And the rage I feel, it twists and contorts, metamorphizing into something so much worse—pure, undiluted hatred—when he opens his mouth for another round: "The world doesn't see you the way that you do. Ugly. Emotionless. You've done that to yourself."

"You have no idea what you're talking about."

"Don't I? You think you're mad at me and I can take it. I've dealt with shit you will never understand, felt worse pain than you could ever imagine. Broken bones don't even crest the surface." He taps his face, over the bleeding wound that I hand-delivered personally. "But you're no martyr. You locked her up. You looked her in the eye and betrayed her trust. Fact is, *you're* the reason why she'll hate you, and you can't fucking deal with it."

Anger tears through me, potent and visceral. It ignites my blood. Steels every one of my muscles until it feels as though I'm a living, breathing anomaly—human derived from granite. "Don't pretend you wouldn't have something to say if I let her walk free."

Coolly, his gaze flicks over me. "Don't pretend that you didn't choose the queen over her."

Prove it to your son that the Crown must always come first.

Pain registers in my chest.

A crippling, unwieldy sensation that drives my lungs inward.

As if sensing that I'm coming undone, Damien releases me and I stumble away from him, away from Guy, away from what's left of my family. It's been the three of us for so long that to tear at the fibers of our relationship feels like slicing the limbs from my body.

I chose Holyrood.

I chose the queen.

I chose us Godwins.

I'm barely aware of grabbing the first object I see—a chair, dating back three centuries—and hurling it across the room. It crashes against the wall, splintering upon impact. I see nothing but red. The red of my father's eyes when he begged me to look at him. The red of the king's ring, just before he slid the knife behind my ear and scoured my flesh. The red of my own blood, now, as shadowed recognition hits that I've shattered glass.

Crystallized shards cling like teardrops to my butchered skin.

"*Jesus*, someone get me the kit. I'll clean him up." *Damien*.

"And here we've always thought you were the unstable one, Damien." *Paul*.

"Everyone, out." *Guy*.

My voice booms over the din: "No."

"If I don't sew you up, we'll be standing over your dead carcass by midnight."

Ignoring the blood dripping from my palms onto the prized Persian rug, I look at Damien. "I'll do it myself."

"Absolutely, fucking mental," grunts Hamish, shaking his head. "It must run in the family. Not a sane one in the whole lot of ye."

Nostrils flaring, I ignore him too. "No one pays Isla a visit but me."

The lot of them all exchange wary glances, but it's Guy who speaks up. "You have two choices here: death or imprisonment. She's a traitor."

Is she? Or was her assassination of the king only a symptom of the debilitating anger stirred deep within her after her parents were murdered? She turned to fire and I turned to ice, and it's that ice that's been my constant companion for twenty-five years. I conned her into that prison cell like the coldhearted bastard I've always been. And she... She was all too easy to manipulate with her trusting gaze and the eager way with which she'd followed me, as though willing to bend to my every whim.

Am I to call you boss, now? she asked me, days ago.

If only I'd known then what I know now—that I've always been trouble, a true Godwin, and that whatever heart I do own has been wired, over decades' worth of subjugation, to spurn every ounce of warmth that comes my way.

I captured a warrior and dragged her into the darkest pits of hell.

"No one," I repeat softly, with a hard edge that will not be defied, "but me."

CHAPTER 35

ISLA

I've been encased in darkness for an eternity.

"Hours," I whisper to myself, staring up at the ceiling from where I'm sprawled out on the cold slate floor. "It's only been hours." I think.

More likely than not it's been less than a day.

Without artificial light, without even a single window, there's no sense of up or down. I could be splayed out on my stomach, my nose grazing the dusty floor, and I wouldn't know the difference.

I know that I stopped screaming Saxon's name after my voice went hoarse.

I know that Alfie Barker could hear every one of my pitiful cries because he shouted for me to shut the hell up right around the time hopelessness became a suffocating shroud and I sank to the ground.

My shins and kneecaps are bruised from posturing before that door, as though if I begged, however silently, that help might come.

That I might be saved.

It's only taken hours inside this miserable cell for me

to recognize the truth: Saxon Priest tricked me, manipulated me, and then he left me to die.

Bastard.

Rolling onto my side, I push onto all fours and crawl toward the shared wall between my cell and Alfie Barker's. To keep my healing wound clean, I drag my sleeve down over my palm and offer up a silent plea that I won't contract an infection. The crown of my head bumps the wall first, and I twist immediately, planting my arse on the floor and my back against the stone.

At this point, I have nothing left to lose.

"Alfie." A small pause. "*Alfie*, I know you can hear me."

"Sod off," comes his aggravated reply.

Admittedly, I'm desperate enough not to care that he's being a complete wanker. If I find myself locked in this prison for more days yet, I'll be ten times worse than he'll ever be. "How long have you been here?"

"Didn't I tell you to piss off?"

"It's a courtesy I'll allow since you look like absolute hell."

"How gallant of you to say so."

Ignoring the residual ache in my stiff legs, I drape my wrists over my bent knees. Peer out into the pure blackness that envelops the cell. "Have you been fed? Watered?"

Nary a pause before his sarcastic retort filters in through what I suspect are the ceiling ducts: "If I were a plant, I would be a cactus on its last leg. I piss in one corner, shit in another. Any other pertinent details you want to know before I go back to wishing I were dead?"

"Yes. Why are you *really* here?"

I tilt my head, listening for any sort of response from my fellow inmate. A tiny sliver of me—the indestructible sliver that always seeks out the good in people—believes that this is somehow a test, that Peter and Josie will be waiting for me with open arms as soon as I'm set free.

The rest of me prays that my siblings are simply alive. *Don't go there. Don't you dare think that way.*

"Alfie?" I try again.

Then, finally, "I had orders to kill the queen."

My back goes ramrod straight. "Orders? Orders from whom?"

I can practically see him shaking his head when he admits, "I don't know and, truthfully, I didn't care. My wife is dead—last year's riot on Easter—and I just . . . I just—"

Sobs fill my cell, wrecked and tormented, and I turn onto my knees and place one hand against the roughened stone wall. "Alfie." More sobs, this set louder and tinged with sorrow. "*Alfie*, you mustn't cry. Do you hear me? If you want to—"

"If I want to *what*?" he expels on an unmistakable water-logged exhale. "Survive? I'm lucky that I'm alive! And you know who'll suffer if I do die? My two little girls. They'll be the ones to suffer, not me."

The same fate will meet Peter and Josie, I know that all too well. But I hope . . . Well, I hope that the two of them are stronger together. *Where are they now?* I've asked myself that question no less than twenty times since being trapped in this cell and, like every other instance, I suppress the bad, lurking thoughts and place them in a mental box with an impenetrable lock.

First I need to escape.

Then I can go about saving them.

"Whoever you had orders from," I say, my brain working overtime as I run through the beginnings of a hazy plan, "would they realize you've gone missing?"

"Are you asking if they'll save me? Or if they'll save

you, considering that you shot the king?"

"The two aren't mutually exclusive." I swallow, tightly. "We must help each other, Alfie. However we can."

I expect Barker to issue another derisive rejection. But even as I strain my ears, listening for the increasingly familiar timbre of his nasally voice, there's no further activity from his side of the wall. *Dammit, Barker.* Another moment of silence passes, and then yet another, until concern slams into me. There's nothing in this cell that could inflict self-harm—I've checked what feels like every nook and cranny for a weapon I might use to escape—but that doesn't mean he hasn't found another, more sinister, method to get the job done.

Like bashing his head on the wall and ending his misery.
Oh, God.

Still on my knees, I bang a closed fist against the stone. "Alfie, think rationally. Do you hear me? Whatever you're feeling, it'll get better. It *must* get better. We've spent our lives fighting for this and you can*not* give up now."

"He hasn't."

At the familiar, dark-pitched voice, I swing my gaze toward where the door is vaguely located—only to spot Saxon standing there. As it was when we first entered the hallway, the two-sided glass is crystal clear, quite literally, which means that even if I didn't want to see his blasted face ever again, I'm not given the luxury.

The overhead lights flicker on as I push to my feet, not bothering to wipe the grime away from my joggers or the betrayal from my heart.

"Have you come to kill me, then?" I ask, not the least bit flippantly.

"Not quite." Saxon's expression doesn't so much as twitch, but he does move his foot against something on the floor. It's only then that I realize he's brought me a tray of food. "I prefer other methods of intimidation. Starving my victims tends to lessen the fun of stealing every one of their secrets."

"How unfortunate for you, then, that I'm all out of those." Kicking my chin up, I stare him down over the slope of my nose. "The same can't be said for you, can it, Saxon Priest?" The straight set to my shoulders falters as a staggering thought hits me. "Is that even your real name or have you lied about that too?"

When his only answer is to avert his gaze, I wrap my arms around my middle and hold on tight. It's either that or cry, and I refuse to shed a single tear for this man. At least, not any more tears than I already have. And certainly not while he can bear witness to their existence.

Even so, I can't silence the bitter laugh that climbs my throat any more than I can the hostile retort that leaps free: "I shouldn't be surprised. You've done nothing but lie from the start. Once again, I've unveiled everything there is to know about myself. Willingly. Because I trusted you. Meanwhile, it was all a ploy—"

His fist connecting with the glass has me damn-near jumping out of my skin.

"I turned you away," he snarls, his scarred mouth pulling angrily, his bruised knuckles flush with the door. "I'm no hero, Isla. I've never claimed to be one. But don't you dare fucking say that I welcomed you with wide open arms."

As though the barrier doesn't even exist, I march forward and jab a single finger into the glass. If it weren't there, I hope I'd puncture his good-for-nothing heart. "No, let me rephrase that for you—you wanted to *use* me. Not for my body, as I expected, but for information." My lips turn up in a thin, dangerous smile. "You promised to steal every piece of me—to, what did you say?" I snap my fingers. "Oh, yes. *To fill every broken and misshapen part of you*. Do you feel better now? Do you feel anything but *hollow* for proving the world right? That you're nothing but a savage, coldhearted—"

"*I feel lost!*" he roars, so forcefully that I actually stagger back. His chest heaves, expanding sharply. The tension in his harsh face remains tragically visceral. "You've had five years to walk alone. Try doing so for your entire bloody life."

"Saxon . . ."

"*No.*" Despite the glass, I feel the anger radiating from him. Pulsing, threatening, gathering tangibility like a whip bound to flay trembling flesh. "You want me to *unveil* myself? Then I will, and you'll see"—his voice catches, a vulnerable crack in his icy veneer—"you'll see that you should have stayed far away from me. I don't inhale, Isla. I consume, I devour, and then I destroy whatever's left."

Nerves eat away at my stomach as I rub my dry lips together. "I won't allow myself to be frightened by you."

An acrimonious smile curves his mouth. "Oh, yes. Because you've killed the king, you think that you can take on the world." He drops his voice to a sardonic whisper. "Your night terrors would prove otherwise."

I rear back, hurt. "I told you that in confidence—not to have it thrown back in my face."

"Christ, you are so"—he rakes his fingers through his hair, tugging sharply on the thick strands—"so incredibly *naïve*. This is war, Isla, and we are not on the same team. And even if I had the choice to jump ship and stand by your side, I . . . I—"

"You *what*? Just say it." I wave my hands at him, frustration turning my tone merciless. "Whatever you want to say, just *say* it!"

"I would still choose the Crown over you."

In that moment, I learn the true meaning of self-loathing.

Oh, how I wish I could remain strong and impassive and rigid. Like stone, like *him*. But I'm the same girl who cried after losing her parents and I'm still the same woman who lies in bed each night, discovering new circles of hell for knowing that her actions have led to hundreds, if not thousands, of deaths.

Tears bleed to the surface.

I feel them and do nothing to wipe them away.

Sometimes warriors cry, too.

When I blink to clear my vision, Saxon has twisted around. His shoulders are broad, and his back tightly muscled, and do I disgust him *that* much that he can't even bear to look at me? I ought to tell him to take his stupid food and toss off, but I find myself standing in place, unable to move, because this man—this cold, cruel man—should not have the opportunity to ignore me like I don't exist.

He stuck me in this cell.

He abused my trust to satisfy his own motivations.

While I can understand that we aren't on the same side, I would have thought—I *do* think—we are so much more than our divided beliefs on the royal family.

And then, so softly that I almost miss the words, he says, "I was eight when I learned my lesson." Something in his tone prompts a shiver down my spine, and instead of stepping away, I move closer. Because I'm a glutton for punishment, for him, with no hopes of recovery, it seems. "The king made sure of it."

"I don't understand."

"No, you wouldn't." He turns, only slightly, but it's enough to reveal the contours of his profile. The dark, heavy brows. The crooked, broken nose. The misshapen, scarred mouth. Vicious. Beautiful. And, until only hours ago, *mine*. "Your hatred for John started later but mine, it was born in terror." His lids flutter shut, like he's frozen in time, seeing whatever it is that devastated him. His powerful frame shudders. "I used to beg my father to let me attend to the king with him. Holyrood was in our blood. Has been since our ancestor saved a prince back in the nineteenth century. From birth, I knew that my life's mission was to protect the royal family."

Holyrood . . . the name is unfamiliar, but my gut tells me that it's the government organization. The secret, spy one that Josie first guessed in teasing before he himself confirmed it.

With me locked inside this cell.

I force the bitterness down before it chokes me to death.

"And my father," he continues on a rasp, "he was never the sort to tell anyone no. Princess Evangeline was dead, and the king's sanity balanced on a tightrope made of steel knives. But still I begged and still Pa brought me." His lids flick open and he twists his head to pin those eerie green-yellow eyes on me. "They argued from the start. Angry words that made me wish I were anywhere else but in that room. I said nothing, barely breathed. It wouldn't have mattered if I'd made all the noise in the world because John, he—*Christ*."

My throat works with a rough swallow. "You're alive."

"What?"

"It's what I tell myself," I say, tangling my fingers before me, "when the anxiety spikes. *I'm alive.*"

The chiseled line of his jaw stiffens. "I don't have anxiety."

"Then why are your hands trembling?"

As if in doubt, Saxon splays his palms open and lifts them to chest-level. Even from where I stand, there's no mistaking their visible tremor. Slowly, as though embarrassed by his body's betrayal, he curls those lean fingers inward and clenches them into fists.

"You're not a block of ice, Saxon, no matter how much you might wish that you were." I keep my tone level, though it's a struggle to sound unaffected. In the deepest part of my heart, I want to beg for him to open this door—not to escape, but so that I might wrap my arms around him and soothe his battered soul. *Pitiful, absolutely pitiful.* "It's human to feel."

"Until you, it was never a problem."

"That's not fair." Frustration restricts my lungs, squeezing tight. "You can't throw that accusation at my feet, like it's my fault that you aren't . . . that you aren't some emotionless robot!"

"Bloody hell, Isla, I didn't know what I was missing!" He storms toward my prison cage, not stopping until his hot breath mists the door, he stands so close. His eyes are turbulent, wild. "I drowned every bit of me that day. He held me down. Kept me fucking strapped to that chair while my father watched, utterly *useless* to save me."

Heat, the sort that always foreshadows the arrival of something bad, warms my skin to a feverish pitch. "What did he do?"

"He branded me."

"I-I don't understand. How—where—?"

His fingers drift north to find the shell of his ear before tracing the sensitive flesh behind his lobe. *Exactly where he flinched when I touched him, days ago.*

My heart thunders as he husks, "There's a certain level of fear that comes with pain, no matter the age. Broken bones. Torn ligaments. But there's something to be said about when you realize, even at a young age, that power is the most frightening thing of all. The king's power kept my father silent. The king's power meant I would not have gotten away with fleeing, if I'd even had the chance. And then the king turned the power he wielded into a lesson by carving my Holyrood code into my skin."

A horrified gasp escapes me before I can smother the sound.

"Pa was dead within months," Saxon continues, without outward inflection, dropping his hand to his side. "We suspect on John's order but we'll never know for certain."

"How could you"—I shake my head, trying to find the right words for a situation that is all so *wrong*—"how could you stay working for that man, knowing what he did to you? What he did to your father?"

"Because Paris showed me a different type of fear." He runs his tongue along the ragged perimeter of his upper lip. "For our safety, we were exiled. Whether that was the actual truth or not mattered little. We had nothing. We *were* nothing. Begging for scraps, stealing whatever we could. It was brutal. Hopeless. Holyrood sent us money, but it never went as far as it should have, not with Mum sick and hospital bills eating every last quid we had."

Realization spreads through my veins like liquid truth. "So you wanted power. Returning to Holyrood gave you that."

He holds my gaze, never once looking away. "I wanted a life where death sat around every corner."

"Why?" I demand, flushed with confusion. "Why in

the world would you want that for yourself?"

"It was the only time that I didn't feel numb."

Until you.

He doesn't say the words out loud, but I hear them anyway. Stark and raw and *real*.

My lids fall shut.

There is so much to say and yet nothing can overrule one single, sobering fact: Saxon Priest did not choose me. No, he chose the life that he's always known, the life that lets him cling to the shadows forever.

And those shadows, they'll swallow me whole.

"If you hurt Peter or Josie . . ." I open my eyes, letting him read the threat raging within me. "I will murder you, even if I have to claw myself out of this hellhole first."

His troubled green eyes search my face. "Won't you beg?"

"Like Barker has for days?" I ask, never severing eye contact. "No, I won't make that mistake."

He clutches the back of his neck, frustration engraved in the movement. "Just—"

"I won't make this easy for you." Planting my hands on the cool glass, I hold my ground. Hold myself from breaking down, again. *Don't you dare shed a tear.* "You made your choice, same as I did. Holyrood or me. Your family or me. I don't blame you. I can't even fault you. But I'll be damned if I roll over and fit neatly into your plans. If I'm to die, then you'll do it."

"*Fuck!*"

The curse explodes from his mouth like cannon fire, startling me, but not more than the shocking way he violently pummels a fist into the wall beside the door. I can't see his knuckles, nor the unlikely damage he's wrought on the stone itself, but there's no mistaking the emotion that shatters his expression.

Good.

I hope he feels exactly as I do: hopeless, ruined, *broken.*

Coolly, I tilt my chin toward the tray that he left abandoned on the floor. "And take that with you," I tell him, stepping away from the door, "I'm not hungry."

Fury winds its way down his powerful limbs as he glowers at me. "You need to eat."

"I would prefer to starve."

And then I turn my back on the man who I once thought would be my destiny. Or maybe he still is—after all, his will be the last face I see before I die.

CHAPTER 36

SAXON

"You've a death wish coming here, you know that?"

"When doesn't he?" Hamish snorts derisively as he shuts the office door behind us.

I slide a hard look toward the Scot, then another to Marcus Guthram, the Metropolitan's police commissioner. The only child to a former Holyrood agent, Guthram shouldn't know anything about our world—per organizational guidelines—but Guthram Sr. was never one to follow the rules. In a twist of fate, having the commissioner in our back pocket has been an ace that's benefited us more times than not. When he's not fucking us over, that is.

Without prompting, I drop a stack of banknotes onto his cluttered desk.

"There's nothing I can do about what happened at Queen Mary." Tone laden with exaggerated pity, the look he throws the green is greedy. Utterly famished. He clears his throat. "There were witnesses."

Setting a duffel bag down by our feet, Hamish rolls one bulky shoulder.

I nudge it to the side with my boot. "They haven't

released the survivor's name, which means either you're withholding information or—"

"I wouldn't," Guthram interjects swiftly. His dark eyes dart to the money again, reminding me, as if I've forgotten, that Marcus Guthram recognizes only one currency: financial gluttony. "You know I wouldn't do that."

"But you have." Leaning forward, I rest my knuckles on the desk, effectively blocking his only escape route. "And now," I murmur, my voice eerily pleasant, "we have Damien on house arrest."

"That wasn't—I mean, I didn't plan for—"

Idly, I trace a finger over King John's face on the banknote, waiting out Guthram's panicked sputtering. When he finally dissolves into uncomfortable silence, I take the opportunity to skim my thumb over the money. Fifty-thousand quid. Guthram tracks the taunting caress like an addict.

He's so transfixed, he notices too late that I've withdrawn a lighter from my trousers.

"Oy, now." Hands up, palms facing me, he straightens in his chair. "Priest, let's not be hasty."

I flick the spark and watch the flame flicker to life. It teases the crisp corner of the stack, turning the edges a murky brown.

"*Jesus*," Guthram breathes, the flickering flame reflected in his pupils, "you're absolutely mad."

"You have two options." Grabbing the chair beside me, I draw it backward. Its feet scrape the floor with a pained whine. The flame continues to dance, turning King John into bitter smoke. And when my ass hits the seat, it's in sync with a squirming, desperate Guthram, whose frantic stare never leaves the burning money on his desk. On an apathetic murmur, I continue, "You'll tell me everything you know or—"

"You can't just be bursting in here and throwing out demands! I won't stand for it."

This negotiation is not his to control. And if he hasn't yet realized that I don't broker deals with traitorous bastards, then he will. Immediately.

"Take the money I'm offering, or you'll find yourself so deep in the Thames, your body will never be recovered."

The commissioner hisses through his teeth. "If my father found out that you've threatened me, he—"

"Your father has been locked in an asylum for the better part of a decade," I finish, removing my thumb from the spark. The acrid scent of burning paper permeates the room. "And by your own doing."

"Thanks to Holyrood, he lost his bloody mind." His dark eyes flit to Hamish, as if looking for support. When the Scotsman merely plucks at his shirtsleeve, blatantly ignoring the commissioner, Guthram visibly steels his shoulders. "It was either an institution where he'd have some modicum of freedom or putting the man out of his damn misery."

Liar.

My lips curve in a humorless smile. "We both know the only reason that your old man is still breathing is because you aren't done collecting his pension."

"That isn't—"

"And I allow it to happen," I cut in, speaking over him, "so long as you're useful. So, let me repeat your choices, Commissioner. Tell me what you know or you'll be taking a permanent dip in the Thames. What will it be?"

Defeat chases away the last strains of Guthram's arrogance, as I knew it would, when he passes a trembling hand over his angel-white hair. "There were no survivors.

No one made it to the hospital"—a small, monumental pause that drives me to the edge of my seat—"and no one lived long enough to give us your name."

What?

If I killed everyone, then . . . "Who."

It's not a question.

"I wish we knew." Tugging open a drawer, Guthram pulls out a folder and sets it on the desk. "See here."

Photographs scatter, their glossy paper refracting the overhead light.

Not even the slight glare can hide the images for what they are: namely, me mowing down every loyalist at The Octagon. Picture after picture, death after death. And not just of me but of Isla, too. Her fight with Ian Coney for the knife. Her strangling him with her bare hands.

Every picture has been captured from a high vantage point.

The galleries.

Someone had watched the mayhem unfold from The Octagon's second or third balconies.

Bloody fucking hell.

Over my shoulder, Hamish curses so loudly that I wouldn't be surprised if the president of the United States heard him, too, clear across the Atlantic.

"You didn't think to come to me with this?" Behind my rib cage, the organ that's failed to beat for decades pounds frantically. *Anxiety,* Isla called it two days ago. I wouldn't admit it then, not out loud, but Christ, I feel it now. Dread clogs every airway as I fight for oxygen. Nearly half the photographs have Isla in them, bloodied, struggling, her beautiful face contorted with fear.

Each one leaves me feeling more nauseated than the last.

And each one reminds me, once and for all, that I will always be a savage, coldhearted bastard.

"I'm going to bury them where they fucking stand."

A thread of air rushes past Guthram's lips. "We don't know who it is."

My gaze jerks north. "What did you say?"

Clearly aware that he's treading a fine line, Guthram fingers the starched collar of his police uniform. "The photographs . . . They're being sent anonymously."

"Give me more than that, Commissioner, or I'll bury you first."

"They've arrived on our doorstep every morning for five days now," he mutters hastily, flicking a finger toward the photographs. Copies of the originals, I'm sure. "No fingerprints. No notes. Whoever is sending them wants you behind bars, Priest, which means you *really* shouldn't be here right now."

Hamish drops his big body into the chair beside mine. "I find it unlikely that ye don't have any real leads."

"You think any of this looks good on me, MacDonald?" The commissioner steeples his fingers on the desk, pointedly angling his chin. Scorn practically seeps from his pores. "It makes me look *inept*. Five days and we've no more leads than we did that first morning. I have one bastard angling for my job and now the country's most wanted criminal is seated across from me. And there's not a damn thing I can do about any of it."

"You could."

Guthram's shoulders twitch. "What the hell are you going on about, Priest?"

With one last glance at the photographs from The Octagon, I brush them out of the way. *Focus, man.*

I've done nothing else but lose my focus for the last

forty-eight hours.

Six mealtimes of Isla refusing every tray of food I've brought to her cell. Two days without her taking even the smallest sip of water. She's hurtling toward dehydration, if she isn't there already. No matter how she gives me her back when I step before the cell, with her clearly determined to pretend that I don't exist, there's no denying the yellow pallor of her skin and the delicate blue veins which appear ever more visible.

If she dies . . .

Holyrood will celebrate a job well done. Queen Margaret will breathe a sigh of relief, knowing that her father's killer has been stripped of this world. And I—*I* . . .

For the sake of self-preservation, I slam the door on that mental black hole and return to my mission.

Reaching down, I nab the straps of the duffel bag resting by my feet. It's heavy. Weighted down with enough money to sway even the most faithful. It goes without saying that Marcus Guthram has not a sentimental, loyal bone in his body.

The bag lands with an audible *thunk* on the commissioner's desk, who only blinks warily. "Jesus, man. Who are you wanting me to kill?"

"He's already dead."

"Already dead?" The man's brows knit together. "If we're talking resurrections, I'm no miracle-maker. And you won't be catching me digging up any graves. Not for any amount of money."

"He's wanting to see William Bootham's body."

"*Bootham*? You mean the reverend who was murdered this week?" Slack-jawed, Guthram's head swings from Hamish to me. "Hold on. You're wanting me to bring you to the Coroner's Court?"

Simply, resolutely, I answer: "Yes."

Guthram blanches. "Are you out of your goddamn mind? I can't just *waltz* you in there, as though—"

"I'm offering you your only lifeline." Gripping the bag's strap, I tug, upending all the money we carefully laid inside not even two hours ago. Stacks of banknotes spill across the desk. "You get me in, and this becomes yours. Or you don't and we both know what comes next."

"Doesn't seem like a difficult choice, Commissioner. Life or death." Hamish offers a sinister grin. "Had yer father still had his wits about him, I'm sure he would have offered the same deal. Especially after he learned what it is ye do with his pension."

Guthram pales beneath his already alabaster skin. "MacDonald, I'm warning you—do not go there."

The Scot unfolds from his seat, grabs the burnt stack, and drops the money in the commissioner's lap. "Ye're a bought man, Guthram," he murmurs tightly, "willing to sway with any direction of the wind, so long as ye come out richer. I'm sure it's easier to lock away dear, old Papa than it is to face the facts: ye betrayed us all, and if it were up to me, ye'd already be swimming with the fish."

By the time we reach the Coroner's Court in Poplar, the street is bathed in the first stretches of dusk. Under the setting sun, the building's brick façade glows orange while the diamond-paned windows reflect the pink cotton candy clouds dotting the sky.

Beautiful. Picturesque, even.

A sight that William Bootham will never appreciate again, thanks to me.

Ignoring the foreign tightening in my chest, I resettle the Met-issued custodian helmet on my head. Narrow my eyes on Guthram fumbling with the lock code. "Faster, Commissioner."

He shoots me a tight-lipped smile. "We're here after hours, just as you wanted. Give me a moment."

The longer he takes, the more likely that we'll be caught, even dressed as we are in borrowed Metropolitan patrol uniforms. After exchanging a look with Hamish, I bite down on a harsh retort and resort to counting every second that passes. If it weren't for Guthram's penchant for following the trail of money, I'd be concerned that he's playing us for a set of fools.

Or maybe he still is.

After all, he's the reason why Damien faces a future of house arrest within the Palace's sixteenth-century walls.

"Ah, there we go," the commissioner exhales on a grateful breath.

Cracking the door open, he shoves it wide and steps through. The hairs on the back of my neck stand tall as I follow closely, with Hamish taking up the rear. The foyer offers nothing more than an entryway table set off to the side and an accompanying solitary chair. No check-in points. No signs of artwork or décor. The atmosphere is morbid, and that has nothing all to do with the fact that we're standing in a house of the dead.

"This way." Guthram waves us forward.

When Hamish's heavy tread echoes behind me, I throw up a hand and look back at him. "Watch that door."

He nods, his stride falling short. "Done."

The commissioner spares Hamish a halted glance before turning to lead me down a hallway. Picture frames hang on the beige-painted walls. Almost all boast botanical flower renderings, as though it's the coroner's hope to soothe the distraught friends and families of the deceased.

Henry Godwin never made it to a coroner.

Never made it into a cemetery, either.

Like all the Godwins before him—at least those whose fates were tied to the Crown—Pa was cremated, his ashes scattered over the historic remains of Holyrood Abbey in Edinburgh. In death, he returned to the same place as his forebearers.

Ghosts, the lot of us, for over a century now.

For a split second in time, though, I came alive.

Isla Quinn, the king killer, did that. She removed the cloak of ice from my shoulders and wrapped me in an embrace so hot, it's a miracle my skin didn't singe. And then I backstabbed her, chose the queen and my loyalty to Holyrood instead.

If I'm to die, then you'll do it.

A sharp breath immediately has me inhaling the pungent scent of formaldehyde. Slowly, my eyes adjust to the dimmed lighting as we enter the morgue. Stainless-steel wall vaults line both sides of the room, enticing me to find Bootham within one of them, but there's no time to waste. I head straight for the computer in the back-right corner of the room.

"Priest," Guthram protests, following, "what the hell are you doing?"

I don't answer.

Even though tech is my younger brother's domain, my movements are practiced, efficient. The flash drive I've brought with me plugs into the monitor and, seconds later, I'm completely bypassing the need to enter a password to access the coroner's database. Another one of Damien's genius inventions. Ironic, maybe, that I'm using it now just as my brother had, months ago, to anonymously infiltrate Westminster. Both times, Guthram witnessed all. This time, I'll blow his brains out if he tries anything even remotely suspicious.

"I thought you wanted to see the body."

I do, and I will, but only once I have the coroner's notes at my fingertips.

It takes me twenty seconds to find William Bootham's file, and another forty-three to absorb its entirety:

Legal Name: William Aurelius Bootham
Sex: M
DOB: 13/04/1973

Any lingering doubt I had that the priest's death and the loyalists from The Octagon are related disappears the moment I come across the previously unmentioned cause of death: asphyxiation. Exactly how Isla killed Ian Coney.

"*Fuck.*"

I tab down with the mouse.

Aside from the handprint around Bootham's neck, there were no other visible signs of struggle. His clothes remained intact, even after his transport from the unknown scene of the crime to Isla's flat in Stepney. No traces of DNA left behind, either around Bootham's neck—aside from the size of the hand prints themselves—or beneath his fingernails.

There's nothing but a dead man abandoned in an innocent woman's flat. But it's enough. Enough for a trial, enough for a conviction, enough to see Isla behind bars for the rest of her life.

Guthram steps beside me, eyeing the monitor over my shoulder. "Well," he says, almost flippantly, "you've come all this way to, what? Sift through medical records?"

With my hand hovering over the mouse, my heart hammers so ruthlessly that I feel its twin echo in my temples, in my lungs, in every limb and artery that was dead until she strolled into The Bell & Hand and threw my carefully orchestrated life into chaos.

You know what you have to do.

I don't allow myself the chance to think twice—with a stroke of the keyboard, I delete Bootham's file from record.

Guthram gasps. Grips my shoulder. Tugs, hard, but not hard enough to move me even a millimeter. "*Priest,*" he hisses, "what the *fuck* do you think you're doing?"

"Making you earn your thousands."

"Earn my . . ." The commissioner mirrors my step away from the computer, remaining in front of me. His dark eyes flash, but not from fury. Panic. It oozes from his frame, warps his features, and cloaks his voice. "The priest's funeral must be any day now, and you've j-just *deleted* his autopsy report!"

"Demand another be done."

"Demand *another?*" Guthram gapes at me, so shocked that I manage to skate around him, heading for the vaults to my right. "There will be *questions.* Questions I won't have a bloody chance in hell of answering. The coroner will be suspicious. I could lose my post. And that's saying nothing about the fact that you're tampering with a case."

"If you want the money, you'll make it work."

"Who do you think I am? Fucking *God?*"

"Let me rephrase," I tell him, "if you want to keep breathing without the use of an oxygen tank, you'll make it work."

When I stop three rows away from the door, Guthram's feet grind to a halt. "Priest," he says, keeping his distance. "Priest, whatever you're planning to do, I wouldn't."

But I do.

The handle to Bootham's vault is cool to the touch as

I draw it open. There's the quiet *clink* of metal scraping open, and the immediate astringent scent that wafts up toward my nose as the priest is revealed. First, the top of his shorn, balding head. Then, his eerie, sunken eyes that have yet to be touched up by a mortician for his funeral. They peer back at me, lifeless but somehow still condemnatory.

You did this to me, they seem to say. *You killed me.*

And I did.

Every time that I stepped into his place of worship, I collected little pieces of his life, shard by shard. I lied to him. Stole from him. And now . . . And now, *this*.

"I'm sorry, Father," I whisper, for him—the dead man.

Bending down, I lift the hem of my trousers and remove Isla's knife from the leather holster cinched around my calf. The knife that I confiscated from her, just before we left my house in Camden, without her noticing. I hear Guthram's panicked footsteps approaching, but I ignore him. Bring the serrated edge of the knife to the calloused pads of my fingertips.

I cut myself, enduring the pinch of pain as my punishment.

And then I pick up Bootham's cold, limp hand, and smear my blood beneath his nails.

"Jesus, Mary, and Joseph," Guthram breathes from beyond my right shoulder, "You've lost your bloody mind. You. Have. Lost. Your. Bloody. Mind."

Except that it isn't my mind that I've lost, it's my soul, and I've lost it to a blond warrior who killed the king then demanded that I kill her next.

I look down at Bootham, fresh blood coating the ivory whites of his fingertips.

If I'm to die, you'll do it.

It seems that I can't.

CHAPTER 37

ISLA

Death lingers like an unwanted guest.

It sits in the empty pit of my stomach and on the cracked bed of my lips. It strains every one of my muscles as I debate the inevitable: accepting defeat. Quenching my thirst would give me strength. Eating would go a long way toward revitalizing my fatigued limbs.

But at what cost?

To then die at the hands of my lover, who hid everything that he is from me?

A spy. A loyalist. A man not adverse to putting his mission above all else, including me.

I told Saxon that I would rather starve, and I would, but this . . . I have never felt so drained as I do now. Emotionally, physically. Mentally, too. My mind is nothing but a foggy disarray of scattered thoughts.

In The Octagon, I prayed for him to save me.

Now, I hope for the opposite: I wish he would put me out of this godawful misery.

A bullet to the head.

A sharp twist of a blade to the heart.

Anything to end the sobering reality of being locked inside this cell for years to come.

Tapping into what's left of my reserve, I roll myself over onto my front. Curl my knees beneath me and tuck my hands under my forehead, a makeshift pillow. *Don't think of Peter. Don't think of Josie.* When I do, I cry. When I don't, I manage to float on the edge of darkness, resigned to my fate.

Isla Quinn, the king killer.

Click.

At the sound, my ears strain for the source.

Click.

A groan slips from my mouth when a sliver of florescent light hits the floor, directly beneath my nose.

Click.

Light-footed steps echo off the unforgiving slate, coming closer, closer still. I should defend myself, just as I did at The Octagon. Fight to be the last woman standing, no matter what. *Get up, get up, get up.* But when I try, my shoulders protest and my stomach cramps with hunger, and bloody hell, won't it *end?* The pain and the heartache—especially the heartache.

Warm fingers graze the ridged line of my spine before settling on my nape. To kill me? To strangle me as I did Ian Coney? The irony would be one for the books, and yet . . .

"Stop," I whisper, my throat so dry that the command breaks on the single syllable. Weak. Fragile. Running my tongue over the roof of my mouth, I try again. "Stop. Please."

Those fingers smooth into my hair, following the curvature of my skull. "I can't," a deep voice rumbles, staking me right in the heart with its ragged vulnerability, "I *can't.*"

A big hand repositions me onto my back, and this time, when I blink, there's enough light seeping into the cell from the hallway that Saxon's hard features are unmistakable—as is the shiny, metal pistol aimed directly at my head.

Oh, God.

A startled cry threatens to surface, and immediately I slam my eyes shut. Burrow my arms down by my sides like I've already been stuck in a narrow coffin and lowered into the earth.

How many more seconds until he pulls the trigger?

How long will consciousness last before the darkness consumes me forever?

The king lived only minutes before he bled out. I'd aimed for his torso, the largest surface area on a human body. Vengeance may have guided my mission but practicality dictated where I aimed. And, in that moment, as I stood by the window and observed the crowd gathered below to witness his speech, I gave no passing thought to the king's last moments.

How terrified he must have been.

Shot from what must have seemed like thin air. Assassinated before his only surviving child, after having already lost his first.

I have no doubt that this is better than what I deserve.

Karma served swiftly.

Unable to tear my lids open and stare down the barrel of the pistol, or the man wielding it, I move one hand, finding a part of his body. His calf, I think. Strong, muscled, even through the thin fabric of his trousers. I cling to him, seeking warmth to take away the ice in my blood.

"Just do it," I tell him, my voice quivering. "Kill me

and be done with it."

Metal touches my forehead, a chilled kiss of imminent death.

This time, there's no restraining the pitiful cry that wrenches itself from my soul. I choke on the sound, every ounce of strength vacating my body as reality sets in. In a matter of seconds, this will all be gone forever. Josie. Peter. *Him*, Saxon, the man who awoke something inside me and lit me on fire. I've never believed in the afterlife. I've never believed in much of anything, really, and now the alternative emptiness seems excruciatingly bleak.

The pistol skirts south, to the notch between my eyes, silently baiting me to open them.

I obey on instinct.

And then, so softly that I strain to pick up the individual words, he orders, "Reach for your knife."

"*What?*"

"We'll have two minutes to get you to the car. Maybe less." His pale eyes dart up, fixating somewhere behind me, before returning swiftly. In them, I see nothing but grim determination. "They're watching us now. Guy, Damien, the others. I know you're tired, sweetheart, but I need you to run for me. I need you to give me everything you have because if you don't—fuck, we don't have time for this."

Sweetheart. He called me *sweetheart*.

Pulse racing, my fingers tighten on his leg. Beneath, I feel the delineation of a leg holster, as well as the sharp edge of a blade. *My* blade. "Why aren't I dead?"

"This isn't the time—"

"*Why?*"

Unexpectedly, his weight falls forward, one hand planted beside my head, the other still gripping the pistol. He keeps it locked in place, cold metal to vulnerable human flesh. "Because," he husks out next to my ear, his voice so untethered, so raw, that I feel pressure building behind my eyes, "I've been a prisoner my entire life. I was born with shackles on my wrists, and centuries-old oaths contracted on my soul, and I won't have that for you. I *can't*. I need you to breathe, Isla. For you, for me." He swallows, roughly, and perhaps it's a trick of the light, but his unholy eyes glitter with what looks like unshed tears. Opening his scarred mouth, he adds, "For us and what could have been."

I choke on grief. "Saxon, then come with—"

He cuts me off with a calloused palm over my mouth. "No one leaves Holyrood, least of all a Priest. This is the way it has to be." His thumb caresses my cheek before he seems to catch himself. "Grab the knife and slice my forearm. Turn left down the hall and don't stop until you hit the woods. I'll be right behind you. Do you understand?"

Behind the weight of his hand, I nod.

I nod, even though I'm not sure I'll have the strength to do as he says. I nod, even though I suspect this will be the last time I ever see him, and even though he's kept me locked in this darkened cell for days now, my heart still calls to his.

Destiny.

Fate.

Whatever you want to call it, this is not how it was meant to play out between us.

Still, I don't disappoint him.

The moment he lifts his hand, I swipe the blade from the holster and thrust it toward him. A sharp jab to ward him off, followed by a wide arc that actually glances his golden skin. His lips pull back with an audible hiss—lips that I've kissed, lips that have kissed me—and then he drops sideways, as though I've shocked him.

It's an invitation to flee, and I seize it with both hands.

Get up. The second I scramble to my feet, black clouds roll across my vision. *Don't you dare fall!* On weak legs, I stumble to the right, like a drunk after a long night. Reach out a hand, as if expecting someone to stabilize me before I end up sprawled out all over again.

"Isla," Saxon growls from behind me, "*go.*"

Do or die trying.

Escaping the cell, I careen into the far wall and bite back a moan. *Faster, move faster!* I can hear Alfie Barker screaming for help. I want to turn, I want to save him, too, but then I hear the piercing sound of a siren, so eerily similar to the ones that play during a riot in London, and suddenly I'm sprinting for all that I'm worth.

Down the darkened hallway with the diamond-paned windows.

Run.

Down past a rickety stairwell that winds up to the first floor.

Run.

A gun explodes. My skin twitches at the sound, and I crash into the wall, instinctively twisting to look behind me with wild eyes, my knife poised to slash first and ask questions later. The dim hallway remains blessedly empty, and I—

Boom!

I take off again, not slowing down until I spot an old-fashioned door that must lead outside. But where it may have been clamped tight before, the lock now hangs loose from its hinge. *Saxon.* Only Saxon would have anticipated this escape and destroyed any obstacle standing in my way. Without hesitation, I fling open the door and am immediately purged from the darkness.

Stars twinkle like diamonds in the sky, and the full moon hangs heavy within the clouds, illuminating the wooden drawbridge extending over the darkened moat. It's a sight out of a fairy tale, beautiful and hair-raising, all at once.

On shaky legs, I run across, only to hear thundering footsteps behind me. *Shite!* Hilt in hand, I spin around, expecting Guy or the Mad Priest or another faceless spy assigned to take me out.

But it's Saxon who bears down on me.

The drawbridge trembles under the weight of his powerful frame; the moon above casts shadow over his hard features; and then his muscular arm loops around my waist as he hauls me into his embrace like some ancient warlord claiming his prize.

He carries me like a bride.

Like I'm *his* bride.

"I told you to run," he grunts.

"I *was* running."

"Not fast enough." He cuts through a small courtyard, enclosed by what looks like trimmed bushes, with me locked against his chest. He grips me so possessively that I barely bounce in his hold. "We have forty-five seconds."

"Until what?"

"Until Damien realizes I've blown the cameras to smithereens and they'll start blocking the road." When we clear an opening, I spy a car nestled within the trees, some five meters away. "You'll need to drive out," he says, "but I've already programmed the GPS to take you to where Josie and Peter are in Oxford."

Four meters.

Desperation controls my tongue when I beg, "Come with me."

Three meters.

"Don't stop driving," he replies instead, his breathing unlabored, despite the run, despite the fact that he's carrying me as if I weigh nothing at all, "no matter what you think you see."

Two meters.

"*Saxon*—"

"You're free, sweetheart." Stopping in front of the car, he lowers me to the ground. Snaps open the driver's side door and promptly nudges me inside. I'm so weak that I all but collapse in the seat, my energy zapped from that initial sprint. "Free of this life and free of Father Bootham. You don't have to worry."

Free of Father Bootham? But the man is already dead. Not by my hand, of course, but still *dead*.

"What did you do?" Dread pervades the rush of adrenaline when I clutch Saxon's thigh. "Saxon, answer me. *Please.*"

He ducks down, swiftly bending at the knees, so that we're at eye level. "I chose," he rasps, pressing a soft, devastating kiss to my mouth, "and I chose you."

Framing his face with my hands, I stop him from retreating. "But what did you *do*?"

His unholy gaze flickers between mine, once, twice, before he clasps my hands. Mine are sweaty, his cool to the touch. But I feel them trembling, as though he's seconds away from coming undone. Then he physically pulls back.

His absence hits me like I've been dunked in a frozen lake.

"You need to leave."

Violently, I shake my head. "Get in the car. Come

with me, dammit!"

His hand curves over the door frame. "The devil always collects his due, sweetheart, and I bargained everything I had on you."

Before I can edge out another word, he slams the door shut and the car—the car that should not be moving without my foot on the accelerator—shifts into gear, all on its own, and slowly takes off down the dark, tree-lined road.

Darting a glance to the rearview mirror, I spot Saxon standing there, with what looks like a remote control in his hand. He waits no more than a beat before dropping it to the ground and smashing his heavy boot down upon it. The car immediately jerks in response, as if the control has been revoked, and unexpectedly swerves to the right, toward a tree.

"Shite!"

Instinct has me latching onto the steering wheel and yanking hard to avoid collision. I manage, just barely, but my heart . . . my stupid, bloody heart is locked on what I've left behind.

The last I see of Saxon Priest are figures stepping out from the dense thicket to surround him. One catches him behind the kneecaps, nailing him down to the ground. Another grasps him by what looks like his shirt, hauling him forward across the dirt path. The thick wood gathering behind me insulates the scene after that, and a sob breaks from my throat.

What have I done?

CHAPTER 38

SAXON

Dulled pain registers in my hamstrings seconds before I hit the ground.

Familiar bodies circle me, men whose faces I've known for years, but are now silhouetted by splintered moonlight. They swarm like locusts, all frenetic energy and pulsing anger. I stare through them all, as if they don't even exist, and watch Isla's taillights fade into the pitch-black night.

She's gone, safe, and I'm—

"You helped her escape!" Roughened hands bunch the fabric of my shirt, jerking me forward. Thin nose. Hollow, weathered cheeks. Jayme Paul's pungent breath wafts over my face, whisky soaked. "What the hell were you thinking?"

The same as I'd thought when I found her, unconscious and curled on her side, in front of Buckingham Palace. *Nothing*. Nothing beyond an inexplicable need to see her safe—even if *safe* entails sending her far, far away from me.

The devil.

The monster.

The man who doesn't even deserve to kiss the ground she walks on.

When Paul, my father's old replacement, shakes me like I'm nothing but a rag doll, I clamp a warning hand around his wrist. "Let me go, old man."

"She killed the fucking *king*, you dimwit. The king!"

"She did, but she doesn't deserve to die."

"Doesn't deserve to die?" Startled astonishment flatlines Paul's rabid expression. With his fingers still clasping my shirt, he gapes at me, then at Jude and Benjamin, another of our agents, before visibly pulling himself together. "Did you hear that, lads? Apparently, Isla Quinn doesn't deserve what's coming to her, even though she murdered the one person we're sworn to protect."

"Utterly daft," Jude clips out.

Benji shakes his head. "You risked everything—our location, our mission, *each of us*—and for what? Half-rate pussy? Come off it, Priest, you're better than—"

The rest of his sentence hinges on silence when I lunge for him, practically taking Paul along with me, and undercut my throw to nail him in the chin. His head snaps backward; his body sways in place. Like any Holyrood agent, he's formidable, lethal, and instead of retreating, he grabs my arm and digs his thumb into the shallow flesh wound left behind by Isla's knife.

I see red.

"The big, bad Saxon Priest," he sneers, "taken down by a woman with a set of balls bigger than your own. Has your knob shriveled up too?"

"I don't advise playing that game with me, Benjamin."

His dark eyes glitter in the moonlight. "A game? This isn't a game. *You* helped her escape. You, a Godwin, a Priest, the foundation of this godforsaken agency. You betrayed the Crown, not me."

I smell the scent of whisky before I feel the telltale shape of a pistol on the nape of my neck. "Which is a crime punishable by death, according to Holyrood," Paul says, drawing the pistol north until it sits at the back of my head. A silent threat. One wrong move of his finger and my brains will paint the night red. *Boom.* "How many agents have you killed for this exact transgression, Priest? Can you even count them all?"

Only two.

A number lower than expected, considering how many of us have sworn to serve the royal family, all across the country. I don't regret much in life but them—Quill and Sanders—I do, still. Years later.

Tonight, the miscreant group of Holyrood spies, who have turned on the Crown, gains another reluctant member.

Me.

I don't know what love is. Not the sort of love, at any rate, that appears on television with heart-shaped boxes of chocolates or slow dances spent under the starry skies. What I feel is darker. Animalistic. The tightening sensation in my gut and the burn in my heart as though she's personally set fire to the organ. I understand stark possession. Frenzied desire, too. I understand that, with Isla, I'm driven by an unidentifiable motive that asks for nothing in return—not a favor given, nor a favor owed. All I know is that as I stand here now, with my life hanging in the balance, there's only relief swimming in my chest because she's *free*.

Free to live.

Free to breathe.

Free to find love with a different man, a better man, who's capable of sweeping her off her feet and buying the chocolates and the flowers and anything else she might ever want.

And that is *enough*.

It has to be.

Inviting death to the circle, I bow my head and drop one knee to the ground, then the other. Blood from my wound coats my sleeve. My pistol, the same one I've kept on me since returning from Paris, remains in my holster like dismissed sentry.

"Let's not pretend," I husk out, "that you haven't been waiting for this moment for years."

There's an audible swallow from Paul and the distant, familiar whine of the drawbridge from the main house lowering. No doubt whoever it is will be joining the hunting party—where I'm the only course ready to be served.

"You're mad, Priest. Utterly mad." The pistol jams into my skull, making my ears ring. "You broke the law. You committed a *crime*. Don't put any of that on me."

"I'm accepting my due, aren't I?"

"Your father would be disappointed in everything that you are," he grinds out, ignoring Jude and Benji, his attention trained solely on me. "He *died* for the Crown and here you are, spitting in his memory for a woman who is everything that we—"

A scream splits through the night.

Masculine. Infused with pain.

Loud, so loud and so close, that it echoes in my ears, slow realization subsequently dawning that I'm sprawled out on the ground with Paul's weight atop me. My chin slams into the dirt, coating my lips, the roof of my mouth.

Christ.

"Kill him," declares a familiar, gruff voice, "and I'll shove this knife straight into your heart and gut you where you stand."

Damien.

Grasping fistfuls of dirt, I shove Paul off me and roll onto my hands and knees. One glimpse of the older man reveals the blunt handle of a knife sticking out from his thick, flabby shoulder.

Stunned, my gaze snaps to my brother. "You stabbed him."

"Old bastard doesn't know how to die," Damien mutters, bending at the hip to rip the blade straight from Paul's back. Ignoring the man's anguished wail, Damien wipes the bloodied edge of the knife across his sleeve. Then, "Guy wants you out."

Are you in or out?

Guy had asked me that before. Holyrood or Isla. Him and Damien or Isla.

I choose her. Always, always her.

Climbing to my feet, I purposely show my back to Jude and Benji. Of all people for them to support, fucking Jayme Paul. "Naturally. The Crown must always come first."

Catching my sarcasm, Damien's blue eyes appear almost translucent under the cast of the moon. "He heard what you did about that priest, Bootham."

The muscles along my spine go taunt. "I did what I had to do."

"You're a dead man walking," my younger brother tells me, re-holstering the knife to his forearm, "a total liability."

I toss a look toward where the Palace is, behind the swath of trees. Like a king, it's obvious that Guy has sent Damien to do his bidding. "No one leaves Holyrood, not alive."

"Well, today is your lucky day, brother. You're allowed to leave—and not in a body bag."

"The catch?"

"You're banned from Holyrood. Persona non grata. And if you ever come back..." On the ground, Paul emits a soft groan, to which Damien lifts his booted foot and grinds it down on the wound. Hard and harder still, until Paul passes out cold. "You're dead."

CHAPTER 39

ISLA

The tears won't stop.

"You have until Loudwater to pull it together," I tell myself when I pass the exit for Iver Heath, some forty minutes outside of London.

Loudwater comes, Loudwater goes, and I remain an utter wreck.

Kilometer after kilometer, I'm plagued with the visual of Saxon, a man so composed and indestructible, being driven down to his knees.

Did they hurt him? Will his brothers throw him to the wolves as a traitor?

And the question that won't be silenced: *is he alive?*

"Please," I whisper, strangling the steering wheel, "please, *please* be alive."

It takes me another fifteen kilometers to accept the fact that I'm an emotional disaster who shouldn't be on the road. Foggy-headed and drunk on a debilitating cocktail of grief and adrenaline, I pull off the motorway at Stokenchurch and drift through the village until I spot a white-stucco pub with a large car park.

Seeking privacy, I back the car beneath a tree with a great canopy of branches.

I want to rage, to harness the fury that's propelled me forward for years now. But it's gone, replaced with a bleak emptiness more terrifying than all the hate in the world. At least before, I had a plan. At least before, I didn't know what it feels like to mourn the living.

Tears well again.

With my sleeves already soaked through, I stretch across the gear shift and fling open the glove box, in search of tissues.

Stacks of banknotes tumble out, falling to the mat below.

"What in the world—"

I pick them up, one by one. Lay them out on the passenger seat, in a line, as though that might help me make sense of it all. It doesn't. I count five hundred thousand quid. A proper fortune. Enough to skate us by for years, if we watch our spending and avoid extravagant things.

"Damn you, Saxon."

My heart teeters in my chest, torn between feeling grateful for the unexpected gift and guilty for even considering accepting it. This sort of money could move us to America, just as I'd planned five years ago. It could set us up somewhere new, in a country not wracked with political turmoil and death around every corner. Peter could transfer universities. Josie could take that gap year she so wants, exploring the States or Canada or anywhere, really, that isn't England. And I could . . . I could start over, couldn't I? A fancy new job, perhaps—something in my field. Lease a flat that isn't on the verge of collapse—or stacked with the bodies of dead priests.

And then Saxon will be gone forever.

I drop my forehead onto the backs of my hands on the wheel.

"Stop crying," I order, but I've been a liar for so long that I last only seconds before I'm drying my eyes with my wet sleeve for what must be the hundredth time. Tissues. I need tissues.

Leaning back over, I stick my hand into the glove box and riffle through the junk. Papers, a smattering of receipts, a pair of sunglasses, and then—

A mobile?

My palm closes over the object, and sure enough, it's a phone. New. Sleek. Did Saxon put this in here for me? I brush my thumb over the glass, watching as the wallpaper illuminates from the pressure of my touch. The picture is basic: a set of roses blooming—a stock image, at best—but it's the unread message that captures my attention.

With no password to plug in, I swipe the text open:

I'm a Godwin.

I once heard someone ask the question, what's in a name? According to a book Guy stole from a library in Paris, Godwins are fierce protectors. Ironic that thanks to a fluke chance during the Second Boer War, we became our name in truth.

Fierce. Deadly. Guardians to the Crown and whoever claimed the throne.

But it wasn't until you that I realized the scope of being a Godwin.

There is not a man I wouldn't kill, a mountain I wouldn't scale, a pain I wouldn't endure, to keep you safe.

I'm loyal to the queen out of habit—out of an expectation, an oath, spanning generations—but you are the only person, man or woman, who owns me.

> I was cold until you. Numb. Like the skin the king scarred, like my heart which wouldn't beat.
>
> One touch from you—one kiss—and you've left me burning, still.
>
> You are my first, Isla Quinn, and my only.
>
> Breathe for me, sweetheart, and know that somewhere I'm inhaling and taking up the torch for us both.

A noise like a wounded animal shatters the quiet, and it's only after a moment that I realize that the sound belonged to me. I sit with my legs drawn up on the seat, my entire body curled around the mobile as though it's my only lifeline. Tears coat my cheeks, and I don't need to look in the mirror to know that my eyes are red-rimmed.

Acting on instinct, I tap on the phone app and wait for the callback.

It rings, only to answer with a curt, "The number you have rung is not in service."

I try again.

And again.

Each time more fraught with dread and frustration, until I throw the mobile onto the passenger seat, atop all those banknotes, and scream at the top of my lungs.

He's left me with more money than I know what to do with, a car to shuttle me away to safety, and a note that's effectively torn me in two. In return, he stole my heart—and I'm never, ever getting it back.

I don't know how long I sit in that car park, watching the tree limbs sway in the breeze. Despite the late hour, customers go in and out of the brightly lit pub: couples holding hands, mothers pushing their babies in prams, fathers hoisting their toddlers up onto their shoulders.

I roll down the window and draw in fistfuls of fresh air.

And I dream: of ducking down before a pram of my own to stare at a baby boy. A son with his papa's black hair and his unholy, glittering green eyes; of the solid weight of my husband standing behind me, his fingers playing with my hair as he stares down at the boy who is the perfect blend of us both.

Brave and stubborn and loyal, to a fault.

You are my first, Isla Quinn, and my only.

With my elbow planted on the open window, I press my mouth to my balled fist. There's nothing but the hum of activity from the pub and the gentle wind blowing into the car, which teases at my hair. It's quiet. Safe. Peaceful.

Inside my chest, there is nothing but chaos and desperation and aching need.

"I love you, Saxon Godwin," I whisper, to myself, to the empty car, to the midnight sky with its diamond stars and faraway galaxies. I whisper the words like a prayer, as if, by saying them out loud, they might summon him to me.

They don't.

By the time I pull up to the safehouse he plugged into the GPS, with Peter and Josie spilling out from the cottage and rushing toward me, I whisper another, "Please come for me, Saxon. Please, please come for me."

He never does.

CHAPTER 40

ISLA

"How long do you suppose she'll let the sadness get to her and go without bathing?"

"*Oh*, so that's the stench I keep smelling. I thought you'd forgotten to take out the rubbish."

"Peter Quinn, I'll have you know that you're a proper arsehole."

"As opposed to what? An *improper* arsehole?"

"I can hear you both, you know." Cupping a mug of steaming tea, I glance over my shoulder to where my brother and sister are hovering in the doorway. "Jos, no cursing. Peter, I'll bathe when I feel like it."

Which will be right around the time I swallow my misery and stop thinking about Saxon around the clock. At this rate, I'm looking at the prospect of *never*.

Red hair dancing behind her as she skips to the sofa, Josie swings herself over the arm and plops down beside me. She bends her knees and perches her chin atop them. "Tell me, since you've killed the king, I think I should be allowed certain freedoms. Like the right to say *arsehole* whenever I feel like it."

I arch a brow. "Is that really the bargaining chip you want to use?"

"At least it's creative." Peter chuckles as he bypasses the sofa and props himself up on the coffee table, his gangly legs sprawled out. "Especially since you've dragged us to the middle of nowhere."

Grimacing into my mug, I take another sip. "It's Stokenchurch, not Thurso."

"I wake up to peeping Toms staring at me through my window every morning." When I gawk at him, concern swelling at the thought of us being discovered by the authorities, my brother takes pity, adding, "The deer, Isla. I'm talking about the deer."

Oh, thank God.

Perhaps it was pitiful to return here, to a village I've only driven through, but the bed and breakfast I booked comes with a fully furnished wing, large enough to fit all three of us without always bumping elbows. Not that the quaint farmhouse is anything to drool over. The matching wallpaper from room to room dates back to the seventies, at least, and the furniture is threadbare and on the verge of passing over to wherever furniture goes to die. And, while I haven't used the shower yet, there's no mistaking the startled yelp I hear from Josie whenever the water suddenly turns cold mid-wash.

The benefits to staying here: it's cheap and Stokenchurch is tiny.

And it's close enough to London should there be any . . . news.

Josie's elbow glances my side as she scoots closer, resting her head on my shoulder. "It's been three days. Maybe we should venture out. I would *die* for some crisps right now."

"Maybe I ought to go first," Peter says, clasping his hands together in his lap. On the floor, his toes tap out an uneven rhythm. "No one knows my name"—he throws an apologetic look my way—"or my face. What if someone recognizes you from the telly?"

We've been lucky so far.

The owners accepted the banknotes without question, and we used Peter's license to check in, instead of my own. Just in case. For three days, we've stayed far away from the news. No turning on the car for a listen to the radio or popping on the telly. Not that the latter works—I tried, that very first night we stayed here. Seventy-two hours after I fled London, and we've been cocooned in a bubble of ignorance ever since.

Shaking my head, I pass the mug over to Josie when she taps the handle, silently asking for a sip. "We go together, or we don't go at all. Same as we did when we went shopping yesterday. I don't . . . I don't want us separated again."

Lips flattening, Peter hangs his head forward. "If I'd known . . . if I'd known what that bloody bastard was prepared to do to you, I wouldn't have allowed him to send us to Oxford."

"Peter . . ." The sofa cushion squeaks under my bum when I stretch out a hand, settling it on his knee. "You can't blame yourself. You *can't*. He said I'd be following the next morning—how were you to know that wouldn't be the case?"

"I should have known better than to trust a Priest." He lifts his chin, his gaze finding mine. The blue of his irises is rimmed with remorse. "I told you not to trust them, and then I went ahead and did just that. You almost died!"

"Peter . . ." I rub my lips together, sliding my arse forward until I sit on the edge of the sofa. "Do you remember the time you threw yourself from the tree?"

Josie mimics me to my right, dropping her feet to the scratchy beige rug. "I do," she announces, hooking an arm around mine. "He screamed bloody murder."

My brother shoots her a dirty look. "I didn't anticipate breaking my leg."

"You thought you could fly."

"And you," he deadpans, "thought it'd be a grand idea to follow in my footsteps."

I hold up my hands between them, making the universal gesture for time-out. "The point is, you had no idea how you might feel after you jumped. You just did it, because Mum and Dad always taught us to be brave and to take chances and to remember that there are no bad decisions. The prospect of consequences didn't even enter the picture until you were limping around in a cast for months on end."

Squirming beside me, Josie splays her hands out wide. "Killing the king was—"

"A bad decision," I finish for her, "which is exactly what I'm trying to get at. Anger ruled my emotions. Revenge, too. I spent years watching the two of you struggle after Mum and Dad died, and never... Well, I should have shined the lens back on myself, perhaps, because I was the one struggling most of all. I assassinated him in cold blood, and I've spent months living in fear because of it."

Peter drops his stare to his crossed ankles. "So, what you're trying to say is, we should forgive Priest."

My heart pinches at the memory of Saxon being shoved to the damp earth. No matter how much I try, there's been no forgetting that moment. And I've tried, over and over again, since leaving London. Since reading the message that he sent me, only to realize that he'd purposely cut off all other communication.

The damned man thought of everything.

On a whisper, I admit, "I think that he's spent his entire life putting the Crown first. Tricking me into that cell was the equivalent of him jumping from the tree. Or, in my case, pulling the trigger on the king."

But unlike Peter, who whined and griped about his scratchy skin beneath the hard plaster, or even me, who took to hiding in plain sight, Saxon faced down the consequences and flashed it the appropriate two fingers— knowing, all the while, that it would lead to his own demise.

I chose you, he told me. *I chose you.*

"Don't cry," Josie murmurs from beside me, her arm snaking around my waist, "please don't cry."

"I'm not."

Peter kicks my foot with his. "You definitely are."

Blast it, not again.

With my knuckles, I wipe away the dampness from beneath my eyes. "I'm all right. See?" The smile I give them threatens to crack my cheeks in two, as if I'm made of porcelain and not human flesh. "Just fine. Really."

"You love him."

"I-I—"

"You *love* him," Peter repeats, harder this time.

My vision shimmers and my breath quickens, and tearfully, I confess, "I do. I love him with everything that I am."

And then I crumble, right there before them both. For years, I've held myself composed. The rock of the family. The foundation keeping us all afloat. Any hope of turning my emotions to stone disintegrates completely when Peter takes the empty cushion beside mine, hugging me on one side while Josie maintains her post on my right.

Their arms surround me, a tight cocoon.

For the first time since Mum and Dad died, and I stepped up as head of the family, I let my siblings catch me.

And then, as true siblings do, Peter coughs not so delicately into my neck, muttering, "You really need a shower."

"I was just thinking that," Josie says, on the other side of me. "It's quite bad."

"Like rubbish."

"No, like B.O."

Laughter climbs my throat. "I can hear everything you two are saying."

Peter grumbles, "I'm hoping you'll get the point."

"The point being," Josie adds, patting my leg like I'm a dog, "that I want crisps more than anything and you need a shower. Immediately. Right now. Before I pass out from sitting too close to you."

"Duly noted." Chuckling for what feels like the first time in weeks, I push up from the sofa and smooth my palms over my shirt. Maybe this is what we need—the chance to eat out like nothing is wrong, that I'm not a criminal on the loose, or that my heart wasn't captured by the devil himself.

I can pretend, for a few hours, that I'm happy.

"Isla?"

At Josie's sweet-tempered voice, I turn on my heel. "Yes?"

Her blue eyes pin me in place. "Everything you've done, everything that you've sacrificed . . . We would do the same for you."

Perhaps it was an omen, foreshadowing at its finest, that Josie would repeat the same words that I said to her, weeks ago.

It takes twenty minutes for me to wash all the grime from my body.

Another five before we're on the road.

And only thirty seconds for Peter to switch on the radio and for us all to hear the same, bone-chilling announcement: *"The Metropolitan Police have just come forward with a shocking update on the murder of Reverend William Bootham. During a second autopsy, which was apparently required after complications with the first, dried blood was discovered under Bootham's fingernails. Police Commissioner Marcus Guthram has confirmed that Isla Quinn, whose flat Bootham was discovered in, is no longer a suspect in the case. The DNA belongs to the infamous anti-loyalist, Saxon Priest."*

"Isla! *Isla.*"

Hands slide over mine, gripping tightly, and twist the car back into the two-lane road.

"Pull over." Peter's tone leaves no room for rebuttal. "Isla, pull the bloody car over right now. You can't drive like this."

With trembling hands, I pull the car over, rolling into a grassy embankment.

"He lied," Josie says from the backseat. "Saxon didn't kill the priest, did he?"

Leaning forward, Peter drops his forehead onto his upturned hands. "No. He took the blame, so—"

"I would go free," I whisper. *Free of Father Bootham*, he'd said, just before he slammed the car door shut. "He did it, so I could live."

So I could *breathe.*

Damn him.

Damn him!

Palms sweaty, I grit my teeth. "I need to find him. I need to—"

"We know," Josie says softly, settling a hand on my shoulder, squeezing. "We know."

Peter digs his thumbs into his eye sockets. "You can't go back to the Palace. They'll kill you, if you do."

Where else might he be, though? If not the manor house in Kent, we could try his home in Camden. Or . . . "The Bell & Hand. He might be at The Bell & Hand."

"We'll come with you," Josie says.

I shake my head. "It's too dangerous. I couldn't forgive myself if something happened to either of you."

"We come with you," Peter repeats, his voice rough, "together or not at all."

CHAPTER 41

SAXON

"You're a bloody idiot."

"I could say the same for you," I utter tonelessly into the mobile, my gaze fixed on Christ Church Spitalfields. It feels like months since I've stood under its shadow, not a matter of days. "How long before big brother dearest finds out you've phoned me?"

Damien's low growl echoes through the receiver. "I don't give a damn about that."

"You should."

"I *don't*," he clips out. "But I do care that you paid off Guthram to falsify the coroner's report. Fucking hell, what were you thinking?"

Pushing away from the roughened brick wall, I re-settle the hat on my head as I cross Fournier Street. I've made this walk thousands of times, at all times of the day, but never as I am now: With my face plastered across every storefront and news network. Without the backing of Holyrood to stay handcuff-free, should someone from the Met spot me.

With my heart and mind continuously circling back

to a certain blond warrior.

Damien's agitated voice drags me back to the conversation when he snaps, "Guthram is a snake. Trusting him is like feasting with the devil and expecting not to end up in hell."

"I know the risk I took."

"Do you? Because from where I'm sitting, it's starting to look like you've a death wish. Just like Pa."

Sighing, I ask, "Why did you ring me, Damien?"

Barely sparing The Bell & Hand a glance, I approach the side entrance door to Christ Church. The same one I nudged Isla through. Feeling the now-familiar pinch in my chest at the thought of her, I rub my heart with the flat of my palm. Once, twice. The sensation doesn't lessen, or loosen, not that I thought it would. I've resigned myself to this miserable fate: wanting a woman who will never be mine.

Life was so much simpler when I didn't know what lay beyond the ice.

"I want you to tell me that you haven't thrown away everything for a woman," Damien says, frustration brewing in his gruff voice. "Holyrood, the other men, Guy, *me*. Fuck, you threw it all away, and for what?"

"If you have to ask, then you won't understand."

"Then make me understand!" he explodes, and I'm instantly reminded that he's been nicknamed the Mad Priest. A boy genius with a heart of gold, but with a dark underbelly that I've never understood. "Guy never plans to speak to you again. The rest are too terrified to cross him. But me . . . For fuck's sake, Saxon, make me understand."

"She made me human." Pressing my eyes shut, I drop my forehead to the door, taking care to keep my profile averted from the street. "I've spent years waiting to die.

Hell, I've spent years as Death itself. Who I murdered didn't matter. Who I saved mattered even less. I existed, Damien. Existed like some shattered version of myself, and then she . . ."

When I trail off, my brother impatiently prompts, "And then she what?"

I swallow, roughly. "She made me want."

Her hands on my ravaged skin, her sweet mouth lifting to mine, her quick smiles and her husky laughter, and her ill-timed humor that never failed to make me grin. Isla Quinn snuck into my life, an untamable storm. She hammered my walls open, lodged blistering fire in my chest, and reminded me that I am a man like any other.

A man who craves.

A man who bleeds.

And a man willing to drag himself through the darkest pits of hell just to keep her safe.

Gritting my teeth, I fist the doorknob and tug it open. "I have to go."

"No, hold on—"

"Watch your back, brother. You don't want to end up like me."

"Saxon, *dammit*, don't hang up on—"

I hang up.

With my chin dipped, I let the door close behind me as I enter the left flank of the nave. I've been in this church countless times, enough to know that at this time of day, the pews will remain empty as the afternoon light filters through the windows and dances across the marbled floor.

One could argue that I shouldn't be here.

I might not have killed Bootham, but the taint of my life sullied him anyhow.

For over a century, Holyrood has functioned like our mission overrules all else. We have a monarchy to uphold, to protect, and to hell with anyone who stands in our way.

I don't know how many deaths I've doled out. Upward of one hundred. Probably more. Doubtful less. At some point, the little boy who eagerly accompanied his father to St. James's Palace lost his humanity along with his moral compass. The Crown, as the king had threatened me, should always come first. And then I became the monster John created.

No victims remembered.

No victims mourned.

But Bootham . . .

I slip into a pew at the front of the church, the old wood creaking under my weight as I lower the kneeler and sink down. The blood-red cushion cradles my knees as I clasp my hands together, head bowed, and give voice to my penance.

"Forgive me, Father, for I have sinned . . ."

CHAPTER 42

ISLA

"Stay here."

Peter slips an arm around the back of my headrest and leans forward, his eyes locked on my face as I climb out of the car. "What did we say? Together or not at all, right?"

"I won't be long. Promise."

"It's all a front." His mouth firms as he slants a look back at Josie. "An infamous anti-loyalist pub when the lot of them are monarchists. Bloody brilliant, really, but who knows *what* the staff knows?" His Adam's apple bobs with a convulsive swallow. "What if they've heard about you and the king?"

"Impossible. There's no way Saxon has told them anything." Despite my protest, my stomach churns at the mere thought of what I might be walking into—everything ranging from bad to horribly deadly. Saxon may have said nothing to the staff, but that doesn't mean his brothers have kept quiet. *Don't go there.* I shake off the fear the same way a dog rids its fur of water. "I'm only asking for his mobile number. We'll be back to Stokenchurch before you know it."

"What if Guy is in there?" Josie asks, poking her head into the front of the car, between the two seats. "What if he sees you?"

Then I have my knife and my wits to save me.

Unwilling to unnerve them any more than I have, I shake my head. It's probably best not to dwell on the fact that the man's flat is above the pub. "He won't see me."

"You don't know that, not for sure."

"Twenty minutes," I tell them both, offering a fleeting smile. "If I'm not out by then, you have the right to drag my arse out for a lecture."

Josie quirks a brow. "You're bribing me with blasphemous words. Don't think I don't know it."

"Is it working?"

"It is for me," Josie quips at the same time Peter rolls his eyes and grumbles, "Hardly."

Choking out a weak laugh, I tap the hood of the car. "Twenty minutes. Time me, if you want."

Slamming the door shut, I purposely avoid looking at Christ Church Spitalfields as I take to the pavement. Guilt and I have become intimately acquainted these last few months, but still, knowing that Father Bootham was killed—and that his real murderer is still on the loose—does little to relieve me of my remorse.

"Think of Saxon," I mutter, sidestepping around a small group when they spill across the pavement, leaving no room for me to squeeze past.

Déjà vu strikes for a third time when I approach the glossy black door. It swings open, an older gentleman stepping out, and my pulse immediately spikes. *Ian Coney is dead*, I remind myself, as the man moves around me and heads for Commercial Street.

In the span of days, I've gone from being wanted by the police to yet another nameless face in the crowd.

All at Saxon's expense.

The scent of pastries and coffee fills my lungs as soon as I step inside. No matter that one of its owners has been accused of murder, The Bell & Hand is busy as usual. Customers fill nearly every seat in the pub, while the bar remains standing room only. Above the din, a melody dances to a light, airy rhythm.

Time to get to it, then.

The first server I try waves me off with a dismissive, "Busy, sorry. Can't help." The second doesn't even stop as she balances a tray heavy with croissants and coffee.

It's not until I'm at my wit's end, boldly stepping in front of a middle-aged woman with vibrant red hair and clear green eyes that I get anywhere. Tucking the tray beneath her armpit, she throws an impatient look at a new group entering the pub. "Look," she starts, flustered, "if you really need it, the office has all the Priests' numbers listed on a whiteboard behind the desk."

She's gone before I can even thank her.

Not that it matters; I'm already hightailing it down the hallway.

The longer I stay, the greater the chance that someone might alert Guy or the other brother, Damien, that I've stormed enemy territory. It was a risk coming here, but compared to scaling the sixteenth-century walls of the Palace—and that bloody drawbridge, of all things—The Bell & Hand seemed like a safer bet.

The soles of my shoes step to the same staccato as the anxious ringing in my ears. Hand to the brass knob, I push the office door open and—

My eyes go wide at the figure standing behind the

desk, one hand rifling through a drawer. I know that bushy gray beard. Those brown eyes stinging with animosity. The craggy features that declared war before we'd even been formally introduced.

As if he doesn't care that he's been caught, Jack offers an indulgent smile. "Well, well, look who's come to join the party."

"You shouldn't be in here."

"The same could be said for you."

"What were you doing?" I ask, leaving the door ajar as I step inside the office.

His smile turns brittle, all trace of indulgence gone. He looks old—older, even, than the last time I saw him. Beard straggly and unkempt. A red mark extending from the underside of his chin to halfway down his neck. With a quirk of his gray brows, he plants his arse on the corner of the desk, as if he owns it. Beside him, the drawer remains open as he treats me to a once-over.

"Body like a twig, personality like a rock," he drawls, fiddling with the corner of the desk. "Priest's lost his damn mind over ye, and for nothin'."

Coming from anyone else, the insult might land a solid jab to my self-esteem, but Jack is the last person whose opinion I care about. *Chauvinistic bastard.* "Jealousy isn't a good look on you."

"Trust me, I ain't jealous." Sneering, his crowded front teeth make an appearance. "Not of you."

"Of course not."

At my dismissive shrug, he pushes away from the desk with the backs of his thighs. "That right there?" He jabs a bandaged finger in my direction. "*That's* why I don't like ye. High and mighty, thinkin' you're better than e'eryone else. You ain't the queen, love. You ain't even the dirt beneath her shoes."

"I wouldn't dare to think I am." The second his features turn rapier sharp, I know that I should have ditched the sarcasm. *Shite.* Clearing my throat, I send a sideways glance to the drawer he's yet to close. "You really shouldn't be here." A small pause then, with a step to the left, closer to that desk, I add gently, "You were let go."

"Because of *you*."

He spits out the words with such force that actual spittle flies from his mouth. Instinct begs me to turn around and escape out the door, but pride, fickle emotion that it is, cements me in place. "Blaming me won't do you any good. I don't even work here, so whatever problem you think you have with me, I suggest that you shelve it."

"*Shelve* it, eh?"

"Or don't," I say, palms lifting to the ceiling. "We aren't mates. I honestly don't care what you think of me, but if you think I won't tell Saxon that you've been here, going through his office, then you have another—"

"Bints like you, thinkin' you can come in and change things"—the tips of his boots graze my shoes, intimidation charging the air with high-voltage friction—"but I've been workin' this place for years now. There ain't one thing about this pub I don't know."

"Then maybe you ought to take what you've learned and apply it someplace new."

"I had plans here. Big plans."

When his hand presumptuously touches my shoulder, I duck away on light feet. Meet his stare, head-on. "Don't. Touch. Me."

"Or *what*?" Jack watches my backward trajectory with nary a blink. But he follows. One step, two, tracking me across the room. I feel the hair raise on the backs of my arms. "You think Priest will be here to save ye?" he taunts, moving closer. "It's me and you, little bird. Me. And. You."

"I'll scream."

An unidentifiable emotion nips away his earlier frustration, something cold and deranged settling in its place. Trailing a finger along the desk as he nears, he goes so far as to close the drawer with an audible *snick*. And then, "Will you scream as loud as last time?"

As loud as last time?

A sick sensation lands in my gut, twisting, mounting. I stare at him, visualizing his face in an entirely different setting. One with gorgeous herringbone floors and octagonal walls and galleries that allow secret visitors to never show their faces to those down on the ground floor.

But there's no way . . .

We would have seen him. *Heard* him, at the least. Right?

Those astute brown eyes shine with delight as I shuffle backward, adding another meter between us. And they positively gleam when I shoot a hasty look toward the door, marking the number of steps it would take me to flee.

One.

Two.

"Screaming—really?" I swallow, as I make step number three. "I hate to say this, but I have no idea what you're talking about."

"A little reminder, then."

I don't move fast enough.

He launches toward me, catching me around the middle, and drives me to the ground with so much power that we skid, together, across the tile. My head glances off the desk's corner leg.

Pain ricochets though my skull and the ceiling, it spins and spins and—

A hand seizes my nape, his thumb digging into my pulse while my fingers scrape the floor, determined to drag myself away.

"Get off! *Get off!*"

"Won't you scream for me?" The question comes in a heavy pant beside my ear. "The way you did for Ian?" When I stiffen at the name, the implication truly settling in, Jack releases a noisy, sinister laugh. "Oh, yes, I was there. Up on the gallery. I watched you fight to live, little bird. Shaking legs. Graspin' hands. Even from up there, I could see it all."

My lungs pump for oxygen, dragging in air through my nose.

Saliva builds in my mouth, from his hand locked around my throat, but still I manage a choked, "A-a loyalist."

Another laugh, this one accompanied with more spittle that lands on my cheek. "An opportunist. I go where the money takes me, and I had it real good, workin' them both. But then Priest sacked me because of *you*."

"J-jealous."

His other elbow clamps down across my back, roughly angling my cheek into the hard floor. "I turned on him before he even met you," he hisses. "You think you know e'erythin', and I already told ye"—he squeezes my neck, and a gurgling noise erupts from my throat—"I ain't jealous. Now scream for me, little bird, just like your priest did."

Father Bootham.

Oh, God. Oh, God. *OhGod.*

"You k-killed him—"

Lips land on my temple. Wet. Chilled. They part to whisper, "Suppose I am a little jealous. The good father did nothin' to me. Always said 'ello when I saw him. But it's yer fault, anyway." Panic wells within me, and I thrash my legs beneath the weight of his, barely able to raise my hips from the floor. "Had you just been in your flat when I showed up, the priest wouldn't be dead. How was I goin' to get information for the lads when I was sacked? No information, no money. You had to go. You *have* to go."

My vision blurs.

My heart stampedes.

I've crossed Lady Luck too many times now to expect another slice of mercy.

The knife. Grab the knife.

A stifled moan reverberates in my chest. I have seconds, no more, before those deceitful hands squeeze the life out of me. My head feels swollen, a balloon on the verge of imploding. No one is coming for me, not this time.

Josie and Peter—

Oh, dear God. The twenty-minute countdown.

Move, move, move.

With weak fingers, I fumble for my trousers. For Dad's blade that I stuck in an oversized pocket. I find the handle, pulling it out, but my grip is so weak that it clatters noisily to the floor.

Jack's hold on me imperceptibly slackens when he realizes what I've dropped.

Silence reigns, a throne of impending doom, and then he lunges for the knife while I drag myself away on unbalanced hands and knees. I sway. Elbows giving out beneath my weight. I can't breathe. I can barely see, not with the dancing black dots swarming the office.

Run. Run. *Run.*

"You'll scream," Jack growls from behind me, "and then maybe I'll drop yer body at Saxon's house, for a little present. A dead priest. A dead bitch. Oh, Ian would be so happy."

The air beside my right ear sings—

And the knife plummets south a meter past me, having only just missed its mark.

Me.

I need to hustle.

I need to run.

Heavy footsteps stalk around me, blocking my path to the door. Not wasting time, I turn and rise on trembling legs. There must be another way out. Saxon, Guy—neither of them would allow only for a single exit point. I gasp for breath, swinging right, then left.

"Nowhere to go," Jack drawls casually, like he's enjoying himself immensely, "no one to save you."

I whirl around, hands raised to ward off another attack. Only, I shouldn't have bothered.

Sunlight from the window catches on the silver pistol in Jack's hand. A pistol that is unerringly pointed . . . at me.

"You don't have to do this," I whisper, winding backward on legs as weak as a newborn fawn's. "Please, Jack, you don't have to—"

"You killed Ian. You killed my *brother*."

My mouth parts in shock then clamps shut. The two look nothing alike, but that's saying nothing. Both men are unhinged. And both men want me dead because of my relationship with Saxon. If only they knew . . . if only they knew of Holyrood, that they're all on the same side.

The *queen*'s side.

I slide my gaze south, to the gun. "Jack, don't. You don't understand. Saxon, he's with you. It's all a front. A ploy. He's loyal to the—"

"Scream for me, little bird."

The gun erupts, and I hear myself cry out when I lurch away. I scream, just as he demanded, as a trail of fire explodes within me. Burning sensations crawling over my flesh. Heat, so much *heat*. I glance down, just for a second, and all I see is red. Red oozing from the ring-sized hole in my chest—a deep, dark maroon. Nearly black.

I clutch my chest, smearing the blood as I stumble. Collapse. Arms and legs sprawled as my lungs heave with the effort to breathe.

A blurry figure steps above me. There are two of them, swaying, bending, coming closer and closer, until his face is all that I see.

Jack.

My murderer.

My own ruthless, broken monster.

"Sweet dreams, Isla."

A hand presses down on me, driving into the wound itself, and another cry shatters the room. My tears. My pain. I'm sinking. Drowning. Gasping for air, for life itself. And then there's nothing . . . Nothing but agony and darkness and the deep, endless abyss of oblivion.

CHAPTER 43

SAXON

I feel no better leaving Christ Church than I did stepping within its hallowed walls.

William Bootham will never attend another mass, hold another confession, or—fuck—just *breathe*. Selfish. It was so bloody selfish of me to use him, knowing that if anyone were to find out, it would end just as it did.

Quietly, I slip the door closed and step out into the sunshine.

Considering my dark mood, it ought to be storming. Black clouds, heavy downpour. I want to soak in the misery, let it consume me. If not that, then let it try and purge the guilt away.

Scrubbing a palm over my jaw, I step onto the street. Life without Holyrood hasn't settled in yet. I have more money than I know what to do with. More time, too.

I could do without the latter.

Every unhurried minute of the day only allows for more time spent thinking about Isla. Does she sleep in Oxford, at the secret safehouse that I sent Peter and Josie to, knowing that my brothers have no idea of its existence? Has she brought her siblings somewhere else, somewhere she can grow roots and start a new life, away from the anger and the vengeance and the deceit?

Does she miss me?

My chest squeezes with a ragged breath. Anxiety. Another newfound emotion that Isla has given me a name for. A feeling I could do well without.

Lifting my hat, I thread my fingers through my hair before resettling the brim back in place. Briefly, I shoot a glance to The Bell & Hand. Another loss, there. I shouldn't miss it—the needy customers and the waitstaff that drove me insane with their random requests. But still I stand here, on Fournier, stuck between two folds of my past.

The Bell & Hand. Christ Church Spitalfields.

I turn away from them both, only to freeze mid-step when I spot a familiar car parked along the curb. Eyes narrowing, I move to the left, searching for the number plate.

Isla's car.

Something twists inside me, all-consuming and devastating, all at once. If she's in there, I'm going to . . . to—

Kiss her.

Demand that she never leave me.

—rip the passenger's side door open, fuming.

At the sight of me, Peter practically spills out of his seat. "Bloody hell! What are you doing here?"

"What am *I* doing here?" I jab a thumb into my chest, bending low so I can look him in the eye. "What the fuck are you—"

"Language, Saxon," quips a female voice from the backseat. Josie. If I ever reproduce, I pray not to have a daughter like her. Full of sarcasm. Headstrong. On second thought, she's a younger version of her older sister. *And when have you ever thought about children of your own?*

Swallowing a hot retort, I return my attention to Isla's brother. "You're supposed to be hundreds of kilometers away right now. On the other blasted side of the island. Anywhere, *anywhere*, but here."

Peter folds his lanky arms across his chest. "She heard what you did."

I stare at him, unblinking. "I stuck her in a jail cell then left her to die."

"You didn't, though," Josie pipes up, sticking her face between her brother's seat and the open door. "Because you love her, which is clearly the only reason why you told the world that you killed that priest when you didn't."

"I don't—"

"You have hearts in your eyes right now," Josie adds, cutting me off. Bravely, she flicks her finger near my face, twirling it in a half-circle. "Big pink ones. Googly-eyed ones."

Do I?

The fact that I'm considering that she might be right has my mouth tugging to one side. "I'm not going to answer that."

"Because it's true."

"Because I—"

"We came because she figured one of the staff must have your mobile number." The youngest Quinn blinks up at me, wriggling her brows. "She misses you. She hasn't bathed in days."

Peter smacks a palm over her forehead, gently shoving his sister into the backseat. "Don't tell her we mentioned the bathing thing. She'll never forgive us."

She misses you.

Bloody fucking hell. I'm a total goner. She's turned me into a sap—the sick, annoying kind, at that—and

I find my palm rubbing my chest, right over my heart. Happiness, something so entirely elusive, settles within me. Unicorns. Treasure chests of gold. I could die here, in this moment, and I would at least know what it feels like to be adored.

She didn't bathe because she *missed* me.

My mouth curves upward, and though I catch Peter's poorly concealed blanching, I don't take offense. Isla wants me just fine, deformed upper lip and all.

"I'll get her now," I say, pulling back. "Two minutes."

Isla shouldn't be anywhere near London, but she's single-handedly weakened my resolve. She's here. I'm here. And, clearly, there's no choice left on the docket but to kiss the hell out of her.

Releasing an aggrieved sigh, Josie mutters, "We'll be here. As was already promised."

Long strides bring me to the front door of The Bell & Hand, and I experience only a moment of self-doubt when I step inside. Damien may be battling a severe case of regret over me leaving Holyrood but the same can't be said for our older brother. In the days since I left the Palace, I've not heard a single word from him.

No phone calls. No text messages. Not even an email.

This pub was never Damien's passion, but it was mine and Guy's. We bled hours into The Bell & Hand. Found the best chefs in the area. Hired waitstaff that could have hacked it at London's premiere restaurants, had they ever decided to leave us. Though it started as nothing more than a front to entice anti-loyalists into our midst, The Bell & Hand was our tiny slice of normal. Here, we were business owners. Here, we were brothers—not spies for the Crown.

Will Guy run it on his own?

Is he here now, upstairs in his flat?

My heart doesn't race. My palms don't sweat. But I'm acutely aware of a . . . a sort of *loss* that threads through my body. The same that I felt when Mum took her last breath. Back then, at nine, I'd turned to my older brother and soaked his shirt through with my tears.

This time, I don't cry.

"Saxon? Is that you?"

I turn at the sound of my name, and find one of my servers, Sara, standing beside an empty table. I draw the brim of my hat lower, to ward off any curious glances. "It's best if you don't mention me being here to anyone."

To the world, I'm a killer now.

A killer of a priest, a potential suspect in King John's assassination.

Her head bobs in a hasty nod. "Yes, yes, of course. Is there"—she shifts the tray onto one hand, leveraging it up by her shoulder—"something you needed? We received all your instructions. Everything is under control."

Feeling slightly uncomfortable, I shift my weight. "Was there a woman who came in here within the last few minutes? Blond? Slim? She—"

BOOM!

"Dear God, was that gunfire?"

"Was it outside? Please tell me it was outside."

A scream renders the pub silent, chilling, nightmare-inducing, and as chaos erupts all around, I surge forward through the crowd stampeding toward the front door. That cry. That *voice*. Undiluted fear slams into me as I shove patrons out of my way.

"Isla!" I bellow, at the top of my lungs. "*Isla!*"

My feet pound the floor as I enter the hallway leading toward the office, as well as the stairwell up to Guy's flat. *Guy*. Did he find her here? Did he *shoot* her? I'll rip him limb from limb. Tear his cold, black heart straight from his chest, and—

A man stumbles out from the office.

Blood coats his right hand, the leg of one trouser. A pistol is clamped in his opposite hand, one that's still adorned with a splint around his index finger.

The red wings of fury sweep me into flight.

I charge down the hall, arms pumping at my sides, legs churning fast, faster. His chin jerks up at the sound of my footsteps, features blanching. Immediately, he fumbles with the pistol. Lifts his arm. Aligns the mouth of the gun with me.

Crack!

Lifelong experience of literally dodging bullets has me dropping to my knees. The air above my head crackles with the force of the discharged weapon. It crackles with my rage, too. Dragging up the hem of my trousers, I grab the knife from its holster and tease the weight of the hilt in my hand.

"Priest. Hold on now, yeah?"

"I heard her scream," I grit out, swiftly covering the ground between us. "And you've blood all over you, which means you have five seconds to prove that you didn't shoot her. That, when I open the door, I'm going to find her sitting behind my desk. Sleek. Beautiful. *Alive*."

His gaze turns flinty. "We were friends."

"Not the right answer, Jack."

"You ruined e'erythin'! *E'erythin'*."

It's all the admission I need. His hand visibly shakes, and I pin my attention on it. Gripping the blade, I wind my arm back and send the knife hurtling through the air. It finds its mark in the crease of his shoulder and armpit, rendering his shooting arm useless. His pained shout echoes down the hall, the pistol crashing to the floor.

He wobbles to the side, his shoulder colliding with the wall.

I step up to him, wrenching the blade from his torn flesh. Look him dead in the eye as I leverage my forearm across his heaving chest and drag the point of the knife down over his sternum. A new scar splits his throat. Recently fresh, only a matter of days old. I narrow my eyes. "I told you what would happen if you came back."

Sweat beads on his flushed temple. "And I told ye she'd be the end of you. All this given up for a cunt—"

I plunge the blade deep into his middle.

His mouth gapes open but no sound emerges. His bloodied hand circles my arm, using my weight to keep himself standing. I step away. Let him slither to the ground, his legs giving out. Dark blood streaks down the wall, but I'm already stepping away and throwing open the office door. I have to find her—now.

"Isla? Isla, are you—*oh, fucking hell.*"

What's left of my heart shrivels at the sight of her.

It's déjà vu, a damn near recreation of the moment that I spotted her at the riot. Blond hair haloed around her head. Legs drawn up tight into her chest. But her face is tipped up to the ceiling and her arms are splayed outward, like a cross, and her chest . . . her *chest* . . .

Blood. There's so much blood.

Horror turns my limbs into a trembling mess as I demolish the space between us. One step. Two. The third has me sinking to my knees beside her, my shaking hands moving to frame her face. I fan my thumbs over her cheekbones, my other fingers cradling the back of her skull. Blood coats the corner seams of her mouth. More dot the ivory white of her upper teeth.

Fuck, fuck, *fuck!*

"Isla." Her name leaves my lips on a battered plea. "Isla, sweetheart. I'm here. *I'm here.*"

I wait for her lids to pop open as though the sound of my voice has the ability to perform miracles. But I've only been friendly with the devil, the conductor of destruction himself, and her eyes remain shut, her face pale from loss of blood.

Terror mounts, gathering in my throat, my chest.

Hurriedly, my fingers skim her neck, searching for her pulse. Weak, too weak. Her chest looks ravaged by a sea of red. She needs pressure. Christ, what she needs is a surgeon but we're too far away from the Palace. Lifting the hem of my shirt, I tear the fabric in two. It would be better if the cloth were clean, if we were within driving distance of Holyrood, but there's no time to dwell on what isn't reality. I need to get her to a hospital—now.

Pressing my shirt to her open wound, I shift her weight and gently gather her in my arms.

Her breath ghosts over my neck, faint but there. Barely.

"Stay with me, sweetheart. Fucking *stay with me.*"

With her limp frame tucked into my chest, I tear out of the office, barely sparing Jack's hunched-over frame another look.

The dining area is completely empty. Chairs turned over. Splintered stemware glittering on the floor. I ignore it all, too focused on the woman in my arms. "I'm breathing for us both. Every breath. Every hope. Do you hear me, Isla? Don't give up. Please, please don't give up." My face heats; eyes prick with moisture. "I need you," I rasp, aware of my voice cracking, "*I love you.*"

The heavy weight of my boot has the front door sailing open. It flings wide, nearly coming off the hinges, and then I'm cutting left, toward where I left Peter and Josie. Her brother must spot us in the rearview mirror because the passenger's side door flies open and then his lean frame is sprinting toward me.

"What happened? Saxon, what happened to my sister?"

He shot her.

I can't say the words out loud. They're crammed in my throat, lodged there with panic and grief and love. So much love for this woman, and *fuck!*

"Recline your seat." When Peter hesitates, clearly hating the thought of leaving Isla's side, I bark, "*Now!*"

His face whitens, and with a short nod, he's moving and I'm trailing behind, hot on his heels. The passenger seat goes horizontal and Peter inches to the side, waiting. *Waiting.* I look down at Isla. Her lips are blue and her skin so very pale, and I drop my head, praying to feel the shallow ghost of her breath on my—

"Saxon," Peter argues, "lay her down."

I can't let her go. *Won't* let her go.

My fingers dig into her flesh, pulling her tighter against me. If I put her on that seat . . . if I release her for any amount of time—

"*Priest.*"

"Help me," I grunt, and then we're carefully lowering her onto the seat together. Josie's whimpers are more strokes of terror down my spine. I'm aware of ordering her to keep Isla in place while I drive, of Peter clambering into the backseat along with his younger sister. Six minutes. That's all it'll take to deliver her straight to the front doors of the closest hospital.

I punch the petrol, grab Isla's limp hand in mine, and don't let go.

I'll hold on for the two of us forever, if it means she'll stay by my side.

"Who did this?" Peter demands, anger undercutting the obvious worry in his voice. "Who did this to her? Was it your brother? *Was it?*"

"No."

"Priest, you better tell me who it was or so help me God, I will—"

"*Stop!*"

It's Josie's cry that snaps her brother into silence. "Stop! We have to be calm for her. We have to b-be *calm*. What if"—a sharp sob escapes her—"what if she c-can hear us yelling?"

In the rearview mirror, I see Peter's shoulders begin to tremor. "She can't die. She *can't*."

"I won't let her." Two pairs of eyes find mine before I return my gaze to the road. Softly, I speak only to Isla, "Do you hear that, sweetheart? I won't let you. Don't you dare disappoint me. I—I need you. Now, tomorrow, forever. You're my only, and if you die on me, I'll fucking drag you back from heaven myself."

The moment a member of staff spots our car pulling up in the emergency lane, controlled mayhem ensues.

There's clear, concise shouting about stretchers and body scans and then Isla is being ripped from my arms. I feel her loss immediately, and I flex my fingers, as though in doing so, I might retain the feel of her warm weight within my embrace.

"I'm her brother," Peter announces to a nurse in scrubs. "We have to go with her. Please."

The nurse turns dark eyes on Josie, who sticks her tear-stained face in the air with complete defiance.

"Younger sister," she says primly, before pointing a finger at me. "And that's her husband."

Peter doesn't bat an eye at her claim, nor does the nurse, and I . . .

I step forward, linking an arm around Josie's thin shoulders. "We need to be with her, however we can. The waiting room. The cafeteria. I don't give a fuck where we are, so long as we're seconds away when she comes out of surgery."

Blinking back at me, the nurse offers a gallic shrug and turns on his heel.

We follow like a dog trailing its master's heels.

"She'll be fine, right?" Josie asks me.

I swallow, tightly. "Yes. Yes, she'll be fine."

Peter slants me a disbelieving look, and I avert my gaze. I've seen men survive worse injuries, and others die from a wound that shouldn't have amounted to more than a scrape. And never have I been as terrified as I am now.

The nurse leads us to a small room with green-painted walls and uncomfortable chairs scattered throughout the space. He points to a water fountain with a dismissive wave of his hand, and then mentions something about food being available right around the corner and down the hall.

Peter and Josie collapse onto chairs, side by side, and I stalk the empty space.

I meet the gaze of every nurse and doctor that walks past, as though daring them to tell me the worst. They drop their eyes to the floor, every one of them. *Cowards.* Anxiety ripples through me as an hour turns into two with no updates from the trauma surgeon. And then, finally, commotion starts from down the hall.

Isla's siblings launch from their respective chairs, moving to my side.

But it's not the doctor's grim-set face that I spot

striding toward us.

It's Marcus Guthram's, and the satisfied smirk he's wearing has me growling obscenities beneath my breath. He's sandwiched by four other Met officers, all donned in the same navy-blue uniform that I wore, just days ago when I broke into the Coroner's Court.

Josie's small hand lands on my arm. "What's happening? Did they find the shooter?"

"No," I mutter, clenching my teeth, "they've found me."

The Metropolitan's police commissioner stops in front of me then snaps his fingers at the officer to his right. "Cuffs, Barnaby."

The younger officer leaps into action, nudging Josie and Peter aside and coming around to my back. Aggressively, he grabs my arms and jerks my wrists together at the base of my spine. The second that cool metal encircles my flesh, I try to wrench away, only for three of the other officers to swarm me.

Josie cries out and Peter shouts at the men to let me go and Guthram only picks at invisible lint from his cuff. "Saxon Priest, you're under arrest for the murder of William Bootham."

For the first time since I spotted Isla comatose on the floor, something other than fear roots itself in my veins. Anger. Retaliation. "You fucking bastard," I growl, spitting at his feet. "You know that I didn't kill him."

*Tsk*ing his disapproval, Guthram only cups my shoulder and brings his mouth to my ear. "Don't insult an officer of the law, *Godwin*." He steps back, then motions toward his men. "Come on, lads. Time to pack him up and bring him to the station—and don't be afraid to rough him up a little. I daresay he might even enjoy it."

CHAPTER 44

ISLA

A breeze settles over my skin.

Cool. Damp. Like wind before a heavy summer rain, when the sky threatens with ominous clouds but the sun still manages to peek through.

Too cold.

It's much too cold.

I lift my arm to push whatever it is away but don't get very far. A moan of protest stings my throat, just as I hear, "Miss Quinn, no. Don't pull at that."

I pull anyway, hoping to escape the bite of ice.

"A stubborn one, aren't you," remarks that same voice again, and this time, my prayers are answered. Almost immediately I sense a respite when the damp breeze disappears and I'm no longer squirming.

Where am I squirming?

Flexing my fingers, I feel softness beneath me. A blanket, maybe. Yes. A blanket. It sits heavy across my feet when I wriggle my toes. Am I in bed? If I am, I've been here for ages, it seems. My back is sore, the muscles tight on either side of my spine.

"Miss Quinn, please stop moving or we'll have to sedate you again."

Sedate?

Absolutely not.

"No."

That croak, is that my voice? I swallow. So parched. Why am I so parched? The same as I was in that cell. Hungry and thirsty and angry at Saxon, even as I secretly begged for him to release me, to *love* me.

"You've a fever, girl." Paper touches my lips, the rim curved. Water. It slips against the seam of my lips before I remember to open, to swallow, to open my eyes. A fuzzy figure comes into focus before me. Gray, curly hair. A nurse's cap. Blue scrubs that hug her curvy frame. She pulls the cup away from my mouth, setting it down somewhere off to my right. "We have you on IV, for your liquids. But I suppose there's nothing like fresh water."

There are tranquil photographs on the walls: beaches and castles and dense woods. But nothing feels tranquil within me. "W-what happened?"

Soft brown eyes look down at me in pity. "You were shot, Miss Quinn."

Shot?

As if sensing my confusion, the nurse pats the back of my hand, careful to miss all of the tubes that seem to triple in number each time I look at them. "A little scare is all. You lost quite a lot of blood. And your lung—well, I suppose it's a good thing you arrived when you did. Thank God for small miracles, I say."

I feel as though I've died.

Perhaps I'm still dead and this is all a dream.

"Who—"

"Now, I think that's enough questions for now,

wouldn't you say?" She leans forward, rummaging around with something outside of my periphery. "Perhaps a few more hours of sleep ought to do you some good."

"No," I whisper, trying to move my arms but, dear God, the *pain* that shoots through my chest is unimaginable. "No, please . . ."

"Sweet dreams, Miss Quinn," the nurse says kindly.

Those words. I *know* those words. They spark a memory. A memory I should remember—something dark and sinister and damning.

But then there's no more discomfort. I slip away on the breeze, cool and calming.

"Is she awake?"

"You told us she'd be awake by now!"

"Mr. and Miss Quinn, while I'm sure you're desperate to see your sister, she's *healing*."

"Dr. Longstrom, if you value your life worth a damn, you'll let us at least *see* her."

"Lad, threatening me is not going to get you far. Now, please, go and sit down."

With every ounce of strength that I can summon, I reach over and smack the nurse's bell. Although it's more like a tap. A weakened, feeble tap that barely emits a peep. I try again. Better, but not great. *Again.* There . . . there—

The door props open as I suck in fistfuls of air into my lungs. There's a flurry of blue, of orange doused in red, and then the foot of the bed is crowded by Peter and Josie. They stare at me with tear-stained, anguished faces.

"Mr. and Miss Quinn," starts the doctor, stiffly.

"Let them stay." I fist the bed cover in one hand, grounding myself. "Please."

I hear his disgruntled cough. Then, "Ten minutes."

"Twenty," Peter returns sharply, never taking his eyes off me, "and we won't make a fuss about leaving."

"Twenty and not a minute more, boy."

The door clicks shut a moment later, and Josie comes around to my right side. Dragging a chair close, she sits and reaches for my hand but seems to think better of it when she spies all the IVs running into my veins.

"You almost left me," she says quietly, a small hitch in her words.

"Not by choice," Peter butts in, leaning against the footboard. "She was *shot*, Jos. We've been over this."

Josie's blue eyes dart to our brother. "We need to tell her."

He shakes his head. "No. Not right now."

"Peter, we can't *not*."

"I just said, not right now. Later, when she's feeling better."

"I feel fine," I interject, trying to draw myself upward on the bed. But the tightening in my chest—the wound that nearly killed me—keeps me horizontal but for the slight tilt in the mattress. I've gathered bits and pieces of what happened at The Bell & Hand each time I've awoken. Jack coming after me with the gun, him calling me *little bird*. I should have realized it then, in that moment. Ian Coney had said the same thing to me at The Octagon. Both times I'd been too determined not to die that I hadn't it given much thought. "Did they get him?" I ask, flicking my attention between my brother and sister. "Please tell me they got him."

Josie stares at me, her teeth sinking into her bottom lip. "They did," she says. And then, louder, "They did! They put handcuffs on him, Isla. Said that he killed the priest!"

A dead priest. A dead bitch.

Self-righteous anger, both for myself and for Father

Bootham, has me edging out, "Good. He bloody deserves everything that's coming to him."

Josie blinks.

Peter clears his throat. "I thought we were on Saxon's side?"

Everything in me goes still. "What? I don't understand. Saxon—"

"Oh, hell." Peter drops onto the corner of the bed, near my feet. "Oh, hell, you don't remember."

"Dr. Longstrom said I passed out from the blood loss. What don't I remember?" I feel the telltale swell of worry rise within me. "Peter, what don't I remember?"

He exchanges an inscrutable look with Josie. Rakes his fingers through his messy hair and then drops his head forward. "Saxon saved you, Isla. We were . . . we were waiting in the car like you told us to, and he was at—he was at the church. You know, the one across the street from the pub. He went in to find you and when he came out you were . . . Well, you were—" He gestures at me, apparently unable to find the appropriate words.

Doing my best to ignore the erratic thud of my heartbeat, I run my tongue along my bottom lip. "Who took him?" I look to Josie. "You said someone took him. *Who?*"

She stares just past me, as if unable to make direct eye contact when she admits, "The Met. They came and they took him."

I spend a full day fighting every doctor and nurse to allow police entry into my room. Finally, at the twenty-fourth hour, an older gentleman in the classic navy blues of the Met's uniform strolls inside, his custodian helmet tucked under one arm. On his chest, his badge reads T. CRAWFORD.

"Miss Quinn," he greets, his tone dripping with the sort of saccharine sweetness that implies pity, "I heard you were in need of an officer."

Pushing from my heels, I shove myself farther up in the bed. The IV tubes and other medical equipment aren't doing me any favors in looking like a woman ready to issue any warning, any threat, to get her man released from prison.

"I have evidence that Saxon Priest was not the one who killed Father William Bootham."

Indolently, the officer lifts one brow. "That case is closed. Priest's blood was found on Bootham."

"He *put* it there," I argue, all too aware of how ridiculous I sound. "But only afterward, so that I would . . ."

"I'm aware that the priest's body was found in your flat."

I press my tongue to the roof of my mouth. "He was, yes. But neither of us murdered Bootham. It was—"

"The Commissioner himself confirmed with the coroner, Miss Quinn. There's no doubt about who the murderer is. Now, why would Priest then drag the poor fellow over to your place? That's an answer we don't have." He sets his hands on the metal footboard and leans in, his helmet still stuck beneath his armpit. "Care to tell us why that was?"

"Because it wasn't him!" My heart rate spikes and the residual ache from the gunshot wound tugs at the surrounding muscles and tendons. Dr. Longstrom told me that I'm lucky that the bullet only glanced a lung as it went through my chest. In one way, out the other. But Jack's damn powerplay of digging his fingers where they didn't belong pushed me over. I breathe, heavily, and press a hand to my clavicle. "It wasn't him," I repeat, evenly this time. "Jack—he shot me at The Bell & Hand. He was rifling through the Priests' desk. Told me that he—that he wanted me to scream, just as Father Bootham had when he'd killed him."

Tapping on his helmet, Crawford studies me thoughtfully. "Jack, what?"

"Pardon?"

"His last name? This Jack who supposedly shot you."

"*Supposedly?*" I echo, my jaw falling open. "Sir, he did shoot me."

"I'm only trying to gather all the facts."

"And I'm telling them to you!" Bloody hell, I need to calm down. Four days. That's how long the fever ravaged my body. If I'm not careful, I'll end up being sedated for another four to go along with it. Swallowing past the lump in my throat, I muster the strength to try again. Cool. Callous. Cruel. *Be Saxon at his chilliest.* "Officer Crawford, I understand there are certain . . . procedures that I'm not privy to understanding. But I was shot, and it was by Jack, and he *did* confess to killing Father Bootham. Saxon should not be in that jail cell for a crime that he didn't commit."

Straightening, Crawford only palms the curve of his helmet before swinging it down by his side. "I'll see what I can do."

Surprise lands like a boulder in my gut. "You don't believe me."

The look he levels on me is nothing but pity. "I think you've had a bad spell, Miss Quinn, but we have our murderer and I would venture to say that it's in your best interest if you just focus on"—his eyes flick to the IV station beside me—"getting back to form."

When he turns away, I bash my fist on the mattress. "He didn't do it!" I shout at his back. "He didn't bloody do it."

Crawford peers back at me, his dark eyes revealing nothing. "Good day, Miss Quinn."

And then he's gone, and I'm left back at square one.

"This is not a good idea," Peter says, slamming the car door shut behind him. "You've only just been released and you're tempting fate all over again!"

I'm sprawled in the backseat, my head propped up by the window. Eight days of being stuck in that hospital bed. I won't admit it to a single soul, but I almost feel like I could have spent a lifetime there.

Despite the fact that I've been flushed clean of infections and sewn up to tip-top perfection, everything hurts. I survived what King John did not: a bullet to the chest. Mine creased my right lung, then exited between my shoulder blades.

You're lucky that your lung didn't collapse, Dr. Longstrom told me.

"Just drive," I tell Peter, folding my one hand over the edge of the seat for balance. "The sooner we get there, the better."

"For you to *die*," he counters irritably. Turning to Josie, he waves a frantic hand in the air. "Tell her that she's utterly mad."

Josie peeks into the backseat, her hand looped around the headrest. "Are you mad?" she asks pleasantly.

I humor her with a smile. "Just a tad desperate, Jos. You know."

"I know." Straightening back around, she motions for Peter to get a move on. "She's desperate, is all."

"I *heard* her," he grunts, turning the car on.

As we leave London, I try not to let my thoughts turn morbid. Peter isn't all wrong. This may very well be the worst decision of my life. In a week's time, I've been shot, almost lost a lung, and can still barely draw even breaths without wanting to die a little on the inside.

But this—*Saxon*—is more important than anything else.

He's my first, too. The first man to look at me and see who I am, deep inside. The first man I ever truly loved. *Love*, present. I fumble with my coat, sticking my hand into my pocket to grab the mobile he gave me. Coated with blood just days ago, it's good as new again. I tap my way to the messages and pull up his.

Breathe for me, sweetheart.

I'm breathing, all right. I'm willing to breathe right into the face of the one man who wants me dead, if it'll mean seeing Saxon walk free.

As the sun sets, we finally pull down the narrow, tree-lined path that I fled not two weeks ago.

"Are you sure about this?" Peter asks me from the front seat, his hands gripping the steering wheel as though his life depends on it. "They might shoot you on sight."

I drop my legs to the floor mat, ignoring the pinch in my chest. "I'm sure."

"I don't like this."

"You don't have to," I murmur, my hand already reaching for the door handle, "but I would do the same for you. Both of you."

The car idles to a stop and I push the door open, resting my weight heavily upon its sturdy frame. There's no fear lingering in my veins, just cool acceptance. I've returned to the lion's den, knowing that doing so might end with a pistol delivering me my very own third eye.

Boom.

With a deep breath, I move away from the door.

There are eyes, everywhere, watching me. I feel them. On my back, on my face. But I don't stop until I've crossed the drawbridge over the moat to stand before the heavy oak door. I knock, once, just to be polite.

The door opens, slow, deliberate, and then the devil's own eyes stare down at me. Blue. Hard. Wild in hue but unfeeling in nature.

"I have a proposition for you," I murmur, "and I think it would do to hear me out."

CHAPTER 45

SAXON

One hundred and ninety-two hours.

It's approximately how long I've sat with my ass on this bench, my back against this stone wall, and worry staining my soul.

"You goin' to ask again?" My cellmate drops his foot from the bench opposite mine to the floor, perching his ankle over his knee. "It's my only bit of entertainment, you askin' about your girl."

One hundred and ninety-two hours translates to:

The roughly twenty-two times I've demanded to know if Isla came out of surgery, healthy, each time Guthram has strolled past our cell.

The more than a hundred times I've closed my eyes and succumbed to the memory of red. The blood cloaking her chest. The blood that gathered, like tears of mortality, at the corners of her lips. The utter self-loathing that swam in my veins for leaving her alone in the first place. Had I been with her, she wouldn't have gone to The Bell & Hand. Had I fled London at her side, we could be living like hermits in the farthest corners of Britain, just as she once threatened.

And the approximate eight times—once per day—when I've imagined skewering Marl O'Malley where he stands. With a steel bar detached from the cell door. With the plastic spoon we eat with, thrice per day.

Give me a blade, and I'd cut out the bastard's tongue without thinking twice.

"Just about that time, Priest," he says now, his face as delighted as a kid opening presents on Boxing Day. "Hold on, I hear him. Walks like a fuckin' penguin, that one. You ever notice?"

I grunt out a negative.

"Jesus, you're no fun." Rolling his shoulders, he pushes to his feet and saunters to the door. "Anyone ever tell you that?"

Yes. A blond warrior with a fierce heart who gave me my first kiss.

My only kiss.

It's a vow I have no intention of breaking.

"No answer, eh?" O'Malley flashes me a smug grin. "Guess it's no secret that you're one sorry fucking bastard, Priest. Oh, *here we go*. Could be your lucky day yet."

I look at my hand and envision all sorts of ropes, knives, guns that could be used to shut him up. Eight days with O'Malley is eight days too long.

Whistling low, between his teeth, he curls a hand around one of the thick bars. "Well, look at that. Has a new bloke with him, Guthram does. An accomplice, maybe? Another officer with his finger shoved so far up his arse, he can taste his own sh—bloody hell. *Really?*"

I lift my eyes from the floor. "Bloody hell, what?"

O'Malley scratches the back of his head. "Bloody hell, I'll be damned, that's what. It's Guy-fucking-Priest."

Guy?

In two strides, I've got O'Malley shoved aside, crying about me spraining his pinky finger, while I grip the steel bars and watch the progression down the hall. I'd recognize Guy anywhere: the angry-set brows, the narrowed, lethal stare. My brother's face reveals nothing while Guthram waves his hand about before pounding Guy on the back in forced camaraderie.

They stop at our cell.

"Don't tell me you're gettin' out," O'Malley whines behind me. "This ain't fair, I tell you. You killed a *priest* and I did nothing. I took some little old lady's purse. She didn't have nothin' in it anyway, so really, this is some shite karma—"

He shuts up when I pin him with a hard stare.

"You're right," he rambles, nodding rapidly, hands fluttering, "it's been a brilliant time. Just brilliant. Best cellmate I ever did have."

If I never see the man again, it'll be too fucking soon.

Guthram's face reddens as he fumbles with the keys and unlocks the cell. "Your brother has . . . he's, ah, been quite *persuasive* in your case, Mr. Priest. So persuasive, in fact, that it was clear that we were wrong. You . . . They've been dropped, all the charges."

"Have they?" I ask, softly. "How much green did you bend over for this time, Marcus?"

His guilty gaze shifts away. "No money. Only for a gift. Just for a . . . a gift."

Lifting a brow, I turn to my brother, who mirror-images me. One eyebrow arched high. His mouth flat, his gaze impersonal. As if bailing his brother out of jail is a regular occurrence for him. We both know that's not the case. In a long line of Godwins loyal to the Crown, I'm the first to find myself behind bars.

It's an honor I would prefer go to someone else.

Guy steps back. "Ready to go? We'll be hitting traffic."

Thirty minutes later, I've changed out of the bloodied clothes I've been wearing for the last week and into the new set Guy brought me. The dirtied set lands in the rubbish the minute I've finished the necessary paperwork allowing me to leave without a single charge to my fake name. Not the murder of Father Bootham, nor the seven deaths that I dealt at The Octagon. Not even my supposed assassination of King John. I'm no innocent man walking free, just a former spy for the Crown, whose connections are wide and varied.

I run my tongue along the curved ridge of my upper lip as I settle in Guy's car.

This life has molded me, broken me.

Only one light has graced my darkness: Isla Quinn.

And while my brother speeds us along A20, she's most likely still stuck in a hospital bed in London. It's on the tip of my tongue to demand that he turn us around and head for the Royal Hospital. I need to see her with my own two eyes. I need to see that she . . . that she—

Fucking hell.

I twist my head and look out the window—not that I note anything of the passing landscape. All I feel is suffocation and desperation and the dread skimming my spine at the thought of Guy calling me out on the emotion that's no doubt straining my features. With my thumb and forefinger, I pinch the bridge of my nose. Breathe through the worry until I can deal with it later. Later, when I can visit Isla on my own, positive that Guy won't appear from behind me to stab her in the heart.

Hold on for me, sweetheart. Please, hold on.

Clearing my throat, I drop my hand to my thigh. "How much money did you shell out?"

Knowing exactly what I'm referring to, Guy doesn't bother with small talk. "No money."

"You really gave the bastard a gift in exchange for getting me out?" I ask, incredulous.

"I gave him Jack's head on a silver platter."

"I'm sorry, you did *what*?"

Swinging my gaze to the right, I seek out my brother's profile. He stares straight ahead, his grip loose on the steering wheel, his expression apathetic. "Left it on Guthram's bed," he says, drumming his finger to an indistinct rhythm. "Tucked it in real nice, too, beneath the covers."

Staring at him, the only thing I can even think to say is, "You're full of shit."

He smooths his palm over the leather wheel. "It was Damien's idea."

"You're both absolutely mad."

"Or just brilliantly creative."

"I don't even know what to say."

"I'm sorry."

My brows shoot up in surprise. The last time Guy apologized—*never*. It's happened approximately zero times in my entire life. And I can't deny that it feels good to hear the words, to know that he cares—

"You should say *I'm sorry*," he finishes.

I open my mouth . . . I open it, and absolutely nothing comes out. My palms land on my thighs, just north of my knees, and I squeeze the muscles through the fabric of my fresh trousers. *Keep your cool. Find your calm.* Teeth clenched, I bite out, "Why the hell would I apologize?"

"For choosing her."

An animalistic sound claws its way up my throat. "I

will *always* choose her."

"I know."

"If you know, then why ask for the apology? Why bother springing me from jail when you know . . ." I suck in a sharp breath of air, letting it fill my lungs. "Why bother," I try again, my voice laced with grit, "with anything, when you know I'll wait all of minutes to find my way back to her again?"

"Because she's made you weak."

Never taking my eyes off my brother, I issue a single-word command: "Fuck off."

"Let me show you something." He tilts his head toward the glove box.

Muscles coiled tight, I snap it open and pull out a leather-shelled briefcase. It's no bigger than a purse. Tugging on the zipper, I fold one half of the leather back.

Photographs slip across each other.

Their primary subject makes my stomach churn.

"Where did you get these?" I ask, quietly, as I stare down at William Bootham's tortured body. Picture after picture all reveal more of the same: handprints circling the priest's throat, the man's blank stare, the broken chairs and furniture beneath him—all signs point to him putting up a struggle. I lay my hand flat over the last one, unable to take anymore. Not of this. Not of him.

"Jack was hiding them in our desk when Isla stumbled upon him. Most likely to implicate you as co-conspirator to the murder. That's my guess."

Shocked, I blink. "Jack? *He* did this?"

"Playing two sides of the field, it seems." Guy never diverts his attention away from the motorway to the photographs in my lap. While he wasn't friends with Father Bootham, the two were acquainted. Friendly enough, at least, that I know my older brother feels uneasy about what happened. After a moment, he adds, "Guthram will be placing the blame where it belongs."

"On a dead man whose decapitated head he found in his bed?" *Christ*. What a shitshow. With both hands, I drag my palms over my face. "It won't hold up. Not in court. Which means we'll be in the same position within months."

A position I'd been more than willing to undertake if it meant keeping the heat off Isla. But sitting in prison in place of Jack, who *actually* murdered Father Bootham? No shot. Not in this lifetime, not in the next one either.

"Jack killed him in his own flat." Guy gestures toward the briefcase. "I don't know how he lured Bootham there. I don't know what he said to the priest. But I recognize those chairs, that table—we helped him bring them up to his flat years ago. He left everything as is. Guthram confirmed it."

"Only a fool would conspire to murder someone in your own home."

"Jack was a fool."

I'd said as much to him weeks ago when I sacked him. Only, I'd been a fool too. Then, now. I never saw the evidence laid out before me. Maybe I hadn't *wanted* to see it. Hadn't wanted to consider that Jack was a two-timing bastard.

"Who was the other side?" I ask. "If we were one, then who—"

"Ian Coney."

My mouth falls open. "No."

"Jack claimed they were brothers but Damien, he's already figured out that Jack didn't mean so literally. They belonged to a . . . political cult, if you will. The pay was good, so recruitment was high. We're looking into it, seeing how it might pose a threat to Holyrood."

My back collides with the seat. "Bloody fucking hell. How? How do you know all this?"

"Because she chose you."

He says it like she's alive. Like she's *breathing* and healthy and wasn't just mowed down with a gunshot wound to the chest last week. Gut instinct has me wanting to lean into the visceral relief, to bask in the knowledge that *she is alive*. But something . . . something does not feel right. "Elaborate," I demand, "right now."

Guy lifts one hand off the wheel to scrape down his clean-shaven jaw. "Trust you to find the one woman in this country who has balls bigger than any man."

"Christ, get on with—"

"She came to the Palace."

White noise rings in my ears, startling in its ferocity. Beneath it, I hear the roar of tires ripping down A20, toward Kent; there's the sound of my brother's steady breaths, too. The white noise, I think, is the sound of my soul shattering.

The photographs fall to the floor, between my seat and the center console, and I can't find it in myself to pick them up. To do anything but whisper, horrified, "Tell me you didn't."

"Saxon—"

"*Tell me you didn't!*" I roar the words, breathing fire into every syllable. "Tell me you didn't put her back in that fucking cell. That you didn't"—I gasp for air, my hands clawing fruitlessly at my chest—"tell me that you didn't . . . Fuck, I can't say it. *I can't say it.*"

An arm flies across my torso, the way a parent might with their child to keep them from going headfirst into the dashboard. Guy twists his arm, so that his fingers dig into my clavicle, keeping me restrained.

"She's alive. A little worse for wear after what Jack did to her, but she's fine, Saxon. She's *fine.*"

A wretched noise climbs my throat, and I find myself gripping my brother's arm. Holding tight, the way I did as a child frightened by the world that we were thrust into, alone. My head falls back, my lids slam shut. Emotion assaults me from every angle: joy that she's alive and safe; relief that my brother is still the honorable man I've always known him to be; greed because I need years more with Isla Quinn and I'm selfish enough to demand that she spend each one with me.

Swallowing, roughly, I jerk my head in a short nod. "Is she there now? At the Palace?"

Is she waiting for me?

Guy tugs his arm back, then drives us down the narrow one-lane road that leads directly to Holyrood's main compound. "She is, yes."

Thank fuck.

I'm going to devour her where she stands. Throw her over my damn shoulder, the way I did that first day, and carry her to the first flat surface that we find. The floor will do, too. So long as she's in my arms, I won't be—

"She made a deal."

Stiffening, my gaze cuts to Guy, just as he pulls the car into the car park to the left of the manor house. "What the hell do you mean, she made a deal?"

Without giving an immediate answer, he throws open his door and slides out. I follow suit, tagging his heels as we wind through the small courtyard before stepping through a set of trees that brackets the entrance to the Palace itself.

I wrap a hand around Guy's forearm. "What deal?"

"She chose you," he says, meeting my stare, "and sacrificed herself in the process. If only our forebears knew that one day, the woman who killed a king would take the oath for Holyrood."

My feet come to an abrupt halt, my mouth parting and closing. "I'm sorry, I thought you said that—"

"Holyrood owns her now." Guy's smile is nothing short of humorless. Before I can even react, he claps me on the shoulder and brings me in for a hug. By my ear, he murmurs, "Her contract is in the vault in your office. Signed on the dotted line. Yours to do with as you wish."

Chin snapping back, I stare at him. "Why would you—"

"Let her go?" He shrugs one shoulder, casually, then steps away. "Because I'm not a total heartless bastard." Another step, this one accompanied with a mirthless grin. "And because I prefer to keep my enemies close, brother. As you well know."

Then he turns, hands stuffed inside the pockets of his trousers, and ambles away.

I follow at a more sedate pace, my eyes scouring the estate for a head of strawberry-blond waves. I find her, ten minutes later, by the stream and the stone bridge. With her shoes kicked off to the side, and her feet splashing in the water, she stares up at the early morning sky.

Beautiful.

Perfect.

Mine.

I kick my shoes off as I approach her. Pull off my shirt, leaving it to flutter away in the breeze as I let the fabric go. And then I destroy what's left of the space between us, and say the only words rattling around in my chest: "Holyrood will never own you."

CHAPTER 46

ISLA

I feel him before I see him.

Feel the way his gaze hungrily roams my body. Feel the way he'd strip me naked, if he could, and take me until I come screaming his name, to hell with whoever might stumble upon us here. Feel his heat and the raw strength of his power, both of which leave me desperate to fold myself into his arms where I belong.

My first and only.

The same goes for me, too.

Saxon Godwin is my destiny, and there is nothing that—

"Holyrood will never own you."

Heat scrapes through my lungs as I turn, too fast, and see him coming toward me with smooth, long strides. His shirt is gone, leaving him bare-chested in the brisk morning chill. But true to form, Saxon is like some ancient god, untouched by human weaknesses. The first sweep of the sun glances off his golden skin, turning his already pale eyes nearly yellow. Tawny, in its truest hue. His muscles contract with each step, as do the scars that litter his chest and abdomen and arms.

He's a portrait of pain and bravery and . . . And then his declaration sinks in.

My mouth goes dry. "Saxon, I—"

"You aren't a woman meant to be owned," he says, eclipsing the final distance between us. He sinks to his knees before me in the dewy grass, his thighs slightly spread apart, his big, calloused hands reaching for me, as if he can't bear the thought of us being so close and not touching. "No one owns the king killer."

On instinct, I retreat. From his touch, from that label that feels like less of a compliment and more like a noose around my neck. A noose I placed upon myself, but a noose, nonetheless. "Please . . . please don't call me that."

His palm skates under the curve of my jaw, lifting. "Look at me, Isla."

Feeling more vulnerable than I'd like to admit, I do as he says.

An answering smile hitches the corner of his mouth. And then his palm smooths north until he's tucking a lock of blond hair behind my ear. "You told me once that we all bear scars. Mine exist for all to see, and yours . . . Yours you keep buried inside your heart."

Right now, my heart is beating in overdrive. From his closeness, from the tangible warmth in his husky baritone.

"I see you, Isla Quinn," he tells me, letting his big hand fold over the back of my neck. Gentle. Affectionate. His Adam's apple bobs with a tight swallow. "I see *all* of you. Your strength and your bravery, your hard-headedness and your grit."

"Saxon," I start, but he quickly shakes his head.

"Let me get this out—please."

Rubbing my dry lips together, I stare up at him. Give

a small nod for him to continue.

"You are the king killer, Isla. But you're also the woman who sheltered your siblings after your parents died, and the woman who took a position to give our fellow countrymen the truth. You take risks because you rely on your gut. Right from wrong, good versus evil. For my whole life, I've done the opposite. I stick to what I know—I fucking *burrow* myself in the familiar—because it's what I can control and manipulate and put an end to, should I want." His thumb grazes down the length of my throat, so softly that his touch feels like nothing more than a kiss from the breeze. "Seeing you is like learning to look at the world through a brand-new lens."

Feeling the flutter of my pulse, I reach up and place my hand over his. "You risked a lot by saving me. We were on two sides of this war, you said."

As if embarrassed by the praise, his dark lashes lower over his pale eyes. "I did it without thought."

"On the night of the riot?"

His hand flexes against my flesh as he confesses, "I had you in my arms before I even knew it. You fit. Christ, you fit there, against my chest, in a way that every part of me rebelled. But still I carried you. *Still*."

My throat tightens with emotion. "What of The Octagon?"

"I would do it all over again, just to have you next to me now."

"And . . . and about what happened at The Bell & Hand? D-Did you react without thought then, too?"

Tension seeps into his frame, and then his hand is lowering to my spine, between my shoulder blades where the bullet from Jack's gun exited. He stays just like that, linking us together, his palm lingering over the dressing covering my wound. Our breathing is rhythmic, completely in sync, the rise and fall of my chest dictating when he inhales.

"Saxon?" I prompt on a whisper.

His unholy eyes meet mine. "I've chased Death for years, sweetheart. Doled it out like it was my right. Killing Jack was not enough. I almost lost you. I almost lost *years* with you, and I—*Christ*." As if unable to stop himself, he drags me closer, until my legs are straddling his and my knees are buried in the soft grass. He tucks his face into the crook of my neck. Levels my flesh with a soft, agonizing press of his lips. "I've been a wreck without you. I didn't know if you were alive or dead or still in that fucking hospital bed."

Pressed so close to him, my skin turns to fire.

I sink my fingers into his thick hair, scraping my nails over his skull to soothe the rigid fear from his body. And then I press my mouth to the shell of his ear, and murmur, "Holyrood owns me because life without you wouldn't be much of a life at all." When he stiffens, imperceptibly, I settle myself more firmly in his lap. "You sent me that message like it was a good-bye. You gave me the money and the car and a house in the middle of Oxford like those were the only pieces of you I'd ever have left."

"You were better off without me. You're *still* better off without me."

My heart plummets. "Saxon, I only want—"

"But you're *mine*."

Jerking back, I sweep my gaze over his rugged face, noting the notch between his brows and the firm set to his mouth. "I thought . . . you just said that—"

"A girl like you shouldn't be with a man like me," he says, cupping the back of my head so that I have no choice but to be swept away on a sea of glittering green and tawny yellow, "but you lost any chance to walk away the second that I spotted your car outside the pub. You were mine when Josie let it slip that you hadn't bathed, over missing me. You were mine when I heard that gunshot and felt terror the likes of which I've never known. You were *mine*, sweetheart, when your brother begged me to put you in the car and I couldn't fucking let you go."

Tears prick the corners of my eyes, and there's nowhere to hide.

Saxon watches me, and surrounds me, and I let them fall. A warrior at her most vulnerable—for him, for *us*.

"You said that that no one should own a woman like me."

"I don't own you, Isla. I'm choosing to walk by your side."

The dam breaks open, then, and maybe it's a week of being stuck in that bed with my nerves on edge. Or maybe it's the leftover adrenaline of storming the keep, so to speak, and expecting to find myself locked back in that cell beside Alfie Barker for a second time. Either way, I curl myself into Saxon's arms and allow myself the freedom of being comforted by the man I love.

My first, my only.

He rubs my back, careful of my healing wound.

He husks out words that I can't quite make out but nevertheless feel their vibration against my skin.

He holds me like I'm his, now, tomorrow, forevermore.

Only once my tremors have stopped does he raise his dark head, and the look on his face, it's . . . sinful. Downright *sinful.* "I'm going to kiss you."

Answering heat blooms between my legs. "I told you, you don't have to ask permission."

"I'm not asking for anything," he retorts, leveraging

his hand at the base of my head, "it's a promise. A warning. Because once I do, there's no stopping. I'm going to lay you out on this grass and drive myself so damn deep inside you, they'll hear you at the Palace. I'm going to remind us both that we're *alive* because right now . . ." The fingers of his free hand flit over my shirt collar, dragging it down, down, down, until he's exposed the lace of my bralette. "Right now, this still feels like a fucking dream and I'll be damned if I wake up to find you gone again."

"I'm not going any—"

The rest of the word breaks on a stifled gasp, and then Saxon is kissing me.

My back pressed into the damp grass.

My legs spread wide to make room for his brawny frame hovering above me.

My mouth parted, devoured, ravaged.

There's tiny discomfort in the pressure against my battle scar, but it's gone within seconds. Lost to a man who balances pain with pleasure, who offers possession and dominance on the heels of endearing affection.

Saxon kisses me like he may never have another chance, his calloused fingers fluttering over my face. Teasing down my temple, dancing across my cheek, firming over my chin, so he can angle me just right. My eyes are peeled open, and there is nothing beyond him but the wide breadth of his shoulders, and the soft, dark hair that falls over his forehead, and the harsh planes of his face.

And then his eyes meet mine, our mouths still fused, and I might as well be falling.

Raw vulnerability mingled with stark need dances in those pale green depths. He pulls back. Touches his tongue to his upper lip, and rasps, "You asked me, once, if I believe in fate. I said no."

My hand finds the firm contour of his shoulder. "Have you had a change in opinion?"

"The day you walked into the pub," he says, hoarsely, "I should have realized it then. Of all the thousands of people that we meet in our lifetimes, it was you who sat down in front of me. You, just *you*."

His mouth slants over mine, his tongue teasing at my lips until I grant him entry.

There is lust in this kiss, but there's something more. Something that brings an ache to my chest because Saxon . . . there are no walls built around him. I've scaled them, or maybe he tore them down, but as his tongue tangles with mine, there's no denying the possessive roll of his hard cock against my core or the way he breaks from my mouth to utter "fucking beautiful" and "*mine*" against my temple.

This is Saxon Godwin unrestrained by the chains of Holyrood and prescribed loyalties and forever-present ice. And it's *wonderful*.

I strain my neck, arching my back and thrusting my breasts into his body. "Please. *Please*."

"Please, what?" The words are a taunt against my mouth, a dare for me to rise to the occasion and demand what I want from him. "Don't be scared now."

With my fingers raking through his hair, I yank on the strands. "I'm not scared of you."

"You should be, sweetheart. You fucking should be."

His nimble fingers flirt with the elastic waistband of my joggers. An intentional stroke along the seam. Another well-positioned drag over my clit. With his chest pressed flush with mine, he holds me captive as he works me into a writhing, trembling mess. I want *more*, and I part my lips to demand just that, but then he's already moving.

Beneath the cotton of my sweats, beneath the silk of my knickers.

Until I feel the rough pad of his finger coasting along the all-too-sensitive bundle of nerves at the hood of my sex. He strokes me in a soft, barely-there caress, but it's *enough*. Enough for sensation to flare. Enough for me to bury a cry into his shoulder while he rewards me with a guttural groan that has me turning into liquid beneath his body.

"Oh, God. *Saxon*."

He plunges two fingers inside me, then angles his body so that I have a clear view of what he's doing to me. My pulse skips a beat at the sight: my knees propped up, my hips rising again and again, shameless in my desire, his hand tenting the material of my joggers while he curls those fingers inside me and drags a moan from my lips.

The orgasm tickles at the base of my spine.

I feel it, the heat, the pull for me to let go.

Saxon doesn't let me fly.

With one last thrust of his fingers, he pulls his hand out from my bottoms and plants it on the grass beside my head. "You'll come with me," he growls against my mouth, "and not a second before."

"Cruel," I tease on a heavy pant, "so bloody cruel."

"No, not cruel," he rumbles, as he sinks back on his heels and reaches for my shirt, arrogantly gathering the fabric in one fist, which he uses to pull me from the ground. My hands clamp down over his hard shoulders, just as he adds, "Starved. For you, for this."

He whips the shirt over my head, discarding the material a heartbeat later. My bralette follows next.

Silence steals over our small corner of the world, until there's only the gentle trickle of the stream and the birds waking in the trees, and the harsh sound of Saxon's pained groan when he spies the new, finger-length scar that descends like a line drawn in the sand between my breasts. The stitches will come out soon, but not yet.

I lick my lips. "Looks like you're not the only one with visible scars now."

It's a modest attempt at humor, as ill-timed as the rest of my jokes. But Saxon barely gives me the chance to crack another because his lips descend on mine, urgent yet confident. Palm hovering over my scar, he doesn't touch me directly. But he waits, lingers, then ducks down to kiss my collarbone.

I breathe out his name.

He places another kiss a millimeter north. And his eyes never leave my face. "I see you, sweetheart. The scars you bear, inside and out. Just like you see mine."

My mouth trembles as I soak in his frame. "Broken," I whisper, tracing the raised, hardened flesh beneath his arm, down his left side, "ruined."

Dragging my knickers down the length of my legs, Saxon shakes his head. "Beautiful. Brave. Fierce." Stripping off his joggers, he lowers me down to the grass, using my shirt as a blanket, before lining up his cock with my core. Instantly my toes curl, spine arching as his thick crown slips through my wetness. "You pieced me back together, Isla. You saw the broken and misshapen parts of me, and you filled them with warmth. You made me *want*."

On the final word, he thrusts home.

A cry spills from my mouth, and I move my hands to clutch his powerful arms.

"And to a man like me," he growls, gliding his hips in a sensual rhythm that has me straining for more, "wanting is a dangerous thing. It made me curious." Gathering my wrists in his hands, he pins them above my ahead. Holds them there while his gaze holds mine and that rhythm . . . God, I feel it in my toes. So good, *so good*. "It made me desperate. And the wanting, it led to more. It led to love. Christ, I love you."

Love. Love. *Love.*

His gruff admission tears through me, burrowing so deep within my veins that there's no telling where I begin and he ends. Fate. Destiny. "Say it again."

"I love you," he grunts, "my only, Isla. You're my only."

I throw my head back, even as I loop one leg around his waist.

We're in the middle of the estate, the early morning chill rapidly warming under the weight of Saxon's frame. Anyone can see us, hear us, *find us,* but instead of panicking, I bathe in the moment. The sun kissing my naked skin. The stream gently lapping at the grassy bank. Saxon's groans as he winds us both higher, tighter.

The fact that he *loves* me.

I wrestle against his hold, fighting off the urge to last longer before my orgasm claims me, but his green eyes darken and his fingers don't release their cage around my wrists. "Say it back, sweetheart. Say it *back*."

"I love you."

His strokes plunge deeper, hitting harder, rougher.

"I love you."

He groans deep in his chest, a sound so tangible, I swear I can feel it between my legs.

"*I love you.*"

With little fanfare, his tongue thrusts inside my mouth, much the same way that his cock grinds against my core. The kiss is a duel, a power struggle of love and lust and adoration, and I live for every second of it. I nip his upper lip, fearlessly, and he moans against my lips, his thrusts gaining speed.

Sparks ignite down my spine and I whimper into his mouth.

He jerks back, releasing my wrists, and grabs hold of my hips. Fingers digging in hard enough to leave bruises, his abdominal muscles rippling. His dark stubble nearly disguises the curve of his upper lip, and when he throws his head back, his teeth bared, all I know is love.

This man has saved me.

This man has fucked me.

But this man, this one right here, has given me something that he's showed no one else: all-encompassing trust.

I find his hands with mine, linking our fingers together.

"Fuck," he grunts, "you feel good."

He angles his hips, propping one hand up by my shoulder, and that's all the prompting I need. I come, with his name on my lips like a prayer—penance. "I love you," I whisper, as my orgasm tears through me.

Pale eyes bear down on me. "Again," he orders, finding my clit with his fingers. He rubs in a tight circle, drawing the sensations out, determined to make me scream.

A moan wrenches from my throat, and then I give him the words again: "I love you."

He orgasms with a roar, coming so hard that his shoulders tremble and his beautiful green eyes slam shut.

A man unraveled. A man undone.

Because of me.

Only once we've come down from the high do I brush my hand over the crown of his head. "Do you have something to tell me?"

Saxon's fingers trace over my chest, tracing the shape of my breast before dipping down between my legs. "You won't be working for Holyrood, in case that's what you were wondering. It was a noble sacrifice, I'll give you that. But if you even think for one minute that I'll let you surrender the rest of your life to—"

"That's not what I was hoping you'd say," I interrupt, laughter climbing my throat.

"No? What else is there?"

I pinch his rock-hard side. "*Saxon.*"

He rolls on top of me, brushing my hair back from my face. All traces of good humor gone, he meets my stare. "I love you, Isla Quinn. I love you for reaching into the darkness and pulling me back to the light." He takes my hand and lays it over his heart. "This is yours, and you . . . You are my only, sweetheart. I breathe, you inhale—"

"—and we both go up in flames," we finish, as one.

CHAPTER 47

SAXON

Isla sleeps like the dead.

Sprawled across the mattress, stealing my pillows along with hers.

I suspect that these last few nights that we've spent at my house in Oxford are some of the first that she's experienced without night terrors. Maybe, if I hadn't spent years in Holyrood, I would be more prepared to sleep a full eight hours.

I figure I'm lucky if I manage five.

The house is quiet as I rise from the bed, pressing a kiss to Isla's forehead. Her strawberry-blond hair is tangled with her neck, and a gritty chuckle reverberates in my chest as I sweep the strands back before they strangle her. As if attuned to my touch, she follows the path of my hand, turning from her side onto her back, her chin lifting like she's seeking a kiss. I'm no prince out to wake Sleeping Beauty, but still I take what she's offering. A brush of my lips over hers, a nuzzle of my nose by her ear, and a roughly uttered, "I love you."

She snores, none the wiser, and warmth floods my

chest. This is not the life I imagined for myself. I expected the bloodshed. Hell, I even expected betrayal. But what I never expected was love. Isla brought me that hope and then she fed the beast, filling me up with so much emotion that there hasn't been a day in the last week that I haven't looked over at her and just *smiled.*

Like some lovesick fool.

Like *her* lovesick fool.

But as I move from the bedroom on silent feet—so I don't wake Peter or Josie down the hall—it's difficult to keep my brain from turning back to Holyrood.

I'm out, still.

Somehow still welcomed within the fold, out of familial obligation, but no longer a member of the pack, the tribe to which I've always belonged. I'm the first Godwin in over a century to have been booted from Holyrood.

Quietly, I slip into my office. Close the door first before flicking on the overhead light.

I sit at my chair, run my fingers over my desk, and gaze upon the computer where I've spent thousands of hours working.

It sits blank now, unused.

A soft knock comes on the door, and I turn, already knowing who it'll be.

"Come in."

Isla enters with our blanket wrapped around her shoulders and her hair in complete disarray. Christ, she's stunning. Beautiful in a way that sometimes feel otherworldly. Voice still raspy from restless slumber, I ask, "Couldn't sleep?"

"Not without you next to me." Instead of waiting to see if I'll offer an invitation, she settles herself in my lap, her legs swung over mine, her head tucked into the crook of my neck. I sense her eyes wandering the setup before us. Then, with a hand pressed to my chest, she says, "You miss it."

It's not a question. She's entirely too perceptive, but that alone is one of the reasons I fell in love with her. She sees me when no one else does, and never casts judgments, even when maybe she should. I've never claimed to be a good man, but fuck, I want to be one for her.

"I don't know what I feel." Pressing a kiss to her temple, I wrap my arms around her and prop her head up higher on my chest. "I broke the rules. Fuck, I didn't just break them. I treated them like they didn't even exist. For you, I would do it all a million times over."

"But?" she prompts.

I turn my gaze on the blank-screened computer. "But Holyrood is in my blood. I feel . . . I feel itchy to do something. *Anything.*"

"Can you show me Alfie Barker?"

I furrow my brows. "Now?"

She nods against my neck. "Yes."

Despite knowing that I probably shouldn't, I fire up the computer and sort through the various files until I'm clicking on the security cameras at the Palace. Apparently, Damien hasn't scrubbed my clearance yet because within seconds, I'm selecting Room 2's video. The small loading symbol appears. A second passes. And then there's nothing but black . . . and the telltale sound of Alfie Barker snoring somewhere in the cell. Immediately, my gut clenches at the thought of how I'd put Isla in there. Guilt, potent and real, snatches away some of the happiness I've found.

"It's dark," she says softly, as if reading my mind, "a place where a person can easily lose their mind. How long has he been there?"

I count the number of days back, to that first morning when Isla and I met. "A little over three weeks."

"It's a long time to admit to nothing," she murmurs idly, drawing her finger down the length of my arm. Back and forth, back and forth. It's peaceful, affectionate. Familiar heat tugs at the base of my spine. "Whatever you think he knows, I don't think that he does."

Resting my head against the chair, I drag my gaze down to her beautiful face. "Hypothetically," I start, voice steady, "what would you do with him? Let him go?"

She scrunches her nose then turns back to the computer. Reaches out to graze a single finger down the side of the monitor. "Hypothetically," she answers, tapping the screen, "I would be open with him. Transparent. He lost his wife last year during one of the Easter riots. Now he's locked in that cell while his two girls are alone in the world. He's a father, Saxon, a caretaker. To get back to his daughters, you might be surprised at what he would be willing to agree to, given the opportunity."

It's not the way I would go about it.

Brutal intimidation. Mental tactics designed to see a person spiral then break. It's what I do—what I *did*. Now, I . . . Well, I guess now I speak in hypotheticals about an organization I no longer serve.

"I love you," I whisper into the strands of her hair. "And you're probably right about Barker."

She snuggles deeper into my embrace, hiding a yawn behind the back of one hand. "I love you more," she replies, a tired but content smile gracing her face, "and I'm usually right about most things."

A small grin tugs at my mouth. "Anything else you want to see before I drag you back to bed?"

Her blue eyes peer up at me, and already I see the wheels turning. My Isla is a sweetheart, the fiercest sort of protector, but she's cunning. As ruthless as I am savage. And I know exactly what she wants before the words even leave her mouth: "The queen."

She doesn't bother to deny it. "Show me her."

Isla props one forearm on the desk while still maintaining her spot, sprawled across my lap. I hook one arm around her waist, dragging her ass back so that her spine is flush with my chest. She tosses a knowing glance over her shoulder at me, and I don't bother to apologize. I want her. I *always* want her. But I get with the program, hand to the computer mouse, and sift through a series of locations throughout the country that we—*Holyrood*—closely monitor for the queen. Windsor Castle in Berkshire. Dunrobin in the Highlands. Countless others that I've seen only in camera footage but which I have never visited in person. Finally, I settle on Buckingham Palace.

"I used to visit every year," Isla tells me, as I flick through the public rooms on the first floor. At this time of night, there's no one afoot. "I didn't always hate the monarchy, you know."

"No one ever does. The misgivings come later, after you've been burned a time or two."

Sliding her the mouse, I give her free reign to peruse the palace. Once upon a time, these rooms were open to British citizens and people from all over the world. They sit empty now, with white fabric draped over priceless antique furniture and the ghosts of past kings and queens roaming the halls. The only set of rooms actively in use are Queen Margaret's apartments and those used by her staff.

I feel Isla shift on my thigh, her spine going ramrod straight. "Saxon? What time is it?"

Languidly, my gaze moves to the digital clock on the desk. "Just before three. Why?"

The image on the screen jumps backward, rewinding from room to room. Isla shoves her finger toward the monitor, tapping the glass in the upper right-hand corner. "Watch the clock. It doesn't... If these are security cameras, wouldn't they be live? But the time, it's not—"

"Changing," I finish for her.

And they aren't changing, not at all. All are frozen at 2:21:15 AM. Frame to frame. Room to room. Despite the fact that she's been virtually touring Buckingham for the past twenty minutes. A quiet chill of foreboding skirts down my spine as I debate the merits of calling Damien. I'm no Holyrood spy, not anymore. My obligations to the queen ended the moment I chose Isla over Margaret. But still, better safe than sorry.

"Isla, would you—"

"Tell me what you need."

"My mobile. It's on the nightstand in the bedroom."

"Say no more." She scoots from my lap with a brief kiss to my cheek, and then I hear nothing but the quick tread of her feet padding down the hall.

Be calm. Be cool.

Moving through every room of the palace, I continue to note the unchanged time. *2:21:15.* A few years back, we paid a fortune reinstalling new security at Buckingham. King John's paranoia that Princess Evangeline's killer was back had spread throughout Holyrood, forcing the lot of us to put in more hours. I barely slept, barely ate. We never discovered who killed her—an unsolved murder case spanning almost thirty years—but the new security system went a long way in settling the king's ruffled feathers.

And someone's tampered with it now.

"Saxon." Footsteps gain momentum down the hall, and then louder, more urgent, "*Saxon!*"

Isla.

Heart hammering in my chest, I enter the hallway in three strides. She stands there with my mobile in her hand, her blue eyes big in her face.

I crowd her immediately, reaching for her arms to pull her close. "What is it? Sweetheart, tell me what it is."

"Clarke, whoever he—"

Snatching the phone from her hands, I turn it over and see a single, unread message flashing across the home screen: HELLPP FIR

"What the hell does that mean?" I check the timestamp of the text, and my stomach, it bottoms out completely. *2:35 AM.* Sent ten minutes after the security cameras became frozen in time. Something happened. Something bad, something big, and, without pause, I turn on my heel, heading straight for the living room and the telly.

"Is he one of your agents?" Isla asks, following closely. Unmitigated worry scrapes through her voice. "That text, it sent a chill down my spine, Saxon. He's in trouble, wherever he is."

"He's at Buckingham Palace." I find the clicker, stuffed between the sofa cushions, and turn on the television. "We have him stationed with the queen."

To keep her safe. To keep her *alive*.

Dread becomes a fist locked around my lungs.

Isla's hand lands on my back, moving in soothing circles. "Whatever happened, I'm sure it's a misunderstanding. It has to be. Clarke will be fine, and the queen—she'll be fine too."

Except that the second the news station appears on

the screen, I know that it's anything but.

Buckingham Palace is on fire.

Flames flicker toward the sky, angry and volatile. Glass windows implode from the heat stored within, shattering into thousands of broken shards, as the camera crew pans from one wing of the historic palace to the other. And then the entire upper floor detonates with a catastrophic *boom!* loud enough to be heard from London to Edinburgh.

Screams erupt on screen, from the crowds gathered around the front gates of Buckingham. A frenzy stirs, the camera toppling over until the view ends with a sideways shot of the palace on fire, hundreds of feet trampling past in a flurry to flee.

"Oh, my God," Isla whispers. "Oh, my God."

I ring Damien without thought, and he picks up immediately. I hear him panting as though he's running.

"Tell me Clarke got her out," I bark into the phone, the first thing I say. "Tell me you've heard from—"

"She's stuck inside, Saxon. The entire palace is on fucking fire and she's stuck *inside.*"

My ass hits the edge of the sofa as I stumble backward, my eyes rooted to the morose image of stampeding feet on the television and the abject screams filling the quiet space of my safehouse, and the knowledge that whoever did this had it planned.

I see nothing but flames, feel nothing but horror, and hear my hoarse voice rasp only one thing:

"Long live the queen."

TO BE CONTINUED...

***Sound of Madness (Book 2 of the Broken Crown Trilogy)
is now available!*** Damien Priest will meet his match, and life as the Priests know it will shatter forever.

Need to talk all things Road To Fire?
Come find the Spoiler Group on Facebook or join Book Boyfriends Anonymous, my personal reader group!

And before you go!
Are you not ready to leave the *Broken Crown* just yet? I've written a short story prequel about the first Godwin who saved Prince Robert, back in the Second Boer War. You can find it on my website to download for free!

Dear Fabulous Reader

Hi there! I so hope you enjoyed *Road To Fire*, and if you are new to my books, welcome to the family!

In the back of all my books, I love to include a Dear Fabulous Reader section that talks about which locations from the book can be visited in real life or what sparked my inspiration for a particular plot point. (I like to think of it as the Extras on DVD's, LOL).

As always, we'll hit it up bullet-point style—enjoy!

- You might be wondering: "Where in the world did you come up with this series, Maria?" Four words: AMC's *Turn: Washington's Spies*. To say that I'm obsessed with the show is a grave understatement—I've watched all four seasons at least three times through. But in watching it, I began to think, *what if Britain hadn't lost the war? What if America never became what it is today?* After some heavy pondering, I realized it might be difficult to suspend one's disbelief of a modern-day America still fighting for its freedom. England, however, was the *perfect* landscape for such a series. I never once looked back—although I did consider writing an Author Disclaimer, which would have only said, "Queen Elizabeth II was not harmed in the making of this book."

- In my pre-author life, I was a medieval historian. Pretty much, I'm that nerd who thinks translating Old English is fun—Mr. Luis regularly questions my "fun" meter, to which I tell him that he doesn't know what he's missing. Though I specialize in 14th century London gender norms and crime, *Road To Fire* feels like my—admittedly *dark*—love letter to England. In fiction, most alternate universes imply a made-up country; for the *Broken Crown* books, I wanted to cement a fabricated political landscape within the concrete reality of the UK. With some adjustments, of course!

- This means that *many* of the locations that I referenced in *Road To Fire* can be visited. In no specific order, here are some of the lesser known places:

  - **Holyrood Abbey in Edinburgh, Scotland.** The first time I visited, I fell in love with these ruins. They are regal, utterly picturesque. When deciding upon a name for the Godwin's spy ring, I wanted a place where they might return, year after year, through the generations. Holyrood felt like the perfect fit.

  - **Christ Church Spitalfields in London, England.** While living in York, I visited London multiple times—on one visit, I took a Jack the Ripper tour, which brought us right onto Fournier Street. Darkness blanketed the city street, and then there was Christ Church's steeple, lit up like a beacon in the otherwise starless night. It was eerie and beautiful, and five years later, it's remained a visual I still picture clearly. In picking a location for The Bell & Hand, I could think of no better place than that bustling corner of London.

  - Speaking of **The Bell & Hand**, you *can* visit such a pub, but you'd be on the entirely wrong continent! Actually named The Bell *In* Hand, this tavern can be found in my native Boston, Massachusetts. Opened in 1795 by Jimmy Wilson, Wilson was known for talking . . . a *lot*. As the town crier (i.e., an officer of the court who made public announcements), any information you wished to know, Wilson probably knew it. Following the Revolutionary War, he opened The Bell In Hand, and was more than willing to talk shop with anyone who entered his tavern. When creating the Priest brothers' pub, I thought it would be fun to pay a little homage to one of Boston's oldest alehouses.

- **The Octagon at Queen Mary University of London.** It was fate, I think, that I had Peter attend Queen Mary because of its close proximity to their Stepney flat. When creating the scene where Saxon rushes to save Isla, I paused for some online research. I didn't want to fabricate a building, but I would if necessary. And then . . . Well, then I stumbled across The Octagon. I'm almost positive that I gasped. The galleries, the beautiful architecture, the busts of Shakespeare and Byron and all the others. It was the *perfect* setting, and so I dug right in.

- **The Palace, otherwise known as Ightham Mote in Kent, England.** For the sake of full transparency, the first time I ever saw Ightham Mote, my history-loving heart SWOONED. Its history (roughly 700-years-old!); its architecture (a stunning blend of Medieval and Tudor); the *moat*. I mean, the moat. Can it get any better than that? Ightham Mote is on the National Trust list, which means you can visit on your next trip to England.

As always, there are many more (like Æthelred the Unready or, of course, Buckingham Palace) but here is just a sampling! If you're thinking . . . that seems rather fascinating and I want to know more, you are always so welcome to reach out! Pretty much, nothing makes me happier =)

Much love,
Maria

ACKNOWLEDGMENTS

Saxon and Isla have been in my head for so long that to know that they're out in the world is beyond thrilling! But this book wouldn't be what it is without some of my favorite people.

Najla—girl, your talent, your vision. Thank you from the bottom of my heart for listening to me ramble about what I wanted—while simultaneously making no sense whatsoever, LOL—and making it happen. Working with you is such a joy!

Wander & Andrey—I don't know what I would do without the two of you! Thank you for bringing my vision for the photography to life.

Kathy—I won't lie: I broke into tears when I read your first feedback email. Having this story within me for so long, not knowing if it was good or just good in my head . . . you gave me the confidence to know Saxon and Isla were as badass as I thought they were. Fourteen books, three years. I couldn't do this author gig without you.

Brenda—thank you for reading my books early, for giving me your thoughts, and for being a rock I desperately need while navigating this author world. But, truly, just thank you for being *you*.

Viper—no book of mine can enter the world without your eyes on it! It's because of you I now think about generations—ahem, Maria, when were they born??—and I always giggle when I come across something that you've given me feedback on. You are the best!

Ratula—without your excitement for the prologue, nearly two years ago, I don't know if I would have had the conviction to keep writing *Road To Fire*. Thank you for believing in me, for being my friend, for being the cheerleader I need when you push me to give my characters everything. I adore you.

Dawn and Tandy—y'all are the reason my books sparkle as they do! Thank you for kicking the pesky typos off the island, and for being the awesome people that y'all are.

Dani—thank you for helping me to reach my dreams and for being a steady hand of support when I need it. You are the best partner-in-crime!

To my besties/family/awesome-sauce friends Tina, Sam, Jami, Amie, Jen, Jessica, Stephanie, and to all my girls in 30 Days to 60k, Indie AF, and Beach Retreat, I would absolutely be lost without you.

To my VIPers and to my family in BBA, just know that your excitement over the *Broken Crown* books is more than I could have ever hoped for. This series is not my norm and yet you rallied behind me and made me smile each and every time I revealed something new. You are the best family a girl could ask for, and I would be so much lonelier in this journey if you weren't along for the ride.

And, lastly, to you Dear Reader, for picking up *Road To Fire* and giving me a chance. Thank you for allowing me to live my dream, and I can't wait to bring you Damien's story.

Much love,
Maria

ALSO BY MARIA LUIS

NOLA HEART
Say You'll Be Mine
Take A Chance On Me
Dare You To Love Me
Tempt Me With Forever

BLADES HOCKEY
Power Play
Sin Bin
Hat Trick
Body Check

BLOOD DUET
Sworn
Defied

PUT A RING ON IT
Hold Me Today
Kiss Me Tonight
Love Me Tomorrow

BROKEN CROWN TRILOGY
Road To Fire
Sound of Madness
A New King (Spring 2021)

FREEBIES
(AVAILABLE AT WWW.MARIALUIS.ORG)
Breathless (a Love Serial, #1)
Undeniable (a Love Serial, #2)
The First Fix
Kissing the Gentleman
(Put A Ring On It, #4: A Short Story)

MARIA LUIS is the author of sexy contemporary romances.

Historian by day and romance novelist by night, Maria lives in New Orleans, and loves bringing the city's cultural flair into her books. When Maria isn't frantically typing with coffee in hand, she can be found binging on reality TV, going on adventures with her other half and two pups, or plotting her next flirty romance.

STALK MARIA IN THE WILD
AT THE FOLLOWING!

Join Maria's Newsletter
Join Maria's Facebook Reader Group

Printed in Great Britain
by Amazon